It Never Ends – Book One of The Vengeance Cycle

Cover art and design by Jhada Rogue Addams
Cover model: Donna Hirsch

2nd Edition – updated 2012.

ISBN: 978-1-4243-4272-3

Soylent Publications

It Never Ends
Book One of The Vengeance Cycle

Jhada Rogue Addams

I dedicate this book to my sainted mother,
Mary Patricia Morehouse, who crossed the river to
the next life on March 2, 2009.

She was a veritable hell-bound harpy when it came
to typesetting and editing. She was the nonfiction
side of the family and I get the entirety of my love of
books (especially horror) of any kind from her.

I would like to think that she'd be proud that her
daughter finally got this work published, even if
she'd be somewhat scandalized by the content.

I want to give many appreciative thanks to Suzi,
who worked diligently with me to help me hone
these characters back when I still thought I was just
writing a short story.

I also want to thank my dear friends Cjae, Fara, Kim
and Christine who provided me with awesome
feedback and critique – you all entirely rock out.

And thank you to my wonderful editor, Sue Baiman.
You're a rock, darlin'.

Thank you all for helping me make this happen.

Do not kill, do not rape, do not steal.

These are principles, which every man of every faith can embrace.

These are not polite suggestions, these are codes of behavior and those of you that ignore them will pay the dearest cost.

One day you will look behind you and you will see we three.

And on that day, you will reap it.

And we will send you to whatever god you wish.

And shepherds we shall be, for thee my Lord for thee.

Power hath descended forth from thy hand,

that our feet may swiftly carry out thy command.

And we shall flow a river forth to thee,

and teeming with souls shall it ever be.

In nomine Patris, et Filii, et Spiritus Sancti.

– Boondock Saints –

One
A Fresh Start

A stabbing pain in Dani's gut forced her awake, and she winced as she tried to push herself up into a sitting position. Her body still didn't seem to want to cooperate, and it took several tries before she was finally able to prop herself up on her hands and knees. Her limbs trembled as she looked around the room, momentarily disoriented.

What the hell?

She blinked as she spotted a crumpled, somewhat desiccated body across the room. Blood was everywhere, it seemed. The body reeked and her nose wrinkled as she brought a hand up to try to block out the smell.

She peered over at the clock. About two hours had passed since she'd blacked out. Her hands curled into fists that she pressed against her stomach in an attempt to suppress a painful cramping. It was damn near debilitating and she let out a small, pained groan.

After a few minutes, it subsided a little, giving her a moment to think. Unfortunately, the pain was then quickly replaced by a strong hunger. She couldn't remember the last time she'd been this ravenous. She had an overwhelming need to eat something. Anything.

"Dear god," she croaked hoarsely as she tried to stand up.

Dani groaned; pale fingers splaying out against the carpet as she slumped back down and fought to control her breathing. Cradling her stomach, she slowly lurched to her feet. A sibilant hissing echoed through her thoughts, and she shuddered at the sound of a disembodied voice.

:: *You must feed, child. There are animals that need to be put down. Only when you expedite the process of working my will in the world will your pain go away.* ::

The voice was strangely soothing and seemed to quell the cramping a touch, backing it down to a more manageable level. Dani shook her head slowly, trying to think, her head jerking suddenly back as the face of her attacker flashed through her mind. The body against the wall.

Oh god.

She violently threw up into her hand and it spilled out onto the carpet in a crimson spray.

The faint outline of a horrifically beautiful woman swam into view before her. The woman's skin was a strange, non-reflective onyx that seemed to consume the light that touched it, giving nothing back. Three separate sets of arms darted in a surrealistic jerking dance around the woman's curvaceous body, their movements wholly unnatural as a long crimson forked tongue darted between sharp, white teeth. Shiny red lips spread in an unnerving smile reminiscent of a Japanese Demon mask as the woman's full features came quickly into focus.

Dani shuddered at the realization that none of it had been a dream. She could feel the man's hands on her again, and a tear rolled down her cheek as she wrapped her arms around herself. She tried to push away the memories of how slick and tight his skin had been as her clawed finger had accidentally slipped in between his ribs, puncturing his lung. She could still see his mouth opening and closing, like a fish caught on dry land.

She remembered the first words of the entity as it had made its presence known, :: *Child. Be careful what you wish for. I will help you, yes, but for this service I require something rather strenuous in return. Are you certain you would be willing to make such a bargain?* ::

Her voice was unsteady as she replied aloud, "Wait, feed? I..I don't know what you mean. I don't understand."

The image of a raven-haired man with a nasty glint in his eye flared to life in her mind. The visual was disorienting, and it made her head swim. Several quick images of a location flashed through her mind in rapid succession. The man was standing at the edge of a dance floor, eyes sharp as they roved along a sea of dancing people before him, searching for something in earnest. The corner of his mouth twitched and his gaze darted hungrily from one girl to another. The distinct impression that he was hunting something hit her.

It became clear that she was now supposed to go out and find this man. She had to track him down. While Dani wasn't entirely certain what she'd do with the guy once she found him, an alien part of her curled in on itself in anticipation. With a sense of growing unease, she began to get an idea of what needed to happen. The vision cut off abruptly, leaving her sweating in the middle of the room, swaying gently. Dani recognized the location. There was no way she could get there without transportation, and she definitely couldn't drive a car in this condition.

"How am I even supposed to do this? I can barely walk without falling on my ass," she grumbled.

A sense of mild irritation that wasn't her own flickered through her as the sibilant voice rang out again, :: *You must work in alignment with the connection I have forged within you.* ::

Dani frowned, confused. "What does that even mean?"

Dani took another jerky, wobbling step forward. She closed her eyes, letting a slow breath out and then taking another. The body tremors calmed down a little.

Okay, that's a little better.

Another wave of nausea flooded her senses from the stench of the corpse crumpled against the wall. She needed to get the hell out of this room, but had never been entirely comfortable parading around the house naked to begin with, much less in front of a dead body. Dani winced and reached out to collect an over-sized grey night shirt from the back of a chair. After a few graceless and unsuccessful tries at getting her hands in the armholes, she finally pulled it on and stumbled out of the room.

Gotta get downstairs. I can't think with this reek in my nose.

She started coughing, slowly making her way down the stairs. The last thing she needed was to pitch over headfirst and break something. Her movements stayed jerky and ungainly as she navigated her way to the bottom floor. Once she stepped into the foyer, she collapsed again, her body beginning to shake as she hit the floor.

What the hell is happening to me?

The mild seizures lasted for a moment, then abated.

:: Focus your will, daughter. Only then will you be able to control yourself. ::

Dani took a deep breath and closed her eyes. She kept seeing her attacker's shocked expression as he staggered away from her; kept feeling the man's tongue against her skin. The urge to simply break and run was almost overwhelming. She began retching again, and the voice of the strange Dark Lady cracked like a whip as it echoed through her mind.

:: FOCUS. Now. ::

The command snapped something to attention inside her and she felt her body hauled up by an alien internal force. She stood rigidly, hands fisted at her sides, not liking the sensation at all. It was disorienting, but not really painful. Her right foot lurched forward and she heard it hit the floor with a loud thump. Now the left foot. Thump. Dani shuddered and tried to fight the feeling. It was distinctly unsettling.

:: Struggling will only increase the time that it will take you to acclimate to your changes, daughter. You must move with it, not against it. ::

And what, exactly, is this *it* you're referring to? Dani mentally snapped in response.

:: The sensations you experience now will only grow worse in time if you do not act. ::

The sound of someone rapping against the front door brought Dani's head jerking around, breaking her concentration as she slumped to the floor again. She quickly blinked and muttered, "Who the hell would be showing up at this time of night?" As if there wasn't enough going on.

At the sound of keys being slid into a lock, her chest tightened in fear.

Oh shit. The landlord.

The irritating man had the annoying habit of showing up whenever he happened to be in town, no matter the time of day or night, and he'd usually just let himself in to make sure that his tenants weren't ruining his property. Dani was certain that there had to be a law against these impromptu inspections, but she'd usually been away from home when he visited in the past. Most times she would come home to find a note in the kitchen detailing any annoying little issues that he happened to find. The man was remarkably unpleasant, so she tried to avoid him when he visited while she was at home. She scrambled back up against the wall as the front door opened.

The man strode confidently inside, as if he were arriving home at his own house.

Asshole, she grumbled internally.

He took a quick look around, then spotted Dani on the floor and took a quick step back, closing the door behind him.

"Jesus lady, you scared the shit out of me," he stammered, holding a hand up to his heart. He was an older man; Dani always figured he was about fifty.

She felt something inside her thrum with interest as she looked up at him. A strange red haze coiled around the man in wisps all over his body. It was faint, but definitely something that was difficult to miss.

OK, that's freaky.

The feeling grew stronger now as the man peered down at her with a strange expression and asked, "You a friend of that odd bird that lives here?"

His tone made it sound as if he had a hard time believing that Dani had any friends, much less ones that would actually visit her. His gaze swept along the curves of her body appreciatively as he extended a hand out to help her up. Dani frowned back at him, wondering why he didn't recognize her. She then blinked as she remembered her rather drastic appearance makeover. She now no longer looked remotely like the woman she once had been. Whatever else the strange entity in her head had done to her, it had also sculpted her body into a much more appealing form.

:: *To make you more enticing to your prey, daughter.* :: The voice had explained, adding, :: *One must always use the proper bait.* ::

She nodded mutely back at the landlord, accepting his hand and letting him help her up. She wobbled on her feet like a newborn foal and he chuckled, catching her before she fell again.

"You okay little lady? Been drinkin'?"

His voice had an odd timbre to it she didn't remember hearing before. He sounded almost pleasant. She tried to answer, but the words wouldn't come. Her landlord called up the stairs, "Dani, you wanna come check on your friend down here? She looks a little outta sorts."

He seemed nice enough, which baffled her. Dani couldn't remember him being anything but gruff and brusque with her in previous encounters. She finally found her voice and stammered, "Sh-she's not here. She went out to get us..snacks." It was the most plausible explanation she could come up with.

The landlord frowned as he helped her over to the couch and gently sat her down. Something about the man repelled her, but she couldn't quite put her finger on it. At the moment, he seemed pleasant enough.

"She left you alone? In my house?" he asked, his tone dropping into irritation.

Dani couldn't think of a good answer that would placate him, so she simply shrugged, trying to cover herself with the large shirt as best she could. His eyes were getting a little more interested in her new body than she liked.

"Let me go on and get you a glass of water. I'll be right back." he explained as he turned to head to the kitchen.

She heard him open a cabinet door, grumbling to himself as he filled the glass with water from the tap. "Could'a sworn that weird gal had no friends."

Dani had the feeling that he'd said it under his breath, but she'd heard it as clearly as if he had been standing beside her.

The man walked back into the room and handed her the glass. Her hand shook as she reached out to take it and as she clutched at it, the glass shattered in her hand. Startled both at the sound and the pain in her hand, Dani whimpered and cringed. The man peered at her closely, his eyes narrowing.

"You on somethin' girl? You been doin' drugs in my house?" His voice lowered to a dangerous growl as he said, "You're awful cute and all, but I don't brook no drugs bein' done on my property. You know the bank can take this house away from me if you kids do that shit on the premises?"

Ah, there he was. Now he was the asshole that she'd met with before. The man grabbed her wrist, his grip tightening painfully as he looked down at her hand.

"Christ, now you're gonna bleed all over everythin'. I ain't payin' to have the cleaners come out and siphon blood outta this carpet. C'mere." He hauled her to her feet, all false niceties dispensed with now as he grated, "Fuckin' junkies. You kids think you own the god-damned world."

Dani stumbled behind him and he looped an arm around her waist, holding her up as he made his way into the kitchen. His touch was rough and unpleasant, making her skin crawl. Dani shielded her eyes from the near blinding light of the fluorescent bulb.

"What'd you take, girl?" he demanded, unceremoniously dumping her into a chair. "Better tell me before I call the cops."

Dani could hear a low pitched hum that sounded as if it was coming from the man himself. It seemed to be getting louder the angrier he became. The man tossed her a moist hand towel, then sat across from her, his expression stony. As her eyes slowly adjusted, her senses suddenly picked up on a spicy scent that seemed to be emanating from him. A brief, alien emotion flickered through her and she stiffened.

What the hell was that??

A wave of images flared through her mind. *The inside of a house, somebody's living room. A man who looked to be in his thirties sat on a dilapidated couch with a carefree smile watching a football game and sipping a beer. A young girl, possibly thirteen, stepped between the man and the television wearing a very adult outfit that left very little to the imagination.*

"I put it on like you told me to, Uncle Jesse. Just like you said."

The girl's voice was high and reedy as tears slowly trickled down her face.

"That's real good scooter, real good. Now go on back in me an' your auntie's room and wait for me, okay?" he replied, a sickening leer pasted on his face.

The little girl began crying openly now, pleading incoherently with him.

"Now, what'd Uncle Jesse tell you about those tears?" he asked, his tone becoming darker. Angry.

The girl quickly wiped them away and fled the room. The man smiled and put his beer on the table beside the couch, then began softly whistling to himself as he turned the television off and stood up.

Dani looked back into the much older eyes of the man from her vision, shaken. :: *You begin to see now, child. You see the import of our work.* ::

The spicy smell was becoming stronger now as the man's mouth narrowed. "I said what the hell did you take?"

An odd sensation flared through her, bringing her to sit ramrod straight in the chair. She was shocked at the venom in her words as she crooned, "What did that little girl ever do to you to make you treat her like that? To make you hurt her?"

The man looked back at her, confused. "What the hell are you goin' on about?"

A malevolent cackle bubbled out of her throat and Dani shuddered inwardly as she heard herself say, "I put it on like you told me to, Uncle Jesse. Just like you said."

The man paled, then quickly stood up, knocking the chair over. The sharp sound made Dani wince inwardly. "What the fuck did you just say to me?" he whispered, his eyes wide.

Dani felt her lips curl into a smile, surprised to realize that his discomfort was pleasing her. "Oh, I think you heard me just fine, Uncle Jesse." The words dropped from her lips like honeyed poison. Dani had never heard herself sound so cold and seductive.

"How could you know that?" The man hissed. "What the fuck are you?" The man's emotions slid into cold fear and uncertainty as he continued stammering, "That was a lifetime ago, and I made sure she never told a soul." His eyes looked haunted as he backed up against the cabinets.

"Please, Uncle Jesse. It hurts! Please stop!"

Dani heard herself mocking the man in an ugly tone, shocked at her own behavior as well as that of the man before her. How could he have done that to his own niece? The man was sobbing now, holding his hands before him as if trying to ward something off as Dani slowly stood up. Her body moved of its own volition this time, and she remembered the words of the Dark Lady. Dani worked to coordinate her own thoughts to the movements that her body was making as it slowly stalked across the kitchen towards the whimpering man that was slowly sinking to the floor. He dropped his hands to his lap and trembled.

She found herself nose to nose with him and something in her shifted. Dani felt her body wobble slightly, but she seemed more stable now. She slowly inhaled his scent, sniffing him like a cat. "Don't you want to play anymore, Uncle Jesse? I promise I won't tell Aunt Gina."

The man roared and lashed out, knocking Dani over and kicking out at her. "Get the fuck away from me you freak!"

He quickly stood up and tried to get around her, but Dani swung a leg out, tripping him. As he sprawled out face first on the linoleum, she heard a meaty snap and the man began howling. She was on him in a flash. He kicked and thrashed as she pulled him closer. A sharp pain flared through her jaw as the heel of his shoe connected with it. She growled, feeling her fingers lengthening as she jammed the clawed tips into his leg. The man yelped out in pain, reached out and slapped at the side of her head, leaving her with a ringing sound in her ears.

He then kicked out again, hitting the leg of the kitchen table. The sound of a glass vase tipping over, then rolling off the side and crashing to the floor was so crisp and sharp it was agonizing. Dani clapped her hands over her ears, wincing. The man rolled over and began skittering away from her, his hands slipping on the blood spattered linoleum; his broken nose a red faucet. Dani gritted her teeth against the pain of the noise to reached out and grab one of his legs. The other caught her in the stomach and she slid across the kitchen floor. He was old, but strong, and so far he was kicking her ass. Dani struggled with him in earnest, earning herself several more kicks and punches to the shoulder and side, until she was finally able to straddle him, forcing his wrists down to the floor.

:: Now, daughter. Look into his eyes. ::

Dani frowned as the man's head thrashed back and forth. She forced one of his wrists beneath her knee, pinning it, then reached up to grab his jaw, meeting his gaze. The move felt right, as if she'd done it all her life. The man beneath her trembled as a gurgling sound choked out of the back of his throat. His eyes went wide as she felt herself slip into his psyche with an ease that both excited and frightened her. His jaw went slack, and his eyes became glassy as she held him. She was immediately overwhelmed by a dizzying procession of memories that slid through her consciousness, dumping into the grey matter of the man beneath her. She winced at the imagery, not wanting to see it, not wanting to know that there were people that were capable of this in the world. Sure, she'd read about this sort of thing before, but the difference between reading words on a stark page and witnessing the act itself was so vivid it made her sick.

The man's consciousness writhed like a stuck pig as the memories stabbed at it, worming themselves into the darker parts of his psyche and taking root there; sliding into him and forcing him to experience everything that he did to that poor girl through her perspective. Dani felt the beginning of what she could only describe as a memory loop of sorts as the collected fury of his past horrors revisited him and slowly began tearing his mind apart. She felt something in his mind snap, and the voice of the Dark Lady echoed in her mind again.

:: *Now nourish yourself, child. There is much work to be done.* ::

Dani looked down at the twitching form of the man beneath her and hesitated. His mouth quivered, almost as if he were trying to say something, but nothing but a long slow exhalation of a tortured breath came out. The tantalizing scent of him became overwhelming again and she leaned in, startled at how easily her teeth slipped into his neck. It went much smoother with him than it had with the body upstairs and she eagerly drank down the hot, delicious liquid. After a few moments, she heard an erratic flutter in his heartbeat.

:: *You must stop now, child, else he will have no time to appreciate the enormity of the payment for his crime.* ::

Dani quickly pulled away, and immediately felt like throwing up when she saw the agonized expression on his face. Her throat began convulsing and the voice of the Dark Lady rang out painfully in her mind.

:: *You must learn to keep it down, daughter. This is your only true sustenance now. If you keep expelling it, you will sicken and fade.* ::

Dani clapped a hand over her mouth, scrambling off of the man and looking away from him, trying to think of anything but the fact that she'd just killed two men in cold blood in a single night.

And this is better than the life I had before how? She grated internally, forcing the contents of her stomach back down.

:: *You desired my intervention, and this is the payment I demand for services rendered, daughter. However, it does come with certain benefits that will reveal themselves to you in time.* ::

Dani shuddered and backed up against the kitchen cabinets, trying desperately not to scream. She could feel the edges of hysteria pressing against her.

:: *Come child. It is not as bad as all that. Think of the innocent that he corrupted. That he tortured. It is an unforgivable thing, and he must be called to account for it. This justice you mete out in my name, it is your glory.* ::

Dani felt her breath calming, her pulse slowing as the Dark Lady spoke. The sibilant, hissing voice was somehow soothing, reassuring. :: *You dance in divine fury with my blessing, daughter. Never be ashamed of this.* ::

Dani's eyes darted over to the still breathing form of her landlord. Every once in a while the man's foot would twitch, his leg jerking. A strange, savage joy fluttered in her. This man had performed monstrous acts, things that made Dani's stomach roil. The Dark Lady was right. He was finally paying for those savage moments he had stolen from the life of that young girl. The odd thing was that he really had seemed harmless enough in the past, even though he could be an outright prick. She never would've suspected it of him.

:: *Monsters do not always wear a murderous guise, child. Many times, they are the ones whom you least suspect.* ::

Yeah, I'm getting that, Dani replied, her expression tightened with disgust. She found it somewhat odd that she was getting used to having an inner dialog with, well, whatever it was that had changed her life and was now directing her actions. Letting out a long, slow breath, Dani stood up, realizing that the light no longer hurt her eyes as much as it had before. She frowned, then snapped her fingers several times before letting out a sigh of relief. Colors, light, and sound were still vivid, but nowhere near as overwhelming now.

"Oh, thank god. One less thing to worry about." Dani murmured to herself as she leaned back against the counter top. She looked back over at her soon-to-be ex landlord, relieved that there didn't seem to be as much blood all over the place as there had been with the attacker upstairs. Dani's gut churned as she realized that the rest of it was now being processed in the pit of her stomach. She closed her eyes and again forced her gut to settle down. Letting out a slow, shaky breath, she looked around the kitchen.

"I need to get the hell out of here." she muttered, looking around for a towel to clean up the blood smeared on the tile. Collecting a towel from the handle of the refrigerator, she began blinking quickly. It was difficult to process everything that had just happened. At least the blinds in the kitchen were down so nobody could peek in to see the disarray and the body. Had anybody heard anything? The sharp image of the raven-haired man flared through her mind again, as if to remind her that there was something she'd forgotten.

Dani's mouth gaped in astonishment as she said, "Wait – even after all this, you still want me to go out and find that guy? Tonight??"

:: *There are many things to be done, child. Will this not also get you out of your residence? Was this not what you wished?* ::

Dani frowned in irritation. The last thing she wanted to do was stay in this house with everything that had just happened. If there was one thing she'd learned throughout her life, it was to persevere and adapt. She just never thought that this would be so harshly put to the test before. She was still reeling from the night's events, and was having a difficult time regrouping.

:: *If it will put you at ease, this will be the last task I require from you this night, beloved daughter. After your work has concluded, you may rest.* ::

Dani took a deep breath, then walked past the body on the floor, tossing the dishtowel down over its face. She then began the laborious process of cleaning up her mess.

Two
Adjustment

With both bodies safely stashed in the basement, Dani had quickly jumped in the shower to wash off the stink of the night's activities. She leaned forward now, peering back at the strange woman in the mirror. It was still difficult to believe that the image reflected there was her own. Her skin had turned alabaster, almost iridescent in the dim light that radiated in from the other room. Her fingers brushed the surface of the mirror, the tips meeting those of the image looking back at her as she turned to look at her now waist-length indigo hair. A startling shock of white ran through the middle of it. The weight of it was substantial now as it stuck in wet, stringy tendrils against her back. Her eyes, which had been a pale hazel all her life, were now a vibrant, jewel tone, royal blue.

Blinking and pulling her hand away from the mirror, she peered down at it. Her hands were now smooth and graceful as she held both of them before her, turning them over and frowning. She ran a hand down her arm and squinted as she spotted several strange black symbols that looked like tattoos inked around her fingers and wrists. Dani inspected them, marveling again at the arcane sigils that decorated fingers that were now much more delicate than she remembered having. The markings seemed to have no surface to them, reflecting no light whatsoever. It was as if the skin there was just gone. She ran a trembling finger over one of the designs, and was surprised to feel unbroken skin beneath her fingertips. Dani looked back up at her reflection, relieved that all her freckles were now gone, along with the mousy shock of short, reddish brown hair she'd had.

With a jarring shock, she realized that the scar that had caused so much anguish throughout her life was nowhere to be seen. She shook her head gently as she looked back at the alien woman in the mirror. There was no longer even the merest shadow of the scar along her skin.

In fact, there were no traces of any of the various other blemishes she'd acquired over the years. Her eyes rimmed with tears. The only man in her life that had ever wanted to continue touching her after he'd seen what she had to offer, had then brutally raped her. That man now sat in a crumpled heap in the bowels of the house, stone cold dead. She was finding the surreality of the situation a little difficult to deal with.

Dani let her fingers play gently against the soft texture of her new skin, marveling at its smoothness. She then looked back at her reflection before wrapping her hair in a towel and stepping out of the bathroom. The stench was still present, but it was nowhere near as offensive now that the source was secreted away in the basement. She remembered the thump-thump-thump of the landlord's head against the stairs as she'd dragged the body behind her into the bowels of the house. The man had still been somewhat alive when she finally dumped him in a corner. Her opinion was firm – the world was better off without a man like that.

By the time she'd made another trip up the stairs to collect the body from her bedroom, it had been easier to control her movements. It was almost as if she was working out some strange kink in her nerves and muscles. She was adapting quicker than she thought she would, which was a relief.

Another vision of the man in the bar flickered to life in her thoughts. This time it felt less invasive, less painful. The location was a place she remembered visiting once or twice in the past, but she hadn't liked the crowd much. It was a goth/industrial club located in a bad part of town, and there had been entirely too many 'children in black' trying very hard to look bored and disaffected. Their whole social dance had seemed like such a wasted effort to her.

As she made her way over to the closet to find something to wear, she remembered seeing a familiar red haze around the man that coiled in wisps all around his body. Interesting. For an image that lasted about half a second, she certainly seemed to be able to recall it with an amazing amount of detail.

:: It is the shroud of their crime you see, daughter. The brighter it is, the farther the corruption has expanded in their psyche. ::

Good to know, Dani thought to herself, suppressing a small shiver as she reached out to pluck a black mini dress from its perch. Again, she thought of her hand and frowned. She was positive that the glass had cut into her palm deeply, but her skin had been clean and unbroken when she'd finally come out of shock enough to realize it. She wasn't entirely sure what that meant. Maybe the injury hadn't been as bad as she'd thought it was.

She held the dress up and pursed her lips. Would it still fit? She'd picked it up years ago for a company function. Everything else was either business attire or casual clothes. She pulled the black dress over her head, watching it slide down over her legs in the full-length mirror on the inside of her closet door. The fit was a bit loose, with her new body now being slimmer and surprisingly taller. She hadn't noticed the increased height earlier.

The dress would have to do. She wouldn't be able to get anything else to work on such short notice. She zipped herself up and slid her feet into a pair of black heels, grinding her teeth as she realized that they were now a size too small. Lovely. Dani fished through the closet, finding a pair of black flats that she had tossed into the back of the closet a couple of months ago. She'd gotten them for an amazing price, but they had ended up being too big.

She'd picked them up for a special occasion and had to stuff toilet paper into the tips of the shoes in order to get them to fit better, but afterwards had found no use for them. She slid them on, and the fit was only slightly better now. Not perfect, but workable. At least she wouldn't be in agony walking around all damned night. Things were bad enough as it was. Now, what was she going to do with all this hair?

Dani wasn't used to having so much of it and so had nothing lying around with which she could tie it up. She sighed and made her way downstairs, looking around for something that would suffice. On the small marble table in the hallway, she found a set of black lacquer chopsticks in a vase that held black and red silk flowers. Little chrome dragons with tails that ran about an inch down the chopsticks perched at the tips, their teeth bared menacingly. She quickly pulled them out and used them to pin her damp hair up. The finished result wasn't great, but it'd do for now. After all, it wasn't as if she was going out on a date or anything.

Dani looked up, checking out her reflection in the hallway mirror. In the light of the foyer her skin seemed to give off a slight glow, the depths of her blue eyes glittering as she grinned back tentatively at the alien reflection. Taking a deep breath, she spun around, grabbing a black coat and her keys as she headed back to the garage door.

Her lips curled into a grin as she opened it and stepped into the garage. She bent down to open the door to her baby – a flat black '66 Karmann Ghia with white leopard print seats and sharp fins that extended out past the bumper in points. Sliding into the driver's seat, she let out a heavy sigh, happy that her disorientation was receding a little more as she started the car up. Dani wrapped her fingers around the bloodshot eyeball on the top of the gearshift and relaxed.

The carnival of lights on the road took a little getting used to, and Dani forced herself to drive slowly so that she didn't get disoriented and wreck her baby. As she pulled up to the warehouse bar, the worst of the road disorientation seemed to be gone. Dani parked the car in the side lot, more than happy to pay ten bucks to have her pride and joy guarded by club security goons while she was otherwise engaged. She'd be damned if she was going to park it on the street in this neighborhood. Taking a pair of sunglasses out of her purse, she covered up her now unnaturally blue eyes and headed off toward the club.

One look at the crowd was all it took to realize that she looked very out of place. At least nobody seemed to be looking her way. For the most part everybody kept to themselves, intent on keeping up the appearance of being bored by the 'scene' from which they were all so terribly jaded. It was one of the main reasons she'd stopped going out in the first place. Now the club was full of an impressive collection of empty shells in flashy goth and industrial uniforms.

There didn't seem to be any true individuality left in the world, and it depressed the hell out of her. The music echoing from the club had a forceful, driving rhythm, setting her heart to pounding and her hands to shaking slightly. The pain in her gut twisted as she stood in line behind two snotty women who were complaining rather vociferously about one of the DJ's weekly tendencies to rant and rave drunkenly halfway through the night.

An overpowering scent drifted past her on the night air from the gathering of children on the sidewalk as they waited to gain entrance to the building. It was something she didn't remember picking up on before tonight, and she was a little annoyed that she couldn't place it. A boisterous boy bumped into her, not even bothering to apologize to her as he continued to gesticulate wildly to the pack of friends with whom he'd arrived.

This is the problem. Nobody has any goddamned manners anymore.

Dani glared at him, swearing that she could hear his heartbeat over the din.

As the line moved along, she tapped her foot impatiently behind a pair of girlish twits who were arguing with the doorman about what constituted a legal ID. After what seemed like an eternity, she stood in front of a large, beautiful mocha-skinned man with deep chocolate-colored eyes. His voice was a sensual rumble as he looked down at her and asked her for her ID.

She quickly presented it to him, and he frowned. For a moment, her stomach dropped. She'd forgotten that she now looked nothing like the picture on her license. The man cocked an eyebrow at her as if she'd insulted his intelligence. The look said that he was disgusted that she wasn't even trying.

Damn, she grated to herself, her face flushing with color. She stood before him unmoving as she felt a strange electric tingle around her scalp. The man frowned harder as she felt something in her mind reach out to touch his. She felt a gentle push go through her, and watched as the doorman's eyes widened briefly. He sized her up for a moment before finally handing the ID back to her and waving her though with a noncommittal look on his face.

What the hell just happened?

She shook her head and set the thought aside. She'd figure it out later.

She couldn't help noticing that he smelled really good, almost delicious as she walked past him. Dani's mouth began watering slightly at the realization that everybody around her was redolent with their own odor. Some people, like the doorman, had scents that stood out from the others, who smelled bland and unappealing.

The doorman smelled slightly spicy, reminding her of her hunger. She cast a brief glance back at him before heading towards the ticket window just inside. The woman behind the glass looked annoyed at having to actually work as she thrust a begrudging hand out to collect her money before pressing a cornflower blue ticket into Dani's hand and waving her on.

I don't know why people come here if they're all so obviously miserable, she thought to herself before walking up a ramp to another bored individual that was chatting up a grimy graver chick with a truly garish haircut. They both reeked of rancid patchouli oil that smelled as if it had been left in the back of a car for a year in a puddle of grease and urine. The combination was distinctly unpleasant, and her nose wrinkled as she handed her ticket over, not really wanting to come into physical contact with an individual that smelled that odoriferous.

God, had people always smelled this bad without her noticing it? *Ugh.*

The guy took it without acknowledging her presence, which she thought was an interesting trick. Not that she was complaining. The two wretched-smelling individuals could keep well to themselves as far as she was concerned.

The steady thrum of music had been sending delicious little tremors through her since she'd entered and was now almost overpowering as she moved past them, making her way into the club proper.

The place was enormous, its high corrugated warehouse ceilings and grey granite walls decorated with metal art constructs and colored lights. The bright spots of color in the dim club lighting coupled with the sound was extremely disorienting initially, and she moved over to the wall, holding a trembling arm against it as she fought to gain control of herself.

"How the hell am I supposed to function if I'm completely over-whelmed by sensation every five minutes?" She muttered angrily before steeling her resolve and slowly venturing into the crowd.

One of her favorite songs started booming loudly out of the sound system, bringing a heat to her skin that seemed to drift along it, tick-ling along the little hairs on her arm and the back of her neck. It felt as if she'd just taken a hit of adrenaline as the music pumped through her body; her breath coming in hitches as she stepped closer to the dance floor. Dani seemed to pass some imaginary line in the room and was bowled over by sensation. She wrapped trembling arms around herself to try to get it under control. She shivered as she watched the sea of people on the dance floor bounce around to the beat. It was intoxicating.

For the first time, she noticed small, almost ghostly little red threads that extended from those on the dance floor back to her stomach. The threads all seemed to meet at the same focal point on her belly. Something rolled through her, purring inside as she felt a part of herself reach out to pluck, then pull at the little threads.

It felt strange, but also seemed natural at the same time. Her eyes fluttered shut as a lightly pulsating energy flowed into her, taking the sharp edges off the hunger, momentary disorientation, and pain. Cocking her head to the side, she reached out and pulled harder, licking her lips at the fluttering energy that answered. A group of people on the dance floor swooned, and Dani quickly backed off.

Oops.

The now familiar sibilant voice slid through her thoughts again, laughing lightly as it spoke. :: *What you are feeling is the latent energy in those around you. You are tapping into it automatically now because your reserves are so low that you're in pain. As you experience more, you will learn how to effectively utilize this talent to feed in case of an emergency. As you've seen, if you draw too strongly, it will have obvious side effects. For now, open your eyes and look towards the bar.* ::

Dani did as the voice asked, catching a glimpse of the man she'd seen in her earlier vision. The red haze that surrounded him was now churning aggressively, almost stabbing out at the women around him as they passed by. His expression was thick with disdain, which was drawing women to him like a powerful pheromone. She never quite understood why women always seemed to be attracted to assholes.

He wasn't ugly, by any means, but the look in his eyes was enough to turn her stomach. Dani turned back to the dance floor, unsure of how to proceed. She'd been running on autopilot since she decided to leave the house and run this errand. Now she felt a small coil of doubt creep in. With a slow breath, something inside her clicked as a reassuring presence filled her. Suddenly, she had it. Setting her jaw, she turned to head towards the bar, putting a little sway in her hips as she moved through the crowd. The sea of people parted before her, flowing around her like eddies around a rock in a stream.

Dani caught the man's eye as she passed him, her gaze lingering on him for a moment before lazily turning to look back at the dance floor. She leaned back into the bar, her pulse quickening as she felt him move closer. His excitement resonated at an almost painful level. How anybody could stand near him and not know his intentions seemed unthinkable.

The man trembled as he stepped up to her and she found herself briefly swept up into a chaotic swirl of violent thoughts when he leaned into her, presenting her with an even, cocky smile. Various unbidden images of violence scratched through her thoughts as he spoke.

"You are extraordinary. A goddess among us, as I live and breathe. Can I get you something to drink?" His voice was a smooth purr. His eyes glittered dangerously as his smile broadened into a friendly grin. To anybody else, his expression would probably have seemed open and genuine.

Dani forced a smile, her stomach roiling at the desires she found running through his head. She was extremely uneasy at being able to see what was in his thoughts so clearly. So vividly. God knows she wasn't the one coming up with the imagery. She'd never even seen most of the women that flickered through his thoughts, screaming and fighting. It had to be him. Dani nodded and accepted, stating her preference and the pair of them conversed inanely until he was ready to finally make his move.

Thank god. Listening to the man yammer on and on about his business, his money and his position was both tiring and irritating. When he suggested that they 'go somewhere private', she gave an inward sigh, thankful that she'd be able to stop with the charade soon. This shaky, murderous man was really beginning to irk her. Apparently he had taken a cab to the club, so they'd have to use her car.

As they walked up to the Ghia, her hands started to shake. She dropped the keys before being able to insert them into the lock, growling a silent curse to herself. She had been able to kill earlier, but would it come so easily again? Dani didn't want to know what would happen if she found herself unable to follow through with what the strange dark lady wanted. The man chuckled softly and bent down to pick them up, placing them back into her hands and gazing at her with a strange fondness that made her even more uneasy.

Ugh, he thinks it's charming that I'm so jittery, she thought to herself.

Once they were in the car, he placed a hand on her knee and began rattling off various details about his job and expounding upon what he thought 'the scene' was really all about. Dani nodded and tried to act interested as the engine kicked to life. She had agreed to go back to his place, for obvious reasons.

During the drive, she found herself almost wanting to wreck the car just to shut him the hell up. He finally had her pull into an old, run down industrial park. She spotted a lone, decrepit house on the side of the road, knowing that it was his but unsure of where this certainty came from.

Perfect place to hide multiple bodies, Dani thought grimly to herself as she pulled up in front of this house that seemed as out of place as a frog in a liquor store.

She wondered at the age of the house. Had the industrial park just sprung up across from it? Had the original owners been unwilling to sell for some odd reason? The front yard was a disaster area covered in a wide variety of filthy trash bags, rotting mattresses, and shopping carts from various grocery stores. None of the buildings in the park looked like they were currently being used, and everything in the 'neighborhood' was in a general state of disrepair, seemingly forgotten. Several of the buildings in the park were slowly being covered with creeping vines and ivy, and grass crept out through cracks in the pavement in the middle of the street. She was surprised that anybody could actually live in such a place. The man presented her with an eager grin when she looked back at him after assessing the area.

What an utter dump. Did women really fall for this shtick? Dani supposed that once he'd gotten his victims out this far it was likely much too late for them to do anything about it. As she shifted into park and turned the car off, her companion leaned towards her, his hand on her knee squeezing gently as he moved in to kiss her. Dani politely pushed him away, wanting to wait until they were at least out of the confines of the car before she made her move.

The man paused, his face coloring in anger. He grabbed her, his voice quickly changing to a nasty growl as he cocked a hand back. She barely felt the blow as his hand connected with her cheek, and her head jerked back. It was a strike that would've probably knocked a normal woman out, or at the very least into a state of shock. It didn't hurt but it still startled her. He grabbed her arm and yanked hard, pulling her across the gearshift and out the passenger side door. He did his best to wrench her arm as he unceremoniously dumped her out onto the sidewalk.

Dani remained silent, her expression a little frightened as she stared up at him. His face twisted into an ugly smile as he looked down at her. What the hell was she supposed to do now? She felt lost again, unsure of how to proceed before a now familiar little shift happened, filling her with a terrible resolve. He let out a harsh laugh as he took a step away from her, amused at her confusion and fear as he checked his handiwork.

She felt a cold wind blow through her as she turned to look up at him, her face now devoid of expression. He frowned, taking another step back and re-evaluating the situation after sensing that the dynamic had changed. For a moment uncertainty flickered across his face. He then quickly recovered, becoming red with rage as he reached down, grabbing her hair and hauling her up by it. As she wobbled unsteadily on her feet, laughter bubbled up out of her throat and something inside her began to vibrate, sending a delicious tremor through her.

Dani suddenly knew exactly what was going to happen next and that something inside her was going to enjoy it very, very much. Rich, throaty laughter rang out through the night air as she looked back at him, blue eyes glittering. The man seemed taken aback, but only momentarily this time. Effortlessly, Dani dipped into his consciousness, laughing harder as the man began to rage.

He'd be damned if some bitch laughed at him; especially while he was roughing her up. He'd have to teach her, like he had taught the others. He growled at her then, spittle flying in flecks from his lips as he brought his hand back to deliver another blow across her face.

Dani easily blocked it. Her hand moved faster than her own eyes could track as she grabbed his hand and jerked it sharply towards her. She was startled at the ease with which she snapped his bones. She'd barely flicked her wrist and they had broken with a muffled crack. Dani heard the dark laughter of her patroness in the back of her thoughts as she released his wrist and took a step back to watch him cradle his ruined hand.

Dani chuckled darkly as her prey whimpered. Seemingly of their own volition, her hands darted out in a white blur, grabbing his shoulders and tossing him away from her. Her eyes widened as she watched the man sail across the yard, smashing shoulder first into a large green dumpster before crumpling onto a bare patch of grass. She held her hands up and looked at them, her brow furrowing as her gaze flickered back over to the man who was now breathing in rapid, shallow breaths at the other end of the yard.

Picking her way through the garbage as she walked over to him, Dani cocked her head and inspected the damage she'd inflicted so easily. Shards of bone now poked out through the bloody ruin of the man's wrist, his hand twisting back at an unnatural angle. He was still conscious, but being tossed against the dumpster had knocked the wind out of him as well as broken a couple of ribs. Beads of sweat dotted his forehead and his skin had gone very pale.

She felt a nasty grin play at the edges of her lips, her voice harsh as she spat, "Easy pickins', eh? Not this time, little boy. I'm the last woman that you'll set eyes on in this lifetime."

Dani growled as she knelt beside him, twisting his head and forcing his eyes to meet hers. A familiar connection snapped into place between them as a whirlwind of painful memories waited eagerly on the sidelines to scream down the line into his consciousness, wanting desperately to become a furious storm of reckoning in the man's psyche. As she cut through his thoughts, she'd found that he'd gone through about a dozen women so far and had convinced himself that he'd never be caught. He was on top of the world in his own mind. She was surprised to find that he was also apparently involved in pretty shady business dealings, having successfully embezzled over twenty million dollars out of the company at which he was currently a trusted employee. Dani chased the information down through his neural pathways. The details of the various transactions and account numbers settled into her memory, waiting in her grey matter to be recalled, should she happen to need them.

Money and power dominated the man's thoughts, along with the vicious and intense imagery of the various acts performed on the women he'd tortured and murdered. A rough push in her mind directed the images and feelings of his victims back at him, creating a loop of torment that caused him to experience every moment of the violence – through the eyes of his victims – all the pain and fear he'd forced on them – over and over again. She became a conduit that forced him to feel everything that he'd subjected them to, and something inside her lurched forward, pulling from him, greedily consuming his fear.

She delighted in it. It was much stronger than the connection she'd forged with the landlord, and she bared her teeth against the horrific barrage, snarling as he whimpered and choked on the feedback of the collective experienced horror of his victims. Dark laughter scraped through her head as the voice of the lady brushed against her mind again.

:: *You are a natural at this, my daughter. The more he suffers, the better nourishment he will provide you. Drink him, but do not kill him. Leave him to die here amongst the filth, alone and shattered. This will be suitable payment for what he has done.* ::

Dani shuddered before roughly gripping the man's uninjured wrist, yanking it to her mouth and wrapping her lips around the pulse jumping frantically beneath his skin. She bit down and was rewarded with a hot crimson jet across her tongue. It was ambrosial and sent an electric shiver down her spine as she pulled the liquid life out of him. Her eyes fluttered shut as the coil of dull pain in her gut began to fade and was replaced with warmth and satisfaction. After a few moments, she began sensing that she'd kill him outright if she took more.

It took considerable effort to pull away from the hunger and look back at him. His eyes were now completely mad with torment, his features twisted into a gruesome rictus of unimaginable anguish. A small trickle of yellow drool trailed out of the corner of his mouth, dripping from his cheek to the ground below.

Dani cocked her head, pursed her lips, and watched him with a clinical detachment as he sagged to the ground. He'd live just long enough to suffer properly for his actions. The energy from the man's blood sang through her as she slowly stood and looked up into the night sky. In her entire existence, she had never remembered feeling so alive. The stars in the heavens seemed to dance as she watched them glitter against a canopy of darkness. She was now giddy from the power that sang in her veins.

Dani felt a touch nauseous and a little uneasy as she looked back down at her would-be assailant. Her third casualty of the night. Well, he hadn't expired yet, but that was the expected end result of her actions tonight. It was a strange feeling, but she noticed that it didn't really seem to be colored with remorse. After all, the guy had been raping and killing young women as a form of entertainment and had intended the same fate for her. He wasn't exactly innocent. Something felt very right about what she'd just done, but it still made her uncomfortable. She hadn't gotten into so much as a slap fight in her life and now in the space of less than twenty four hours, she'd killed three people. Savagely. Granted, she'd always had moments of imagined violence towards people that had pissed her off, but this was entirely different from vivid daydreams of petty vengeance.

Dani frowned as she thought about her next move.

I should probably bury him. If corpses start piling up in the open, investigations will begin. Best to be smart about this.

She thought briefly about the corpses she'd left in the basement at her old house, before reaching down and grabbing the man's pant legs Dani dragged him to the back of the house, pulling him through the rancid trash littering the lawn. She danced around some of the more squishy patches of ick before propping him up against the base of a mound of garbage, wondering if he happened to have a shovel some-where in this dump.

She scanned the yard, spotting a shed off to the right. A thick pad-locked chain snaked through the handles on the doors. Dani reached down and inspected the lock as the links clinked against one another. Great. No key. Exactly how strong was she now? Could she break it? She shrugged, deciding to give it a try. Grabbing the lock, she gave it a rough tug, yelping in surprise when the handles came off both doors with a cracking sound.

The doors swung open to reveal an array of tools and machines that hadn't seen much use in a long time. Spotting a rusty shovel in the corner, she dropped the chain, reaching in to fetch it. Maybe her luck was changing. There was a dull tug on her hand as she pulled the shovel away from the wall. Bringing it into the light, she noticed a jagged tear in the webbing between her thumb and forefinger.

It didn't really hurt, which she thought odd. Dani looked at her hand closely, inspecting it. It had probably just gotten nicked by a nail or a sharp tool.

Great. At least it wasn't painful. Just gory. She walked back to the body and began digging a hole large enough to drop it into, surprised at how effortlessly she could jam the shovel into the rough earth. Within a few quick minutes, there was a body-sized hole in the ground. Dani figured that she would kick him into it after he finally expired.

After stabbing the shovel into the ground off to the side of the hole, she took another look at her hand, noticing that the wound had closed up completely. She wiped the blood off on her dress and examined it more closely. It was as if the skin had never been broken. There wasn't even a slight discoloration or mottling. Her eyes narrowed as she looked down at her dress, which was now patchy with dirt and muck.

The names of the women that her assailant had killed stayed burned into her memory, as if waiting for something. Their faces twisted in her mind as they held up their hands in self defense, scream-ing as he had attacked them. The combination of the images and the rank odor of rotting garbage was nauseating. Dani brought the back of her hand up to her mouth as she fought to keep from vomiting. The yard swayed in her vision for a moment before she gained control of herself. She looked back over at him, realizing that it would probably be a good idea to relieve him of any plastic or cash that he happened to have on him.

He sure as hell won't be needing any of it now, she thought as she leaned down and began rooting through his pockets for his wallet and any other useful items that he might have. He'd amassed an impressive collection of platinum cards and had a rather tidy sum of cash on him. He was either entirely too egotistical about his financial status or just ridiculously stupid. His driver's license had his address listed in another state entirely.

She turned back to the house, wondering if he actually lived here or if this was just an effective place to bring the women that he tortured and killed. He'd buried quite a few of them in the backyard, she realized with a shiver. She stood, turned away from him, and started towards the back door.

The back porch light was on and she noticed a light in one of the upper rooms was on as well. Were the other utilities on as well? Maybe he did live here. Dani shrugged, hoping the water was still in working order as she made her way to the back door. It'd be a bonus if there were some clothes inside that she could use as well. She wanted to remove the dress as soon as possible. The blood and other fluids were already sticky and she felt fairly soiled.

Dani tested the back door, it was locked. She pushed the door firmly and the wood frame around the lock gave with a loud snap. She stumbled into a sizable kitchen. She looked around, and raised an eyebrow.

The inside looked slightly better than the outside of the house, but was still disgusting. Dishes were piled in the sink and several enormous roaches skittered under a microwave. Dani shuddered. She'd never liked bugs much. Especially roaches. She wondered how fully they had infiltrated the house. She walked over to the sink, turned the faucet knob, and clean water splashed over the dishes.

Good sign. At least she'd be able to take a shower. This would be her fourth tonight, and after all the scrubbing she still felt filthy. Dani turned the water off and walked into the hallway. The floors were dirty and needed mopping, but were still in decent condition. With a little work, the house might actually be turned into a viable living space.

Dani investigated the rest of the house, not wanting to be startled by something nasty while she was in the shower. The house was empty and dilapidated, except for the upper rooms, which her 'gracious host' had filled with modern furnishings and decor. Apparently he had been a bit of a clotheshorse. His closets were practically overflowing with designer suits and shoes. Confident that she'd have something to wear once she cleaned herself up and discarded her sticky garments, she tossed his wallet onto the bed and went to quickly shower off.

Dani sighed as she toweled herself off in front of the bathroom mirror. She stared in the mirror, mesmerized by the movement of muscles beneath her skin, which was now giving off a strange glow under the fluorescent lighting.

She wondered how people could possibly mistake her for a normal person. Her eyes glittered like sharp jewels in their sockets, indigo depths burning. She looked over at her bra soaking in the sink, thinking that it was about time to get another one. She'd apparently gone up a cup size as well. Dani reached up and tossed the towel over the shower curtain bar, leaving it to dry as she walked into the bedroom. After a brief hunt through various dresser drawers, she pulled on a pair of gray drawstring sweats and a white tank top. At least the man knew how to dress casual.

Dani collected the wallet from where she'd tossed it, sat down and pulled her feet up under her as she began plucking credit cards out of it. She spread them around in a pattern on the sheets, leaving the money off to the side. As she ran her fingers over them, she wondered if she should start to head home soon. She frowned as she realized that she didn't want to go back. She had no desire to return to a life of constantly smothering her anger and frustration in order to keep from losing the existence that she'd built for herself. Admittedly, it wasn't that great a life to begin with and she would be more than glad to see the back of it.

She no longer looked anything like the woman that had originally signed the lease. If she returned, the neighbors would likely begin to wonder about the strange woman's comings and goings, wanting to know where the original tenant had gone. Not to mention, if somebody had called the police while she was out, there would be a fair amount of explaining to do if she returned. God only knows how much noise she'd made while she had defended herself. She was lucky that she'd been able to leave the house before the police arrived to investigate.

She sighed, then peered out the window and checked the backyard. The man was still slumped over and drooling onto a pile of garbage.

Why not this place? she thought to herself.

Sure, it would take work to get it livable, but it could definitely be done. She definitely wouldn't mourn her old life. The only thing waiting back at her house was a continuing spiral into severe depression and a grinding search for a new job that she could only hope wasn't crappier than the last one.

Dani had been looking for a way out of everything for so long and now that she was being presented with the perfect opportunity. She was hard pressed not to take it. She'd be damned if she would let a little discomfort with her new occupation keep her from enjoying this new identity. Dani smiled as she felt a palpable weight lift from her, and a short bark of laughter escaped her lips, sounding loud in the small bedroom.

She quickly covered her mouth out of habit, then began to laugh openly. A throaty sound full of joy rang off the walls as she flopped back onto the bed and stretched her arms out, flexing her fingers in the covers. This definitely had possibilities.

Three

Opportunity Strikes

Dani's eyes followed the second hand of the clock on the nightstand as it slowly swept over the tics etched into its face. With everything that had happened she figured that she'd be well and completely exhausted, but was surprised that she was curiously energized. There was a curved sliver of light high in the sky as she turned to look out the window.

What to do now...?

Dani pursed her lips, remembering a room that looked like an office. In a fluid movement of feline grace she was on her feet and padding down the hall. On a meticulously kept desk sat a black laptop and a medium-sized accordion file folder of paperwork. For a murdering psychopath, this guy seemed pretty anal retentive about his workspace.

Not spotting a network cable coming out of the laptop, Dani assumed that the guy had installed a wireless hub somewhere in the house. She couldn't see it in the room anywhere. The room itself was very Spartan, sporting no motivational posters or personal markings of any kind. Dani pulled the black leather office chair away from the desk, rolling her eyes as she caught sight of the bright, bold scrolling text of his screen saver.

"If you can actually count your money then you are not really a rich man."
- J. Paul Getty.

Words to die by.

Dani chuckled to herself as her fingers danced over the keys, her voice having a smoky lilt to it as she murmured, "And here I thought that being a tech geek would never pay off."

She typed a website address into the browser, grinning as the site popped up immediately. She offhandedly found herself wondering what kind of internet service he had. It was at least as speedy as the connection at her office. With the information she pulled from the man's head earlier she was able to access his Swiss bank account. The resident of this hideous little domicile who was quietly expiring on the lawn outside had socked away a truly breathtaking amount of money. Dani figured that it was only a matter of time before somebody went looking for it. Most of it seemed to be kept in an institution called Credit Suisse. Thankfully, they had an international branch in New York.

It only made sense to collect the illicit funds as soon as possible. It would be simple enough to set up an account to transfer the funds over, but the transaction could be too easily tracked for her liking. Given her new job and appearance, she had no desire to have anybody try to come looking for her, for any reason. It would only end up causing problems that she didn't want to deal with on top of everything else.

Dani frowned. She'd be unable to empty the account in an untraceable manner without actually having the man who originally opened it show up at the bank in person. This presented a problem. The thought of all that money sitting and rotting in a bank account that nobody could touch annoyed her, but then she remembered the doorman at the bar earlier. Would she be able to do the same thing in this instance? There was only one way to find out.

After doing some in-depth online research on the dead man's various accounts and holdings, Dani had to give him at least a little credit for keeping such a low profile. Most people that had pulled off similar scams would've been stupid about it, and immediately started living a lavish lifestyle, garnering the rapt attention of the IRS. While he'd been smart about some things, he'd shown very poor judgment in others.

She also rifled through the collected utility bills in the desk drawer, checking to see if he had been stupid enough to put his legal name on the statements.

It turned out that he'd given the various utility companies a false name that seemed to be connected with a set of identity papers in one of his desk drawers. The man definitely had a plan – he had made arrangements to leave the US soon, to hit one of those countries where money talked, and people didn't care so much if women went missing. Good. It meant that she could stay and assume the false identity until she tired of this place and decided to move on. That settled, she spent the rest of the night checking out the damage to the house, trying to figure out where she would need to start making improvements in order to make it into a livable dwelling. She had to admit to herself that she was bouncing back impressively. This newfound productivity both impressed and reassured her. She was going to be just fine.

Dani took a break, spinning around in the chair and leaning back in it to look out into the hallway. She had taken care of as many financial issues as she'd be able to tonight, and it was probably about time that she checked up on the guy in the backyard. Perhaps he was dead now and she could finally dump him into the hole she'd labored over. Dani padded into his bedroom, looking for a pair of shoes. The last thing she wanted to do was trudge around the trash in the yard in bare feet. A pair of white tennis shoes two sizes too big did the trick. She doubled up on socks before slipping her feet into them.

Back outside, she peered down at the now still form of her ex-assailant, poking gently at him with the canvas toe of her newly acquired shoe. The man slumped onto his side, eyes frozen open in a terrified, haunted stare. Once she realized that she could no longer hear the beating of his heart, or the soft rhythm of his breathing, she pushed him into the hole with her foot and pulled the shovel out of the ground.

Dirt rained down into his open eyes as they continued to stare off into the distance, looking dull and empty as his body jerked with the impact of clumps of earth hitting him. It was quick work, and once she finished filling in the hole, Dani began tossing bits of garbage on top of the mound to cover any traces that might lead someone to believe that there was a body buried in her new backyard.

She placed the shovel back in the shed, her thoughts distracted as she tried to figure out what she was going to say to the bank official to get him to let her have as much of the money as she could reasonably leave with.

By the time six o'clock rolled around, Dani had come up with an impressive list of things that she wanted to pick up later. As the sun began creeping over the horizon, she yawned, exhaustion suddenly overtaking her. It had been a long night, and a nice stretch of unbroken sleep was probably just what she needed to get ready for a trip to New York. Heading upstairs to the bedroom, she reminded herself that she wanted to make an appointment to meet with the dead man's account representative as soon as possible.

Luckily, the balances on all the man's credit cards were far from full, and apparently the payments that her victim had made on them had been very earnest. He'd garnered himself several platinum Master Cards and Visas that she'd be able to put to quick use. She gave a brief stretch before reaching down to set the alarm clock for one in the afternoon. Seven hours of sleep should be plenty. Dani crawled into bed, happy that she'd thought to flip the mattress and change the sheets earlier. God only knows what the man had done in this bed before. She would have to pick up a new one later this week. She was out almost before her head hit the pillow.

Four

Retail Therapy

"You're not thinking of fighting back, are you princess?"

Someone had jammed a thumb deep into her mouth, pressing down on the back of her tongue and making her gag.

"That'd be a bad idea."

There was a sharp ache in her tongue as he forced it down and she immediately went still. He slowly pulled his hand away from her mouth and began undoing his trousers. The lips framed by the slotted hole in the ski mask curled into a nasty, smug grin.

Tears trickled out of the corners of her eyes, and she quickly closed them, flinching and choking back a sob at the rough touch of his hands. Her breath came in hitches as she tried to control herself, not wanting to anger him. She had known several people that had been raped before, and their advice had always been to stay silent - to do anything the attacker told them to do. Otherwise, you could make them angry and they'd do - worse things. As if the act itself wasn't horrifying enough.

A cold numbness slowly crept through her body and a whimper bubbled out of her throat as he pawed at her. She hated that she sounded and felt so helpless. The man let out a nasty laugh and smiled, apparently pleased with her reaction.

Dani was willing to do almost anything to keep this man from becoming more violent, so she forced herself to remain silent while her mind screamed in anguish, the ghost of her own voice ripping through her head at the violation.

Oh GOD get this motherfucker OFF ME!!

She turned her face away, tears spilling out hot against her cheeks as the man roughly pulled at the towel covering her, exposing her body - her awful secret, to him.

The man paused for a moment, and Dani fervently hoped that it would disgust him; that it would be enough to make him stop. Her soul cried out in furious indignation as she felt his bare hand clench viciously at her breast.

"Damn, that scar is fuckin' ugly baby, but pussy is pussy, right?"

The man laughed as Dani let out a plaintive cry. She heard something begin to bubble up out of her throat, the beginning of a shriek. The gloved hand was back, this time at the base of her throat.

"Want me to take your tongue?" he growled, his fingers slowly squeezing off her air, his other hand moving in towards her mouth.

The sound died in the back of her throat as her hands balled into shaky fists at her sides. The man let out a growled hiss as he parted her legs with a rough jerk. He quickly penetrated her and began moving in sharp jerks inside her, his breath catching in his throat as he brought his other hand up to clutch and twist in her hair, wrenching her head to the side as he licked the side of her face in a long, wet line.

The sensation of it all was both nauseating and painful, and her throat soured. She wondered if she was going to throw up, and if that was going to stop him. She let out a choking cry, wondering how much she would have to endure before he finally finished and left. The sense of violation was unbearable. Mental anguish tore into her just as effectively as his flesh did.

Dani screamed as she sat bolt upright in bed, her hands fisted in the sheets. Tears rolled down her cheeks as she quickly scanned the room. It took her a moment to realize that the threat was gone, that it had just been a nightmare. She closed her eyes, shivering as she forced herself to calm down.

He's dead. He's gone. He can't do that to you anymore.

It was a mantra in her head as she gently rubbed her forehead, groaning as she shifted in the bed. The harsh sound of the alarm clock startled her out of her rumination and she lashed out angrily at it, flicking it with her hand and sending it smashing into the wall, where it promptly shattered. With a heavy sigh, she flipped the covers off her, swinging her feet down to the floor and sitting up.

I really need to work on this overpowering strength thing, or I'll end up accidentally destroying everything around me.

With a yawn, she stretched and stood up.

*OK, I gotta get moving, stop thinking about... **that,*** she thought as she padded down the hall into the makeshift office. She sat down and her quick fingers began clicking at the keys on the laptop. She was surprised at how easy it was to rent a car through a local agency for the trip to New York. She picked a very plain color and style, mindful of the Ghia's personality. It would be far too easy for passersby to remember her in it and she wanted to get in and out of New York for this trip with as little notice as possible. The nice thing about the internet – you didn't have to verify who you were when you made a credit card purchase. As long as you had all the pertinent information that a given company was looking for, they were more than happy to sell you anything you had your little heart set on. Of course, that was also one of its drawbacks as well. She would also need to stash the Ghia into the garage so it wouldn't be seen from the street. The less obvious indicators that somebody was occupying this place, the better. It was probably a good idea to blackout the windows of the rooms she used most as well.

After that had been taken care of, Dani had picked up some clothes and other essential supplies. A new wardrobe to go with her new body seemed necessary. She'd run into a brief snag earlier at the car rental place. The card had an obviously masculine name on it, and the agent wouldn't listen when she explained that her husband had given her the card for her own use. Remembering the feeling she had experienced the other night with the bouncer at the bar when he became contentious about her ID picture, she'd been able to push into the woman's mind to make her see what she wanted her to see. After that, the clerk just smiled and rang up the rental. Each successive instance had been a little easier.

It seemed as if, all at once, life was finally making up for the amount of shit it had put her through. She figured that it was about damned time.

It crossed her mind to acquire an SUV, or a minivan, when she returned for body transportation purposes if nothing else. She definitely couldn't continue burying people in the back yard. The idea creeped her out just a little too much, and the idea of carting around bodies in the Ghia made her skin crawl. She loved the car far too much to put it through that particular indignity. Picking up construction materials for the house would have to wait until she returned as well.

As she drove back to the house wedged in amongst her whirlwind shopping spree purchases, Dani pondered getting a new motorcycle – one that actually worked instead of crapping out half the time. She was tired of riding and constantly repairing old, broken down cruiser knock offs with atrocious performance. A light danced in her eyes at the thought of finally being able to afford a Harley. This new gig definitely had its perks.

Once back at the house, Dani spent her remaining time trying to find a reliable contractor to finish the basement. The rest of the house she could probably handle herself with a minimum of effort, but the basement was a mess. It was also the perfect place for a master bedroom and bath and she didn't want to bother with the plumbing and electrical wiring that the project would entail.

After making an appointment with a man that assured her that they could start the project this coming weekend, as well as remain discreet for a little extra cash, she went back downstairs and busied herself with cleaning. Oddly enough, she found that she didn't have quite the amount of energy that she'd had last night. Perhaps with her new body came new sleep patterns.

Dani was downstairs, setting out roach traps and hosing everything down when she felt a strange wave of revitalizing energy. She perked up, feeling immensely better, but there didn't seem to be an obvious reason for it. She frowned and looked out the window, noting that the sun had dipped below the horizon. With a brief shrug, she set about cleaning the enormous, foul mess that was the kitchen.

The trip itself wasn't that bad. After setting off over a hundred dollars in bug bombs throughout the house, she'd left in the early morning, arriving at the branch shortly before it opened. She'd selected a fairly conservative wig to go with the outfit, hoping that she looked like any other business commuter on the street.

Once inside, the dead man's account representative seemed very pleased to see her. She had only told him over the phone that she wished to speak with him about opening up a new account with their institution. As he looked at her, his eyes dropped down to eye the large metal suitcases she carried.

"Is there a private room where we can discuss this transaction?" Dani inquired.

The man smiled and replied, "But of course. This way, please."

They stepped into a small office, and the man closed the door. As he turned around, Dani pushed into his thoughts, focusing on the man she'd killed the other night. The account representative winced, then blinked, disoriented for a moment before he greeted her as the man that was now slowly rotting in her backyard.

Dani notified him that she wanted to withdraw as much as would fit in the suitcases from her victim's account, figuring it would be too risky to try to pull out the entire amount. The entire process went smoother with the various mental pushes she'd had to force on him and several others, but the resultant effort had left her with a roaring headache that had taken an hour to die down afterwards. The drive home was uneventful, and she found herself surprised at how relieved she felt as she pulled up to the dilapidated house that she now called home.

The contractors were due to show up tomorrow, and she still had to unpack the computer equipment she had purchased on the drive back. She honestly couldn't remember the last time she'd gotten this much done in as many days. Dani padded upstairs, eager to have it all finished so that she could take a break and relax.

Within a matter of hours, she had several servers up and running in the room upstairs and set up a high-end entertainment center up in a corner of the bedroom upstairs. As she surveyed her handiwork, she realized that the bedroom was uncomfortably small. She looked forward to the new one downstairs being finished.

The contractors worked quickly on remodeling the basement, and Dani had gone ahead and picked up a large SUV. Cleaning out the garage for both cars had been an unpleasant chore, but she felt better having both cars off the street. She was careful to keep the outside appearance of the house and the main floor moderately shabby. She did not want to draw attention to the fact that there was now someone living here on a regular basis. Blacking out the windows insured that no light showed to any outside passersby during the nighttime hours when she was awake. She also planned on having all the doors and windows reinforced to insure that if anyone managed to break in, they would have to go through a dog and pony show from hell to do it. Her new patroness had her out and hunting several times a night now, and Dani was beginning to fall into a smooth rhythm with it. The killing no longer bothered her as much as it used to and she was becoming more adept at tracking and subduing her targets, which was more reassuring than she thought it would be. Getting her ass kicked had been tiring at best and wasn't something she wanted to repeat regularly.

During her downtime, she converted one of the upstairs rooms into a training area of sorts with padded floor mats. She wasn't practicing any particular martial art, but was more trying to keep in sync with the new flow of her body. From time to time, she still felt a strange shift in her consciousness during her kills, but now it only came when she became unsure of herself.

When the work in the basement had finally been finished to her satisfaction, she purchased a very comfortable king-sized bed, placing it within an enormous wrought-iron frame. She draped large, dramatic purple and indigo swaths of organza fabric around the top of it, sweeping them down delicately from the tops of the frame to billow around the posts. Opaque black silk curtains enclosed the entire bed, giving it a tent-like feel. The walls she had painted a rich, dark blue. Coupled with the soft grey that she had chosen for the ceiling and carpeting, it gave the room a very cozy, cave-like feel. Muted lighting from a Chinese paper lantern made the room appear larger than it actually was, but kept the feel intimate. Several Moroccan lanterns of different colors held tea lights that tossed gently flickering light around the room.

An antique mahogany chest sat at the foot of the bed with an extra set of blankets piled on top of it. Off to the left of the bed sat a black wrought iron makeup dresser and a long chest of drawers. Dani surveyed the final finishing touches of her surroundings and smiled. She was finally living in a space in which she was completely comfortable. It was almost too much to take in.

She was finally home.

Five
Settling In

Bubbly water surrounded a smiling Dani as she looked around her new bathroom. The bathtub was easily large enough to fit four people. Across from the tub sat a large glass-enclosed shower. Black and chrome fixtures complimented the plum-colored ceramic tiling in the large room nicely. Wisps of indigo and white hair trailed around her arms and shoulders as she relaxed in the warm water, letting her mind drift.

She had fallen into a predictable pattern over the last six months. When she wasn't exhausted from hunting, she would rise in the late afternoon, head out to the city library and quickly flip through medical textbooks, as well as resourcing references on both state and federal law and criminology. She'd always had a bit of a passion for those particular topics, and since she was no longer holding down an eight-hour-a-day job, Dani found herself with an inordinate amount of free time on her hands. Rather than waste it, she chose to challenge herself and the boundaries of her newfound mental capacity, which had been formidable even before the change.

Testing in the genius IQ levels when she was younger, her parents had held impossibly high hopes for their 'little girl', which Dani had quickly dashed to pieces during her rebel phase. She began coloring her hair, dressing in ratty clothing found at the local Salvation Army, and spending a great deal of time in her room alone, when she wasn't running around doing what her mother often referred to as 'god knows what'.

Dani had tossed around the idea of disseminating the information about the women to the police. She had a strong urge to let somebody know that their killers and tormentors were being brought to justice. At least that way the families of the women would finally know what had happened to their children, wives, and sisters. Unfortunately, the justice system didn't look too kindly on people that decided to take matters into their own hands. The FBI would probably become involved pretty quickly if an unusually high amount of accurate information about interred bodies and murdered women started flooding their network. They'd likely come after her in short order, when all she really wanted was to be left alone.

It was a dilemma that she didn't want to act on without thinking the details through thoroughly. It would likely end up being more of a pain in the ass to deal with than she had the capability to handle at the moment. Perhaps it would be something to focus on later down the road, if she ever decided to leave the area.

Through a little experimentation, Dani had also discovered a number of interesting things about her present condition. First, there was the enhanced strength – which she'd initially tested by lifting her new SUV up by its front end, almost flipping it over by accident. Startled at how light it had been, she had then worked her way up to pushing around one of the large industrial dumpsters in the neighborhood.

Her eyesight was now off the charts; she was capable of picking up subtle visual nuances that most people missed. After the first few days of discomfiting aural sensation, her hearing backed off to something that she could function comfortably with, but certain noises still startled her. Anything shrill was damn near unbearable. She could pick up random sounds throughout the neighborhood without trying, but when she focused on them, she could listen clearly to conversations and noises well out of normal human hearing range. Dani's heart rate had also apparently decreased to about a beat per minute, which would be difficult to explain to trained medical professionals, should she ever find herself in a hospital.

Definitely something to avoid, she mused to herself.

As she lay back against the tub, wiggling her toes up through the soap bubbles in the water, she had a strong desire to come up with a new name to go with this new person she was becoming. Something that better fit her new path in life.

A soft whisper drifted through her thoughts, as though it had been a quiet suggestion.

Jilah.

She thought about it for a moment, unsure of the origin, but liking the sound of it as it rolled off her tongue.

"Jilah..." The name resonated throughout the room, bringing a smile to her lips. It sounded exotic.

Okay. That works. She grinned and settled back into the bubbles. The choosing of a new name seemed to give her a stronger sense of her place in the world, an odd sense of purpose, and a motivation that she had never really felt before. For the first time in her life, she finally felt as if she belonged somewhere. She felt a curl of warmth in her chest, and her smile grew broader. Not only did she belong now, she mattered. She was a force to be reckoned with. It was a heady realization.

During daylight hours, while she found her strength somewhat diminished, she realized that she was still a good deal stronger than the people around her. She found it uncomfortable to be outside in direct sunlight now and had resorted to having prescription sunglasses made that kept out as much ambient light as possible to rid her of the headaches she'd gotten from walking outside during the day or in brightly lit areas. The possibility of vampirism occurred to her, and she had started voraciously reading everything she could get her hands on about the 'affliction'. The only real world accounts she could find resembled rabies or a rare condition known as porphyria more than anything else. Besides, she was still able to consume and enjoy regular food – another legend proven wrong.

Although she still enjoyed the taste of food, she gained very little sustenance from it.

She was still conducting her duties on a nightly basis, and bodies were rapidly beginning to pile up. She never buried more than one body in the same place. *At least I'm not running out of places to put them yet,* she thought. Jilah had started taking a strange sort of pride in her work, actually beginning to enjoy it after the first couple of weeks. She truly felt that she was doing good in the world, making a difference.

Over the last couple of days, she had come to a rather discomforting realization – that her life had become little more than carrying out her patroness' wishes and poring through various textbooks and course materials. Her existence was beginning to seem almost mechanical, and it bothered her. She sighed as she opened the drain, stepped out onto a square mat of black carpet on the tiled floor, pulled a towel from the rack and began drying off. She was filled with the sudden desire to get out and do something non- work related to go dance. She wanted to show off her new body and all the swanky clothes she had purchased months before to go with it. After all, what was impeccable fashion with nobody around to witness it?

She was also tired of concealing her true appearance. She'd gotten quite adept at it now and had perfected the art of dressing down to become socially invisible to people as she walked among them. Forcing people to see what she wanted them to see was draining, and she wasn't able to effectively do it in large groups of people, so the disguises proved fairly useful. There had been tense moments in previous months when disheveled homeless people would walk up to her, their arms waving furiously as they began shouting and pointing, yelling that they could see her and that they knew what she was. It was almost alarming how psychically sensitive some of them were.

She remembered with a shudder one instance where an approaching couple had walked well around her, trying desperately to avoid what they considered an obviously crazy man and his intended target – uncomfortable with the idea of such open conflict. It always amazed her how eager people were to avoid a confrontation, sometimes to the point of ingratiating or outright humiliating themselves.

Her standard mode of dress when she wasn't hunting had become black jean shorts with stray threads around the knees, black motorcycle boots, tank tops of varying colors and styles, and a black leather motorcycle jacket. The outfit was both comfortable and easy to move in, as well as showing off her new body to good advantage. It was decent lounge wear. Tonight she wanted to try wearing something stunning, interested to see if she could turn more than a few heads. Now dry, Jilah padded into the bedroom, enjoying the texture of the plush grey carpet against her naked feet as she strode up to an enormous walk-in closet. It held an impressive collection of clothing and footwear, and she moved down a line of hanging items, letting her fingers trail softly along them as she searched for the right outfit.

Her lips curled into a wicked grin as she selected a black leather bustier with shoulder straps and indigo piping up the sides. Shiny, little chrome buckles crossed in front of a zipper that went up the front. The leather was buttery smooth to the touch and fit her like a glove. It accentuated her breasts perfectly, giving them just the right amount of support. Jilah zipped herself into it, latched the buckles, then pulled on a pair of matching pants, enjoying the feel of the leather as it slid over her skin.

They looked almost painted on, but strangely enough, they didn't really hinder her movement. She had been very careful to find clothing that wouldn't rip in embarrassing ways in an emergency. Jilah stood before a full length mirror on the back of the closet door, turning to inspect the lines of the outfit. She ran her hand down the back of her legs slowly to work out any wrinkles. She looked at her right shoulder,frowning at the clear smooth skin that was a bitter reminder of the tattoo that had faded and disappeared just several days after she'd gotten it a month ago. Her body had slowly pushed the ink out of her skin. In her opinion, this was definitely one of the down sides to her condition.

A set of black, beaten up tanker boots with indigo accents completed the outfit nicely, and kept her from looking like a complete tart. Jilah pulled her hair back into a long, thick blue and white striped braid, not wanting it to get whipped into a tangled mess as she rode down the highway. One of her more extravagant purchases had been a beautifully restored 1951 Harley Pan head. She still took the Karmann Ghia out on the open road from time to time, but the hog had become her favorite mode of travel shortly after buying it. Unfortunately, riding it wreaked holy hell on her hair unless she braided it.

Jilah padded over to the makeup table and began applying a shade of eyeshadow that accentuated the royal blue in her jewel-toned eyes. She kept her eyebrows plucked to razor sharp points now, giving her eyes a very predatory look. Plum lipstick colored her full lips, and she pursed them before placing the lipstick back down on the table. A sharp line of indigo Bettie Page bangs with a shock of white in the middle complimented her face perfectly. Jilah grinned at her reflection, pleased with the results. She then walked back over to the full length mirror, giving herself a once over before heading upstairs.

Oh yeah. She looked good. She was feeling pretty damned good, too.

She had never really been much of a clotheshorse in the past, but Jilah was now truly beginning to enjoy wearing garments that accentuated her new body well. It had always seemed shallow to her, the way women would tart themselves up before they left the house, but now she understood it. Sometimes it really was the little things that mattered, and helped most.

It was going to be a great night. She could feel it. There was a noticeable spring in her step as she grabbed a weather-beaten black leather jacket off the coat rack by the front door and slid her arms into it. She reached over to collect a set of keys and a peanut skullcap motorcycle helmet with a bone white skull and crossbones on the front of it. A vibrant splash of indigo and purple fire licked along the sides of the cap from the skull, reaching the back of the helmet in sharp points. She placed a hand on the doorknob and paused, wondering if she was forgetting anything before heading out to the garage. She opened the garage door, and her eyes glittering as she gazed at her two-wheeled pride and joy.

It was a stunning motorcycle; black and sleek with a set of three skulls on either side of the gas tank that had blue and purple flame licking around them. Azure, purple, and black leather tassels dangled from the handlebars. She liked the way they whipped playfully at her hands as she rode down the highway. A pair of indigo and black leather saddlebags graced its sides, widening out the back end. They rounded out the look of the motorcycle nicely.

Jilah stepped up to it, her expression softening as she kicked a leg up and over, enjoying the feel of the machine beneath her as she sat down and slid the keys into the ignition. She knocked the kickstand up and sharply stomping down on the kick starter. The rumble of the pipes filled the garage as she leaned back in the seat, gently placing the helmet onto her head and securing the strap beneath her chin with a languorous smile. She'd gone for somewhat quieter pipes on the bike, not wanting to draw more attention to herself than she was already. Jilah revved the engine, then pulled out a pair of night shades, sliding them into place. The night was young and by god she was ready to take some time off.

Jilah paused for a moment, eyes sliding shut as she reached out and pulled an extra shield around herself. In her mind's eye, a purple liquid field shimmered up around her toes and quickly slid up and over her legs, extending about a quarter of an inch away from her clothes. She luxuriated in the feel of her power skipping along her skin as the shield flowed up her body. She always kept basic shields up – it had become an automatic reflex by now, but for some reason she felt safer if she strengthened them when she was on the bike. The last thing she needed was a distraction when she was zooming down the highway at ninety plus miles an hour. She was apparently capable of healing most injuries in alarmingly rapid fashion, but had no desire to tempt fate to see if she could fully regenerate from being splattered all over the asphalt. That was definitely an experience that she could do without.

Jilah laughed softly as she backed the motorcycle out of the garage and down the driveway. She wrapped her legs around the body of the thrumming bike and kicked it into gear, tearing off down the street. There was nothing quite like feeling the relaxing vibration of the bike as she finally pulled out onto the highway. Riding was always soothing and strangely restorative for her. No matter how bad her nights could sometimes get, a ride on the Harley would always set her mind right. Luckily, there was very little traffic on the roads tonight, giving her plenty of room to maneuver. In heavy traffic, she usually felt claustrophobic. She had lost count of how many times she'd almost gotten clipped by some idiot that wasn't paying attention to what was going on around them.

A large, grizzled man on a Road King with an enormous POW/MIA flag attached to the back of his bike roared past her, giving her a friendly, interested grin, winking at her as he went by. The large flag tore at the air, flapping wildly as the bike went down the road. It was so nice to finally have some downtime. Appreciative glances were also good, she decided. As long as nobody actually approached her with that interested gleam in their eyes, she could maintain a level of comfort. Getting hit on usually ended up making her skin crawl.

When she pulled in front of the club, she backed the motorcycle into a spot next to three sports bikes. Her brow arched as she looked over at the colorful crotch rockets, having never really understood the fascination with all that brightly colored plastic. As she rocked the Panhead over on its stand, she let her power flow around her, letting her true appearance show through. She had a strong desire to be noticed tonight. A pounding rhythm echoed in the night air from the open air patio/dance floor in the back of the club.

Jilah kicked a leg up and over the motorcycle, pulling her helmet off and hanging it off one of the handle grips before checking herself out in the side mirror. Something sent the wind up her back, setting the short hairs at the base of her neck prickling and she stood stock still.

What the hell was that??

Jilah had experienced something similar several nights ago, but to a much lesser degree. Having it happen twice in one week put her on guard. She had received strange emanations from obviously insane people before, but they had been scattered and weak. This definitely felt stronger, and much more focused. It also didn't have that special crazy taste to it – that sharp, sour bite that made her jaw twinge. Jilah had the distinct feeling that she was being watched.

She quickly spun around, almost bowling over a boy with long, honey-colored hair that was pulled back into a ponytail. He looked back at her, his ice blue eyes wide as he took a step back, startled.

"Whoa! Sorry about that. I ah... wow, you move fast."

The boy stammered as he looked back at her, presenting her with a broad grin. As he spoke the strange sensation fled, leaving Jilah feeling a little uneasy. She sized the boy up, knowing that he couldn't be over twenty. She also realized with a start that he was obviously very interested in her. His eyes were more than a little glassy, and his body fairly vibrated as he looked her over. OK, maybe it'd be a good idea to pull the shields up just a tad. As she did, she watched him blink twice before his expression softened, becoming less awed and hungry.

"It's okay. I should've been paying more attention," she replied, keeping her tone light as she asked, "So, anybody good spinning tonight?"

The last time she'd gone hunting in an alternative club, the DJ had been wretched. He'd called himself something painfully pretentious, like Damiana or Castrata. How people in the club scene came up with their token nicknames was beyond her. She had a fleeting image of a small group of people in all black shuffling to the front of a long line and tossing pennies onto a grid with various combinations of mythical and old alchemical words.

The boy brightened, his smile relaxing as he nodded slowly and replied, "Yeah. Joven's in the main room. Sounds like he's doin' a pretty good set."

He paused, seeming to struggle with what he wanted to say next.

"You, ah, here with anybody?"

She chuckled softly and replied, "Not really. Seeing as how I rode up alone and all."

He presented her with a sheepish grin and nodded again, "Oh. Yeah. I knew that."

He's cute. And sweet, she thought to herself as she reached over and pulled the keys out of the ignition, depositing them in a jacket pocket, her eyes glittering when she turned back to face him. Unfortunately, now that he was seeming honestly interested, she was becoming a little too uncomfortable to continue flirting with him.

Jilah gave his mind a gentle push, and his eyes went blank for a moment before he shook his head and turned to walk back to the club entrance. At least there wasn't much of a line this time. The steady thrum of industrial dance music became louder, her skin tingling as she stepped into the line forming outside. The bassline thumped inside her chest with an intensity that surprised her. The doorman was a short, angry-looking punk kid with a shock of vibrant green hair and sharp eyes. A barely perceptible smile tugged at the edges of his lips as she walked up and handed him a doctored driver's license. It really was remarkable, the things that one could procure when one had the financial means to do so.

He quickly scanned it, then looked up at her, the smile finally winning out and stretching his lips into a sly grin as he reached over and stamped her hand. She responded with a warm smile and a raised eyebrow, causing the grin on his face to broaden as his eyes lit up.

"Sweet ride. Must be hell to maintain."

Jilah shrugged, her tone a little smoky as she answered, "Not if you know what you're doing."

He paused for a moment, sizing her up before nodding slowly and letting out a sharp bark of laughter.

"Not bad." He reached out to return her license and waved her inside, his body language now a little more open and relaxed as his gaze moved to the next person in line.

Once inside, the music pounded through her, her head rocked back, a satisfied smile playing across her lips. The rhythm was a palpable force. Her hips swayed in time with the beat as she strode towards the dance floor. She had never thought of herself as particularly graceful when she danced, and had always felt like a bit of a dork, even when she'd danced alone in her bedroom. Now, Jilah was surprised to find her moves liquid and sensual as she walked over to a dark space by the DJ booth. She slipped her jacket from her shoulders, sliding it down her arms to rest on the floor at her feet as she became caught up in the beat, closing her eyes as she let the rhythm ride her.

The pulse of the music was a living thing, feeling almost as if it were slowly sliding along her skin as she moved, and she was quickly lost in the dance. It was glorious. Jilah tapped into the energy of the rest of the crowd while her body was in motion, being careful to draw gently from them this time. The power lightly brushed along her skin, sending a tremble through her that made her eyes flutter. She soon lost track of time on the dance floor, feeling almost as if she'd been moving for hours when she felt a familiar prickling at the back of her neck. Whatever it was, it was stronger now.

Where the hell was it coming from? Eager to locate the source, if for nothing else than to assuage her own curiosity, Jilah frowned as she leaned down and collected her coat. She slid it on and quickly cut a path through the crowd as she tried to track it. Somebody grabbed her arm as she reached the edge of the dance floor, yelling slurred greetings as he moved towards her.

Jilah whirled around angrily, practically snarling at the drunken idiot who was keeping her from pursuing whatever it was that seemed to be following her. The boy's expression slackened, his eyes going wide. He quickly jerked his hand away from her as if burned, backing away, stumbling into a tall brunette and knocking her drink down the front of her shirt.

"I don't have time for this," Jilah growled as she spun away from him, relieved to find that the strange sensation was still there.

Good. It hasn't gotten away.

It seemed to be coming from outside.

The patio.

Jilah moved quickly through the club now, throwing extra shields up to insure that nobody tried to grab her again. As she stepped outside, she heard a warm, smooth voice drift through her thoughts.

:: You're getting warmer. ::

Jilah froze, blinking. While used to the voice of her patroness in her thoughts now, it was startling to hear this new one echo through her consciousness. Much less that of a male. A low chuckle rolled through her mind, setting her teeth on edge. Whatever or whoever it was, it was now toying with her. Jilah took a breath and scanned the crowd, jeweled eyes narrowing to slits as she searched for the source of the voice. Finding her usual prey was always easy, they were usually surrounded by colored auras. This was proving to be a completely different kind of hunt, and while she found herself interested in the challenge, she wasn't entirely sure that she liked it. She hadn't quite gotten the hang of picking one set of thoughts out of a crowd, and began feeling a distinct sense of unease as she slowly made her way through the throng of people outside.

Jilah tried letting her thoughts drift out into the crowd, hoping that she would at least get something useful back. She blinked as her mind touched something very different.

It was off to the left.

:: Warmer... ::

Yeah, it was definitely male. Whoever he was, she hoped that she'd be strong enough to beat the holy hell out of him when she finally found him. This mental game of cat and mouse was more than a little bothersome. She had never liked being messed with. Jilah set her jaw in a hard line as she made her way towards a set of stairs that led to an upper deck off to the left. The source definitely felt like it was coming from the upper deck now, but it didn't seem malicious. Just playful. She ran up the stairs in a blur of motion, and stopped to look around. A tiny gasp sounded off to her right and she turned to find a diminutive girl with horn-rimmed glasses off in the corner with a group of friends. The girl's eyes were wide with startlement.

Great. A psi-sensitive.

Jilah added another layer to her shields, and the girl blinked twice before looking back over at her friends and babbling quickly. They shook their heads and laughed, asking her how much she'd had to drink so far.

Thank god for skeptics, Jilah thought to herself as she looked over her left shoulder towards a small group of people.

There. It's definitely coming from over there.

Jilah took a step forward and the group dispersed, revealing a man wearing a black leather jacket, a white tank top, tight black leather pants, and black motorcycle boots. He was reclining in a cheap plastic lawn chair. One leg hooked over the right arm of the chair and was swinging gently. The man's eyes seemed to shine from within, chips of bright emeralds in the setting of a very striking face. They glowed with a fiery intensity that was incongruous with his slightly amused expression. His hair was a spiky blue-black shock that contrasted starkly against luminous skin. His thumb moved in slow, deliberate circles around the mouth of the beer bottle in his hand, and she felt a strong heat in his gaze as he looked back at her.

Jilah briefly wondered if he was gay. It had been her experience that straight men with that much confidence were extremely rare, if not downright nonexistent.

He was devastatingly handsome.

A delicious tingle started low in her gut, and she felt a light sheen of dew on her arms as she looked over at him. She clenched her jacket tightly in a fist as she fought to look away, not at all comfortable with the fact that the only thing she seemed to want to do was kneel at this strange man's feet and trail the tip of her tongue along the inseam of his pants.

A slow, liquid thump echoed through her chest as the voice brushed gently through her mind again.

:: *Took you long enough...* ::

Six

An Unexpected Diversion

The man's lips curled in a seductive smile and Jilah stood transfixed at the sight of him. She blinked, forcing herself to look at the wall behind him, desperate to find anything else to focus on. He was too damned distracting.

:: *Am I truly that gruesome?* ::

The voice echoed gently through her thoughts, the tone decidedly amused. This earned him a sidelong glare. He grinned back at her, eyes glittering as he uncoiled from the chair and stood up in a fluid motion. Narrowing her eyes, Jilah took a quick step back, her arms automatically coming up in a defensive posture.

She kept her tone flat and empty as she asked, "What do you want?"

Jesus, he's fast. If he decides to attack...

Her mind raced as she cranked her shields up again. She didn't know if she'd be able to hold her ground against him and felt a rush of adrenaline slide into her veins.

The man raised an eyebrow and leaned slightly forward, cocking his head to the side as he eyed her and purred, "Little jumpy, eh?"

The rest of the bar patrons milled around the two of them, seemingly oblivious to what was going on. Jilah figured this was probably for the best. As a test, she pushed the majority of her energy into her defensive shields, causing what remained of her cosmetic cover to drop completely. Still, nobody seemed to notice. Not a good sign.

"I'll ask again. What do you want?" Jilah kept her expression empty as she waited for him to respond. His eyes widened briefly, emerald depths flashing as he stood stock still for a moment. It was almost as if he'd become an image frozen in time. It was extremely disconcerting. He then sighed and relaxed, his tone slightly aggrieved as he hooked a thumb in the pocket of his leather pants.

"If I had wanted to hurt you, don't you think I would've done it by now instead of 'leaving a trail of breadcrumbs' as it were?" Jilah frowned as she considered his words and the fact that he was actually speaking aloud now.

His voice softened as he continued, "I only wished to speak with you. It has been a great many years since I've run across someone that," He paused, as if searching for the right words, "draws my attention the way you do."

This wasn't necessarily a good thing, in her opinion. Granted, he was extremely easy on the eyes, but something felt very different about him. There was an intensity that radiated from him; it had a rhythm that was completely different from any of the people around them. She blinked quickly and concentrated, opening up her awareness and listening to the crowd surrounding her. It had been something she'd started practicing recently under the minimal guidance of her patroness. The Dark Lady always seemed to give her just enough help to get her through her nightly duties, but if she wanted to know anything else about her abilities, it ended up being a mental tug of war to get the information she needed. The steady rush of pulse and heat flared through the bodies around her, so when she turned her focus back on him, the difference became obvious. Even over the steady thrumming beat of the music, she was startled that she hadn't noticed it until now. She was usually quicker on the uptake than this.

The man in front of her had no discernible heartbeat. And he was awfully pale. Her sense of unease growing, Jilah took a step back. Several key questions that she dearly wanted to ask him sat trapped on her tongue, and her throat closed.

The man laughed softly and she heard his voice once again echo through her thoughts. :: *Yes. I am what you think I am.* ::

Whoa, mind-reader too? This entire 'head conversation' he kept having with her was disorienting enough, without the added irritation of him being able to read her thoughts as well.

"Please stop that." she growled.

"Stop what?"

He was the very picture of innocence as he looked back at her.

Yeah. Definitely annoying. Jilah's expression darkened as she growled. "Stop digging around in my head."

He presented her with a sharp-toothed grin, a wicked gleam in his eyes as he purred, "Oh, I suppose I could always go..." Jilah felt the weight of his gaze as it traveled down the line of her body. "'digging around' in other things. Do you have any suggestions?"

His eyes snapped back up to meet her gaze, his expression playful as a he let out a dark chuckle and rocked back on a heel. Jilah felt a tiny shiver run up her spine, like soft little fingers sliding up and across the back of her neck in tiny, delicate circles. Something inside her tightened, wrapping around itself and bringing a soft sigh to her lips. She shook it off, not entirely certain what had just happened, but more than a little clear that he'd had something to do with it.

Her voice was harsh as she growled, "Now with the threats?"

The man raised an eyebrow and a slight frown marred his features. His expression immediately softened.

"You're right. Please accept my apology. I am afraid that my manners are a little off. It has been quite some time since I've been social. Might we start again from the beginning? I believe an introduction is in order. I am Argent Valentine."

He brought up an alabaster hand, touching it to his chest and presenting her with a gentlemanly bow, his eyes never leaving her face.

"Because I truly wish to converse with you, I won't be a complete ass and continue intruding in your grey matter. Please, is there perhaps somewhere we might go where we can talk?"

He seemed sincere, but Jilah wasn't at all ready to trust him. Her expression remained suspicious as she looked him over. He stood about a full head taller than her and she felt a flush of heat creep into her face as she realized exactly how well proportioned he was.

Man, those leather pants are tight. Her heart skipped a beat and she quickly dropped her gaze to the floor, forcing herself to think about something, anything else. Suddenly he was standing before her, gently gathering her hand up into his. Jilah felt the brush of incredibly soft lips as he kissed it.

She jerked back in a motion that was too quick for the eye to track, blurring over to the wall and glaring back at him. She held her hand to her chest, cradling it as if he'd burned her. Her words came out in a rush, "Christ, that's unnerving."

Argent peered at her strangely, his brow furrowing as he carefully asked, "Pardon?"

Jilah shook her head and stepped away from the wall. "I'm not used to being around anything that moves as fast as you do. It takes a little getting used to."

He nodded slowly, uncertain as to how to react. He wondered why she was behaving so cautiously, noting that she was keeping enough distance between them to ensure a quick getaway should the situation call for it.

Jilah was not at all sure that she wanted to go anywhere with him, but he was right about one thing. If he had wanted to hurt her, why go about it in such a roundabout way? She had a strong feeling that he was easily quick enough to outmaneuver and overpower her, even without knowing exactly how strong he was. Strangely though, she found herself interested in what he might have to say. She'd never come in direct contact with anything supernatural before, and Jilah now found herself facing a strong desire to find out more about him. Books could only tell her so much. The opportunity to converse with and learn from a direct subject was almost worth the risk.

Against her better judgment, Jilah looked back over towards the stairs, her voice noncommittal as she said, "There's a cemetery a couple of miles down the road." She looked back over at him, her expression nonplussed. "Will that do?"

He flashed her a stunning grin and replied, "A little dramatic, don't you think?" He chuckled softly, leaning over to place the beer he'd been holding down on the railing. It was still full.

With a brief shrug, she said, "It's quiet and private, as well as having the added bonus of easy disposal, should you decide to become unfriendly."

The man eyed her, curious. "You're being awfully careful. Are you so certain that I could pose that much of a threat to you?"

Jilah gave him a slow nod in response, her eyes bright and sharp.

"Then you are as intelligent as you are beautiful." Argent's lips curved in a gentle smile as he bent slightly at the waist and offered a hand out to her, his voice a warm purr as he asked, "Shall we?"

Jilah took a step back, cocking her hips as she gestured towards the stairs and replied, "After you."

Argent shook his head gently with a little smile as he walked past, flashing a quick grin back at her as he headed over to the stairs. Jilah couldn't help but notice the easy, feline grace with which he moved. She felt another flush of heat as her gaze traveled down his body, almost mesmerized as she watched him walk.

Yeah. He is supremely well put together. And most definitely dangerous, she thought to herself with a little shiver.

The crowd parted easily before him, giving her just enough space to follow in his wake. Jilah wondered exactly how powerful he was, as well as what his capabilities might be. She began mentally ticking off the pros and cons of vampirism as she had come to know them through the books she'd read.

OK, supposedly sunlight is deadly, garlic, holy water, crosses, all wards against them, greatly enhanced sight, hearing, and – Oh...immense strength. If Argent decided at any point that he didn't like the questions she wanted to ask, things could quickly become very ugly. However, if she really wanted to learn whether all the stories and myths about vampires were true, she wasn't sure that she'd have a better opportunity. It might also give her a chance to test her own abilities against a much more capable opponent. In the last few months, her targets hadn't really presented her with much of a challenge.

As they stepped outside and began walking over to the bike, Jilah blurted out, "So, why the hell do you want to talk to me anyway?"

Argent's expression was inscrutable as he answered, "I am curious about you. You appear to be like me, but there are subtle differences that I would like to speak with you about." His voice grew quiet as he added, "And, it has been a great while since I've run across another of my kind that I wanted to have anything to do with."

Jilah frowned and stepped up to the motorcycle, wondering at the small wave of sadness she felt from Argent in his last statement. As she reached over to collect the helmet from its resting place on the handlebars, she asked, "So, you want to follow me out there?"

She looked back at him and he brightened a little, shaking his head and presenting her with a sheepish grin as he spread his hands and said, "I am afraid I don't have a vehicle."

Of course you don't, she thought to herself. Brow furrowed, she sighed in mild irritation before hitching a leg over the bike. Settling back into the seat, she pulled the helmet on and looked up at him. "There's an extra helmet in the saddlebag. Climb on."

Jilah nodded towards the back of the bike as she stomped on the kick starter, bringing the motorcycle roaring to life. She revved the engine as Argent pulled out a black skullcap covered with little stickers, turning it in his hands and peering at it curiously.

"Why on earth would I wear one of these?" he asked.

"You ride my bike, you wear the cap. Plus, in the unlikely event that we get into an accident, it's not much, but it'll supposedly keep your grey matter from being splattered all over the road." she replied.

He frowned and she added, "Are you really that eager to see if your body can regenerate your brain? Just put it on."

"I see your rather vivid point." he replied in a mild tone before sliding it over his head and strapping it on.

Jilah felt the bike lower as he settled on the seat behind her, tensing when she felt his hands at her sides. He leaned into her and her eyelids fluttered shut as that strange, delicious feeling rode up her spine again. She wasn't at all familiar with this kind of physical contact or sensation, and her body was practically vibrating in tune with the motorcycle.

"Is there a problem?" Argent brushed her ear lightly with his lips as he spoke, his voice lowering to a sensual purr. His arms encircled her waist, pulling her closer.

He knew exactly what his touch was doing to her, and wondered why she kept shying away from it. He could smell the ache on her. It was a powerful, heady scent.

Jilah stiffened and growled, "It's a bad idea to distract the driver when you're on a two-wheeled vehicle wearing nothing but leather to protect you from the asphalt. The road isn't exactly forgiving if you dump over onto it, no matter how fast you can heal."

She felt him pull away a little, his hands moving back to her hips as he asked, "You have a problem with being attracted to me. Why is that?"

Jilah ground her teeth, annoyed that she was so easily read. "I refuse to throw myself at a cut-rate gigolo vampire just because my body wants me to. You're definitely attractive; I'll give you that, but."

He interrupted, his tone amused as a blue-black eyebrow crept up his forehead. "Cut-rate??"

With an exasperated sigh, Jilah closed her eyes before quietly answering, "Look. Just give it a rest on trying to get into my pants, okay? It's making me distinctly uncomfortable."

Assuring herself that his silence was consent, she pulled the Harley away from the curb and directed it toward the highway. As they rounded a corner, Jilah felt him press himself against her back and her heart did a slow roll in her chest. If this continued, she was going to get them both seriously injured because she couldn't control her reactions to him. Her body thrummed at the feel of him pressed against her back. Unbidden images of the last six months of horror flashed in her head, centering her and letting her gain a little distance from her body's eagerly answering lust.

Thank god. At least I won't end up road pizza now. Christ, I need a way to put my hormones on a leash.

Seven
Graveside Manner

When they arrived at Mortmount Cemetery, Jilah relaxed a little. Headstones from the early 1800s peppered the grounds along with others from many other time periods. An enormous wrought-iron fence enclosed the grounds, shuttered by a set of wicked-looking gates of iron and stone at the main entrance. Jilah had always loved the look and feel of this place. She came here often between nightly runs to relax and meditate. She revved the engine and rolled past the front gates, pulling into a darkened parking lot a quarter-mile down the road.

Argent hopped off the back of the motorcycle and Jilah rocked it back onto the stand, pulling the keys out of the ignition and depositing them into her pocket. She swung a leg over and pulled her helmet off as she looked down the road, glad that this had always been a low traffic area, even in the daytime.

"You don't talk much, do you?" Argent's tone was mild as she looked over at him. He held the extra helmet out to her. Jilah shook her head and collected the proffered helmet and reached over to deposit hers onto its customary perch on the handlebars.

"It's been awhile since I've really talked with anybody. I've been.. busy." She placed the extra helmet on the seat and looked back over at him, her expression slightly wistful.

Argent nodded, his expression softening a little. He then peered over at the motorcycle curiously. He cocked his head and frowned as he looked up at her and asked, "What does DILLIGAF stand for?"

Jilah felt her lips curl into a slight smile, her voice quiet as she answered, "'Does It Look Like I Give A Fuck'."

Argent grinned, his eyes sparkling as he replied, "It fits."

He laughed softly, sending a familiar thrum through her. Jilah took a steadying breath as she turned and began walking towards the cemetery.

"Is there any way you can turn that off? Or at least crank it down a little?"

Jilah jumped as Argent seemed to wink into existence next to her, easily keeping in step with her. "I am capable of doing many things. Controlling your desire for me is not one of them."

Jilah glared over at him and he let out a soft chuckle, shrugging as he added, "I'm afraid I can't help it if your body happens to find me irresistible."

She began walking faster, not liking where the conversation was going. Argent matched her pace effortlessly, grinning now. "If it's any consolation, I seem to be having the same problem."

His admission did little to make her feel better. Well, on the bright side, it was beginning to look as if the only thing she had to worry about tonight was becoming a drooling, sex-crazed slut, seduced by the dark side. Okay, there wasn't really a bright side, now that she thought about it. Jilah winced and shook it off, her hands tightening into fists as her eyes fixed on the graveyard ahead.

"So. You wanted to talk."

She felt a gentle hand on her arm. It sent a small jolt of electricity up her spine that set her fingers tingling as a memory flared brightly to life in her mind.

Blinking rapidly, she looks up at her attacker; a nameless, faceless thug in a ski mask. Her assailant quickly climbs over her, straddling her. He barks orders and obscenities at her, and she responds with a frightened nod, letting him know that she understands even though she's so startled and disoriented she can't really make out exactly what he's saying.

"Keep your mouth shut, or I'll pull your tongue out." he murmurs softly as he traces the tip of his thumb along her lower lip.

Jilah blurred over to the fence surrounding the cemetery, glaring at him and holding her arm, quickly rubbing at the spot he'd touched.

"DON'T." She cried out, shaking now. Her voice lowered an octave, her expression tightening as she repeated, "Don't touch me."

Argent stood still, not wanting to do anything else that might spook her. He wasn't quite sure what was causing these reactions, and didn't want to make it any worse. Jilah watched him carefully as he began to slowly walk towards her. This stranger was getting far too friendly for her liking and she remembered painfully familiar ground.

Too many of the women she had avenged had come to horrific ends, and it always seemed to start out like this. That first flare of heated interest. Sure, they all started out like nice enough guys, but then came the hitting and the torment – and the killing. It was becoming difficult to maintain her composure, being torn as she was by her intense attraction to him, and the intense revulsion of being touched or handled in any way. For the first time since he'd introduced himself, she noticed that he had no aura whatsoever. Usually, even non-sensitives resonated with the faint whispers of one, once she began working on how to read them – but from Argent, she saw nothing whatsoever.

:: *The blood children have no aura, daughter. Being dead makes them no less dangerous, though.* ::

The dry whisper of her patroness' voice slid through her consciousness, sending a wave of goosebumps along her skin. Being dead? He looked very much alive to her as he continued walking towards her with that same fluid, catlike grace. Jilah tensed against the fence behind her, annoyed with the tendency that the Dark Lady had for being extremely vague about things.

She watched his hands come up slowly in a placating gesture as he murmured. "It's all right. I won't touch you. Okay?"

Argent looked crestfallen as relief slowly crept across her features. He kept his voice quiet as he said, "You're awfully jumpy. Are you a fledgling?"

A strange expression flickered across his features as he looked down at her, and she had the distinct feeling that she was being inspected, almost as if under a microscope, as his gaze swept her body. Not really sure she had heard him correctly, she asked, "Ah, fledgling?"

Argent frowned slightly as he replied, "Were you recently fostered?"

Jilah looked back at him, confused. "Fostered? What are you talking about?"

Argent patiently explained, "When a creature, such as myself, chooses to bring a child over – turns them from what they are into what I am, we refer to this process as fostering. That individual is then initially referred to as a fledgling."

"No. Not a fledgling," she murmured softly.

Argent peered at her, his expression intense as his eyes narrowed and he whispered, "What are you? You feel like one of us, but you are somehow different."

Jilah's heart raced as she met his gaze. "I'm something that isn't documented, apparently." She paused, her eyes sliding to look away from him as she quietly added, "I know. I've looked."

Jilah turned and began making her way to the entrance gates. Argent's footsteps echoed behind her as he followed. Months ago, she'd gone through every possible resource that she could think of since the change. She had been unable to find even a shred of anything that would give her a good idea of exactly what she'd become. From what she had been able to figure out, she was now a focal point for the energy of an entity that resembled Kali Ma, but other than that, she was pretty much flying by the seat of her pants. It had to be an entity of some kind. From what she had read, gods didn't work through people like this, or if they did, there didn't seem to be any mention of anything remotely like what she was experiencing. Perhaps she was just frequenting the wrong bookstores.

The city kept the cemetery gates closed at night, but getting past them after hours hadn't been a problem for her after that fateful first night. Jilah gripped the bars of the fence and was up and over in a flash of movement. As her feet touched the ground, she stood and turned to see if Argent was following and bumped into him, letting out a little squeak of surprise. Damn, he's a quick little monkey.

Jilah stiffened as she realized that her hand was now gently pressed against his chest. She could feel the chill of his skin through his tank top. She looked up to find him gazing down at her with the eyes of a drowning man, his hunger naked and raw on his face as his eyes shone brightly.

"Shit." Jilah quickly backpedaled and stumbled over a low railing, her teeth clacking together roughly as she hit the ground. She winced and groaned, "Well, that was embarrassing."

Argent extended a hand down to help her up and Jilah tentatively moved to take it. She noticed that his expression had become carefully neutral.

He helped her up and took a step back to keep from crowding her before he asked, "Pardon my impertinence, but – how old are you?"

Jilah began brushing herself off and gave him a funny look. "Thirty-two. Why?"

Argent shook his head, cutting her off, "No. How long has it been since" He tried to put it into words. "You became what you are now?"

Jilah shrugged and straightened her jacket. "About six months or so."

Argent's jaw dropped. He wondered how the hell she had become so powerful in such a short span of time. She practically radiated energy. He composed himself and asked, "Do you have a sire?"

"A what?"

"The one who made you what you are."

Jilah shook her head gently, wondering why it was so important to him. "No. Not in the way you're thinking." She turned away and began walking slowly through the cemetery, knowing that he would follow. "I'm not really comfortable talking about this right now."

Argent followed beside her, his tone soft as he quietly replied, "My apologies. I am afraid that I'm letting my curious nature get the best of me. I will not continue to press."

The singing tension in her back slowly unwound, and Jilah allowed herself a little smile. They walked in silence for a few moments as she let the restful quiet of the cemetery grounds slowly sink in, her tension slowly releasing. As they passed the plot for a family with the surname Bonner, Jilah turned to him and asked, "So. Vampire, huh?"

Argent chuckled, presenting a slight grin as he replied, "We prefer to be called bloodsucking, baby-eating monsters from the nether depths, actually. The collective 'we' find this a far less offensive description."

Jilah let out a short bark of laughter, quickly bringing a hand to her mouth. Her expression was a little guilty as she tried to stop smiling. Okay, so he was gorgeous and funny.

Argent smiled back at her and softly added, "In truth, we prefer the much shortened Sanguine in most cases. The word vampire is so... sordid."

A now familiar coil of warmth slowly started to flare up in her belly and her brow furrowed as she forced it back down, tentatively asking, "So, how long have you been...?"

Argent shrugged and stepped over a small metal railing. "Oh, about three hundred years or so."

Jilah stopped dead in her tracks, incredulous as she gaped back at him. "Three HUNDRED?"

Argent waved it off dismissively, his grin becoming a little wider. "It's just a number."

Jilah shook her head and began walking beside him again, stunned. Three hundred years old and he didn't look much older than she did.

She caught him peeking over at her, and his voice caused her to jump a little as he asked, "Are we wandering around aimlessly or do you have a particular destination in mind?"

"What, are you in a hurry?" Jilah snapped at him, her words coming out angrier than she wanted them to sound.

Argent's reply was patient and quiet. "Actually, I am unfortunately bound to a nocturnal clock. The sun will eventually rise, and at the rate this is going, I'll be a cinder smoking in the grass by the time you finally decide to stop looking at me as something that is going to eat you. Or worse."

Well, when he puts it like that... Jilah sighed softly, then pointed to a small black building off to the right. "There. We're going over there."

"Are you usually this difficult to get to know?" Argent's tone was casual, his eyes fixed on the building ahead as he walked beside her.

"Sorry." Jilah offered, lamely. She was actually beginning to feel a little bad at the way she was treating him. "It's just been a long time since anybody's wanted to just talk to me. It's not something I'm really used to."

Argent's reply was surprisingly soft, "You spend most of your time alone then?"

Nodding, Jilah answered, "Yeah. I don't really socialize much."

They reached a small iron fence surrounding a black marble mausoleum that was weathered with age. A small gate stood at the entrance. Argent promptly reached down to open it, motioning her inside with a gentlemanly flourish.

Her eyes widened a touch and she looked over at him, her tone colored with amusement as she asked, "You're quite the Renaissance man, aren't you?"

"Only when I'm not playing with my food and spitting up, dear lady." Argent bowed politely to her, then brought his gaze back to meet hers, his lips curling in a playful grin as he straightened back up.

Jilah let out a harsh laugh and looked up at him. "You can cut that lady crap out. I was never a lady."

Argent's voice was a husky, playful rumble as he replied, "Please, do accept my apologies. I can be most presumptuous, apparently." Jilah heard the joking sarcasm in his tone and smiled. "And it appears that I've also completely misplaced my manners. I never did properly ask your name."

The sound of his voice thrummed through her in a strangely physical sensation as it rubbed gently against her in all the right spots. Her own voice was a little breathy as she answered, "It's Jilah. I changed it after..."

She quickly looked at a point beyond his shoulder, trying to quell the overpowering flood of sensation. "The old name reminds me too much of the person I was when..." Her voice trailed off and she shuddered at the memory.

Argent nodded, suppressing his strong desire to physically comfort her. He wished that she would at least give him a little leeway to let him in so that he could help, but he supposed that he couldn't really blame her. He kept his voice carefully neutral as he replied, "I couldn't help seeing a fragment of that. Was he the one that changed you?"

Jilah wondered exactly how much he had seen during his merry little jaunt through her head back at the club. She stiffened, not entirely sure that she wanted to know, and shook her head in response. She suddenly felt so very tired as she answered, "No. He was just a catalyst. I don't really know what I am. I'm still finding out."

Argent remained silent as they walked up to the mausoleum, unsure of what to say next. There was definitely something very broken inside her and it seemed that every time he opened his mouth, he poked at it without meaning to.

Jilah broke the silence, blurting out, "Three hundred years, huh?"

Relieved to be on a less volatile topic, he made a mock gesture of annoyance, saying, "Are we back to my age again?" He continued with a soft chuckle, "Well, other than the fact that I'm well past the age where a normal human would require a walker, I assume you have other questions, no?" His eyes glittered playfully as his lips curled into a warm smile.

To be truthful, she had a plethora of questions, but felt that it would be unfair to grill him if she was unwilling to provide him with reciprocal answers about herself. Jilah nodded mutely as they came to a set of black marble steps with large veins of white marble skittering through them like tiny lightning bolts. The stairs led up to an ornate doorway constructed of similar stones. Two black marble gargoyles with ruby red eyes that glittered with an alien light perched precariously on both corners of the house, their claws and wings extended in defensive gestures, as if at any moment they would swoop down and chase off any unwanted visitors in a flurry of gnashing teeth and slashing claws.

The name GRENDEL was etched into the black marble above the archway in deep, gothic script. Jilah cocked her head as she peered up at it and asked, "Wasn't that the mythical beastie that got its arm pulled out of its socket by Beowulf?"

"That is a rather simplistic view of the poem, but yes." Argent chuckled quietly to himself as she drank in the beauty of the mausoleum.

The little iron gate to the crypt was partially open, and sharp spikes protruded out and down over the top of it in a clawed wave. A round metallic medallion with the design of a dragon's head sat in the center of the door. Flames flared out of its mouth in a brilliant wash of red, orange, and yellow; its scales a shiny black onyx. Jilah tentatively reached out to touch the medallion, swearing that she could almost feel the heat of the flames as she gently traced the little tongues of fire with her fingers.

The building itself, constructed out of white marble with black veins running through it, presented itself as an almost exact negative to the steps and the doorway. Jilah peered around the dragon head medallion, spotting a dim outline that looked like a mosaic image of what she imagined was the legendary creature itself in the floor. The artist had rendered it as a cross between what looked like a wolf man and a dragon.

It was rounding on the small figure of a man, claws extended, reaching out to grasp its prey. It seemed a creepy image to place inside a family crypt, but Jilah figured that the family had their reasons. Perhaps it had been commissioned as a protective piece; something that would make trespassers wary of entering and disturbing the remains of the bodies buried within. Soft tones of red splashed across the floor's surface, adding a fair amount of menace to the place. The light looked as if it were filtering in from the stained glass windows on the sides of the mausoleum, but Jilah had never been able to pinpoint its exact source from outside the building.

"I love this place." Her tone was hushed, almost reverent as she continued. "It has more life and vibrance than most of the people I've come into contact with."

Jilah took a step back and sighed softly. "It was never this stunning when I was...well, not the way I am now." She turned to look at him, asking, "Do you know why that is?"

Argent quietly answered, "It is difficult for base humans to pick up on the nuances of things. They tend to have a great deal of banal noise in their heads that keeps them from being as aware of the beauty and the life around them as we are."

She looked back over at him, frowning as she asked, "Base humans?"

"Non-sensitives," he explained, "People that are incapable of seeing what is truly there, walking among them. Some of them purposefully blind themselves; some of them are simply not receptive to it."

"Oh." she responded, absently letting her fingers play along a section of wrought iron.

His gaze followed her hands as they slowly traced the bars of the iron gate. "I have a confession to make."

Her tone became guarded as her fingers curled around one of the bars. "Do tell."

Wary of saying something else that would cause her pain, Argent kept his voice carefully neutral as he answered, "I've been watching you for a while. I wanted to make sure that you were what I thought you were before I approached you."

Jilah turned to face him, her body language becoming slightly defensive as she let out a sigh and replied, "So, you're a stalker?" Her subsequent laugh sounded more than a little bitter. "That's just great. And you're telling me this because?"

Argent backed off, chagrined. "As I stated before, it has been a very long while since I have had contact with another such as myself." He paused for a moment, before adding, "And I take exception to the word stalker. I like to think of myself as a more of a displaced romantic psychotic."

Jilah let out short bark of laughter. Ah, sarcasm. She moved to sit on the stairs. He stood quietly off to the side, unsure if he would discomfit her further by sitting beside her.

She looked up at him, meeting his gaze and quietly asking, "Why fixate on me?"

Argent paused and thought about it for a moment. "You interest me. I can honestly say that I have never found a creature of your nature in any of my previous travels. I would like very much to learn more about you, if you'll let me."

Against her better judgment, she scooted over to make space for him on the stairs beside her. Craning her neck up to look at him would just become painful if he continued standing. Argent slowly moved to sit beside her, not wanting to make any sudden moves that would startle her. He found himself wondering what had happened to her that made her so skittish. His initial glimpse into her thoughts had been brief; the images he'd gotten had been rather jumbled and chaotic. It had been far too easy to dip further in than he had meant to initially, and he felt a little guilty about it.

Jilah kept her eyes fixed on a cluster of headstones surrounded by a foot-high silver-toned railing as she pulled her knees up to her chin and wrapped her arms tightly around them. Her voice stayed quiet and tentative as she spoke. "I must admit, you interest me as well,

Argent. I haven't been around anything but regular people, and very negligible ones at that, ever. I had hoped that there were others like me but never really knew.." Her voice trailed off as she set her chin on her knees.

Argent leaned back, resting his elbows on the top step, long legs stretching down the stairs as he crossed them. He turned to gaze up at the stars and sighed. Jilah looked over at him, unable to help herself as her gaze traveled down the length of his body. A warm, electric thrum fluttered in her gut and brought a pink flush to her skin.

"I don't want you to be scared of me, Jilah." She jumped a little at the sound of his voice, now sharply aware of the delicious sound of leather creaking as he shifted and looked over at her, his expression sincere as he murmured, "I want you to be able to trust me."

Her gaze darted away from him, her voice distant and hushed as she replied, "I think that I might just have seen too much at this point to trust anybody again."

A slow tear rolled down Jilah's cheek, her expression steely as she now fought to keep from breaking down in front of this man she'd met less than an hour ago. Talking to him was bringing up too many painful memories, things that she had shoved to the back of the 'deal with it later' pile since her new life started. She had worked vigilantly at keeping her emotions out of her work, knowing that they would eventually become septic, that she would be forced to deal with them at some point. Unfortunately, Jilah didn't feel that she'd had much of a choice. The protective walls she'd so carefully constructed now seemed paper thin, barely able to contain it all.

Jilah shook her head to force it to clear, digging her nails sharply into her palms. The pain quickly brought her back to the present. She had absolutely no desire, and no reason, to fall to pieces in front this man. Or anybody else. She refused to be a victim again.

"I myself reached that point many years ago." Argent paused for a moment, sat up and continued, "At the time, I was certain that it was a permanent condition." His features softened, and he smiled gently as he looked over at her. "I am happy to say that I was incorrect in my assumption."

Jilah laughed weakly and replied, "You realize you're dispelling the entire notion that I had about vampires.." She winced and corrected herself, "Sanguine being evil, right?"

Argent laughed. Jilah blinked at the sight of the sharp eyeteeth that peeked out from behind his lips. He shook his head slowly, chuckling as he said, "Would it put you more at ease if I wore a cape and a cheap tuxedo?"

As Jilah fought the urge to smile, a giggle slipped out before she could stop it. She put a hand to her mouth, looking over at him, unable to stop grinning. After a moment, they both collapsed into fits of laughter, the tension between them dissolving, forgotten. Minutes passed, and the laughter slowly faded as they both leaned back on the steps to look up into the night sky.

Jilah broke the silence first. "Thanks for not forcing the answers to the questions you have out of me. I get the feeling that you could have done it pretty easily."

She turned to look over at him and he smiled, his eyes lighting up as he met her gaze.

"I want you to trust me. It's really important to me." He turned to look back up at the stars, sighing softly. "I find that I have grown lonely in the decades spent away from my own kind. I've been so separate for a great while." His tone became wistful as he continued, "Life goes very slowly when there is nobody to share it with."

Argent turned to look at her, emerald eyes full of hesitation as he finished, "I genuinely like you, and wish for us to be friends. I find that over the years, I've grown weary of not having somebody in my life that I will not outlive." A strange sadness washed over her in an almost painful wave at his words, but Argent remained still, waiting for her to respond.

Oh shit. She thought to herself, blinking quickly, *I hadn't even thought about that.*

Eight

Playing Well With Others

Jilah had so thoroughly devoted herself to this new path her life had taken that she hadn't really given much thought to anything outside of it. There really hadn't been time for much else. It had been a busy and, at times, exhausting process – learning about and dealing with the darker side of life almost exclusively. It hadn't really occurred to Jilah exactly how high the emotional toll would be when she was finally forced to come to terms with all the changes.

Her patroness had been very clear about her life expectancy. As long as she continued in her steadfast devotion to the cause, she would show no signs of aging, remaining in the peak of health, beauty and stamina. Her only companionship to speak of had been the echo of her patroness as she prowled through her mind, directing her actions when it felt that she needed to be guided. The Dark Lady seemed to prefer making her presence known only when it was time to work.

Argent's words weighed heavy on her. She felt a dull ache in her chest as she came to the sharp realization of exactly how lonely she'd been as well. She simply hadn't had time to notice it until now. Jilah felt an odd pulling sensation as she looked over at Argent, unsure how to respond to what he'd said. If she started talking now, she wasn't sure that she would be able to stop without falling apart. It felt as if she were walking a razor thin line and it was taking almost everything she had to stay on the safe, sane side of it. Unbidden, her gaze quickly swept over his frame again, drinking in the sight of him. Argent was beautiful, yet somehow still extremely masculine. Jilah found herself wondering how he managed to pull it off. Then again, she hadn't run across anybody, male or female, that seemed so comfortable in their own skin before.

It also didn't help that the types of men that she'd been hunting down in the last several months had completely killed off any romantic or sexual sentiment she'd ever nurtured in the past. They had all behaved like psychotic animals in the end. Any boldness or smooth self-confidence they displayed ended up being just a fragile facade that was easily cracked open once she showed them her true face.

Her attraction to Argent warred with the deep-seated revulsion that she had come to feel for the entire male gender, and Jilah didn't know how to resolve it without breaking and running to someplace safe. But, if she continued running, how much worse off would she be when she finally stopped and dealt with what was now clearly coming to a head? Jilah silently cursed herself for reading all those psychological textbooks a month ago. Not knowing that you lived in a given box made it easier to exist in a state of contentment within it. She intently studied a pile of leaves at her feet, her voice low and soft as she gently pushed one of them around with the toe of her boot.

"I had to completely sever my ties with my old life. Not one of my friends or family members know what became of me." A sharp laugh rang out of her throat. The sound was so bitter it made his heart ache. "Not that any of them would have actually gone to the trouble of finding out what happened. My appearance has changed so dramatically that it would be difficult, if not impossible to explain. And, to be fair, we were never all that close to begin with." Jilah reached over to collect a dead leaf from the pile and began tearing at it as she spoke.

"I haven't had anybody to confide in – to talk to, since. To compensate I buried myself in work and learning everything I could, hoping that it would distract me enough so that I could ignore it all."

She paused for a moment, sighing softly, "It's always been there. It just seemed more convenient at the time to forget about it. To shut it away, or to try to find a way to turn it off."

Ah, crap. Now I'm gonna cry, dammit. Jilah struggled to keep her voice even as a tear rolled slowly down her cheek. Argent sat up and reached a tentative hand out, letting it rest gently on her shoulder, his body tensing as he waited for her reaction. She froze for a moment, a little shaky as she drew in a deep breath. With a trembling sigh, she then leaned into the touch, her expression pained as she struggled with her inner demons.

Argent relaxed, his voice a soft rumble as he replied, "I know what you're going through, Jilah. Trust me on this." He brought a hand up to trace the delicate line of her jaw and she tensed, pulling away. He let her go, dropping his hand. Jilah closed her eyes, taking another deep breath before opening them and looking back out in the direction of the highway.

"There's so much more to it than that."

She wiped away the tear on her cheek, her voice a little more stable now, stronger as she pulled back from the pain and loneliness, determined to stuff it all back behind its mental door to quell the distress it caused.

"I guess I have what clinical psychologists would call.." A tired laugh croaked out of her throat as she stood up and looked back at him, "intimacy issues."

Argent looked up at her, concerned as he watched her close herself up again, wondering if she would ever be able to truly open up to him, or to anybody. He had met others in the past who were beyond reaching, so broken that all they could do was either drown in their own pain or close themselves off from the world and simply exist, shutting off all the wondrous experiences that life had to offer. He had been one of those individuals that had firmly shut everything out, so many years ago. It had taken a supreme amount of effort, and a collection of unusual, extraordinary individuals to bring him back, to teach him to feel something other than empty numbness or unbearable pain.

Jilah quickly looked away from him, hooking a thumb in the pocket of her leather pants and kicking at the leaves on the steps, pushing them along before turning back to him.

"Let's just say that I can't deal with being touched right now. It brings up bad stuff that I'm not at all prepared to deal with yet."

Argent gave her a sad smile and nodded, getting to his feet in one quick, fluid motion to stand across from her. "I will not touch you again unless you invite me to do so."

From the tone of his voice, it was very clear that, should she so desire in the future, he would be more than happy to accommodate her. There was a playful glint in his eyes as the smile became a happy, self assured grin. A slow smile played across her lips as she shook her head and said, "You're incorrigible. But I'm sure you've heard that before."

Argent raised an eyebrow, eyes glittering as he gave a slight shrug. "It seems to be one of the more popular things people say to me."

He laughed softly, taking a moment to stretch before he looked back over at her, brow furrowing as he cocked his head at her.

"You're hungry. Have you fed tonight?"

At that, her stomach gave a rumble of protest at being forgotten. With everything that had happened tonight, she'd completely neglected her hunger, which was becoming more apparent now that he had pointed it out. Her body tightened at the mention of food and she shook her head in response.

"Not really. At least not anything substantial."

Argent flashed her a brief grin before turning to peer off into the darkness. He seemed to be searching for something. His grin widened, becoming broad and hungry, his voice a little heated as he said, "I do believe dinner is being delivered tonight." Jilah frowned, wondering what the hell he was talking about.

Argent turned to look back at her, his face a mask of horrific beauty as he explained, "There. At the south end of the cemetery. There are four of them."

His canines were longer now and his emerald eyes blazed in their sockets. Argent slowly closed them, tracking the scent on the wind. "Can you feel them?"

His eyes snapped back open, his expression uncertain as he asked, "You can't, can you?"

Jilah shook her head, her brow furrowing as her gaze traced the delicate latticework of veins just beneath the surface of his skin. His face now appeared almost translucent. Argent peered at her through eyes that glowed with a fierce intensity, his voice quavering a little as he sensed her hesitation.

"I won't hurt you, Jilah. Trust me. Please." It was the please that did it. She nodded, pushing the nagging doubt about him down as she walked towards him. His grin sharpened, his voice playful as he asked, "Shall we?"

Argent winked at her, then...disappeared. He had been standing in front of her one moment and was simply gone the next. Jilah's eyes widened and her heart skipped a beat as she heard his voice in her mind.

:: *See if you can keep up.* ::

She growled, then took off after him. His scent lingered lightly on the air, leaving a faint trail that she tracked as the landscape blurred by. My god, he's fast.

Jilah was startled to find that she was easily able to catch up to him, matching his stride without breaking a sweat. The wind was loud in her ears as it rushed by, the large pieces of the landscape passing with low whooshing sounds as she made her way through the cemetery. She found herself wondering exactly how fast they were going, making a little mental note to test her speed capabilities at some time in the future. The landscape came to an abrupt halt as she stopped beside him. They had reached the other side of the enormous cemetery in moments.

Jilah blinked twice to reorient herself. She had never moved this fast under her own power before, at least not that she could remember. Her targets, sizable but clumsy, had always been incapable of out-maneuvering her, so she'd never really had to move that all that quickly to catch them.

Argent grinned back at her, his words echoing in her thoughts as he gave an impressed nod.

:: *Not bad. Not bad at all.* :: He raised an eyebrow, chuckling quietly as she scowled back at him.

Jilah stiffened at what sounded like a muffled cry and quickly spun to track the source of the sound. Her eyes widened as she spied two college-aged boys covered with a familiar red haze, standing and looking down at a couple writhing on the ground next to an open grave. The boys were laughing and jostling each other, their faces flushed as they watched their friend wrestle with a nude girl who was struggling weakly against the assault. Another cry echoed out, sounding mournful on the night breeze. A hand rocked back, coming down hard and connecting with a sharp slapping sound as one of the boys struck the girl in the face.

Jilah heard the boy growl, "Hold her, goddammit." The other two quickly knelt down and grabbed her arms, pinning them to the ground while their friend straddled her, unzipping his pants. Their laughter was an ugly thing, setting her teeth on edge as she watched a red haze slowly begin to envelop the third boy as he began moving roughly against the girl.

Witnessing such an act was so awful, so numbing, that Jilah completely froze up. She had never really caught anybody in the act before, and it threw her. She was presented with a violent flashback to that fateful first night, and she gagged as she brought a hand up to cover her mouth. *Why can't I move? Why am I just standing here and watching this happen? Oh god...* The girl's breathing was shallow and ragged as they raped her, and Jilah heard the rough sibilant voice of her patroness as it screamed through her head, angrily calling for the death of these boys.

YES! Finally! Her psyche cried out in triumph. Jilah latched onto the anger in the voice, letting it build as it slowly clawed its way through her; welcoming it with open arms. Everything else went away as she focused on that point of white-hot rage that was now finally here, finally ready. Argent watched as her fingers lengthened into sharp, wicked claws. Jilah's royal blue eyes glittered dangerously as a murderous rage shot up her spine, shrieking as it tore through her system.

Her voice was low and guttural as she growled, "Sons of bitches must pay."

Argent's eyes widened as he looked over at her. He took a wary step back, feeling a cold wave of fury rolling off of her. It was heady and more than a little biting. What the hell had gotten her so angry? Unable to help himself, he tentatively dipped into her thoughts and reeled as if physically slapped by the furious maelstrom he found within.

At its epicenter stood a fearsome woman with skin of onyx, multiple arms darting about her head and torso as she fixed him with a fiery, baleful gaze. Her grin was feral, savage, and sharp toothed, her voice sounding like the hiss of a snake as she spat at him.

:: *Keep well out of the path of vengeance, dead one. If you keep my vessel from her appointed task, I will send her to destroy you as well as these three despoilers.* ::

Argent reflexively jerked away from the image, throwing up a mental shield as he stared over at Jilah. He watched her intently, his eyes bright as she darted forward, grabbing the back of the neck of the boy hunching into the poor girl on the ground. She effortlessly hauled him up over her head, then slammed him to the ground with enough force to shatter the bones in his face. The body impacted with a meaty thud and instantly began seizing, arms and legs twitching as she turned to look over at his two companions. Jilah's eyes blazed with righteous fury as she snapped a hand out, catching the one closest to her by the scrotum and twisting.

Her lips pulled away from her teeth in a ghastly grin and she cooed almost lovingly as she felt the boy's terror and agony sing through her. A low chuckle bubbled out of her throat as she pulled him down to the ground by his testicles. The boy screamed as he kicked and punched at her in a feeble attempt to escape. Jilah was laughing now, throaty and loud as the third boy uttered a high-pitched shriek and took off into the night, blindly fleeing through the cemetery.

Jilah took a moment to look down at their victim, seeing a mass of bruises on the girl's pelvis and breasts. Jilah winced as she realized that this wasn't the first time the girl had been sexually assaulted. The girl lay passed out in a small pool of blood that was now gathering at the apex between her legs. Her breathing was shallow. She would probably live if she received medical attention in time. Jilah could do basic first aid on her, but she didn't want to chance possible field surgery without the proper equipment. It was best to leave that to medical professionals. At least the girl wouldn't need an ER rape kit to try to track down her attackers, although they'd likely do one anyway given her condition.

The avatar's gaze rested back on the boy in her grip and the hideous grin returned, her voice sultry and heated as she pulled him closer and purred, "Oooh, let's just see what's in that nasty little head of yours."

Jilah locked eyes with him and pushed, a thrill running through her as she sent the girl's memories of the experience looping back on themselves in his mind until his eyes became glassy, his face going slack. She chuckled darkly as a line of spittle slid down the boy's cheek and she turned his head to the side. Leaning forward, she bit down into the soft flesh of his neck. His fear was delicious, a sensual feast.

She drank it down in long, slow swallows as hot crimson ambrosia pumped into her mouth.

Jilah pulled the boy's body closer, grinning as she felt several of the bones in his back snap under her grip. A sudden prickling at the back of her neck sent a little electric jolt up her spine and she pulled away from the boy's neck to look for the source.

Argent crouched beside her, eyes glassy and fluttering as he watched her feed. He dropped to his knees beside the now very dead body of the third boy, clawed fingers slowly trailing wet red scores across the boy's torso as he groaned in pleasure. Jilah felt a answering curl of desire flare in her gut, and she watched his expression become reverent as he stared back at her.

She turned back to her meal, looking intently into the boy's eyes to ensure that he was thoroughly ensnared in the loop of suffering that her patroness had sent through her. She could feel the quiet agony of the boy's mind as it ate at itself. Good enough. Tossing the limp body away from her with a disgusted noise, she spat at it before turning to look down at the boy face down on the ground at her feet

A high-pitched whining sound was now issuing from his throat, and his fingers scrabbled at the air as she moved over to him. Jilah reached out and rolled him over onto his back, and the whining became a wet gurgling moan. The boy's face was a ruined, bloody mess. She frowned and leaned over to peer into his eyes, seeing the barest spark of light in them. Unfortunately, the majority of his mind was already gone due to the initial trauma she had inflicted on him. There was nothing left to work with. She gave a disappointed sigh, annoyed that he'd evaded proper punishment.

An overpowering wave of heat and lust flowed in a heady wave from Argent as she turned to look back over at him. It slammed into her with a force that made her knees buckle. Her pulse raced and her clawed fingers dug furrows in the ground at her sides as she dropped to her knees. Argent's voice came out in a croak, sounding as if it were coming from very far away for some strange reason. Jilah noticed that he was now trembling as he met her gaze.

"My god." His eyes fluttered, and he was suddenly before her, reaching a shaking hand out to trace along the trails of blood that had dripped down her chin. His fingers seemed warmer now as they slid along her jawline, and she leaned into the touch, her skin tightening as he brushed soft lips against her ear.

"You are indeed a savage beauty."

Argent let out a shaking breath, unable to remember the last time that somebody had gotten to him this badly. He hadn't fed off of terror like this in decades and honestly couldn't remember the last time he had eaten quite this well. He could still feel the sharp tang of fear and anguish thick in the night air as he drank it down. He let out a shaky breath as the heady mixture of her answering desire rolled through him.

One could not possibly hope to ask for more than this, he thought to himself as his fingers brushed against her temples, leaving a little smear of red there.

Jilah felt betrayed by her own body as she rubbed gently against his hand. His touch was so warm, so soft. So comforting. It stoked the curl of flame in the pit of her stomach, coaxing it into a fire that threatened to roar out of control if she didn't pull away from it. She shuddered, her voice tight with the effort of forcing it back as she breathed, "Please. Stop." She pulled away, her body shaking as she looked away from him.

Sensing the struggle within her, Argent let her go. "My apologies, I have forgotten myself again," he rasped, trying to look elsewhere. Anywhere but at her. "I am afraid that you caught me off guard." If he didn't back away, he was going to end up doing something he was very certain that she would make him regret. The time wasn't right yet. He pulled away from her, firmly shackling his desire.

But oh, when she finally gives in. He trembled just thinking about it.

As he moved away, Jilah couldn't help feeling somehow diminished, colder. It helped to ground her. Digging sharp claws into the ground at her sides, she fixed her gaze on a tree in the distance, determined to master her composure. She was not at all ready to be intimate with this strange man, but her body seemed bound and determined to make the decision for her.

I just met this guy, and now all I can think of is having his hands on me. What the hell is up with that?, she thought angrily, *I run across ONE vampire and now all of a sudden I'm a wanton slut?*

Jilah quickly stood up and moved over to look down at the slow breathing form of the girl by the grave. She really wanted to cover her up with something. There was a weird sense of wanting to preserve the girl's modesty now that she was no longer in immediate danger. There was a meaty thump behind her, and she turned to see Argent tossing the body of one of the boys into the open grave. He looked up in time to see her wiping the blood from her chin with the back of her hand, drawing bloody smears across her cheek. He wanted very badly to lick them from her skin, and fought to keep from running his tongue across his lips.

His voice quavered a little as he asked, "What do you want to do with the girl?"

Jilah seemed lost as she gazed back at him, her voice distant as she replied, "We need to get her to a hospital."

Jilah turned to look back down at the girl, concerned as she watched the slow rise and fall of the girl's ribcage. At least her breathing seemed regular. She knelt down and began noting the girl's vital signs, relieved that they were within somewhat normal levels. The bleeding seemed to be slowing, which was reassuring.

"She won't survive if we leave her out here."

Argent looked back at her with a curious expression, unsure that he had heard her correctly. Was this the same creature who, moments ago, had given him the most awe inspiring meal he'd ever had? Was she joking? "You want to help her?" he ventured, eyes glittering as he waited for her response.

Jilah's jaw dropped, a look of disbelief flooding her features as she gaped back at him. She blinked twice, then shook it off, her voice indignant as she stood and snapped, "How can you ask me that? After what you saw them doing to her?"

Argent was taken aback, mystified as to why she was so angry. Animals fought amongst themselves and raped each other all the time, but humans had never seemed to give a damn about that. These usually ended up being the same kinds of humans who were always going on and on about how they were in full control over their animal urges.

Sure. Whatever they wanted to believe.

Over the decades, his outlook on the sea of humanity had become that of a predator looking out over a field of particularly ill-behaved sheep. Sheep that happened to be very tasty, depending on who you chose to dine on. The bottom line was that he was at the top of the food chain, and they were beneath him, therefore – his natural prey. What should it matter to him what they did to one another?

Argent cocked his head at her in confusion as he answered, matter of factly, "They are animals. Food." He shrugged, "Did you feel this much anguish for the meat from the cows and chickens that you consumed when you were still one of them?"

Jilah reeled back as if slapped. Her mouth hung open again and she stared at him blankly before recovering and narrowing her eyes, her voice becoming sharp as she growled, "It's not the same thing."

Argent arched an eyebrow at her as he licked a splash of crimson from a finger. "It most certainly is. Do you honestly think that the animals that you dined on then were pleased to be butchered simply to provide food for you?"

Jilah began to stammer, her face flushing red as she argued, "No. I don't. But these are people. With lives and feelings. They matter."

Argent gave her a sidelong glance. "And you think animals don't? Surely you are not of the opinion that they exist solely to trot off to the slaughterhouse when their usefulness as something other than food comes to an end? That this is their sole purpose in life?" His voice remained calm as he spoke, truly intrigued.

Jilah let out an annoyed sigh and bent down to pick the girl up, hefting her gently into her arms as she asked, "So you just see humanity as this huge smorgasbord, waiting for you to swoop down and tear into it?"

He shrugged and said, "Why not? I am at the top of the food chain, for the moment, and it's not as if I kill every time I feed." A wicked smile curled the edges of his lips as he continued, "Besides, most of them find it quite enjoyable."

"I'll just bet." Jilah's expression soured as she glared back at him.

Argent laughed and replied, "Face it. As a human, something always had to perish so that you could continue living, be it flora or fauna. Think of this transition as just a generous bump further up the food chain." Her logic was confounding, but it was also one of the reasons he found her so fascinating.

Jilah opened her mouth to deliver a sharp retort before closing it and looking off into the distance. Her brow furrowed as she thought about it for a moment. She hated to admit it, but he was right. Plant or animal, anything she'd consumed had once been a living thing, and thus, must have died to feed her. She shook her head angrily, wanting to be free of him and his uncomfortable logic.

She ground her teeth and growled, "Just humor me, okay? I have to do this. I can't explain why right now."

Argent nodded quietly, then ventured a look down at the girl in Jilah's arms. She was still out cold. "Where will you fit her on the motorcycle? There doesn't appear to be room for three on it."

Jilah took a deep breath, stifling another growl as she realized that he was right again. The entire night was becoming newly annoying. She could always leave him here and take the girl to the hospital. Surely he could find his own way home.

"There is that," Argent interrupted, reading her train of thought, "But she is currently unconscious. Can you handle a limp body while you're going down the road on a motorcycle? What if she wakes up?"

Jilah cut him off with an irritated look and snapped, "Stop doing that."

Argent let out a soft sigh, keeping his tone patient as he said, "Your only option would seem to be calling an ambulance. You can do it anonymously. They will collect her and it won't be on your conscience anymore."

Jilah nodded numbly, hating how he kept being right. Smug bastard. She glared over at him as if daring him to comment.

Argent presented her with a supremely innocent look. "What? I am only trying to help."

He held a cell phone out to her and smiled. "I liberated it from one of the bodies. They won't miss it."

Jilah sighed and muttered, "Good god, you're frustrating."

Argent laughed softly. "It is odd that everybody seems to notice that very thing about me."

Nine

Guess Who's Coming to Breakfast?

Jilah decided it best to leave the girl by the side of the road. She brought an orange emergency poncho she had retrieved from the saddlebags of her bike to cover her up. She hoped that it would make it easier for the ambulance crew to spot the girl from the road. There hadn't been much traffic since they had arrived, so she hoped that the girl would be relatively safe until the EMT's could get to her.

Argent watched as Jilah gently placed the girl down and knelt beside her. The avatar's eyes fluttered shut, her brows knitting in pain as she gently brushed a few stray hairs from the girl's temples. He remained silent as he bore witness, unsure of what she was doing but not really wanting to dip into her thoughts again. He didn't know what the creature in her mind was, but he was pretty certain he didn't want to run across it again – much less piss it off.

Jilah winced as she worked at purging the girl's memory of this nasty incident. As she slipped through the tender images of the young woman's life, she was horrified to find that the girl's father had molested her repeatedly, starting when she was about eight. She slowly pulled out the vivid scenes from earlier tonight, as well as those from her childhood, being guided by the tender touch of her patroness. It was the only time she had ever been gentle.

As Jilah finished and broke the connection, she choked and quickly blurred over to a tree to vomit up some of her earlier meal. A splash of crimson spattered the roots of the tree and surrounding grass as she heaved, holding a hand against the trunk to steady herself.

Argent appeared at her side, his expression deeply concerned as he asked, "My god. What just happened back there? Are you all right?"

Jilah choked up another mouthful of blood, spitting it at the base of the tree and wiping her mouth before looking up at him, feeling strangely out of breath as she asked, "You're actually worried about me?"

Argent gave her a strange look and replied, "That is a stupid question."

Jilah sighed as she got to her feet, wiping her mouth with the back of her hand. She coughed, then nodded and replied, "Yeah. I guess it was."

She turned to look back over at the girl who now appeared to be resting peacefully at the side of the road. At least she'd be safe now. One down. Uncountable numbers remaining. No rest for the wicked. She thought to herself before looking back over at him. "I'm fine. I just had to unburden her, that's all."

Argent raised an eyebrow and peered at her intently, his voice dropping an octave as he asked, "Forgive my curiosity. Can you please elaborate?"

Jilah sighed, running pale fingers over the long braid that had become somewhat disheveled during the night's activities. A bath would definitely be in order when she finally arrived home. She always felt as if she'd been dipped into something sticky and filthy when she sifted through people's poisonous memories.

Her tone became almost clinical as she replied, "She had various... episodes like this in the past as well. I essentially removed the pain of them from her memory so she isn't haunted by them anymore."

Her voice dropped into a venomous growl as she added, "Her father is already in the ground, so I don't need to be visiting him. Hopefully it was painful."

Her words sent a little thrilled shiver through Argent as he looked down at her. "Can I help in any way?"

Jilah shook her head grimly. "No. It's okay. I walk with much worse already."

Sensing his need to ask further questions, she pulled the cell phone out of her pocket and said, "I'll explain later. Right now, let's just get this taken care of, okay?"

Argent hesitated for a moment, and Jilah frowned. "What?" she asked, wondering why he suddenly seemed uncomfortable.

"We've left a bit of a mess back there. It needs to be tended to. There will likely be a police car accompanying the ambulance, and if they find the bodies..."

His voice trailed off as Jilah nodded, irritated with herself that she hadn't thought of it first. Of course, they'd need to dispose of the bodies. She silently cursed herself for not bringing the SUV. "I'll make the call from here. There's better reception by the road. I'll meet you back at the grave site to help you clean up."

Argent replied, "You will want to hurry. We need to bury them far back in the woods. I'll see if I can find a pair of shovels." He darted off in the direction of the cemetery, and Jilah dialed 911.

"Emergency services, please describe the nature of your call." The woman on the other end of the phone sounded official, but almost bored. Perhaps it was an unusually slow night.

"There's a young girl out by the south side of Mortmont Cemetery. It looks as if somebody's attacked her and covered her up with something." Jilah explained, hoping they would be able to get paramedics out here quickly.

"Can you describe the extent of her injuries?" the woman inquired.

Jilah shook her head and replied, "She's pretty bruised up and she's bleeding."

Jilah was hesitant to use medical terminology or to go into too much detail. This needed to sound like a random, clueless call. They just needed to know somebody was hurt. The girl's injuries could be treated quickly enough once they arrived.

"How soon can you get somebody out there?" she asked.

"There's a unit on the way. They should be there in twenty minutes. Ma'am, can you please tell me..?"

Jilah cut her off, not wanting to stay on the phone any longer. She had to help Argent get the bodies of those frat boys into the woods well before the police showed up. "I'm sorry, I need to go. Thanks for getting somebody out here to help her." She quickly hung up and blurred back to the cemetery.

At the grave site, there was a single body left. She reached down and hefted it in her arms as she darted off in the direction of the scents of the other two. The stink of death was easily traced on the night wind; it led her right to him.

Argent turned as he was unceremoniously dropping one of the bodies to the ground. "I was just about to go back for him. How did the call go?"

Jilah tossed the body in her arms on top of the other two at Argent's feet. "They're going to be here in twenty minutes, if the operator can be believed. They might be here sooner, might be later. It's hard to tell."

Argent reached down to pick up the shovels, handing one to her.

"Should we put them all in one hole?" She asked, looking over at the three crumpled bodies with distaste.

"It will go quicker if we do, but we're going to need to dig deep and cover our tracks. We should be far enough in the woods that the authorities' search will not lead them out here." Argent pressed the shovel into the soft ground and began digging.

They proceeded to open a hole in the earth that, quicker than she thought possible, was deep enough for Argent to stand in with his head a foot below the grass line. Once finished, they both leapt out of the makeshift grave and kicked the bodies in. They landed in a tangled jumble of limbs, the expressions on their faces glassy and empty. Jilah and Argent worked quickly to fill in the grave, silent but for the sound of their exertions.

As they tamped the last of the earth down, Argent frowned and looked over at Jilah. "Make sure you cover it thoroughly. I am going to go back to the cemetery to insure that there is nothing that we left behind."

She heard the faint sound of sirens in the distance and nodded. "Be careful," she murmured.

Argent responded with a surprised smile and quietly said, "I didn't know you cared." He then darted off into the night.

Jilah grinned and began pulling leaves and other ground cover over the freshly overturned earth. He was beginning to grow on her. Who knew that spending a night burying bodies could be such a bonding experience?

She had almost finished when he returned. "The site is clean. The police shouldn't be able to find much of anything useful." He explained.

Jilah murmured, "If I had known how this night would end up, I would've driven the truck."

Argent quirked an eyebrow as he looked over at her. Jilah quickly said, "Long story."

Argent nodded. "We need to leave."

Jilah looked down at their handiwork, frowning. "I need to see them put her in the ambulance."

Argent quietly replied, "Then we should watch from a safe distance."

Jilah let out a relieved sigh as the paramedics retrieved the girl. Several police cars had shown up as well, and officers were milling around, disappointed that the girl was unconscious. Argent had respected her wishes and remained silent while they waited for the emergency crew to show up. Afterwards, they destroyed the cell phones from the bodies and had thrown them far into the woods on the other side of the street.

He was now looking up at the sky with a hesitant expression. It was definitely high time to head back home. It had been a more productive night than she had originally planned. Now all she wanted was to soak in a nice hot bath and fall into bed. Pulling memories out of the girl's head had drained her more than she wanted to admit. They quietly walked back over to the bike and she collected her helmet, frowning as she looked back over at him. He was still peering into the sky, seemingly mesmerized by something.

"You okay? It's probably time we headed back." Jilah kicked a leg over the bike, sliding the keys into the ignition. "Where do you want me to drop you off?"

Argent turned towards her, his tone uncertain as he replied, "Actually, I was hoping that you would be so kind as to offer me shelter from the coming day. It's getting a little too close to dawn for my liking, and I'm afraid that I am not near enough to my current living quarters to make it there in time."

Jilah looked around, confused. The sky was still pitch black. Surely it couldn't be that late, could it?

Argent cursed himself for not paying more close attention to the time. He was usually more aware of these things, but then he also hadn't been subjected to a distraction like this in decades. He looked over at her, an odd expression creeping into his features as he said, "It is still dark now, but trust me. When dawn breaks, it breaks quickly. I would prefer to be somewhere protected from it when it does."

Jilah responded with a quick nod, convinced that his concern was genuine. Her expression became thoughtful as she asked, "You don't need a coffin or anything, do you?"

Argent laughed lightly, replying, "No. No coffin. Any place where the daylight is unable to reach me will be sufficient." He shook his head and murmured, "Coffin. How droll," as he walked towards her.

"So," she ventured as Argent picked the helmet up and settled himself on the seat behind her, "is there anything else about your condition that I should know about? Books have obviously gotten a lot of things wrong, and I don't want to seem like a total mo'."

"Moe?" he asked.

Jilah looked back at him and explained, "Oh, you know, Moron?"

Argent chuckled and nodded. "An intriguing way of putting it." He presented her with an amused grin. "Well, I don't get along too well with sunlight, but that's about it." Argent began pulling the helmet on as he continued, "As for the other things – garlic, religious symbols of any sort, holy ground, that's all twaddle."

Jilah raised an eyebrow, a hint of amusement in her voice as she inquired, "Twaddle?"

"Yes, twaddle. You know, full of crap? You'll recall that I did not burn to a cinder the moment we set foot within the consecrated grounds of the cemetery earlier."

Jilah laughed as the motorcycle roared to life. The large chrome pipes rumbled in the night air, and she tensed for a moment again as she felt strong arms wrap around her waist, then called back, "How about that entire 'stake through the heart' thing? Or silver weapons?"

As they pulled away, Argent switched to mental conversation, his thoughts echoing through her mind as he shrugged and answered, :: *To be honest, a stake through the heart would kill anything, including me.*

Take the heart or the head and the body degenerates. All at once. It is not a pretty sight. ::

Argent paused for a moment, then continued, :: *As to silver weapons, those only affect the Tribes. They've never had much of an effect on my kind. ::*

Jilah was actually beginning to get used to conversing with him in this way, finding that it was definitely better than yelling at the person behind you as you went down the highway.

:: *The tribes? ::*

:: *Shapeshifters. Folklore usually refers to them as werewolves and the like. ::*

Jilah was incredulous as they rounded a corner, her mind reeling. So they were real as well.

:: *Oh yes. Many of the old legends are true. How about you? Is there anything about.. ::* Argent paused for effect, his hands flexing on her hips as he continued, :: *Your condition that I should know about? ::*

Jilah shrugged, noticing that she was becoming a little less jumpy about him touching her. She wasn't quite sure whether this was a good thing or not. They turned a sharp corner and he leaned into her with it, his touch still making it a little hard to concentrate.

:: *Sunlight isn't exactly pleasant, but it doesn't damage me, ::* she explained. :: *I just get headaches and nausea along with a little lethargy. It sucks, but it's nice to know that if I have to go out in it that I won't go up in flames. ::*

:: *Guess it just sucks to be me then, eh? ::* He smiled and laughed softly.

Jilah was startled to find that she was beginning to feel comfortable around him. It was a nice feeling. She honestly couldn't remember the last time she'd been at ease with anybody. Had she ever been? It seemed that her entire life before the change had been spent trying to avoid people. Granted, Argent could be annoying as hell in some ways, but he was comfy too. She wasn't quite sure why. Jilah sighed and smiled into the wind as they continued down the road in silence. When they arrived in her neighborhood, she felt his hands tense on her hips.

:: *You actually LIVE here? ::*

:: *Beggars can't be choosers. Besides, nobody fucks with me out here. ::*

The garage door opened as she pulled up to the house and drove the bike up the driveway. She cut the engine off and braked it to a stop inside the garage. Jilah pulled her helmet off, arching an eyebrow as she looked back at him and asked, "Is that a problem?"

Argent ran his fingers through his hair in an effort to tame what had become a considerably less pointy hairstyle over the course of the night. It now had a much softer look to it. He reached down to place the helmet in the saddlebags as he looked over at her SUV and the Ghia.

"Not at all." He said aloud, continuing, "It just caught me a little off guard."

Jilah found herself smiling as well, enjoying the way he moved as he hooked a leg over the back of the bike and walked out of the garage, scrutinizing the outside of the house. She placed her helmet on the handlebars, rocking the bike back onto the stand and swinging a leg over before hitting a button on the keys to close the garage door. She slipped out of the garage and crept up behind him, grinning as she watched him survey her place.

Argent winced at the appearance of the rundown house surrounded by piles of discarded, rotting furniture, shopping carts, and various other broken items. It was a disaster area. Jilah chuckled softly as she walked to the porch and jiggled the keys in the lock, wondering if he was beginning to question his judgment over asking her if she could put him up for the day. Argent moved to stand behind her, wondering if the house looked as bad on the inside as it did on the outside. As Jilah opened the door, he winced again at the state of disarray in the front room. It looked like a junkie flophouse.

He tentatively asked, "Uh, where will I be sleeping?" Granted, the place he was currently holed up in wasn't much better, but he had made the now rather questionable assumption that she lived in better conditions than he did. He'd seen nicer crack houses.

Jilah turned and grinned at the expression on his face, answering, "Downstairs. My bedroom." She stepped inside, gesturing for him to follow. "I wouldn't feel right making you stay in some of the more vivid parts of the house. That okay?"

Argent blinked and quickly replied, "I wouldn't want to impose. Are you sure?"

Jilah couldn't help laughing, more than a little reassured to find that he was just as nervous about bunking together as she was. She waved to the meager furnishings and dirty drapes, "This is just a front.

That way people don't bother breaking in to find out what's really in the house."

Jilah reached out and took his hand, gently pulling him through the doorway.

Curious, he looked back at her. She dropped his hand and explained, "You have to come inside before I can set the alarm."

Argent blinked. Alarm? She had an alarm system to protect this hovel? Would wonders never cease? He heard a series of beeps before she turned to face him, and he smiled gamely.

He could only hope that the other parts of the house were more habitable as she said, "C'mon. Let's get you settled in." Argent nodded, mutely following her as she headed down the back hallway.

"I'll show you the rest of the house when you wake up tonight, if you like."

The entire basement provided a very stark contrast to the rest of the house. The room's decor had a very soothing effect, and he found himself relaxing as he took in the lush surroundings. The mixture of indigo, purple, black, and gray was perfect for the room. The bed was positively enormous. Chinese wind chimes rang out softly in the breeze from a small fan in the corner.

Argent surveyed the room, his eyes widening as he saw the size of the closet. Lord only knew if she'd ever be able to wear all the outfits in it in one lifetime, not to mention all the shoes and boots she'd collected. His tone was soft as he breathed, "Oh my. I had no idea."

He smiled as he let himself settle into the nuance of the bedroom. Considering how suspicious she was, he felt honored to have been invited into such a space, much less offered a place of sanctuary within it.

Jilah turned to face him, her expression hopeful as she asked, "So, you like it?"

Argent nodded slowly as he responded, "I haven't the words." He turned to face her and asked, "Are you sure about this? I am quite capable of staying in another part of the house, if you're uncomfortable."

Jilah gave him a reassuring smile before walking towards the bathroom. She slipped out of her leather jacket, calling back, "I can hardly put you upstairs in a closet. It wouldn't be right. Besides, there are no windows down here – so, no chance of you becoming a crispy critter. I'm going to get out of these dirty clothes and clean up."

Jilah turned to look back at him, arching an eyebrow as she reconsidered and said, "Actually, you might want to go first. You're a little more grimy than I am right now."

Argent looked down, noticing the generous splatters of blood across his jacket and tank top for the first time. He presented her with a sheepish grin and replied, "Oh. You wouldn't happen to have anything that fits?"

Jilah nodded, thinking that she still had some of the original occupant's clothes kicking around here somewhere.

"I'll see if I can scare something up. Just put your clothes on the sink and jump in the shower. I'll throw your washables in with mine. Towels are over there."

She pointed to a set of plush black and purple towels hanging from a bar across from the shower before running upstairs, leaving him to get himself cleaned up. Once in the upper bedroom, she started going through the boxes that she had stored all the unused clothing in, finding a pair of grey sweatpants that looked like they would fit her new guest. Unfortunately Argent was too broad shouldered to fit into any of the available shirts.

Jilah headed back downstairs to dig through her own clothes, remembering an over-sized nightshirt that she'd stashed somewhere. As she reached the kitchen hallway, Argent's voice trailed up the basement stairs.

With cat-like tread, Upon our prey we steal
In silence dread, Our cautious way we feel.
No sound at all, We never speak a word
A fly's foot-fall would be distinctly heard.

He sings in the shower?

She was surprised to find that her new guest was a very talented tenor. Jilah giggled, shaking her head as she padded down into the basement and began searching through a chest of drawers.

Finding the shirt in question, she knew immediately that it wasn't going to fit him either. She sighed and walked to the bathroom, reaching over to rap softly on the door. The singing came to an abrupt halt.

"I'm coming in to get your clothes so I can run them through the washer, okay?" she asked, disappointed that he'd stopped. When he remained silent, she grinned and added, "You have a beautiful voice. Pirates of Penzance is actually one of my favorites."

Jilah opened the door and quickly collected his clothes from the counter, replacing them with the sweats. "I found a pair of sweat pants, but I wasn't able to find a shirt that would fit you."

A furious blush colored her face as she caught the hazy outline of his body through the pebbled glass of the shower door. The view was just enticing enough to send a shiver through her. She averted her gaze as she quickly exited the bathroom.

She left the door open just a crack as she said, "I'll be right back. Want anything to drink?"

Argent sounded a touch wistful as he replied, "Actually, I'm afraid that I'm only capable of digesting blood. Anything else makes me violently ill."

"Wow. That sucks." Jilah winced as she quietly slapped her forehead, adding, "No pun intended," as she darted up the stairs.

Not being able to eat or drink regular food would drive her crazy. She actually felt a little sorry for him. He would never be able to enjoy a rare steak again. Or chocolate. Or ice cream. After a stressful day the mere taste of certain foods would comfort her, something she'd pretty much taken for granted up until now. The idea of losing that made her stomach quiver.

Jilah tossed his tank top into the washing machine along with the rest of the clothes that had been waiting for their turn in the wash. Blood and other odious fluids had already caked onto the leather items, the blood now flaking off in some parts. She ran a moist washcloth over them, wiping down what she could. A thorough cleaning would have to wait for later, though. She just didn't have the energy for it now.

After turning the washing machine on, she went into the kitchen, leaning down to open the refrigerator door. Jilah grinned as she spotted the colorful, happy green cans collected on the bottom shelves. Mountain Dew had been one of her big dietary downfalls when she was alive. Now it was merely a remembered pleasure. Her body couldn't process the caffeine any longer, but she recalled the familiar zing from when she drank it in the past, and she'd always loved the taste. She grabbed a can and closed the door, pulling the tab and knocking the nuclear green soda back, rolling it around briefly on her tongue. How all her teeth hadn't rotted out of her head with the sheer amount of the damned stuff she'd gone through in the past, she would never know.

Jilah dropped into one of the kitchen chairs, her fingers playing along the rim of the can as she pondered everything that had happened in the last couple of hours. It had been quite the enlightening night. Jilah wasn't quite certain what to do with the painfully attractive man now occupying her shower and very soon her bed.

"I'm going to make him sleep on top of the sheets, just for my own damned sanity..." she muttered quietly. Thinking about it made her head hurt. Jilah drained the last of the soda, tossing the can into the trashbag by the sink. As she made her way back downstairs, she hoped that tomorrow would be less angst-ridden.

The sight of Argent coming out of the bathroom stopped her in her tracks. He was rubbing at his hair with a towel. Her heart hammered behind her ribcage as her gaze slowly swept up his body. He had an athlete's build, tight and muscular, his pale skin standing out in stark contrast against the color of the walls. Something that felt very much like a small electric shock shot up her spine as their eyes met. A light pink flush slowly crept into her face and shoulders. Jilah placed a shaky hand on the wall to steady herself as Argent's interest became plainly evident through the loose sweatpants she'd provided for him.

He watched her eyes widen in surprise and quickly placed the towel in front of him, his voice slightly hoarse as he gave an apologetic grin and said, "Whoa. Sorry."

Jilah felt a little weak in the knees as she watched the muscles slowly slide against one another beneath his skin. Her hand fluttered to her throat as her gaze slowly traveled back up his torso, before she quickly stammered, "It's okay. I'm, ah, just gonna go take that shower now."

She quickly darted around him and into the bathroom, slamming the door closed and leaning back against it. She took a moment to collect herself before beginning to strip down with shaky hands.

Dear god. I don't know how much longer I can keep this up.

Jilah turned the water on and stepped into the warm spray, trying to concentrate on how relaxing the warm liquid felt cascading down her body. Anything to get her mind off the man that drove her body crazy in the next room. She leaned her head forward against the tile of the shower wall, annoyed that she was too dirty to simply take a bath and feel clean afterwards. She'd have to soak in the tub after rinsing off, just to get in the mood to go to sleep. Her breath came out in a long, soft sigh as her thoughts began to drift.

A vivid mental flash of pale bodies rocking together, crying out as they moved against one another made her knees buckle, and her hand shot out to catch the wall to steady herself. A loud slap and thump resonated through the bathroom. This was getting downright annoying.

The bathroom door flew open and he was suddenly there on the other side of the pebbled glass asking, "Are you alright?"

Jilah's voice was more than a little shaky as she responded, "Yeah. Just a little slippery in here. Goddamned soap."

She let out a weak laugh and glanced nervously over at his wavy outline, hoping that he would just go back into the bedroom, leaving her to her own little internal drama. Jilah watched him nod before he strode out, politely closing the door behind him. She forced her focus back on washing the grime off, annoyed that her chest and neck were spattered with caked blood. She wasn't usually such a messy eater. Pale trails of red ran down her hips and legs to swirl around the drain as she scrubbed herself clean.

Once she finished, she drew a quick bath, happy that she'd taken the time to do so as she leaned back into the relaxing heat of the water. The tension in her muscles slowly began to release and she smiled as she dunked her head under the water. Afterwards, she toweled off, pushing away the flurry of feelings that tapped at her like a moth batting against a light bulb. She then slipped into a purple silk chemise, sighing as the fabric slid against her skin. She usually slept nude, but today she was definitely covering up. The next twenty minutes were spent on her daily ritual of detangling and braiding her hair so that it wouldn't strangle her in her sleep. It was too much of a pain in the ass to comb out all the snarls that always ended up in it otherwise.

Jilah opened the door to find Argent curled up on the floor, off to the side of the bed. The long, slightly damp braid gently thumped against her back as she walked over to him. She stopped to peer down at him, looking for the familiar movements that people usually made when they slept, shivering as she realized that he had gone completely still. She reached out to touch him, wanting to reassure herself that he was still alive, and shrank back when she found his skin cold and unpliable, like the surface of a statue. It was extremely disconcerting.

"Man, that's just creepy," she said to no-one in particular as she looked over at the bed.

She didn't feel right just leaving him on the floor. Jilah sighed as she crouched down, easily hefting him into her arms. His body had become a fully articulated mannequin that had no control over its arms and legs. He was completely limp, but still rock solid. She wrestled for a few moments to get him settled under the top cover on the unoccupied side of the bed, then stood back and looked down at him. How awkward, she thought to herself as she moved to tuck him in. He looked so vulnerable – so helpless, just laying there unable to move. It made her realize how much trust he must have in her already, to know that he would be safe here.

She frowned, watching him for a few moments as she wondered if she had ever trusted anybody in her life that implicitly. She turned to make her way upstairs to throw their clothes in the dryer. Out the back kitchen window, the sky was slowly becoming an ever-lightening shade of blue as the sun chased the night back across the sky. Jilah moved to stand at the back door to watch the rising of the great ball of fire as it began its journey into the daytime sky, happy that she could still witness such a thing. She stood transfixed as the first brilliant fingers of light crept out from behind the warehouse across the way, her head resting propped against her arm as she leaned into the wall and sighed.

To never see something like this again. She shuddered at the thought and turned to head back downstairs. As she reached the bottom of the steps, she looked back over at Argent and felt a cold chill rush along her skin at the fact that he seemed, for the most part – well, dead to the world. She padded over to the bed, sliding beneath the covers as she turned facing away from him. At least she didn't have to worry about him making a move on her during the day. The thought reassured her as sleep came quickly, and she hoped that she'd be able to make it through a dreamless day.

Ten

Intimacy Issues

A loud thumping noise startled her awake. Jilah was up in a blur of motion, an enormous knife in her hand, her eyes narrowing as she surveyed the room. She held her body in a defensive posture, ready to react to whatever had dared to break into her house – much less trespass in her bedroom. She was going to ensure that it had the chance to appreciate the seriousness of the transgression.

She looked over to see Argent flattening his palms against the wall and watching her with a very careful expression. He brought up a hand, holding it out in a warding gesture as he stammered, "I know I chose to retire on the floor. I honestly have no idea how I woke up in the bed beside you."

After a moment, Jilah blinked then burst into laughter and lowered the blade. Argent visibly relaxed as he watched her place the weapon back in its hiding place in the bed frame. She continued to chuckle as she explained, "It's okay. I slid you under the covers after you fell asleep. I didn't want you bedding down on the floor. You're my guest. The first I've had, really."

Argent breathed a sigh of relief and slid down into a pile of pillows propped up against the wall. He was still more than a little wary of the fact that she slept with a large hunting knife in her bed. What the hell did she need with such an item, or any other weapon for that matter? Perhaps it was a comfort piece. Yes, a razor-sharp teddy bear. He shuddered. Weapons were so archaic. He much preferred an up close and personal kill when it came down to it, choosing to get his hands dirty instead. Weapons just dulled the feel of the whole process, in his opinion.

Noting his wary expression, Jilah grinned as she reassured him, "I'm not going to bite. Really." Wanting to put him at ease, she laughed lightly and beckoned for him to come over and sit on the bed.

A smile played at the edges of his lips as he replied, "Then why would I want to get on the bed with you? Tease."

Jilah rolled her eyes, waving him over again. "C'mon, you can't stay on the floor. I feel like I'm being a terrible hostess." Argent slowly stood up and moved over to the bed.

As she watched him, Jilah felt a now entirely too familiar tingling at the base of her spine. It was almost as if invisible fingers were brushing gently against her skin. He gingerly sat at the foot of the bed. Argent had no desire to spook her, feeling that it was a great deal more sensible to err on the side of caution where she was concerned. She had made it sound as if there was still a great deal she didn't know about her capabilities, and it would be rather embarrassing to get himself killed by accident after everything else he had lived through.

Jilah smiled, fingering her braid as she asked, "How did you sleep?"

Argent smiled, casually responding, "Really well, actually. The best sleep I've had in ages. One could almost say that I slept like," He paused for effect, giving a little mock gasp, "The dead."

Argent grinned as she rolled her eyes at him again. He continued cheerily, "And you? My heroine. My splendorous shelter from the rays of deadly dawn's light." His hand fluttered up to his chest in a dramatic gesture, "My beautiful.."

Jilah cut him off with a playful growl, waving a hand at him, "Okay, that's enough, Romeo." Her voice was still husky with sleep as she continued, "I slept so well that I wasn't even aware I rested. I put my head down and the next thing I knew, you were scooting across the room as if I was going to kill you."

Argent sobered, his voice quiet as he replied, "I'm afraid that the reaction is due to negative past experiences. Old habits apparently die hard." He gave her an apologetic smile.

Jilah raised an eyebrow, cocking her head at him. "Just what kind of, ah, creatures are you used to being around?" She was almost certain that she didn't want to know.

"Oh, minor demons mostly."

Jilah blinked at him, unsure that she'd heard him correctly. His expression became a touch wistful as he continued, his eyes shining as he looked over at her, hoping that she didn't react negatively to what he was about to tell her.

"I tend to be a bit over-enthusiastic for certain partners. Demons are very resilient. It's much easier for them to keep up with me without incurring permanent damage." Argent let his voice trail off as he realized that Jilah was now staring at him openly.

"That was probably a little more information than you needed, right?" He winced and let out a halfhearted laugh.

"Well, I did ask." Jilah responded and looked away, feeling her skin flush, her voice slightly breathy as she said, "You're quite the enigma, Mr. Valentine. I'm not sure what to make of you."

Turning back to meet his gaze, she continued, "I thought about what you said last night, and it occurred to me that I could probably use a friend. Someone I could talk to from time to time."

Argent watched her intently as she spoke. Once again, her eyes began to wander over his features, eventually leading down to linger on his well-muscled torso. He made a small coughing noise, and she shook her head once before meeting his gaze again. His expression was now tinged with a mixture of hunger and amusement.

Jilah looked away, quickly getting up as she began searching for a set of clothing in the dresser. Getting dressed. I'm focusing on getting dressed...Tra Lala, here's me getting dressed, yessir..

It became a singsong mantra in her head as she pawed through the drawer in front of her. Anything to keep from thinking about the beautiful male now leaning back to recline on the bed behind her.

A warm rush tickled its way over her shoulders and up the back of her neck as she heard him murmur, "My god, you're beautiful."

Jilah kept her back to him, her eyes sliding shut as she clutched a pair of ragged black jean shorts to her chest, her voice quiet as she replied, "You keep saying that."

Argent's tone was sultry and she swore that she could feel his gaze as a physical caress that slowly slid along her body as he spoke. "That is because it is entirely true."

Jilah took a slow breath, closing her eyes. "I didn't always look like this."

She stood before a bathroom mirror, frowning at her reflection. Her hair fell around her head in a wet reddish brown mop, her bangs clawing over her forehead into little spiky, dripping points in front of hazel eyes. Freckles peppered her nose and cheeks as well as dotting various sun kissed points on her body. She'd always hated them. Inevitably, her gaze trailed down to her abdomen. No matter how much she didn't want to look, her eyes were always drawn to it – like a car crash or a medical video that you couldn't turn away from while it was playing out.

There had been an operation on her heart when she was a baby, and the scar bisected her torso, leaving little puckered pockets of flesh in its wake as it trailed along her skin. It had been the bane of her existence throughout her teen years, making it impossible to wear midriff shirts or anything other than a one-piece bathing suit.

She had always been terrified of anybody seeing it and vividly remembered the derisive jeering she had received in gym class because she refused to change in the locker room with anybody else. She had hated having to sneak off to the stalls to cover her secret. Her shame.

Would he have found me beautiful back then? The way I was? Jilah thought to herself and frowned, not entirely sure how to feel.

She heard Argent shift against the sheets as he murmured, "The true beauty of a woman is not always entirely measured by her physical appearance."

Jilah turned to face him, the shorts still clutched in her hands. "But it matters."

Argent cocked his head and responded, "Not as much as you might think. Time changes perspective on what the packaging of a given person reflects."

"Then why say anything at all?" she murmured. "This isn't my face, my body. This isn't who I was." It seemed cheating to admit otherwise.

Argent sighed softly and replied, "And yet, it is who you are now." Jilah turned back to the dresser as he purred, "And – you are beautiful."

Jilah shook her head slowly, and she heard his body slide against the sheets as he moved off of the bed, heading towards her. A little zing of electricity skittered up her spine at the feel of cool fingers gently sliding over her shoulder. His voice set every hair on her body on end as his fingertips trailed softly along her skin.

"You are breathtaking, Jilah."

The cool touch slowly slid down along the length of her arm. He enjoyed watching goose flesh rush along her skin as he gave her elbow a gentle squeeze.

Jilah felt the heat in the room rise exponentially as her eyes fluttered shut. The sensations racing through her were overwhelming. Almost painfully so. The knuckles of his other hand began exploring her back and his soft, cool fingers moved to curl around her hip as he leaned into her, brushing soft lips against her shoulder. Her memories and her body's natural attraction to him warred with each other as her grip on the jeans in her hand tightened and she let out a small sigh, completely lost as to how to react now.

"Should I stop?" he murmured softly.

It was so difficult to think clearly, her senses drowning at the feel of his hands on her. It was so gentle; an inquiring touch, not forcing or roughly demanding. A muted cry escaped her as she felt the cool skin of his chest press against her back, the fabric in her hands shredding as he placed a soft kiss behind her ear.

"Please." Jilah's voice was hoarse as she felt him smile against her skin.

His hands slid around to cup her stomach as he gently pulled her against him. The hard, hot length of him pressed against her through the sweatpants and she shuddered, letting the black ragged strips of fabric that used to resemble clothing fall from her hands. Her fingers lengthened into claws as she slapped her hands back on the dresser. Small, puckered furrows opened in the wood beneath them as his hands slid lower, and she gave a small groan.

His voice was a low purr as soft lips brushed against her ear. "Please what?"

Jilah flexed her fingers and heard the wood splinter and snap. It was enough to clear her mind, to break free of the seductive thrill of his touch. A sharp, ugly memory came stabbing back and her voice dropped an octave.

"Stop. Now."

Immediately, his hands were gone and she felt him take a step away from her.

Argent's tone was cautious and quiet as he murmured, "I do apologize. I seem to be quite unable to control myself around you."

With a shaky sigh, Jilah pulled her fingers out of the ruined wood on the top of the dresser. Her body shivered as she hugged an arm around herself and tried to rein in her galloping hormones. Abusive, violent images from the past were now starting to blend in with flashes of true passion and abandon. The mixture was almost making her nauseous. She closed her eyes and a tear trickled down her cheek, dropping to stain the wood.

Argent sounded sad as he murmured, "Perhaps I should go to give you a little breathing room."

She ground her teeth against the urge to vomit as her assailant worked at her, dipping his head down to bite into her shoulder, his teeth leaving bruising marks as he let out a low, grunting growl. Her mind was a white-hot fury as she continued to scream and rail in her head, quickly becoming desperate to escape what was being done to her.

The man became still, as if pausing in thought. He then reached over and pulled out a knife, holding it in front of her face so she could get a good look at it before placing it beside her head.

Oh Jesus. Did he intend to kill her afterwards? She began struggling instinctively against him, no longer caring about the consequences for a brief moment. The man sharply backhanded her, sending sparks across her vision. As she turned her head to the side, she felt something wet and warm trickle from her nose across her cheek.

Jilah choked down a sob as the memory overwhelmed her. It overpowered and washed away everything else. Damn him. She thought about all the meticulous work that had gone into locking everything out and here it had taken what seemed like moments for it all to come crashing down.

Argent frowned as he watched her tremble, unsure of how to help as she held herself up against the dresser and tried to master her emotions. He let out a heavy sigh, frustrated that he didn't really know what was wrong, and therefore had no idea how to make it better. The only certainty he had was that touching her would only make things worse.

"Please. Don't."

Her voice was shaky and ragged as she slowly turned to look at him, her eyes brimming with tears. "Don't go."

Argent replied with a silent nod, padding over to the bed and sitting down. The graceful curves of his face were etched with worry as he asked, "Is there anything I can do?"

Jilah let out a shaky sigh, gently brushing tears away as she leaned back against the dresser. "I just can't... I can't do this right now." Her lips curled into a sad smile, her eyes shining as she looked away and continued, "It's just too much. I'm afraid I'll fly apart."

Her gaze slid back over to meet his glittering emerald eyes. "You frighten the hell out of me, Argent. Not because of what you are, but because of what you bring out in me."

Argent sat, listening intently as she spoke. He didn't understand. Why was she so scared? His jaw dropped as something suddenly occurred to him. He carefully asked, "Jilah, are you a virgin?" It would explain some of her reluctance, but not her screaming fear.

Jilah's expression echoed an infinite sadness as she shook her head, her voice tight and low as she responded, "No."

Argent cocked his head at her, wondering what else could be causing her distress. He was about to ask when she moved to sit at the foot of the dresser, gathering her knees up to her chin. Her expression was haunted as she took a deep breath and continued, "My first – my only physical experience with a man was one of violation. And violence."

Jilah looked over at him with a shaky laugh, her face filled with pain.

"It hasn't gotten much better since that."

Argent reeled back as if slapped. His eyes narrowed, his tone empty as he asked, "Does this man still live?"

Jilah shook her head slowly, sounding so very tired as she answered, "No. He's quite dead now." Her lips pulled back in a grim, thin smile, and she took comfort in the fact that the bastard hadn't gone on to victimize anybody else after her.

"You killed him," he murmured.

"Yep," she replied, her voice barely above a whisper.

Argent moved to the edge of the bed, then slid to the floor to sit across from her. Jilah watched him with wary eyes, wrapping her arms tighter around her legs. Things were starting to make much more sense for him now.

His voice was tender as he met her gaze and asked, "How many other women have you helped, like the one last night?"

"By the time I end up doing what it is that I do, the women are usually long dead." Jilah felt her tension abate when she realized that he wasn't attempting to come any closer. His eyes held a quiet intensity that was somehow reassuring. "I'm the one that ties up the loose ends by exacting vengeance on the men that have..." Her expression hardened and she looked away. "Destroyed them."

Argent prompted, "Is this the 'work' you spoke of earlier? What you've buried yourself in?"

Jilah looked back over at him, nodding slowly and looking a great deal like a puppy that had been swatted on the nose for doing something wrong.

Argent frowned and quietly asked, "How often do you 'work'?"

A harsh laugh echoed in the room, her expression empty as she answered, "Every night for the last six months. Since that first night."

"First night?"

Jilah reached up and collected the tattered shorts from the top of the dresser, pulled them down and began to fidget with them as she replied, "Something that I can't quite define decided to intervene that night. It changed me, giving me the ability to overpower and kill him."

Her words came out in a rush. Now that she'd started talking about it, she found that she wanted it all out, hoping that telling him would make some of the weight of it easier to bear. Her tone was casual now, as if she were talking about an event that had happened to somebody else.

"It was my first time. With anybody. Since then, I've been going out every night to make my appointed rounds." Jilah quickly stood and began pacing, the words coming faster now as she continued.

"The memories of the women they rape and kill stay long enough for me to get the details into a database that I'll eventually use to let the police know what happened to all those poor girls. Well, when I figure out how to do it without having them come after me, that is. Unfortunately, some of the more vivid ones spring up from time to time."

Jilah took a deep breath and turned back to face him, a bitter chuckle bubbling out of her throat. "The thing is, I didn't really take time out of my busy new schedule to think about how all of this would affect me if I happened to run into somebody that I was actually attracted to. It just didn't even cross my mind as a possibility."

Jilah walked over towards the bathroom, still speaking in that same rapid, disaffected voice. "Consequently, my only experience with the opposite sex has been extremely unpleasant. It's kinda like the way that some cops become biased against civilians because they see the very worst in people every day. I don't know how to react to the way you touch me. Well, mentally that is. It's something that I just don't have a frame of reference for. I mean" she began to stammer, "i-it's not as if I never read romance novels before or anything, but..." Her face was etched with lines of frustration as she reached out and gripped the door frame behind her. "A very large part of me is terrified to let my body have what it so desperately wants and it's tearing me apart. It feels like I'm betraying something very basic in myself by even being attracted to you."

Argent sat silently watching her go through an array of emotions that obviously caused her considerable pain, unable to conceive of a torment worse than what she was putting herself through. No wonder she was so jumpy about being touched. He shifted on the bed, an idea forming in his mind.

"I might be able to assist you in the resolution of the conflict you're enduring, if you'll let me."

Jilah watched him with wary eyes as he moved, and when it became clear that he wasn't going to stand up and walk towards her, she tentatively asked, "What, exactly, do you propose?"

"With some of my kind, when we feed there is a," he paused, searching for the correct word, "quality that lends itself to a kind of release. I've been told by many that this quality sometimes assists in overcoming such obstacles."

"You're suggesting that I let you bite me?? Are you high?" Jilah looked back at him, incredulous.

Argent shrugged, bringing his feet under him and placing his hands in his lap. "I can think of no other way to help you. The kind of trauma you've been subjected to sometimes takes years to overcome. Since you seem to continually experience it from a new perspective on a nightly basis, it's likely not going to reach a point of resolution anytime soon. It sounds as if you are afforded no respite to heal from the mental and emotional wounds that you've incurred from your given vocation. I would offer you an alternate solution."

Jilah thought about it for a moment, extremely skeptical of this offered 'solution', but also curious to find out if what he suggested would actually help. She ground her teeth as her gaze slid along his body, once again distracted by the play of muscles beneath his skin. It was becoming evident that something needed to change, or he would need to leave to preserve her sanity – but she didn't want him to go. Jilah nodded as she made up her mind, her voice a low growl as she walked back over to the bed.

"If you don't behave yourself, I'll kick you the fuck out, if I don't end up killing you first. Got it?"

Argent responded with a patient nod, understanding her reluctance completely now. She stepped up to him and she flinched as he reached out and took her hand. "This will be a great deal more effective if you are relaxed."

Jilah let out a sharp bark of laughter, her voice harsh as she said, "That's not going to happen anytime soon. It's taking everything I've got to let you hold my hand."

"You're going to want to sit on the bed, at the very least. I don't want you injuring yourself." His voice was soft and reassuring as he indicated a spot on the bed next to him.

Jilah glared at him before joining him on the bed and turning to stare straight ahead, her voice empty as she said, "Just do it. Quickly. Before I lose my nerve."

"Is the wrist okay? I fear that anything else will only make you more tense." He was being so very careful. Jilah nodded, closing her eyes tightly and hoping that it didn't hurt too much.

Argent slowly raised her hand to his lips, wanting to kiss it to reassure her but knowing that it would likely send her shrieking across the room in her current state. He drank in her scent, his eyes fluttering shut as he turned her wrist up, exposing the tender underside and brushing it softly with his lips. To just bite into her with no sensual preamble of any kind seemed crass. Jilah tensed at the contact, not wanting it to be this intimate.

She was about to say something about it when she felt him bite down, the sharp pain making her cry out before a slow wash of warmth rolled through her. Her eyes fluttered and she drew a long, shaky breath as a flicker of heat coiled in her belly. The sensation began slowly building, matching the rhythm of the faint tugging sensation at her wrist.

Her lips parted, her mouth making a little O shape as she fell back against the sheets in slow motion. Everything became sluggish and slurry. Jilah arched against the bed with a moan as the pulsing tide of warmth rolled into a slow burn that washed over her, her body singing as it slowly slid into every part of her being. Sensations that she never thought herself capable of experiencing rolled through her in a fiery wave, overwhelming the memories that bubbled to the surface and gently pushing them away.

Off in the distance, she thought she heard Argent moan as well, and she felt it unlock something in her. The burn immediately became a blinding flame of pleasure, threatening to consume her. Jilah rode the intensity of the feeling with little gasps, almost frightened to find out what would happen next. When the sensation became almost more than she was certain she could bear, the wave broke, sending her over in a roaring rush, a scream tore out of her throat as she clawed at the bed beneath her with her free hand. Argent watched her as she went over, riding her pleasure as she shuddered beside him.

Good god. So much potential, he thought to himself, wanting so badly to take her then, to show her what it could truly be like between them. It took a great deal of effort to hold back as he gently licked at the rapidly closing bite marks in her wrist, kissing the spot lightly and placing her hand at her side. Jilah went limp against the bed, and he looked down at her with a hopeful expression, his eyes glinting sharply as he watched her lips curl into a slow, dopey grin.

Argent felt the tightness in his chest release, and he relaxed. As he watched her chest slowly rise and fall, he was clear that he definitely wanted to continue but was unsure of his next move, uncertain if she'd respond to further advances. He didn't want to press it in case she was still skittish, but he was also aware that if he didn't do something soon about his own condition, he would be unable to stop himself.

Jilah's eyes fluttered open, her voice hoarse as she croaked, "I..I had no idea."

Argent smiled as he she turned to look up at him, his voice hopeful as he asked, "Did that help?"

Jilah was surprised to find herself giddy and lightheaded, a strange feeling of euphoria making her giggle as she said, "I think so. Is it always like that?"

Argent laughed and nodded slowly. "If one goes about it correctly, yes."

Jilah shook her head, blinking several times before looking back over at him, her voice dreamy. "Wow. My head feels all fuzzy now."

"Good." Argent grinned and reached over to brush a strand of hair out of her eyes. He wanted so badly to kiss her.

Jilah closed her eyes at the touch of his fingers and smiled, "Thank you."

"Trust me, it was both my honor and pleasure."

Argent took a deep breath, then stood up and made his way toward the bathroom.

"Where are you going?" Jilah positioned herself to look over at him, her expression forlorn.

Argent turned back and presented her with a sheepish grin, "To take a cold shower. I'm afraid that I am sorely in need of one."

Jilah frowned and tried to sit up, failing miserably as she slumped back into the sheets. "Why? Didn't you...?"

With a gentle shake of his head, Argent chuckled, his eyes glittering with a light that burned from within as he said, "I'm afraid not. What we have just now indulged in I consider foreplay. I don't want to take advantage of you, thus," he nodded towards the bathroom, "the other alternative."

Although he wasn't really sure how much it would help. Perhaps if they went hunting very soon, he could bleed off some of the need.

Jilah's eyes widened in surprise, both eyebrows creeping up her forehead as she cried, "Wait, that was your idea of foreplay?"

Argent gave a little shrug, amused as he replied, "I believe I stated earlier that I could be more than a little enthusiastic. Add to that unusually high endurance and it tends to make for a bit of a sensation marathon." He flashed her a stunning grin and padded into the bathroom.

Jilah thought about that for a long moment, then yelled, "Hey!"

Argent popped his head back out of the bathroom, his brow furrowing as he asked, "What?"

Jilah wobbled and rocked herself back up on her elbows, clearing her throat before asking in a voice that cracked slightly, "Just to clarify, are you saying it gets better than that?"

Argent's lips curled in a wicked grin and a little more of his torso slid into view, his voice full of promise as he purred, "You have no idea."

Her eyes narrowed as she tried to scoot up towards the pillows, still more than a little fuzzy from his bite. She wanted more. Oh, definitely more. Her tone was halfheartedly petulant as she propped herself up against the headboard and said, "Then show me."

His eyes grew wide, wondering if he'd heard her right. "Show you?"

Jilah rolled her eyes and let out a frustrated huff. "Don't be a jackass."

Argent's expression darkened as he replied, "I want you to be absolutely clear on this. If I end up starting something along those lines with you, I can assure you that I will be incapable of stopping. Do not tease me."

Jilah took the measure of his words, realizing that she wouldn't be able to stop again either. It would be extremely cruel to both of them if she ended up unable to handle it. She could also tell that something felt different inside her now. She licked her lips, looking back up at him as if he were a predator, bearing down on her. She also realized with a start that she now wanted this almost as badly as he did, if not more. Her voice quavered a little, and she let the need show in her eyes as she held out a hand and quietly said, "Please. Show me."

Argent was suddenly beside her, his body seeming to hum as he leaned forward and cupped her face in his hand. Jilah sighed and leaned into the touch, reaching up and covering his hand with hers. His eyes ached with hunger as he gently stroked her cheek with a thumb.

"You're cool to the touch," she breathed, reaching a tentative hand out to let her fingertips brush his chest.

Argent shivered as her fingers trailed up his torso, slowly moving up to his shoulder then down his arm as she explored him. She was fascinated with the planes of his body, her fingertips sliding along the grooves of muscle. He felt like a living sculpture and she found herself wanting to explore every inch of him. She brought her hand back up to his neck, trailing her thumb gently along the curve of his jaw line, causing him to shiver.

His voice was a soft murmur. "I gain warmth from those on whom I feed."

"But, you just drank from me. Didn't that...?"

He shook his head, cutting her off as he softly answered, "I didn't take enough to warm me up."

Jilah's gaze trailed down his body, lingering for a moment on the trail of black, curly hair that vanished into the top of the sweat pants. His interest was evident and a flush crept across her skin as her gaze traveled back up to meet his. Argent leaned in, pulling her into a gentle kiss and she swooned. He let out a soft moan as she slid a hand over his shoulder, pulling him closer. He broke the kiss, then quickly moved and shifted her so that she straddled him. He brought up a hand to stroke her face tenderly.

His tone was reverent as he breathed, "I've wanted to touch you like this since I first laid eyes on you."

Argent slid both hands down and over her hips, cupping her ass and squeezing lightly. Jilah felt the hard length of him pressing against her – the only warm spot on his body. Shivering, she slowly sat up to look back at him. She brought her hands to play along the cool skin of his chest, delighting in the delicious contours of his body as she slowly leaned down to taste him. Argent sighed as her tongue flicked out, the warmth of it burning as she trailed it along his skin. Jilah rubbed her face against him like a cat, breathing in his scent and letting it surround her as she felt him tremble beneath her. She came back to a sitting position above him, positively drunk with emotion and sensory overload.

She'd never felt anything like it.

Argent ran pale hands slowly over her hips, sliding the silk chemise gently along her sides as they traveled up the length of her body. He moved to slide fingers over her breasts, squeezing them through the material, and she rocked her head back, sighing softly.

"Lift your arms." he murmured.

She happily obliged, loving the feel of the material on her skin and the feel of his hands as he slid the fabric along her body. Once she was free of it, he tossed it off to the side with a flick of the wrist. Letting his fingers trail along the underside of her chin, he slowly slid them down her neck and shoulders. Jilah looked down at him with a shaky sigh, then let out a little squeak of surprise as she suddenly found herself pinned beneath him. Argent wrapped her legs around his waist and gazed down at her, his eyes hungry as they traced the curves of her body. His gaze locked with hers as he traced fingers delicately over her breast.

Her eyes fluttered shut and she curved into the touch, her pulse jumping as he squeezed her nipple lightly, then pinched it. Argent's mouth met hers again and she eagerly returned the kiss, wrapping her arms around his neck and arching up into him. Jilah's voice was a breathy moan as she moved questing hands down his back, delighting in the feel of his cool skin under her fingers. He was tight and chiseled in all the right places.

As he pulled out of the kiss, his eyes burned with an intensity that took her breath away. Jilah's heart fluttered behind her ribcage like a trapped bird trying desperately to escape as he smiled down at her, his eyes dancing. Her lips curled in a slow smile as she reached up to trail tentative fingers along his neck.

He disappeared for a moment, but before she had time to react, a flare of heat rushed over her skin as he appeared over her again. She felt him hot and hard against her, realizing that he'd ditched the sweats. Argent's smile grew broad, and he leaned down and offered his neck to her, trembling slightly as her lips brushed against it. Her teeth grazed him and his voice became breathy as he moaned and leaned into the embrace. He then quickly pulled back and looked down at her, his eyes burning with need and an unspoken question. Jilah's breath hitched as she felt the tip of him gently slide against her slickness.

She nodded, her voice husky as she breathed, "Please."

His voice, gentle but commanding, drifted through her thoughts. :: Drink me. ::

Jilah ran her nails over his back, her eyeteeth lengthening as he again turned to expose his neck to her, slowly pressing against her. Argent hesitated as she kissed and licked his neck softly, then cried out as she bit down, sliding inside her at the same moment. The mixed sensation of penetration and the hot splash of fluid on her tongue came close to driving her over the edge. His blood was hot and spicy, and she felt it zing through her as she drank slowly, wanting to savor the taste of him. Her fingers lengthened into claws that ripped into his back as he slid all the way inside her, his hips pressing against her.

Jilah felt him shudder as she carved shallow, bloody furrows into his back, gasping as he slowly slid all the way out and slammed roughly back into her. Argent let out a guttural moan as he began to rock into her, his body humming as he fed from the desire that rolled off her in wave after glorious wave. She wrapped muscular legs around him, trying to drive him deeper, moaning against his throat as she felt herself dance along that bright shining edge.

Her pleasure ripped through her, blinding as she crashed over, and she pulled away from his neck, shrieking as she arched against him. Crimson droplets from his throat spattered her cheek as he followed her over, his voice becoming an almost deafening roar, and he stiffened against her, clutching at the sheets. Her body shuddered and arched beneath him, little red ribbons of skin curling out from under her fingernails as she clawed viciously at his back. He hissed as she tore at him, groaning loudly into her shoulder before they both slumped back to the bed, spent.

After a few moments Argent moved, nuzzling at her neck before pulling away, his smile soft and beautiful as he looked back at her.

"Thank you." He breathed, his voice husky as he bent down to trail soft kisses along her jawline.

Jilah responded with a weak laugh and wrapped strong arms around him, her fingers sliding in the slick trails of blood that now snaked down his back and over his sides. She winced, chagrined that she'd torn him up so badly.

"Whoops." She could feel the grooved slices in his skin healing as her fingers trailed over them.

Argent laughed, giving her a quick kiss. "It's okay. I'm not damaged." He leaned down, playfully nipping at her ear. "Not permanently, anyway."

"I guess I got a little carried away. Sorry about that."

Argent's response was a low, sultry growl as he answered, "I enjoyed it. The pain," he made a noise between a chuckle and a growl, "definitely adds to the experience."

Jilah felt energized now, almost hyper. She wondered if it was from the sex, or his blood.

"You are an extremely talented young lady." Argent purred as he nipped her earlobe.

She giggled as she ran a blood-slicked hand up into his hair. His body was beginning to look like a large, bloody finger-painting project. "I could very well say the same thing about you."

Jilah took a shaky breath and relaxed into the bed, enjoying the feel of his blood as it pumped through her system. A shy smile crept across her features as Argent moved to kiss her again, his fingers trailing across her stomach as she sensed his body recovering.

Her body responded quickly and she slid slick, crimson fingers around the length of him as the heat between them began to grow again. Argent groaned and nipped at her shoulder, his voice shaky. "I was hoping you weren't tired yet."

Her lips curled in a wicked grin and she shook her head in response, "Oh, not by a long shot."

Eleven
Gone Huntin'

The next two nights blended into a blur of sensation. At times it almost seemed as though they were indulging themselves in an experiment specifically designed to destroy certain sections of the house. Jilah still found it hard to believe that he could wring such wonderful pleasure from her, even though he had proven it time and time again. He was very adept at scrambling her senses. She was surprised at how strongly she'd fallen for him and was a bit surprised that he seemed to be equally smitten with her.

Argent found himself equally overwhelmed, elated that she was indeed everything he'd hoped for when he had first noticed her. In each other they found a kind of respite and release from the rough tides they had ridden in the past. At times, they held tightly to each other as if this simple act was the only thing keeping them both from flying apart inside.

Jilah stirred beside him, waking with a loopy, sated smile as she turned to look over at the sleeping form of her lover. She winced as she noticed the larger dings in the walls and varying rips and tears in the mattress. The bedding was wrecked – the bloodstains would never come out. She chuckled softly at the realization that the canopy was still intact, if a bit tattered.

Once Argent had helped her past her initial fear about physical contact, her inhibitions had disappeared. Their activities had become increasingly violent and dangerously playful, causing quite a bit of damage to the rest of the house as well. There were several body-sized dents in the walls on the middle floor, and there was also a bit of cosmetic damage to the kitchen that she'd need to see to. The house had gotten off lightly, given the circumstances.

Jilah turned towards Argent, giving a catlike stretch before reaching out to trail delicate fingers along his shoulder. She frowned at the realization that he was getting a little colder each night. Sleeping next to the equivalent of a cold corpse when he was down for the day was still a little creepy, and she hoped that it would stop being so unsettling over time. It was the only thing that discomfited her about this new situation, but it seemed like such a small thing. It could be easily overlooked for someone that had come to mean so much to her in such a small stretch of time.

She had fallen quickly and hard, a little frightened at how strong her feelings for him had become. It wasn't just his rather explosive awakening of her sexuality that motivated her to love him. There was definitely something different, something deeper there, but she couldn't quite put her finger on it. Jilah sighed and slid closer to him, kissing his chest softly as she felt him come into awareness. His eyes opened, their depths shimmering as he turned to look at her, his lips curling into a relaxed smile.

"I hope I haven't kept you waiting long." He purred, reaching over to stroke the line of her jaw tenderly, pulling her into a kiss.

Her hand slid across his chest, curling around his neck as she leaned into him, and he felt a low thrum of hunger flare in his belly. He'd eaten sparsely since he started tracking her and hadn't really allowed himself to indulge until that wondrous night with her in the cemetery. After several days of bloodletting and marathon sex, his body was now eager to go out and feed properly.

He couldn't help noticing a small amount of discomfort in her about the temperature of his skin. Another reason to feed, he thought as he slowly pulled out of the kiss and stroked her cheek. Jilah's smile was radiant as she gazed back at him, her hand warm as she caressed his cheek.

Argent sighed softly, realizing that it had been at least a century since he'd felt such a strong bond with anyone. His stomach growled and he knew that he'd have to hunt tonight. He hoped that she would come along with him. They hadn't left the house since their first night together, and he figured she was now probably as hungry as he was. He was about to speak up about it when her eyes fluttered shut and she winced, pressing fingertips to her temple as she groaned.

"Are you all right?" His brow furrowed with concern.

Jilah nodded slowly as a pounding headache plowed into her out of nowhere, accompanied by a barrage of vivid images. "Ow."

She cried out as brief flashes of a businessman sipping drinks with a diminutive blond strobed through her thoughts. Damn, she'd almost forgotten. At least her patroness had allowed her this mini vacation of sorts for a couple of days before sending more work her way. She shook her head to clear it and looked over at him, blinking quickly before answering.

"Yeah. I just get these," Jilah winced again, her voice sounding tired as she murmured, "visions."

She gently pushed him away and sat up, taking a deep breath and putting her head between her knees, hoping that it would chase away some of the headache. "Although, they don't usually hurt this bad."

She felt a cold hand on her thigh as he moved to brush soft lips against her shoulder. "How may I help?"

Jilah turned towards him, her grin sly as she asked, "Feel like watching me work?"

Argent nodded and squeezed her knee gently. "I'd be delighted."

Argent smiled as she sat up, brushing a strand of hair away from her face. "I must feed as well. As the saying goes, we will kill two birds with one stone."

Jilah laughed lightly, nuzzling his temple. "Good. I'm going to jump in the shower." Jilah gave him a quick kiss, then pulled away and began padding towards the bathroom.

"Would you like some company?" he called after her, hopeful.

Jilah turned and shook her head, grinning. "We'll never get out of here if you join me."

He shrugged, grinning as he replied, "You can't blame me for trying."

Argent lay back on the bed with a sated grin, eyes bright as he stretched back against the bed covers. His stomach tightened with the anticipation of seeing her eyes shine with that delicious righteous fire he'd experienced before. Death and sex wrapped up in a painfully delicious little package. He definitely couldn't beat that with a stick.

Argent was sliding back into his black leather pants as Jilah slipped into a demure black cocktail dress, her hair swept up and forced tightly into a nylon stocking cap with a small knot at the top.

He gave her a strange look, his expression bemused as he commented, "You're looking rather restrained tonight."

Jilah turned, checking her reflection out in the full-length mirror in her closet, not entirely pleased with the look herself. It annoyed her, having to dress up to suit her prey. She was able to make people see what she wanted them to see, but she hadn't yet figured out a way to do it without putting considerable strain on her mental reserves. Putting on a 'monkey suit', as she called it, was much less taxing and let her focus on the job at hand. Economy of movement and energy, this was key.

Jilah leaned into the mirror, dabbing at meticulously applied makeup as she replied, "It all depends on the prey. It's usually easier to get them on the hook if I look like a potential victim."

Argent raised an eyebrow and asked, "Isn't it easier to just influence them?" He walked over and zipped her up.

"Individuals? Yeah. Crowds, I can't do much with. There end up being too many questions, and I stand out too much unless I happen to be hunting on alternative grounds."

Jilah expended less energy if she tried to concentrate on simply making herself look human. There weren't really any books available on this sort of thing, and the Dark Lady wasn't always forthcoming with information, unless it was to help her with something that would keep her from fulfilling her role. She'd come to learn that if there was a workaround, she usually had to find it herself. Huge learning curve, this new existence.

Argent slipped his white tank top over his head, wondering how to explain it to her. "You," he searched for the correct wording, "reach out and just.." He frowned, somewhat at a loss as he switched over to mental communication.

:: *It would be easier to show you. To see if you have an aptitude for it. It's a remarkably handy skill.* ::

Argent paused for a moment, then continued, :: *You would need to welcome me into your mind in order to do it, however. Are you comfortable with that?* ::

Jilah thought about it for a moment, then nodded, her voice quiet as she breathed, "Just don't get too pokey in there. A girl likes to believe that she has some secrets."

Oh, he'd be careful. He had no desire to cross paths with the creature he had first encountered in her mind. :: *You have my word. I shall poke no further than I need to.* ::

Jilah nodded, reassured as she sent back, :: *You're so cool.* ::

Argent laughed and slid his arms around her waist, pulling her into a deep, slow kiss. It was as if he could pull her desire – her very soul out to caress it as their lips met. When they parted, she blinked and smiled, almost dazed.

Dear god, he's entirely too good at that. She looked back at him, impressed. "How is it that you're able to do that without getting any lipstick on you?"

He shrugged and reached over to collect his leather jacket from the bed. "It's a gift. Where are we headed?"

Jilah grinned and walked past him to pick up a demure-looking black dinner jacket.

"Some yuppie dive called the Pit Stop downtown. You should fit right in."

Jilah slid the jacket on and walked over to the closet to pick through her collection of disguise wigs. Argent arched an eyebrow at the display, wondering why anybody would need so many hairpieces, much less somebody with such an impressive mane already. He watched as she reached up to pull down a shoulder-length, honey-colored wig from its perch atop a featureless styrofoam head.

After expertly placing it over her restrained indigo tresses and primping it into place, she turned around with a flair and asked him, "How do I look?"

Argent stroked his chin with a dubious expression as he murmured, "I much prefer your natural appearance."

Jilah turned to look back at the mirror and frowned. She wasn't overly fond of the wigs either. They were uncomfortable, and they muted her appearance too much for her liking, but seeing as how that was pretty much the point, she sighed and replied, "Yeah. Me too."

Her eyes glittered playfully as she looked back at him. "Okay, let's bolt."

"Will we arrive there in time to intercept him?"

He found himself immensely curious about how she received the information about the people that she was supposed to be hunting, and was hoping that he wasn't being overly nosy with his questions.

"We should. But even if he leaves, I'll be able to track him," she replied.

"Track him? How?"

She frowned, then explained, "It's kinda like this weird, supernatural pseudo-GPS thing. I just get images, vague notions, that kind of thing. And then there's the aura."

"Curious. Would you say that this aura is visual or otherwise sensory?"

"It's a mix. I can feel the target when I get close enough. Depending on how nasty the person is, it can be a little rough."

Jilah grabbed a set of keys off of the table in the foyer as Argent opened the front door. "Are you usually this inquisitive, or are you trying to humor me?"

Argent looked back at her, chagrined. "I am honestly interested in your condition. If I'm asking too many questions..."

Jilah shook her head and chuckled as they headed towards the garage. "I'm just giving you a hard time."

Argent grinned as she opened the door, then blinked as she walked over to an enormous dark blue SUV. An eyebrow crooked up over a beautiful emerald eye as he watched her open the driver's side door. Jilah chuckled at his reaction and asked, "Like it?"

She wasn't sure if it was too soccer mom or not, but given that it had been so very handy over the last couple of months, she didn't really care. It was innocuous, and that was all that mattered. Argent reached out to open the passenger side door, giving a small shrug before smoothly sliding into the seat.

"It looks like a cave on wheels," he murmured.

Jilah chuckled as she climbed inside and closed the door, pulling the seatbelt and clicking it home. "Buckle up, buttercup."

Argent looked over at her, examining the two-inch wide strip of nylon that crossed her chest. He had never had much use for cars, much less their safety devices. "Would it not be safer to be simply thrown clear of the car in the case of a sudden impact instead of being trapped in a potentially explosive machine? I mean, it's not as if you would be unable to heal most of the injuries that you would incur after such an event."

Jilah cringed at the possibility, her expression grim as she answered, "Fine. You go on and get thrown out of the car. I'd rather stick with the possibility of being trapped than having the steering wheel attempt to fuse my lungs and heart into my spine. It's not as if the airbags won't trap you in here in an accident. When was the last time you were in a car, anyway?"

Argent's expression was a moue of distaste as he replied, "I've never been much for driving, or riding in these tin boxes with wheels. Besides, when you can run as fast as we can, who needs a car?"

"Point taken." she murmured.

"How about this – if you happen to get trapped and I'm thrown clear, I'll rescue you." Argent presented her with an amused grin as she looked over at him and laughed.

"Smartass." Jilah swatted at his arm, then started the car.

Argent's voice was a smooth rumble as he leaned back into the seat with a satisfied grin and purred.

"It's all part of the charm."

The bar turned out to be a basic yuppie joint, crowded with teeming shoals of yapping twenty-somethings eager to drink themselves into oblivion so they could forget all about their bright, shining lives full of goals and wretched deadlines. Argent found the atmosphere cloying and banal as he cranked his shields up.

Jilah couldn't help but notice that although he stood out like a sore thumb in this environment, nobody seemed to notice him. Now that, she thought, is impressive. She looked back over at him, an eyebrow crooking up as she sent, :: *They really can't see you?* ::

Argent shrugged and smiled, his tone casual as he looked around the room, drinking in the entirety of the bland features of the bar. :: *They're unable to see or hear me. It's part of that influence thing I told you about.* ::

He eyed a collection of people at the bar. A pair of drunken urban professionals were burbling and chatting up a bleary-eyed brunette with a raggedy bob cut and a sensible dress. Every once in a while, a shrill cackle would ring through the bar, sounding strangely like the sharp cry of a dying rabbit.

Argent asked, :: *Is he here?* ::

Jilah scanned the room, looking for the distinct red aura that usually surrounded the people she hunted. She quickly located the woman she'd seen her target with in her vision, but the man was nowhere to be seen. There was a resonance in the air that told her that he was still here, though. Jilah gently reached out with her mind and dipped into the woman's thoughts. The target was in the bathroom. The woman was eagerly awaiting his return.

Jilah watched the woman nervously fidget with an olive in her martini and answered, :: *Yeah. He's in the little boy's room. He should be out shortly.* ::

Argent perked up as he followed her gaze, his eyes narrowing slightly as they focused on the woman. She was now sipping tentatively at her drink, her eyes scanning the crowd. Jilah's voice was edged with distaste as it drifted through his thoughts. :: *He's definitely got a live one in her. She's all prepped and ready to go with him wherever he wants to take her.* ::

:: *This is an optimal time for our lesson, I think. Allow me to guide your thoughts...* ::

Argent slid his hands over her hips and leaned into her, nuzzling her neck as he gently slid into her thoughts. Jilah felt a light tug in her mind and tensed as it pulled her along with it. There was a strange sense of disorientation as he led her consciousness to touch everybody in the room. With a light push, he directed her to block any images of herself from the mind of the crowd. It was as if she were closing a specific memory door in their heads and, now that she'd done it, she was astonished at the simplicity of the action. She was also happy to find that she didn't have a blazing headache afterwards.

:: Now for the woman. ::

Jilah felt the press of a palpable wave of discomfort and unease as it rolled through her and into the small conduit that Argent had connected to the woman's mind. Jilah watched as the woman began looking around nervously before reaching down to collect her purse from the tabletop. The woman clutched it to her chest with a tight grip, her eyes darting around in their sockets like those of a frightened animal. The woman rose from her seat and began walking quickly towards the front of the bar, her pace hurried and her hands trembling as she pushed open the door and rushed out into the street.

Jilah blinked twice, stunned. Her jaw dropped as she realized that it had taken a matter of moments for the woman to go from being completely at ease to terrified and paranoid.

:: Wow. Now that was impressive. You're a very good teacher. ::

She gently pulled away from him and made her way towards the bar, putting a generous sway in her hips.

A shiver jittered up Argent's spine as he watched her go. He moved over to lean back against the wall as Jilah stepped up to the bar and asked for a drink. A hungry grin quirked the edges of his mouth as he hooked his thumbs into the pockets of his pants. A handsome man with a smug smile emerged from the bathroom and headed back towards the recently occupied table. An ugly look flashed across his features for a brief moment as he realized his date had disappeared, but it was quickly forced back behind a thin veneer of self assurance and civility. The man shrugged it off and turned to head back to the bar, his gait casual and disaffected as he moved.

Argent chuckled as Jilah turned and bumped into the man as he passed, spilling her drink onto his overpriced Italian suit. She looked up at him with an apologetic expression and blurted out, "OhmigodI'msosorry."

Argent watched as the man's expression briefly clouded over with anger until he took a good look at Jilah. Dipping into the man's thoughts, Argent's lips curled into a snarl at what he found. If he wasn't already well aware of his new companion's capabilities, he would've immediately pulled the man's entrails from his stomach and forced them down his throat for his ill intentions.

The man brightened and smoothly shrugged it off, replying, "Oh, it's okay. Nothing to worry about. It's a basic social hazard in a bar, really."

He presented her with an easy, suave smile, chuckling as Jilah reached over and began patting at the stain with an expression of utter embarrassment.

"I'm sure it'll wash out. My dry cleaner is a wizard at getting these kinds of stains out. Really, it's fine."

He flashed her a brilliant smile that set Jilah's teeth on edge. She forced a grateful grin and fluttered her eyelashes at him, her voice a little breathy as she said, "You're so sweet for reassuring me like this after I went and ruined your beautiful suit. I'm usually not so clumsy.."

Argent's eyes glittered as he watched the two of them interact. The man was at least twice her size, outweighing her by at least fifty pounds, but he knew that it wouldn't be an issue. The fool was by no means well-matched against her. Argent shifted against the bar as he watched them, shaking his head at the vacuous nature of the conversation and wondering why she hadn't just reached into his head and forced him to follow her outside.

:: *Playing with your food? For shame.* :: He chided, his tone amused as it drifted through her mind.

Argent heard her laughter across the room, warm and sincere as her voice touched his mind, :: *It's more satisfying this way. He thinks he's the one in control; that he has all the power. It makes it that much sweeter when they realize that they're goatfucked, and that a woman got the drop on them.* ::

Desire fluttered in his chest at the vicious tone in her response. His eyebrows rose as he felt a mixture of both lust and revulsion in her as her prey leaned in and whispered something into her ear. Jilah moved closer to her target, her voice heated as she murmured, "I'm Ginger. It's silly, I know, but it's a family name."

She paused to watch him react, his eyes flashing as he replied in a seductive tone, "I'm Patrick. You're not from around here are you?"

Jilah chose to play it coy, looking away as she murmured, "You could tell, huh?"

Patrick leaned into her, brushing gentle lips against her ear as he breathed, "It's a gorgeous night out and this place is a little too crowded. Care for a bit of a walk?"

She slowly pulled back and looked up at him, her grin growing wide as she nodded and tentatively replied, "I'd like that."

Argent rolled his eyes and chuckled, thoroughly amused by her victim persona. Her 'date' held Jilah's hand as he directed her to the exit. Argent let out a low growl as he moved to follow them. He hoped that what she was going to do to this man was going to hurt a great deal. Once outside, Argent stayed directly behind them as they proceeded to stroll down the block.

Jilah kept chattering animatedly about inanities that had her newfound friend nodding and grinning politely as he began to scope out places that weren't visible from the street. Argent shook his head as he paced them, walking directly beside Jilah now as they headed towards the next block. It was almost impressive how she just kept rattling on, playing the blond bubblehead act to the hilt. How she continued to come up with the constant stream of empty conversation was a mystery to him.

Spotting a possibility ahead, Argent saw her prey roll his shoulders back, his smile relaxing as he shifted and began gently rubbing the thumb and forefinger on his right hand together in small circles. There weren't many people walking around at this time of night. Apparently they had chosen to spend the latter part of the night indoors getting tanked. Patrick walked her up to the mouth of an alleyway, then gently grabbed her wrist and pulled her towards him, grinning as he began backing into the alley and saying, "Jen, you look amazing tonight."

The man's carefully constructed mask of civility shifted to one of utter disbelief as Jilah let out a sharp bark of laughter. She wasn't at all surprised that he couldn't be bothered to remember the fake name she had given him. Women were usually little more than pieces of reactive meat to rapists. For some reason, the more she thought about it, the funnier it became. The man pulled away from her and she began laughing openly.

He blinked as he stared back at her, astonished. He recovered quickly enough, though, and his expression grew furious. The corner of his mouth twitched slightly as he growled, "What the fuck are you laughing at?"

Jilah dipped into his thoughts and began laughing harder. He had apparently been emasculated throughout his young life by strong, self-assured women that wouldn't put up with his arrogant, self-important bullshit. Women who were more than happy to say this to his face as they dismissively walked away from him. The fact that she, his newest conquest, was now laughing at him had him so wound up it looked as if steam was about to shoot out his ears. It was the main motivation for his hatred, the reason for the horrific mutilation he visited upon his victims.

It's what they all deserve, she heard echo in his thoughts.

She looked past him to peer down the alleyway, pleased to find it poorly lit and full of garbage. It would make a fine place to take care of business. Incensed at being ignored as well now, Patrick snarled and grabbed her shoulders, slamming her up against a wall as his anger took control. His tone was low and nasty as he hissed, "Shut up. Whore."

Jilah's mouth snapped shut and she looked back at him, her expression irritated as she asked, "Now, is that really the best that you can come up with?"

She couldn't help thinking that he sounded like a petulant, whiny little boy, and the laughter began to bubble up again. Patrick's hand connected with her cheek, sending her head rocking back into the wall. Jilah looked back at him and just grinned.

"Nope. Wanna try again?" The man was damned near purple with rage as he cocked back a fist.

"What, no weapons?" she asked as she easily dodged it, chuckling as the man's hand slammed into the wall behind her. He yelped out and quickly pulled his fist back to cradle it, his eyes brimming with tears of pain and frustration as he glared back at her.

"Wow, you're really pissed off. How's that paw doin'?" Jilah chuckled darkly as she circled him.

He gaped, and shook his head as if to clear it. His voice cracked as he snapped, "What the fuck are you?"

She presented him with a sharp-toothed grin and purred in a fake southern drawl, "Patrick, mah boy, if that is indeed yer name – Ah'm all the women you done wrong. And now Ah'm comin' to collect."

His grew wide as Jilah's hand darted out and grabbed his throat, her fingers lengthening into sharp claws as they curled around his neck. He barely had time to react before she tossed him down the alleyway, her voice a low growl as she spat, "Bad dog." Jilah cocked her head to the side as she watched him land squarely in a pile of garbage bags, murmuring, "Two points" before blurring over to him.

She dug clawed fingers deep into the meat of his shoulder, and he let out a high-pitched scream. She yanked him towards her, forcing him down onto his knees, watching the little trails of blood that trickled down his neck. His eyes rolled into the back of his head, then he convulsed and passed out. Jilah watched as a long string of spittle slowly slid down from his lips to meet the concrete.

"Shit," she sighed and turned to Argent. "I was too rough with him." The tips of her claws still in his shoulder, she shook then limp man gently. "I think I broke him."

Argent walked slowly towards them, his lips curled in an amused grin as he murmured, "Let me see what I can do. First, you might want to take your claws out of him."

Jilah nodded and complied, unable to hide her disappointment as the man slumped to the ground. She watched as Argent crouched down, jumping a little when the man's eyes snapped open. His breathing was labored, and his eyes rolled wildly in their sockets. His breathing slowed, and Argent looked back at her with a relaxed smile. "Better?"

Jilah nodded numbly as she asked, "What'd you do?"

"Let's just say that I gave him a neural nudge of sorts." Argent replied.

"That's more than a little creepy." Jilah murmured, feeling a cold chill go up her spine. Still, he'd made it so that she could now proceed with finishing tonight's hunt.

"Does it bother you that I can do this?" Argent asked, curious.

"A little," she admitted, "but this guy's only got so much time left. We can talk about the weirdness of this later."

Argent chuckled and stood up, shaking his head. "We're stand-ing in an alley with a man who wanted to take you home and remove the skin from your face. You're about to kill him in one of the most truly delicious ways possible, and you think what I just did to him is creepy?"

Jilah frowned and replied, "Can we just bring this up later?"

"Of course." Argent shrugged and took a step back as she crouched down to peer into the man's eyes, grabbing his chin and forcing him to meet her gaze. A rush of terror rolled off the man in a heady wave, and Argent swayed on his feet. Jilah's grin was ghastly now as she leaned down towards the man at her feet, exposing canines that were curving into razor-sharp points. She let out a dark chuckle as Patrick began seizing violently, his mouth snapping open and shut like a fish out of water trying desperately to breathe. He then stiffened, his jaw going slack and a low whining sound bubbling out of his throat as he slumped into the garbage again. An acrid smell filled the air as he soiled himself.

Argent reached out to place a hand on the wall behind him, steady-ing himself as Jilah delivered a swift and devastating justice to her prey. The man's fear was ambrosial, almost overwhelming.

My god.

A surge of desire flared through him, and a pale pink sheen of sweat dotted his face as the man at Jilah's feet gurgled and began to twitch. She knelt down, gently tilting the man's head to the side before leaning in and biting down. After a few moments, she pulled away, a little trickle of blood running down her chin as she turned to look up at Argent. Her voice was thick, her pupils dilated so wide that the royal blue of her irises barely rimmed them as she breathed, "Where are my manners?"

She took a step away from the man's jerking body, watching Argent as he let out a low growl, his eyes full of need as he blurred over and fed. She opened her mind to him, sending, :: *Don't kill him.* ::

Jilah slowly stood up, licking her fingertips clean as she backed up against the brick wall behind her. :: *Drain him to the point of shallow breathing. He needs to suffer before he dies...* ::

Argent moaned against the man's neck at her words. He loved the fact that she was so damned merciless, providing him with one of the most thoroughly satisfying meals he'd enjoyed in years. Jilah moved forward to touch him, trailing clawed fingers gently along the nape of Argent's neck as his mouth worked against the man's skin.

:: *Is he going to be enough?* ::

She moved to kneel by Argent's side. It took a considerable force of will for Argent to pull away in time and he placed a hand on the pavement to steady himself.

Argent blinked and looked over at Jilah, his irises enormous as he nodded slowly and leaned into her, his voice drifting through her thoughts. :: *My god.* ::

Jilah heard a giddy giggle trail through her thoughts as she helped him to his feet. Argent had an enormous lopsided grin as he looked back at her and he swooned in her arms, his tone breathy as he sent, :: *Oh, that was delightful.* ::

She chuckled softly, nuzzling him as she ran clawed fingers through his hair.

:: *Are you usually this woozy after you've just eaten?* ::

He giggled aloud this time, sounding immensely pleased with himself. :: *Actually, no. I haven't had a meal this..* :: *He stumbled, placing his hands on her shoulders and blinking several times before laughing out loud.* :: *Exquisite in ages.* ::

Jilah shook her head, highly amused at his level of ecstatic disorientation as she looked back towards the open mouth of the alleyway. So far, so good. Nobody had stumbled upon their mess yet.

Argent nuzzled her neck, cooing softly as she peered down at the twitching body of the man at their feet. She kicked his side gently with a toe.

:: *Are you coherent enough to do that mass influence thing you do to the three of us until I can get his body to the truck?* ::

Argent frowned down at the man on the ground, then replied, :: *I should be able to.* ::

He let go of her shoulders and began to sway backwards. Jilah quickly caught him and held him up.

:: *Release me. If I'm to do this at all, I'll do it while standing up of my own accord.* ::

He sounded childishly petulant. She narrowed her eyes at him and muttered, :: *Okay, but if you fall over, I'm carrying you over my shoulder to the truck.* ::

As she set him back on his feet, he let out another giggle then wobbled slightly before grabbing her shoulder again. Jilah raised an eyebrow at him, hands on her hips as he shook his head and pulled away from her, blinking.

:: *Wow. You do tend to put quite a kick into your meals.* ::

Argent closed his eyes for a moment, then looked back at her, edges of emerald beginning to rim the enormous black pupils that filled his eyes. He vibrated with an odd resonance as she met his gaze, and she felt a palpable warm wind blow across her skin that tickled the hair on her arms.

:: *OK. Want me to grab him?* ::

Jilah cocked her head and frowned back at him. :: *What did you just do? You feel different.* ::

Argent replied with a sly grin before grabbing the man and hefting him effortlessly over a shoulder. He made sure to hold the man's head well away from his arm since the body still seemed to be leaking an unappetizing mixture of spittle, bile and blood.

:: *Got a napkin or something?* :: He asked, wincing.

"Don't change the subject." Jilah replied aloud, reaching down to pull off one of the man's socks. She wiped Patrick's face clean, then jammed the sock into his mouth.

"Better? A little fluid and you're all, 'Eww, napkin'." She joked with him, laughing as he looked over at her, feigning offense with a jaw drop and a huff. Unable to help herself, she slapped his ass and waved him off towards the mouth of the alley.

"Come on. Let's get this meat puppet out of here."

Argent let out a sharp bark of laughter as they began walking back to the vehicle. "Meat puppet? I learn so many interesting colloquialisms when I'm around you."

More of the jewel-tone blue was starting to creep out from behind the pupils of her eyes as Jilah shrugged and responded, "It's a gift."

Patrick started making a guttural gibbering noise, and Argent gave him a rough shake, growling, "Cut it out. The drooling is bad enough." Ugh, as is the odor, he thought to himself. The leather jacket would need to be thoroughly scrubbed when they arrived back home. Humans were always so full of a variety of nauseating fluids.

Jilah giggled and called back in a singsong voice, "Remember, don't snap his neck."

"In answer to your earlier question, I had to bleed off a little of the excess energy. As I stated before, I haven't eaten anything quite this rich in years, if not decades." Argent walked beside her, astonished at how much power had flooded into him in a single meal. It had to be more than a simple mixture of blood and intense emotion. He had terrorized people when he'd fed in the distant past, sometimes driving his dinner mad in the process; but it had never been this heady. This overpowering.

He had reached her at the end of her meal in the graveyard the first night they'd met, and even then there had been a great deal of zing to it. But being able to catch it from beginning to end? It ended up being quite a high.

The back of the SUV was easily able to accommodate the body, and Jilah was glad that she'd developed the habit of putting a tarp down so that the carpet beneath wouldn't stain. As it was, they were going to have to deal with the acrid smell of urine the entire way home. She made a note to drive with the windows down. Argent tossed his leather jacket in back as well to be free of the stench.

Closing the back, she sighed and looked up at him as he extended a hand out to her. She took it, and he pulled her into his arms, his lips curling into a wicked grin as his other hand slowly slid down her body. He moaned lightly as he leaned in and placed a soft kiss on her neck.

Jilah laughed and slapped playfully at his back in mock indignation. "Hey! Not in the middle of the street."

Argent chuckled and and breathed, "Why not? It's not as if anybody can see us."

Jilah growled and gave his ear a playful flick. "Why is it that after only three days in bed with you, I feel like such a slut?"

"Perhaps it is because he tends to have that affect on almost everybody he comes into contact with."

Jilah's skin prickled at the sound of an unfamiliar male voice, and she wondered who the hell could've spotted them, much less gotten so close to them without being detected.

She stiffened against Argent as soft, feminine laughter echoed from behind her. Her body started preparing for a fight, and she could feel her eyeteeth lengthening as her clawed fingers bit into Argent's arm.

Argent stiffened, his voice growing cold and empty as he growled, "Aurelian."

His tone spooked her, but Jilah couldn't quite figure out if he was angry or not. It was as if in one moment, she could feel him and his emotions, and the next, it was as if she were standing alone, holding herself against a statue with all the emotional resonance of a pristine kitchen floor.

Jilah blurred out of his arms, standing beside him and meeting the gaze of the tall, bronze-skinned man that stood before them. The man's irises reflected a stunning, metallic gold under the light of the street lamps, and a mixture of honey and platinum-colored locks spilled over his shoulders and down his back in a tangle of soft waves. He was over six feet tall and had the physique of a swimmer. He had the easy, disaffected look of someone who had just walked off the beaches of Malibu, sans surfboard.

The man's lips slid into an easy grin as his appreciative gaze traveled down her body, his eyes glittering. "Man, you really know how to pick 'em. She's definitely *un morceau doux d'âne.*"

Jilah's eyes narrowed at the stranger's words. She let out an annoyed growl, irritated that she couldn't understand part of what the man had said. She had never been very adept with languages, but could hazard a guess as to what he'd meant.

"It would be to your benefit to show some respect, Aurelian."

Argent's tone now held the faintest edge of anger, and Jilah looked over at him, noting that his expression had become very careful; calculating.

The short hairs at the nape of her neck fluttered, giving her the distinct feeling that something very bad was about to happen. She tried sending to Argent and was surprised to find herself locked out, unable to communicate with him mind to mind. She took a deep breath and looked back over at the surfer. He seemed somewhat more subdued now, his expression sobering as he kept his gaze locked on Argent.

The man held out a hand in a placatory gesture, his voice becoming uneasy as he murmured, "I meant no harm, Strigaisha. Please."

Something really strange was going on. The blond looked a little hurt, almost pleading. The air around Jilah grew a little colder as Argent softly murmured, "Too much time has passed for you to use that honorific with me, Aurelian. Why are you here?"

"Because I asked him to locate you. You really are a pain in the ass to track down."

The blond rolled his shoulders back as a diminutive Asian woman winked into existence next to him. She simply hadn't been there before.

Ah, crap. Is she one too? Jilah thought to herself as she looked the woman over.

Her delicate face was framed with long, straight mahogany-colored hair that flowed down to her waist in a shimmering wave. She looked like she'd stepped right out of a hair care commercial. Bright flecks of gold peppered her reddish brown irises. Her voice had an almost musical lilt to it as she met Argent's gaze.

Jilah figured the woman to be about five feet tall, if that. A bronze dress constructed of a strange fabric that looked as if it had been hammered from the metal itself shimmered against her body, clinging tightly to her as she moved to place a small hand in the grip of the tall blond man at her side.

"Mira."

The change in Argent's tone caused Jilah to raise an eyebrow. This was becoming an interesting turn of events, in a bad way. Argent's voice was becoming somewhat warm and familiar, but still wary. Starting to get a little tired of people showing up without explanations and being providing only with what sounded like coded conversations, she quietly breathed, "Somebody'd better fill me in on what's going on here before I make a dangerous assumption."

Jilah flexed razor-sharp claws as she looked back at the small woman. The open street was beginning to feel entirely too crowded now with the appearance of Argent's old acquaintances. She began wondering how many more were going to show up.

Jilah felt a hand on her shoulder and flinched, spinning and backing away from the offending hand, her fingers twitching and wanting to tear into something. She looked back at Argent, who was now reaching out to her, his expression chagrined. She eased down a little, taking a breath before stepping towards him and looking back at the small woman who now had a secretive smile playing at the edges of her shiny gold lips.

Oh, I don't like her, Jilah decided as she felt Argent's fingers intertwine with hers. She allowed him to gently pull her closer to him.

The woman raised an eyebrow, sounding amused as she purred, "It's been far too long." She gave a little bow, her tone just a touch mocking as she added, "Strigaisha."

Jilah frowned, her hand tightening in Argent's grip as she whispered, "Why do they keep calling you that?"

Argent's thoughts slid through her consciousness, reassuring but edged with urgency, :: *It is something that will take a great deal of time to explain. Can it wait until they have gone?* ::

With an annoyed sigh, she gripped his hand harder, sending, :: *OK. But I'm not happy with it.* ::

The woman's soft laughter set Jilah's teeth on edge. The Avatar's eyes narrowed as she looked back at the strange pair before them.

Oh yeah. Not at all happy.

"Is she one of yours? Nouveau-né?"

The woman had a strange accent that Jilah couldn't quite place.

:: *What, exactly, is that supposed to mean?* :: she snapped.

Argent gently rubbed a thumb along Jilah's hand, his voice a soft rumble in her thoughts as he answered, :: *She's asking if you are my get. My offspring, if you will.* ::

Jilah took a slow, deep breath as Argent quietly addressed the diminutive woman, "No. She is something.." He turned to look at Jilah with the ghost of a smile as he squeezed her hand gently and murmured, "entirely different."

A brief tremble went through her as she met his gaze. Dear god, she was acting like a schoolgirl with a new crush. It was embarrassing.

"If I remember correctly, you always did tend to favor the unusual, lover." Mira's voice had an edge to it as she added, "Sometimes I think that was the only reason you chose to share our bed."

Ah, so it's a pissing contest, is it?

Well aware that the woman was just attempting to rattle her cage, Jilah ground her teeth as her thoughts grazed Argent's. She was becoming very uncomfortable with where the conversation was going.

:: *That's just ducky. She's a jealous ex?* ::

:: *It is more complicated than that.* ::

Argent winced, patently annoyed with the way things were playing out as well, and he tersely responded, "I sincerely hope that the pair of you didn't embark on this quest for the sole purpose of chastising me. If so, I'm afraid that you will be entirely disappointed with the results. Now, if we've dispensed with social niceties, what on earth made you think that it was a good idea to seek me out after all this time?"

Mira smiled and shrugged, her voice dropping back into that same musical lilt as she answered, "Politics. What else?"

Twelve

Argent's Past Comes Calling

"You must be either joking, or deranged," Argent responded with a harsh laugh, his eyes glittering with amusement as he rocked back on a heel and asked, "Is it not a little late in the game to be thinking of me as a viable player?"

Mira's lips thinned, her voice tight as she answered, "Strigaisha," She pulled away from her companion, irritation ringing in her voice as she took a step towards Argent. "You may have walked away, but there are things in motion now that even you cannot outrun."

Argent regarded her with narrowed eyes, his tone unforgiving and becoming clipped as he replied, "I am no longer part of that particular game, Mira. Who are you to be telling me my place in it?"

A cold wave of anger rolled off him, sending a chill through Jilah. Having now taken as much of this petulant, presumptive woman as she was prepared to take, she pulled her hand free of Argent's grasp and took a menacing step towards her.

"Back off. Now," she growled.

Mira ignored her, never taking her eyes off Argent as she calmly murmured, "Judiana's dead."

Argent reeled back as if slapped. The news sent a cold rush through him, and he felt his fingers go numb. He mumbled something under his breath that Jilah couldn't quite catch, then took a step back and turned away, bringing a hand to his temple. Startled that the dynamic of this confrontation had changed so quickly, Jilah frowned and reached out to touch his arm, shuddering as a wave of sadness now emanated from him. Jilah wrapped a comforting arm around his waist, not knowing what else to do. The social dynamic was shifting too quickly, and it was too disorienting to try to keep up.

"We had little choice but to track you down." Mira's voice was soft now.

Argent turned to face her, his expression pained as he asked, "How?"

Mira looked uneasy as the tall blond walked over to her, almost as if unsure of what to say. She quietly murmured, "She was given to the morning sun by The Sisters."

Argent's eyes widened, his voice full of disbelief, "The Sisters?? How in holy hell did they find her daytime resting place? Surely she would have been surrounded by..."

Mira cut him off, her voice forceful. "Strigaisha. Should we be discussing this in front of," She inclined her head towards Jilah, "an outsider?"

Okay, that's done it, Jilah thought to herself angrily as she pulled away from Argent and took a step towards the woman. Aurelian quickly moved to intercept her, liquid gold burning in the inner depths of his eyes as he stared back at her. Mira growled, eyes glittering as she glared back at Jilah with a sharp-toothed grin.

"No, let the stripling come. It appears that she has yet to learn manners."

Jilah's hand flexed before snapping out and clocking the tall blond squarely in the jaw. Aurelian's head rocked back with the force of the blow, and he ended up on his ass in the street.

"ENOUGH!" Argent roared.

Jilah blinked and took a step back, unsure where his anger was being directed. Aurelian slowly got to his feet and stepped back, brushing himself off. Argent's expression hardened, his voice dropping an octave as he growled, "You do not want to make the mistake of antagonizing her further, Mira. She is my chosen, my trusted. Answer my questions before her if you want my help."

Mira's jaw dropped, her expression incredulous as she stammered, "You would trust this stray infant with the lives of..?"

Argent took a slow, patient breath, his expression distant as he answered, "It is unwise to continue to question me on her loyalty."

As Jilah witnessed their interaction, she couldn't help being pleased that he'd stood up for her.

The woman composed herself and nodded, "As you wish. There is dissension and has been for some time. Not everybody was satisfied with the way Judiana was running the prefecture towards the end of her rule. I wouldn't be surprised if a few of them didn't arrange this assassination, but we have yet to find an individual that we've been able to break during interrogation."

Argent frowned as she continued, "To make matters worse, the prefecture is slowly fragmenting into warring factions. A foolish few have tried to take the reins of power, to bring the city back under heel, but with Judiana gone things have rapidly dissolved into chaos."

Mira finished and stepped back into Aurelian's arms. The blond watched Argent closely, his expression tinged with sadness as he brought his hands to rest gently on Mira's shoulders.

Argent turned to lean back against the SUV, crossing his arms as he looked back at them. "Surely Judiana had groomed a suitable replacement?"

"Judiana was fair and just, but she was unfortunately short-sighted in regards to that particular choice."

"Meaning what, exactly?" Argent cocked his head to the side, his mouth forming a tight line as Mira spoke.

"Her standards were flawed. When the moment of truth came, her chosen successor crumbled under the pressure and constant demands of her given position. Usurpers kept testing her – small tests at first, to see how much they could get away with. When it became clear that she was unsure of how to react to the multiple and varied challenges to her authority, they sent assassins after her, and she didn't have the faculties to properly deal with the threat." Mira stared back at him, expressionless as she waited for him to respond.

"This does not speak too highly of your capabilities, Mira, or those of your associates." he replied in a dour tone.

Mira answered with a sad smile and nodded. "I would take full responsibility, had I still been in the court to affect any direct change when this occurred."

Argent stared back at her, stunned. "Are you telling me that Judiana dismissed you?"

The diminutive woman shifted, clearly uncomfortable now. "Towards the end, she was behaving in an entirely uncharacteristic and erratic manner, as did a great many crucial members of the court. She completely disbanded the inner circle. Apparently after a certain point she felt that she could no longer trust anybody around her."

Argent stood silent, processing it all. How could his chosen successor have let things get so out of hand so quickly? What had caused her to take such rash action? To become so overly paranoid that she dismissed the very elements that could have saved her?

"And with this revelation you are hoping that I'll just offer to come back and take matters back in hand?"

Mira and Aurelian nodded slowly in unison, looking lost as they leaned into each other.

Argent laughed in disbelief. "You do realize that it's been over seventy years. Who is to say that anyone will accept my authority if I decide to come back with you?"

As Jilah listened, she frowned. She wasn't at all sure that she liked what she was hearing. There hadn't been enough time to get used to his presence, and now it was looking as if he was going to have to leave.

Mira perked up at his response, eyes shining as she answered, "There are many of the old guard that remain in the city, Strigaisha. Enough to keep the young ones in check, if need be."

Argent winced and let out a tired sigh. "Please stop. I left that title behind a lifetime ago."

Mira nodded, but her expression remained hopeful as she continued, "Cynette and Alain have once again offered the blood oath of the Pack to you, should you wish to return. Brigliadoro and Roane.."

Argent cut her off with a dismissive wave, his tone weary now as he replied, "Surely there is someone better suited than I for this task. It would be a lie to say that I didn't wish to see my old home again, as well as the others I left behind, but I removed myself from political life to avoid the conflict it always inspired in others."

He glanced over at Jilah, looking suddenly exhausted as he continued, "Judiana was much better equipped to handle this sort of nonsense, thus my reason for leaving everything in what I thought were more than capable hands. While it is unfortunate that she chose her replacement unwisely, I am afraid that there is little I can do."

"Please," Mira's tone became more strenuous. "Argent."

His actual name sounded rough and unfamiliar on her tongue. Her voice tightened as she explained, "There is no one better suited than you. Even after you left, fear of reprisals from you were what kept a great many people loyal to Judiana. You are still respected. And feared. Even among the Nouveau-né in the city, you are..."

Argent shook his head and grated. "No. I will not be pulled back into this mess. That life is behind me now, and it is best left in the past."

He looked back at Jilah and held a beckoning hand out to her. :: *Come. We should get going.* ::

Jilah took his hand, letting him pull her close as he opened the driver's side door to let her in. She ventured a look back at the woman, something in her heart pulling as Mira pleaded with him now, her voice rising as she cried out, "The city will tear itself apart, Strigaisha! Please!"

The woman's eyes were brimming with emotion as she trembled in Aurelian's arms. Jilah looked up at Argent, her brow furrowing as she sent, :: *I don't want to be responsible for this.* :: She took a deep breath and asked, :: *You'd probably be gone for a while, right?* ::

Argent's eyes widened, and he pulled away from her, his tone slightly wounded as he asked, :: *You could let me go so easily?* ::

Jilah grabbed him and gave him a gentle shake, growling, :: *No, jackass. It's not easy. Give me a little credit.* ::

Argent relaxed and shook his head, his voice soft in her thoughts as he cupped the side of her face.

:: *If I did choose to go, it would probably be a very long time before I saw you again. I am unwilling to leave your side so soon without a fight.* ::

Jilah wasn't quite certain if she wanted to offer this, but knew that in the last few days she'd passed a point where she didn't think she would be comfortable going back to being alone. She wasn't sure if she'd be able to handle it. She took a slow breath, then leaned into him and sent, :: *Then take me with you.* ::

Argent gently kissed the top of her head, then took a deep breath.

"I will have an answer for you in two nights' time, but know this now; if I go, she comes with me as my Striaga."

"Does she even know what that means?" Mira sounded faintly derisive, obviously unhappy with this pronouncement.

Jilah turned to face her, but before she could open her mouth to respond, Argent growled. "Do not push it, Mira. I will not say this again."

The woman paled and stepped back from the force in his voice before she composed herself and tilted her head towards him. "Then we will see you two nights from now. We eagerly await your decision, Strigaisha."

She turned and grabbed Aurelian's hand, and Jilah blinked as they both disappeared.

With a mild shiver, Jilah grumbled, "I really hate that disappearing act you guys do. It's extremely disconcerting."

Argent sighed heavily and leaned back against the vehicle. "You no doubt have many questions about what just happened, but it would probably be a good idea to get the body to a place where we can dump it first." Argent winced as he looked down at her, his voice tentatively joking as he said, "I'm betting that you're pretty pissed at me."

Jilah took a deep breath and said, "Honestly? I'm more annoyed at the complications and curve balls that I end up having to roll with than anything else." She nodded towards the other side of the car. "Get in. Let's get this body run done with."

As Argent slid into the passenger seat, she growled, "And oh, by the way? Your friends have shitty manners."

He laughed weakly as he closed the door, "You noticed that, eh?"

Thirteen
An Explanation

As they headed out of the city, Argent leaned back into the seat and placed a hand on her knee, gently rubbing his thumb in small circles against her skin as he murmured, "I don't think I can express in words exactly how sorry I am about that scene back there. I will explain everything that I can to you."

Jilah did her best to remain focused on the road, gripping the steering wheel tightly as she asked, "First question. What the hell was that word they kept calling you?"

"It's a modernization of an old Romany word that denoted a bogeyman of sorts. It is an honorific title given to a provincial ruler of a given city." Argent grimaced slightly as he continued, "It is a title that I had hoped not to hear again in this lifetime."

Jilah glanced over at him, frowning as she asked, "So, what is the name of this place you provincially ruled over?"

From the unusual names bandied about earlier, she figured it probably had to be in Europe somewhere.

"New Orleans." Argent replied, peering over at her to gauge her reaction.

Jilah gave him a sidelong glance and repeated. "New Orleans."

He nodded and looked back at her, silent.

"So, why New Orleans? Why not Kansas or Detroit – or San Francisco?" Jilah asked.

Argent shrugged and explained, "It is just where I ended up."

Jilah eyed him and asked, "And this was how long ago, exactly?"

"I abdicated in the early 1930's." Argent frowned, trying to remember the exact dates. Not much had happened in the interim, but then he had worked diligently to blot the past out.

A weak laugh croaked out of her throat, and she shook her head. "I, ah, keep forgetting how old you are for some reason."

Argent shrugged as he presented her with a lopsided grin. "I've always had good skin. It conceals age well."

Jilah shook a chiding finger at him. "Don't change the subject."

She tried to keep her tone casual, forcing her eyes back on the road. She definitely didn't want to look at him as she ventured, "So. You had sex with her?"

"Both of them, actually."

Jilah's mind reeled, barely being able to keep track of having sex with one person at a time. She wasn't entirely sure how she should feel about this revelation.

When she remained silent, Argent looked over at her and quietly murmured, "If there is going to be an issue over the number of individuals that I've had dalliances with throughout the years, I am afraid that it's going to be a bit of a problem. Surely you can't have expected me to remain celibate for the last three hundred years."

Jilah glared at him, her tone sarcastic as she grated, "You'll have to forgive my prudery, seeing as how you're only the second man I've ever been with. It's going to take me a little time to adjust to the sheer volume, I'm sure."

She winced, not wanting to appear jealous but failing miserably. That had come out more harshly than she had intended, and she quickly added, "Sorry. It's just that the adjustment curve is looking a little steep at the moment."

Argent held up his hands in a placatory gesture and asked, "New topic?"

Eager to stop talking, much less thinking about his infinite sexual conquests, Jilah nodded and replied, "Okay, back to that whole ruling New Orleans thing."

"It's a little difficult to explain. There is a fair amount of background that you need to be aware of first. Human laws and morals are extremely inhibiting for," he paused, searching for the right word. "Preternatural creatures. One could say that we can only exist outside of the perceived reality of humanity, for all intents and purposes, so there were those among us that came up with modes of governing ourselves to ensure that it stayed that way."

"Elaborate, please?"

Argent shifted in his seat, settling in for a long explanation. "Let me first begin by saying that most of the dark myths and faerie tales that have been disseminated throughout the years all have a founding basis in reality. These stories were usually derived from real-life accounts of people who had actually interacted with such creatures. They slowly evolved into a wide and rather colorful variety of bogey-man stories that humans would tell to their offspring in an effort to promote discipline.

"Many centuries ago, in an attempt to keep from being extermi-nated by humans as we had been in parts of the old countries that knew better about such stories, a council of elders took it upon them-selves to come up with a method to rectify the situation. It was their intention to maintain a sort of order to insure that the creatures from these stories wouldn't manifest themselves physically to the public. In other words, their job was to keep the preternaturals on a short leash so that they didn't step out of line and provide the humans with evi-dence that their folklore legends were true. Make sense?"

Jilah frowned as she asked, "What happened to those that didn't stay on the leash?"

Argent gazed back at her, his tone devoid of emotion. "They were destroyed outright, their remains utilized as reminders to the rest of the wayward populace that were experiencing similar issues with being controlled."

Jilah shuddered as he continued.

"Now, every major city has a sizable population of both humans and preternaturals. The rulers of each city are aware of the others throughout the world and, for the most part, they are allowed to operate as separate entities unto themselves, but the basic rules and terms of conduct within each city vary little.

"If you truly wish to come with me back to New Orleans, I want you to know what you're getting into. It is by no means pretty, and it will be unsafe if not downright dangerous for the first few days."

"Sounds like a war zone." Jilah winced, knowing that if she chose to do this, she'd probably end up well out of her depth.

Argent grinned, chuckling darkly as he replied, "You tend to have this flair for understatement."

Jilah slapped at his chest playfully, then said, "But that woman said that you had lots of supporters. That they would welcome you back."

"While I may still have supporters within factions of the city, I can guarantee that there will be challenges, either covert or open, to anybody that shows up to claim the position. There are a great many residents in the prefecture who will no doubt remember me, but I am fairly certain that many of them will not be entirely pleased to see me return."

Argent had been far from a benevolent ruler towards the end, and he grimaced at the memory. It wasn't so much the remembered acts that bothered him as much as the fact that he had been affected to the point of losing control over himself.

In the end, he had been convinced to step down and get as far away as he could from the situation. Without the protection of the office he once commanded, Argent quickly found himself the target of multiple assassins. He had hidden under the radar from his kind before, many years ago, having to remove himself completely from the society he once knew in order to find any semblance of peace or rest. Having to go through it again had been painful, but had also been necessary.

Returning to a life that had very nearly pushed him past the point of no return was not something he was eager to do. However, he felt a strong sense of guilt that his chosen successor had failed so utterly in the end. While this wasn't a situation that he had directly caused, he was aware of the possible consequences for the friends he'd left behind if nobody stepped in to help – if the council themselves chose to intervene. It was not a pleasant realization.

Argent continued with a heavy sigh, "I am extremely disappointed that Judiana failed to groom a more suitable individual to reign in her stead. Because of her inability to properly judge the character of her replacement, old companions of mine could suffer, and quite possibly perish."

Not to mention that it was doing far more than merely inconveniencing him. He had been positive that Judiana had been solid in her ability and intelligence. Had he really been that far gone before he'd chosen to leave to make such a grievous error in judgment?

Jilah's eyes widened, her voice incredulous as she said, "You make it sound like it's going to be a constant struggle from the minute you put your foot in the door."

"Exactly." He explained, "It is the very nature of politics. You begin to see why I left it behind."

Jilah frowned as they headed down the highway, feeling as if her head were filling up with information too quickly to process it. The sensation wasn't entirely pleasant. "You said something about me being your Striaga, if you decided to go?"

"A Striaga is the official chosen consort or mate to the provincial ruler of a given prefecture. What this essentially means is that everyone in obeisance to me would have to recognize you as my equal and act accordingly. Without question."

Whoa. It sounded as if the position was going to be a great deal like being a queen of sorts. Jilah had no idea how to behave within that kind of social framework, having no reference point whatsoever for such a thing. Being a social peon or pariah was all she had ever known. She blinked, opening her mouth, then closing it before tentatively asking, "Just so that we're both on the same page here, does that mean the same thing for you that it means for me?"

Argent's eyes glittered in the darkness of the vehicle as he answered, "It is not a title given lightly, Jilah. There are many customs, many rules that go along with such an honorific. You are probably still tied enough to human ideals that you believe that this means marriage of a sort, but in fact this is so very much more."

Jilah wrinkled her nose, unsure if she was being insulted or not as she glanced over at him and said, "You say human like it's a bad thing."

Argent shook his head, his voice smoothly reassuring, "Not at all. Just limiting. You're still holding yourself to the rules and morals that you followed when you were still one of them. It's been six months, and you still live the same cluttered existence that most of them lead, wrapping yourself in mortal issues and problems."

Jilah opened her mouth to argue, but he held a hand up, continuing, "Hear me out. You're young. This brave new world you've been unceremoniously thrust into is an enormous, overwhelming change from what you're used to. It is only natural that you would stick to the familiar, holding close the comfort of your past life, trying to convince yourself that not so much has changed. Over time, you would eventually come to realize that these things hinder you as much as you perceive them as helping." His words discomfited her, and Jilah shifted in her seat, as if this simple act could help her escape what he was saying.

Argent leaned towards her, his tone soft and tender as he placed a hand on her arm.

"Unfortunately, if you choose to cast your lot with mine in this and come with me to New Orleans, I'm afraid that these differences will come as an extreme shock. You will have to adapt very quickly to keep your footing. At the moment, you are not at all prepared to handle it. There is much that I will have to instruct you in before we leave, and I am not entirely certain that you will be comfortable with any of it."

Jilah turned the vehicle into the industrial park and drove towards the house. The realization that this horrible-looking domicile had become home, that it was now such a source of stability, jarred her. With what she had gone through in such a short time already, she thought that she'd dealt pretty well with the new life that had been presented to her. Still, , since the change, she'd really done little more than establish a decent base of operations and gotten to work. Granted, between studying and working, there hadn't been much time for anything else.

Now she was being told that the bogeyman was real and that he and his extended family held positions of power all over the world. There was an entire segment of society, of reality, that she had yet to encounter. The learning curve of navigating through society after being so socially closed off all her life had been difficult at first, and not at all pleasant. She was being presented with the enormity of a reality of which she had truly never conceived. She knew she was strong, but was she up to this? Did she want to go down this path with him?

Too much was happening, all of it too quickly for her to trust her reactions – and if she went with him it sounded as if it would only get exponentially worse. Jilah silently cursed fate, giving it a vicious finger in her mind as they pulled into the driveway and rolled into the garage. She turned the engine off and stared at the blank walls of the garage as her head buzzed with all this new information.

Is this what going into shock feels like? I wonder.

Argent peered over at her, his heart heavy as he watched her strain to keep her emotions under control. She hadn't hit him yet, so he figured that this was a good sign. He was well aware that she needed time to adjust to everything he'd just told her, and he was pleased that she hadn't told him off outright. That was also a good sign.

Jilah opened the door, climbed out and closed it quietly behind her, and pulled the wig off as she walked out of the garage. Operating on autopilot now, she realized that the first order of business was getting changed. She wanted to put on more comfortable clothes that wouldn't restrict her movement while she buried the remains of 'Patrick' in the backyard. With everything that had happened tonight, she really had no desire to spend time cruising around town to find a suitable dumping spot.

Argent watched her go, slowly getting out of the car and popping the back open before reaching in and tossing the now motionless body over a shoulder. He wanted to help her somehow, to make this easier on her. He reached out to touch her mind, his voice gentle as he asked, :: *Where do you want him?* ::

Jilah headed through the front hallway, not bothering to close the door behind her; unzipping the dress as his words drifted through her thoughts. She sighed and slid her fingers out to trail along the wall as she walked through the hall, sending back, :: *At this point, I have to admit that I don't really care that much. Put him anywhere in the back.* ::

Jilah numbly made her way downstairs, walking into the bedroom and sliding the dress off, kicking it into a corner. She surveyed the disaster area that her room had become and gave a shaky sigh. She really needed to get a new mattress, but she didn't care if they ended up sleeping on the floor at the moment. She was so very tired as she pulled her undergarments off and tossed them on top of the dress, walking over to the dresser.

Argent's voice echoed in her mind again. :: *I'll bury him and come inside afterwards.* ::

She smiled at his thoughtful consideration, relieved as she walked into the bathroom and began drawing a hot bath.

:: *Thank you. I'm going to sit in the tub. For about an hour. Or two. Or the rest of the night, maybe.* ::

Fourteen

Thinking Back, Acting Forward

Argent unceremoniously dumped the body on the ground and headed over to the shed to get the shovel. He exchanged his jacket for the shovel on the hook and headed back to the body. He wondered what could have happened to Judiana in those last weeks. What had caused her act in such a bizarre fashion? Was it paranoia based on actual events, or did she lose her sanity somehow?

There were too many questions, and in order to get the answers to any of them, he would have to return and resume a job that had nearly driven him mad. He wondered if he would be able to deal with it again, hoping that if he chose to go back that it wouldn't end up being permanent. He had every intention of quickly grooming another replacement, reassuring himself that he would now be better able to judge the character of those around him. Reconnecting with one's sanity had that affect on a man.

Then, there was the matter of Jilah.

If she said yes, he would agree to go; but only on the condition that it was clear that he was going to stay just long enough to find a suitable replacement. He owed it to Judiana, after all. Argent shuddered at the thought of what her last moments must have been like. Even at his most suicidal, he'd never thought about leaving himself vulnerable to the sun to end it. Only the truly masochistic or afflicted ever chose that way out. The pain had to have been unimaginable.

He grunted gruffly and started digging. It took a minimum of effort, and he found himself revisiting past memories. It had been at least forty years since his last encounter with another of his kind. He had avoided heavily populated areas with an almost paranoid fanaticism after abdicating. He'd dispatched the assassin sent after him quickly enough, but Argent was left wondering why a stripling a quarter his age had been sent to track him down and bring back his head.

He had made a great many enemies while in power, and most of them nursed very enduring grudges. He wondered if time had eased their anger, their need for retribution. There was only one way to find out. What was worse, he now felt the almost painful pull of his past and the memories of the people he had left behind. He had to admit that part of him did miss that life, the excitement of the struggle to maintain power and being able to deliver a swift and vicious justice upon those who sorely deserved it. He had been very good at what he did.

He shook his head to clear it, not wanting to think about that particular time. That way laid madness and anguish. It had taken him a very long time to recover and was best left in the past.

His thoughts turned to Jilah, and he found himself surprised at how exciting it was to be with an inexperienced woman again. It brought out a fervor in him that left him eagerly wanting to teach her everything he knew, everything he'd experienced in his long, debauched life. It reassured him that she had been drawn out as easily as he was drawn to her. He'd met and bedded many individuals in his long life, but none of them had so many qualities that he both admired and desired in a single individual.

Her presence comforted him, and he had been surprised to find that he was able to truly relax in her embrace. It had been uncountable years since he'd found peace in someone's arms, and he'd been certain that he'd never find it again. With Jilah there were no angles, no machinations. It was truly just the two of them.

He would have given a great deal to stay with her here, enjoying her relatively uncomplicated life for a good long while. Argent sighed and kicked the body into the hole with a booted foot, then looked down at the streaks of blood and caked dirt that spotted the white tank top and his shoulder. Why was it that he always seemed to get filthy around her? He chuckled softly as he began filling the grave with dirt and wondered what he'd do if she chose not to accompany him. The thought chilled him.

He shook his head angrily and grumbled, "They will simply have to find a way out of it themselves if that turns out to be the case."

The last few clumps of dirt filled the hole, and Argent collected his jacket, placing the shovel back in the rickety shed before heading inside. He stripped off the soiled tank top, wiped his shoulder off, placed both the tank top and jacket on the kitchen table before washing his hands and arms. He then grabbed a bright green can of soda out of the refrigerator and padded down the hallway to the stairs.

It seemed a poor conciliatory gesture, but he felt he had little else to give her. The only thing he could offer her was himself, his presence in her life; having left all else behind so many years ago. Was it enough? As he strode towards the bathroom, he hoped so.

Argent stood in the doorway for a few moments, his expression thoughtful as he looked over at her. His gaze gently caressed the curves and lines of her face as she opened her eyes. He presented her with a faint, apologetic smile and held up the can.

How the hell was she supposed to stay angry, when he was so damned sweet? It didn't help that her body had an almost Pavlovian response to him every time she laid eyes on him. A familiar curl of warmth coiled in her belly as she looked up at him.

In a breathy voice she asked, "Join me?"

Argent walked over to the tub, smiling warmly as he reached over to place the can on the counter behind him. Jilah's eyes glittered as she watched him slowly strip out of his black leather pants. He kicked the pants off then bent down to kiss her. She snaked a soapy hand over his shoulder, pulling him down to her, and he placed a hand on the side of the tub to steady himself. His voice was a warning singsong as he said, "I'll fall in if you keep this up."

Jilah grinned and patted the top of the water in the space next to her in the enormous tub, "Then get your ass in here. Time's a wastin'."

Argent gave a mock gasp of shock, as he pulled away from her and stood up. Jilah thrilled as his lips curled into a wicked grin; her eyes riveted as he slid his hand down his stomach.

"So forceful."

Jilah laughed and slapped at the water. Argent looked back at her, droplets now peppering his chest and stomach. Right now, she just wanted to be with him, to forget about everything that had happened earlier tonight. Even if it was only for a few hours.

She raised an eyebrow, growling, "The gauntlet has been thrown, old man. You up to it?"

She laughed as her gaze slowly slid down his torso, her grin widening as she added, "Well, hey, you're definitely up for something."

Argent's resultant grin was savage, his pupils dilating as he chuckled darkly and reached a hand towards the bubbly surface of the water.

"If you insist."

The next few minutes quickly devolved into an earnest water fight that left enormous wet patches on the rug outside of the bathroom, along with large puddles that had collected in the sink, on the counters and all over the floor. When the splashing finally died down, they were both giggling like loons and leaning into one another.

Still laughing, Jilah ventured a look around, her face falling when she saw how much water had gotten all over the place. It was going to take hours to dry the carpet in the bedroom alone. She'd have to bring down the box fans from upstairs to keep mold from setting in.

"Ah, crap."

She looked back over at Argent, who was now watching her with the expectant expression of a child awaiting possible punishment. She blinked as they stared at one another, then let out a sharp bark of laughter, causing them both to collapse into helpless giggles again. Jilah leaned into him and grinned, "You're really far too goofy to be a creature of the night. I think you should have your business cards changed. You got gypped."

Argent wrapped an arm around her, sobering as he murmured, "I haven't had cause to laugh like this in a long while. It is entirely your fault."

Jilah let out a soft sigh, her brow furrowing a little as she thought about it. "Me either, actually." She sighed, slowly throwing a leg over his lap, straddling him as she leaned into him.

Her scent became sharp and spicy, and he closed his eyes with a soft sigh as he brought his head down to the crook of her neck. He placed a gentle kiss on her collarbone, and he felt sharp teeth brush against his neck. A wave of emotion flowed from her, a sentiment so sublime that using mere words to convey it would have tainted it somehow.

He responded in kind, taking in a sharp breath and rocking his head back as he felt her bite down.

Oh my, his thoughts drifted as the gentle tugging sensation against his skin sent a wonderful sense of both peace and anticipation rolling through him. *I do believe that she's actually going to come with me.*

Much later, Argent smiled warmly as Jilah slowly traced the curve of his lips with a delicate finger. In a quiet voice, she murmured, "So much has happened in the last couple of days." Her smile was tinged with sadness as she continued, "You've turned my entire world upside down."

Argent nodded, brushing a strand of indigo hair back behind her ear, his voice barely audible as he answered, "I know." :: *And you, mine, deadly beauty.* ::

Jilah combed her fingers through his hair, her thumb tracing along the sharp, graceful curve of one of his blue-black eyebrows as she breathed, "I still can't look at you without losing myself in your eyes, and it scares me a little. Your past scares me even more." She paused for a moment, sighing softly. "It makes me feel incredibly inexperienced and out of my depth. I find myself wondering why you sought me out."

Argent reached up and laced her fingers with his and wrapped an arm around her waist, his voice gentle as he replied, "I walked away from others of my kind a long time ago because I no longer wanted to deal with the rather exceptional drama that went along with them. I spent a great deal of time just going from place to place, taking great care to stay away from cities, not wanting to draw attention to myself. The first time I felt your presence, I was struck with the memory of something that I'd lost a lifetime ago."

He caressed her cheek gently, his tone becoming reverent as he breathed, "You are young, yes. And inexperienced in comparison, most assuredly. But you are the only individual that I've run across in the last century that sees me as a man as opposed to a tool to be utilized, or a force to be directed."

Jilah frowned. "Then you've been hanging around with the wrong people."

Argent nodded and gave her a lopsided grin. "Apparently so." He sighed softly, murmuring, "And now you know why I would stay by your side."

As he leaned down to kiss her she realized that no matter how things turned out, they'd be together. It seemed corny and trite, but there it was. It wasn't perfect, and would probably by no means be easy, but it was the best offer she'd ever had. It wasn't exactly as if she could let him go either. Well, why the hell not?

Her voice was soft as she pulled away and looked back at him, "Then I guess I'd better pack."

Fifteen

The Beginning of a Long and Arduous Road

"Please tell me you're joking."

Jilah turned and continued searching through everything that she owned, trying to figure out what she wanted to leave behind, and what she could not bear to part with. The more she learned about this unusual political situation he was heading into, the less she liked it. It came with the territory, she supposed; but it was all a bit much to absorb at one time.

Argent peered at her curiously as she packed, hoping that she wasn't intending to take the entire closet with them.

"I can assure you that there is not much pain involved." he explained smoothly.

She tossed a shirt into one of the bags in the corner of the room and asked, "How would you know? Has anybody ever done the equivalent of what sounds like a forced data dump into your head?"

Argent briefly cleared his throat and replied, "I've been told by others that I've worked with before that the process is not overly unpleasant."

There had never been a reason for him to be on the receiving end of such a transmission. He had always been a very eager student and a quick study. Besides, he'd had the time to learn the proper political protocol necessary for the job. Jilah didn't have this option; and if she didn't receive the proper tutelage, it could end up weakening his political position and endangering both of them. If she wasn't aware of the varying political niceties and policies that went with her title, she could end up proving to be a liability and would likely get both of them killed. Or worse. He had explained the process to her several times already, but she was still balking at the prospect of having him enter her head for any reason other than communication through words or emotions. It was bad enough having another occupant in with her already.

"Is that so?" Jilah eyed him warily and placed her hands on her hips. "That guy in the alley didn't seem to enjoy it all that much."

"That was an entirely different situation," he explained.

"What was that all about, anyway?" she asked, shivering slightly as she remembered the look on the man's face.

"I made the assumption that you needed him to be conscious in order for you to conduct your duty, so I slapped him awake, in a sense. Think of it as mental smelling salts." Argent replied, "It worked out in the end, didn't it?"

Jilah frowned and turned back to her sorting. Offhandedly, she wondered how much she would need to take and how long they were going to be gone.

Without thinking, Argent plucked the surface thoughts from her head and answered, :: *I honestly have no idea. I won't be able to gauge the length of our stay until I witness the events at our reception.* ::

"Stop that." Jilah frowned back at him, then moved deeper into the closet, collecting several pairs of leather pants.

"Sorry." Argent replied, wincing a little. "It's an old habit that I've missed. It really is a far superior..."

Jilah cut him off, playfully mimicking his tone, "Method of communication. Yeah, yeah."

She poked her head out of the closet and added, "You know, I don't mind the telepathic stuff so much now, but finishing sentences as they happen in my head is really - ooky." She grimaced slightly, her lip curling a little. Her head disappeared back into the closet, and she grumbled, "I just don't see why you can't take the time to explain it to me. I'm a fast learner, and I retain information really well."

"As I've explained already, the amount of information you need to absorb would take months, if not years. There have to be flawless points of interest that quickly come to mind without you having to search for them. This is the only reasonable way that I can think of preparing you for what to expect in less than a week."

Jilah remained petulantly silent as she continued to pull selections from the long line of clothes hanging before her.

"Jilah, please."

She stiffened and glared back at him, "You know how much I hate it when you go digging in my head."

She was still unsettled about how quickly he had been able to yank her last target out of unconsciousness the other night. Could he do that to her as well?

Argent winced. That she still feared him, even a little, pained him. His tone was soft as he replied, "My point exactly," he replied softly, "There are unending amounts of odious little head games that these people indulge in. Most of them are far less scrupulous than myself. If you don't want them violating your mind, you're going to need to know how to protect yourself. These are simply not things I can teach you in a linear fashion in a short span of time." He shook his head at her obstinance, understanding it, but thinking it misplaced and inconvenient.

Jilah frowned and murmured. "You know your accent changes when you get annoyed, right?"

Argent blinked as Jilah spun to face him. Her eyes narrowed and she grated, "Alright, dammit. We'll do it your way." Now she was getting downright bitchy. She took a deep breath and tried to relax.

"We could always stay," he offered.

She shook her head, a tired resignation creeping into her voice as she answered, "No. I said I'd go."

She took another deep breath, then walked over and sat on the bed, "Let's just get it over with. Before I have time to change my mind."

Startled, Argent blurted, "What, now?"

Jilah looked back at him with a stoic expression. "Best to get it over with now so that I don't spend a pile of time getting jittery over it because I'm thinking about it too much, which is what I've been doing for the last hour or so now."

Argent sighed heavily as he moved towards her, "You are a truly unpredictable woman at times."

She let out a harsh bark of laughter, her tone impatient as she waved him over, snapping. "You're hardly the first person to point that out, and might I add, you're wasting valuable brain dump time. Let's get it on so I can finish packing."

She tried to calm down as Argent climbed on the bed behind her, wrapping his arms and legs around her waist as he leaned into her. Before she could react positively to the touch, she felt a sharp pain as he bit into her neck, and then the bliss took her.

Argent waited until she was in thrall, then gently pushed, opening a mental connection between them. It had been his intention to transmit the necessary images and information slowly so that she could better adjust to them, but the moment the conduit opened it all pulled from him in a rush.

A pink sheen of sweat broke out on his face as he struggled to control the flow. She didn't have the barriers that even newborns of his kind usually had, so he found it difficult to control the rhythm of it. He growled as he felt the pull of her mind, a rushing vortex that was hungrily trying to absorb everything it could. He felt her stiffen, and tried to ease down, not wanting to hurt her.

Jilah cried out, a long, pained wail that cut through the air as she arched against him, nearly breaking free of his grip.

:: *Relax, beloved. Fighting it will only injure you.* ::

Argent felt a flare as something other woke inside her mind, and a cold voice crept through his thoughts, sending a rippling chill skittering up his spine. His mind recoiled instinctively at the sound, but he held fast. He really didn't want to have to deal with another encounter with the squatter in her head again, but had known and accepted the risks of invading her thoughts before he started.

:: *You fill my vessel with useless trivia, blood drinker. It damages her.* ::

Angry at the added distraction, he calmly explained, :: *It is her choice. It is also essential for her survival, where we are going.* ::

A strange chittering sound echoed through his thoughts as the voice replied, :: *She is foolish to have agreed to such a thing.* :: The voice was dismissive and more than a little disdainful.

This bitch is really beginning to become irksome, he thought to himself, angrily. However, Argent had no desire to start a conflict with the denizen in his lover's head, guessing that it would likely rip Jilah apart in the process. He was also uncertain of the outcome of such an encounter and was in no hurry to find out what would happen. Trying to keep his tone level, he was reminded of the kind of patience necessary when explaining things to a petulant child.

:: *Nevertheless, due to the fact that this is extremely unfamiliar, not to mention painful to her, could you possibly see your way clear to helping her mind slowly accept what she's so greedily yanking from me instead of haranguing me about it?* ::

There was silence for the space of two beats, and Argent growled, :: *If this exchange permanently damages her, she will no longer be able to provide you with what you desire.* ::

When it came down to brass tacks, most of the parasitic creatures that he'd encountered reacted in their own best interests when faced with the possibility of losing their meal ticket. He still wasn't certain of the nature of the connection between this entity and his lover, and he hoped that he'd played his cards right.

Suddenly Jilah slumped against him, a trickle of dark red blood trailing from her nose as her head dropped back onto his shoulder. He felt the connection ease down, the hungry pull of his lover's mind relaxing, wrestling less as the rest of the information finally slid home at a less frantic pace.

:: *It is done, blood drinker. Bear in mind that I only allow your presence because it eases her spirit, making her a more focused weapon. Be aware that if you become a liability, we will have words.* ::

Argent slid free of his lover's mind, pulling away from her neck and moving out from behind her to gently lay her back on the bed. A soft mewling sound bubbled out of Jilah's throat, and he blurred to the bathroom, returning with a cool washcloth and gently dabbed her face. Her movements were groggy, as if she'd been heavily sedated.

Or had just had the crap beaten out of her, he thought to himself, wincing.

His expression was dark with worry as Jilah's eyes slowly fluttered open, her voice a dry croak as she murmured in a voice that sounded so very small, "I thought you said it wouldn't hurt."

His gut twisted sharply as he looked down at her, hoping desperately that she wouldn't pass out. Suddenly, the sound of somebody pounding on the front door trailed down the stairs. He frowned and reached out with his senses to see what who causing the infernal racket and froze when he realized who it was, now angry that they had arrived a night early.

Although, he thought, *perhaps they can help, now that they're here.*

He glanced back at Jilah, who was now grimacing in discomfort as she groaned "Too much, dammit. It's too much. Ow, ow, ow."

She clutched at her head and rolled over onto her side, tears beginning to spill onto the sheets underneath her. Migraine didn't even begin to cover the amount of pain that was racing around in her head. God, it felt as if she'd been split open. And it only seemed to be getting worse.

Argent let out a small noise of frustration and blurred upstairs to the front door, opening it wide and growled, "I have neither the time nor the inclination at the moment to inquire as to why you're a full night early. Get inside."

Mira and Aurelian quickly stepped into the house, followed by a third individual that Argent didn't recognize; a tall boy with intense grey eyes and a shock of short, silver-toned hair that spiked out from his head in an unruly, jagged mess. Sharp edges of what looked like intricate tribal work crept along his skin from beneath the royal blue tank top he was wearing, trailing over the boy's overly muscular shoulders and down well-defined arms. Veins stood out like cables under the intricate designs. Below the knees of baggy black canvas bondage shorts that came down to just above his knees, Argent could see bands of what appeared to be derivative Maori symbols. A beaten up pair of black calf-high grinders graced the boy's feet, the steel of the toes poking out behind some of the torn, scruffy spots in the leather.

He didn't look older than seventeen, albeit very big for his age, but he fairly crackled with energy. As the boy walked inside, his steps were precise and deliberate – a total economy of movement. Enormous, leathery wings the color of stone masonry quivered slightly at his back.

Argent raised an eyebrow and hooked a thumb in the pocket of his leather pants, tasting the boy's scent, his eyes narrowing as he quietly asked, "And this would be?"

Mira gave a slight bow, her tone formal as she replied, "Strigaisha," she made a gesture towards the boy, "This is Brigliadoro's hatchling, Orlando. The Guardian wanted to ensure your safe passage in the event that you decided to accompany us back to the city."

There was an intelligence behind those grey eyes that betrayed the true age of the creature before him as the boy addressed him in a low, guttural rumble. "Le pére envoie ses salutations, Strigaisha, et souhaite..."

Argent smiled thinly, interrupting the boy as he held up a hand and quietly asked, "In English, please?"

The boy nodded slowly, and replied, "Father sends his greetings and has urged us to escort you within the borders of the province within the next fourty-eight hours, for your own safety."

As Orlando finished, Argent felt a strange weight behind the boy's words, knowing that it was rare when such creatures decided to speak. Gargoyles rarely had use for words. They were beings who preferred action in lieu of other forms of communication.

Argent sighed, then glared over at Mira and Aurelian, his voice sharp as he said, "So you now assume that the decision has been taken out of my hands?"

It was Aurelian who answered, his eyes glittering as he stepped forward and said, "The situation is getting really nasty, man. The guardian seems certain that somebody will try to tap you before you're able to reach New Orleans."

Mira quietly added, "The Sisters are leaving a deliberate trail that currently leads north to Georgia. The fact that they were able to eliminate Judiana so easily has bolstered their confidence, but thankfully they are also being careless. Their current behavior is strangely erratic, which defies all explanation, but it appears that they will try to act against you next."

Why the hell would The Sisters move against him? He'd completely removed himself from the game long enough ago that he shouldn't be seen as a viable threat to anybody anymore. Did they know something that he didn't? What exactly had been going on over the last couple of months? This was the last thing he needed.

"I see. At the moment, there is another, more immediate matter that needs to be tended to. Aurelian, I have need of your services."

Argent turned on his heel, heading back to the basement. As he reached the bottom of the stairs, he looked over towards the bed. Jilah was mewling piteously, her feet jittering in fits against the sheets. Her other hand clutched at her forehead. Waves of pain radiated off her. Aurelian took a step into the room and paused, eyes widening as he spotted her.

Argent was immediately at her side, taking her hand from her forehead and dabbing gently at it with a moist cloth, his voice sharp as he waved Aurelian over and snapped, "She needs to eat."

Aurelian nodded, stripping out of his shirt as he strode to the bed. His bronzed skin seemed to glow as he looked over at Argent expectantly, dropping the shirt to the floor as he quietly asked, "Where do you want me?"

Argent moved behind Jilah, raising her up as he reached out to grasp the blonde's wrist, gently pulling it over to her.

"Her kiss does not have the same affect that mine does, so this will probably hurt."

Aurelian's answering smile was gentle and fond as he replied, "It's okay." His voice became a breathy whisper, "She really is a looker, Strigaisha."

Argent responded with a sad smile as he raised Jilah's head up, pressing her lips against Aurelian's wrist. He leaned into her and purred, "Drink, love."

Jilah shivered, letting out a shaky breath before sinking sharp teeth into the proffered wrist. She growled as she tore into warm, tanned skin, drinking deep. The nauseating din in her mind slowly quieted, letting her focus on the delicious crimson fluid as it slid down her throat, noticing that it tasted different. It was somehow richer, warmer – and it sent a lively zing of energy through her as her other hand reached out to clutch at the waist of Aurelian's jeans, gripping tightly and pulling him closer as she moaned against his wrist.

Argent watched Aurelian's head rock back, the blond man's breath coming out in a sharp hiss as Jilah fed from him. After a few moments, her eyes slid open and she roared, tossing Aurelian across the room. He impacted with the wall, knocking a sizable indentation into a section of the drywall that had previously remained unmarred. Jilah scrambled to the other side of the bed, a low growl in her throat as blood dripped from her lips, staining the sheets in a dotted line.

Aurelian was getting to his feet, chuckling as Mira appeared at the bottom of the stairs with an angry scowl. "Wow. She packs quite a kick for a kid." Aurelian's lips curled in a loopy grin as he laughed and asked, "She okay?"

Jilah shook her head, eyes narrowing, darting back and forth from the blond to the woman at the foot of the stairs. Her head swam as she tried to figure out exactly what was going on. She looked over at Argent and snapped, "What the fuck are they doing in my house? Much less, in my bedroom!?" The feeling of vulnerability was overwhelming.

Argent held his hands up in a placatory gesture and explained, "You needed to feed. The transfer took more out of you than I expected."

Jilah swatted at him angrily, growling, "And you thought it would be fine and dandy to just call them over? Christ, couldn't you have found somebody off the street to bring home?"

:: *There was not time, beloved..* :: before he could finish, Mira let out a nasty laugh.

The woman's tone was acidic as she asked, "Trouble in paradise? Already?"

Oh hell no. There is no way this bitch is just going to waltz into MY bedroom as if she belongs here and start shit.

Jilah set her mouth in a grim line as she blurred over to Mira and wrapped lengthening claws around the woman's throat. To her horrified surprise, Mira's head began separating from her shoulders with a wet squelching sound. Jilah screamed, backpedaling in earnest, desperately trying to get away from the woman whose head was now sliding free of her torso.

A wet, crimson mess of what looked very much like internal organs quivered and glistened beneath the woman's head as it floated in the air, the rest of her body slumping to the floor with a thump. Argent sighed in irritation as an unearthly, painful shriek rang through the room. He leapt toward Mira's liberated head as it darted menacingly towards Jilah who was now backed up against the wall, eyes wide as her clawed hands scrabbled furiously at the wall behind her.

Utterly terrified and running on automatic pilot now, Jilah ripped her way through the drywall, pulling out chunks of concrete from behind her. Her thoughts were feverish as the head darted towards her again.

"MIRA!" Argent roared, his tone commanding as he placed himself between them.

Aurelian, still on the floor, was now clutching at his stomach and laughing hysterically at the mayhem unfolding before him. Argent's balled his hands into fists and thundered, "MIRA STAND DOWN!"

The disembodied head, looking extremely irritated, backed off, organs and intestines writhing in a sickening, wet collection beneath it.

Jilah's voice was tight and high-pitched as she cried, "What the fuck is she? What the FUCK did you let in my house??"

She shivered and glared over at him as she pulled her fingers free of the concrete blocks at her back. She'd made a rather impressive dent in the masonry.

Her fingers were bleeding now, and she cradled her hands against her chest as her body began coming down from the surge of adrenaline that flooded her system. Her fingers began to throb and she winced at the sharpness of the pain. Argent glared at Aurelian, who was still on the floor shaking his head and giggling, before turning to face her and explaining, "She's a Penanngalan, the last of her kind."

For a moment, the association clicked. Jilah had remembered reading up on the Malaysian vampire type, but clean, typed print in a book didn't do justice to the truly nauseating reality, and absolutely nothing had been mentioned about that shriek that had torn into Jilah's psyche either. The glistening organs under the head were now sliding back into their home in the tiny body on the floor, making wet shlucking sounds as they slithered back into the top of the woman's torso.

Jilah brought a hand to her mouth and began heaving at the sight. She dropped to her knees, loudly vomiting a large crimson puddle onto the carpet. The pain in her fingers was slowly receding, but it still hurt to hold herself up and away from the now befouled carpet. Argent sighed softly before snapping at Aurelian,who was slowly recovering, his breath coming in hitches now.

"Go upstairs and send Orlando down. She'll need to eat again now."

Argent frowned, kneeling at Jilah's side as she retched, reaching down and pulling her hair out of the way. Aurelian quickly got to his feet and ran upstairs, still chuckling. In between heaves, Jilah tried to speak, her words coming out in between gulps of air, "What. Is. So. Damned. Funny?"

She lurched as another splash of red hit the carpet, and Argent winced as he answered, "Aurelian has a strange sense of humor. Pay him no mind."

Mira got to her feet, her tone nasty as she brushed herself off and spat, "You really mean to take this easily nauseated stripling as your Striaga? They'll tear her apart."

The woman's torso was covered with a clear, viscous fluid, making sections of the crimson silk dress she was wearing cling to her wetly. "And this dress is ruined now," she muttered while trying to scrape off some of the goo.

There was a blur of motion, as Mira's head snapped back, almost sliding out of her torso again as she flew across the room and hit the wall on the opposite side.

Argent stood utterly still next to the space she'd occupied, clawed hands flexing and eyes narrowing as he quietly said, "I will brook no disobedience, Bourreau du Rebelle. You will show her the respect due her title, or I'll strip you of yours and leave you for The Sisters themselves to deal with."

Mira slowly pushed herself to a kneeling position, wiping blood from her mouth and answering, "I see you haven't lost your touch, Strigaisha," her tone ironic as she spat into the carpet.

His voice was clipped and cold as he responded, "You would do well to remember that."

He turned back to Jilah, who was now sitting up and glaring at him.

"I'm glad we're leaving soon. You guys are wrecking my house," Jilah complained, wincing at the sight of the pools of blood at her side and wondering if she should even bother trying to clean it, or whether she should just have new carpet installed. Although, if they were leaving for a long while, the state of the carpet probably wouldn't matter. She sighed as she realized that the blood would attract bugs and rodents. Lovely. She tried not to think too hard about it.

Aurelian appeared at the foot of the stairs as Jilah began wiping her mouth clean. When she tried to stand up, her vision swam and she threw up again. Aurelian shook his head slowly, padding over to help Mira to her feet. Orlando stepped into view, slowly assessing the scene before him.

He turned towards Argent and asked him something in a language that Jilah couldn't understand. Argent padded over to Jilah, picking her up as he reminded the boy, "English, Orlando."

"What do you require of me?" The boy asked again, standing still and awaiting orders.

Argent padded over to the bed and gently set Jilah down. "Nourishment." He murmured as he motioned the boy over.

Orlando slowly walked to the bed, his eyes devoid of emotion as he extended a wrist to Argent in silence.

Argent quietly said, "Orlando, I would present my Striaga, Jilah. It is for her."

The boy's brow furrowed for a moment as he processed the information, then his expression became empty again as he moved to offer his wrist down to her.

Jilah watched the exchange with wide eyes, not quite sure how to react to this large, winged alternative club kid standing in front of her. She opened her mouth to politely refuse, but before she could speak, she frowned at the realization that it would be the very height of rudeness to do so. Somehow, she knew that she had been granted a great honor, but she wasn't quite sure why she knew. Her head began to hurt, and she winced as Argent's voice drifted through her thoughts, his tone soft as he explained, :: *It is part of the benefit of the transfer. When you feed, it will become clearer. The headache should go away as well.* ::

Unbidden, foreign words began to come to her; a respectful acceptance of this gift. Jilah looked up into the eyes of the tall, silver-haired boy and breathed, "Through you I gain nourishment and protection. Through me you gain purpose. May our feet always meet on the same path, Orlando." She blinked as she finished speaking, weirded out by what she'd said and now entirely certain that she didn't want to feed off this boy.

Unfortunately, now that the offer had been made and accepted, she realized that she had to follow through for protocol's sake, if for nothing else. That she knew this didn't help explain things in the larger sense. She sighed and reached up to wrap delicate alabaster fingers around the boy's wrist, steeling herself before pulling it down to her mouth and gently biting down.

The boy's essence burned as it splashed on her tongue, and she cried out against his skin, her body thrumming with heat as she drank. Power shook its way through her, causing her stomach to clench almost painfully. Orlando's expression never changed as he slowly turned to watch the stairs.

After a few moments, Jilah pulled away, unable to take any more. She trembled as she looked up at Argent, her pupils dilated out to the point where the whites of her eyes had disappeared entirely behind them. Argent's skin now seemed to shine with an inner glow, his eyes blazing like emerald coals as he sat down on the bed beside her. Jilah flinched as his hand touched her shoulder, then relaxed as she became transfixed by the intricate violet latticework that seemed to wrap around him. Little bright points of shooting light zigged in and out of the pattern, holding it all together. She reached out to touch his face with an awed expression, her voice a quiet whisper as her fingers pushed through the design to touch him.

She traced a finger along his jawline and breathed, "So beautiful." She slowly cocked her head to the side and asked, "What is it?"

Argent frowned, unsure of what she was referring to. "What do you see?"

Jilah smiled, her face joyous and radiant as she breathed, "It's purple. Something purple surrounds you, like a woven pattern or design. What is it?"

Mira's jaw dropped, and Argent gently moved his lover's hand away from his face, lacing her fingers in his as he asked, "What else do you see?"

"Everything about you just blazes. It's like you have a fire burning behind your eyes and just underneath your skin." She shivered slightly as she leaned into him, her voice dreamy as she purred, "You're so beautiful it makes me ache."

Argent smiled as he wrapped an arm around her and nuzzled her cheek. He sighed and turned to the trio behind him, asking, "What do you see when you look at them?"

She frowned, peering across the room and letting out a small gasp. The ghostly image of an enormous, craggy stone creature with sharp, granite horns, talons, and enormous wings shimmered around Orlando, while Aurelian seemed to be covered in a wet, shiny brown pelt, his hands and feet ending in furry, webbed claws. Mira was surrounded by a pattern similar to Argent's, but hers was darker, almost black. Jilah quickly looked away, her expression distressed. It was apparent that she was having a difficult time processing what she was seeing. It didn't help that it was all being presented so quickly. Jilah had the distinct feeling that she had once again been unceremoniously dumped into a whirling pool and expected to swim effortlessly. It seemed to be happening quite a bit, lately.

Argent leaned into her, sliding his arm around her waist as he murmured, "It's all right. I'm afraid that you're going to be running into that a fair amount over the course of the next few days."

Jilah trembled at his touch as a warm radiance flowed down her spine, tickling parts of her that made her moan softly. It brought a pale pink sheen to her skin.

Argent turned and quietly said, "Leave us."

Aurelian and Orlando made their way to the stairs, and Mira followed, calling back, "We should probably leave soon. We don't know who else might already be on their way here."

Argent nodded and turned back to his lover, who was now gripping his leg in a death lock, her clawed fingers digging into his black leather pants. "Jilah."

She flinched and turned to look up at him, asking in a shaky voice, "What's happening to me?" She plucked her claws from his leg, cradling her hand to her chest.

"You need to bleed off a little energy. Unfortunately, I believe Orlando's blood was a little too intense for your system. It sometimes happens that way with Gargoyles."

Jilah laughed weakly, her voice sounding distant as she murmured, "So that's what he is."

Argent nodded slowly, letting his lips graze her shoulder.

"And Aurelian?"

He explained, "His kind are referred to as the Selkie. They are essentially seals that can become human."

A surge of electricity zipped up her spine. She grinned and began to writhe slowly and sinuously, like a cat in heat. She heard what he was saying, but the only thing that mattered at this moment was having his hands on her.

"Please, just touch me." She begged, falling back to the bed and arching her back against the mattress groaning. As his hand slid over her stomach, she hissed and clawed at the bed.

"Good god," she moaned as a little more of her rational brain kicked in, "It's all so overwhelming. My cortex is gonna short out."

Argent slid next to her, trailing gentle fingers along her collarbone and kissing her shoulder softly. "I know. I'll do what I can to make it easier; less disorienting."

Jilah closed her eyes and let out a shaky breath. "I feel like I'm being pulled apart by my emotions over everything. I don't know how much more I can take. I'm doing the best I can, but..." She let out a sob. Was it really less than a week ago that she was blissfully unaware of everything but her new job?

It seemed like months, no – surely years had passed since she'd met him.

Argent sighed softly and rested his forehead on her shoulder. "I am sorry, Jilah."

Tears rolled down her cheeks as she leaned into him and breathed, "I want so badly to be strong, to be able to shoulder this entire thing effortlessly, to be what you need; 'cause god knows I'm starting to think you're damned near everything I need. Or want."

"Shhh" Argent cooed, pulling her into his arms and nuzzling her gently. "You are strong, beloved. Stronger than you give yourself credit for. It will be difficult, but this will be a fire that will temper you, allowing you to better see those strengths and utilize them. I have a great deal of faith in you; otherwise I would not have sought you out."

Jilah shook her head, muttering, "Mira's right. I'm squeamish, and.."

Argent cut her off, growling, "Mira is a jealous, temperamental bitch, among other things. Take nothing she says to heart. It is spite that prompts her to say the things she does, not insight. She can be extremely immature for her age at times."

He smiled and met her gaze, gently running a thumb along her lower lip. The radiant smile returned to her face as she was again overwhelmed by his beauty and the affect his touch had on her.

"Just kiss me, dammit. Then do what you need to do to yank some of this excess crap out of me. I feel like I'm on a psychoactive chemical of some sort. I'll figure out the rest afterwards." He laughed softly and leaned into her. "Your every wish is my command, my lady."

Argent frowned as he held his pants up to the light, grumbling, "I do believe that you now owe me a new pair."

Jilah laughed as she pulled on a black and purple snake skin leather bodice with silver buckles down the front, then reached for a set of matching leather pants with laces going up the sides. If she had to leave, she was going to leave in style.

"It's about time." She wrinkled her nose as she mused, "I'm not sure I want to know how long you've been wearing them continuously. You never seem to dress in anything else."

She had pulled her hair back into a braid that swayed gently against her back as she moved around the room.

Argent shrugged and answered, "It's a look I like. It favors me, I think."

Jilah buckled the corset up with a sly grin. "I would definitely have to agree. Although your look could use a little variety."

He began slowly sliding the damaged pants back on, his voice playful as he asked, "And what else would you have me wear?"

The grin became a little wider as she walked over to him, trailing gentle fingers down his back as she answered, "Most of the time, I think I'm happiest when you wear nothing at all."

Argent let out a mock gasp. "So bold. I do believe I've created a monster." He sighed softly as she stepped behind him, snaking her hands around his waist and pressing into him. Her hands began to wander down his torso and he chuckled.

"A monster, definitely."

Jilah gently plucked at the dark line of fur that crept up his stomach. He stepped free of her embrace and chided, "Now, now. Remember, we have guests upstairs waiting."

She sighed and turned to look at the holes in the walls. The place was a wreck. "You're right. We need to get out of here." A frown darkened her features as she shook her head and groaned, "I'm really going to hate leaving all this stuff here, dammit."

"It can't be helped, unfortunately. We need to get to New Orleans within the next twenty-four hours. Besides," He collected his tank top from the bed and pulled it over his head, "I'm sure we'll be able to rebuild your collection shortly after we arrive."

Jilah gave him a sidelong glance and a mock pout, "We'd better." She grabbed a pair of purple snake-skin boots with silver buckles running up the sides and slid them on.

Argent smiled, laughing lightly. "I will also send someone up to collect the rest of your wardrobe. I know what a clotheshorse you are. Would I let you suffer such an ignominious fate?"

With a look of mock annoyance, Jilah tossed his jacket at him and said, "Just get upstairs, smartass."

She collected her jacket from the bed as Argent picked up two suitcases and a purple duffel bag. They were packed near to bursting, full of clothing and boots. She blurred towards the stairs, calling back, "I have a few things to take care of on the upper floor. I should be down in a couple minutes, OK?"

:: *Anything I can help with?* ::

His voice echoed through her mind as she walked into the upstairs computer room.

:: *Nah. I got it.* :: She smiled to herself as she began disconnecting the laptop and placing it into a stainless steel crash case she had gotten for it, tossing the rest of the cables and external drives into foam storage slots. She then collected the removable drives from the servers and placed them in the case as well. She didn't want somebody wandering in and going through the incriminating information on them. Once that was finished, she headed back downstairs, setting everything down by the front door. Jilah turned at the sound of an appreciative whistle behind her.

Aurelian was leaning against the wall in the foyer. His grin was heated as he looked her over and raised an eyebrow. He hadn't put his shirt back on and hooked a thumb into the top of his jeans, then slowly slid a bronzed finger along the line of his zipper.

She had to admit that the man was attractive, but his personality and attitude completely ruined it, in her opinion. His openly lewd behavior didn't help any, either.

Jilah muttered, "Are you usually this much of a lounge lizard, or do you have to work at it?" She had always been irritated by men that knew how attractive they were and ended up being cocky pricks about it.

Mira stepped into view from the hallway, chuckling. "Sounds like she's got you all figured out."

The woman had cleaned up and changed into a black silk chimsong dress with a beautifully detailed emerald dragon curling down around the hip. The sides had slits that went almost up to her hips, exposing a great deal of shapely leg. Her black and emerald stiletto heels clicked lightly on the tile as she moved to stand beside him.

Her companion's grin broadened, his eyes sparkling as he rumbled, "You're just jealous because you don't look nearly as good as she does right now."

Mira shrugged, her voice casual as she answered, "She's not interested." She gave a noncommittal sigh as her eyes rested on Jilah. "Besides, I get the feeling that she's the monogamous type."

Coming from her, the word sounded like an insult. Argent appeared at the top of the stairs, two more suitcases in his arms as he joked in a sarcastic voice, "Are you quite sure you don't want to take the entire closet?"

Jilah grinned and playfully growled, "Don't be such a pussy about it. Surely a big, strapping man like yourself can carry ten times that amount."

He chuckled and looked over at Mira, asking, "I assume Orlando's keeping watch over the conveyance?"

She replied with a quiet nod, the ghost of a smile playing at the edges of her lips as she looked towards the door.

Argent looked over at Aurelian and chuckled before walking over to Jilah and raising an eyebrow, "I'm surprised. The three of you alone in a room together, and no signs of violence. Maybe this won't be such a bad trip after all."

Jilah rolled her eyes at him as she shrugged into a black leather motorcycle jacket, then leaned down to pick up the suitcases of electronic equipment at her feet. "Shall we?"

Sixteen

Leaving the Past Behind

Jilah took several steps out the front door before coming to an abrupt stop, dropping the luggage at her feet. An enormous flat black custom tour bus was parked in front of the house. She blinked and stared at it as Mira and Aurelian smoothly navigated around her. There didn't seem to be any windows on the bus, except for those in the driver's compartment. Argent stopped beside her, peering at her with a strange expression.

"Is something wrong?" he asked, gently placing the suitcases on the ground.

"A tour bus?" She blinked. "We're driving down to New Orleans in an oversized recreational vehicle?"

It wasn't a bad idea, now that she thought of it. As long as they didn't wreck during the day, Argent would probably be fine. A nasty thought occurred to her, and she winced as she asked, "Wait, I'm going to have to put up with Heckle and Jeckle all the way down the eastern seaboard?"

Argent looked over at the vehicle and shrugged, casually responding, "It shouldn't be too bad. They travel well, from what I remember."

Jilah looked back at him, horrified as she stammered, "Shouldn't be too bad? Need I remind you that every time I'm near that bitch she ends up saying something snotty that makes me want to break her nose? Not to mention," she waved in Aurelian's direction, "sex boy over there."

She blinked again, then asked, "And what about the bike?"

"That might be a bit of a problem." Argent replied.

On this, she was definitely going to stand her ground. She squared her shoulders and grated, "Ohhh no. I'll leave without the rest of it; the cars, the rest of the clothes, the bed frame – but I'm not leaving the Panhead."

Jilah set her jaw, her eyes narrowing as she watched Aurelian follow Mira into the depths of the tour bus. She actually wasn't at all okay with leaving the Karmann Ghia behind either, but the Panhead would be easier to navigate through traffic, and the idea of driving the Ghia all the way down to New Orleans terrified her. No – if the Ghia moved, they'd have to actually ship it or put it in a covered trailer.

Argent thought about it for a moment, then asked, "Do you trust anyone else riding it down?"

Jilah stared at him as if he'd grown a second head. "And just who exactly did you have in mind?"

Aurelian popped his head out of the bus, then hopped down and started walking towards them. At least he'd put a shirt on.

Jilah looked back over at Argent with a mild expression, "Please tell me you're joking."

Aurelian walked up and presented them with an amused grin, asking, "Strigaisha. How can I be of service?"

"Wow. Uh, yeah, this isn't going to work for me. Tell ya what. I'll follow you guys, how does that sound? 'Cause that's sounding pretty good to me right now."

Jilah quickly picked up her bags and began heading towards the black bus. "Yep, I like this plan. It's both bold and brilliant in its sheer simplicity."

Argent let out a small sigh of frustration as he directed Aurelian to collect the suitcases at his feet. "You are being unreasonable," he called out.

Aurelian collected the bags and walked back towards the baggage compartment on the side of the bus.

Jilah blinked several times, wondering if she'd heard him correctly. She then turned and glared at him, "On the contrary, I think I'm being exceptionally reasonable, considering everything that's happened in the last several days."

She did have a point. Argent shook his head slowly and walked towards her as Aurelian opened a side hatch on the tour bus, revealing a space easily large enough for twice the amount of baggage they had. Jilah tossed two of the enormous suitcases inside, then stalked off towards the garage with the stainless steel laptop case and the duffel bag.

Aurelian chuckled as he placed the other two bags into the compartment. "You always were a sucker for the headstrong ones," he murmured as he slammed the metal door shut, giving Argent a sympathetic look as he walked past him and leaned back up against the bus with a wry grin.

Argent glared back at Aurelian as he made his way over towards the garage, then looked up to see a figure perched on the roof. Orlando was poised at the edge of the shingles, hands in his pockets and a lit cigarette between his lips as he stared off into the distance. Argent took a slow breath and began walking towards the garage, knowing that Brigliadoro had only the best intentions in sending his offspring to guard him.

It would, however, be nice if his hatchling's behavior wasn't so obvious. The boy wasn't even shielding his appearance. At least there were no other neighbors around.

Jilah had gotten the garage door up and was kicking a leg over the motorcycle as she pulled the helmet from the handlebars. She kick-started the bike and slipped the helmet on, backing the motorcycle out of the garage with a determined expression. Argent watched as she carefully navigated around the bus, an eyebrow crooking up as she revved the motorcycle and rumbled loudly through the garbage in the front yard, bouncing in the seat as the bike bounced over the curb. She brought it around, coming to a stop by the mailbox out front.

Argent sauntered over to her, thumbs in his pockets as he sent, :: I can't talk you out of this, can I? ::

Jilah grinned, shaking her head slowly. :: I prefer to travel by motorcycle, and if I end up in that damned bus with those two, bad things will happen. TRUST me on this. ::

As he walked up to her, Jilah slid a finger through one of his belt loops and pulled him towards her. "You could always ride down with me."

Argent raised an eyebrow, his tone mild as he replied, "One, as you well know, the sun and I don't get along too well. Two, that monstrous vehicle over there is covered in glyphs and wards in order to insure that we're able to travel undetected. I'd be a risk to all of us if I stayed out in the open."

Jilah frowned suspiciously, her voice low as she asked, "What aren't you telling me?"

Argent gave her an even look, his voice quiet as he answered, "Those who destroyed Judiana now appear to be heading this way. I believe they mean to do the same to me before I can get to New Orleans."

Jilah's eyes went wide, her tone angry as she growled, "Well now is a great time to tell me. Why didn't you say something earlier?"

Argent shrugged. "I didn't think it would be an issue."

Jilah thought about it for a moment, then replied, "Okay travel in the bus. It should only take, what – seventeen hours of constant driving, right? I haven't taken the Panhead out for a road trip yet, and there's no time like the present."

Aurelian appeared next to them, explaining, "You can't. You reek of him. Both physically and spiritually."

Jilah jumped at the sound of the Selkie's voice, getting entirely too annoyed at this group's penchant for seeming to pop in and out of thin air.

She snapped at him, "What are you, the narrator? Piss off."

Argent nodded, adding, "He's right. The people we're trying to avoid would be able to track you easily. Trust me when I say that you don't want The Sisters targeting you."

Jilah closed her eyes, tightening her fingers on the motorcycle's grips. She was trying so very hard, but it was as if events were conspiring to keep her riding just up to the edge of crazed anger.

It never ends.

She slowly released the grips and rocked back in the seat.

Argent's tone was patient and soothing as he said, "Please. I can arrange to have it either driven or delivered afterwards."

Jilah's eyes snapped open, royal blue irises shining as she glared back at him. Her voice was sharp as she grated, "If there ends up being one – ONE scratch on this fucking ride – or my car, I'll have your head on a pike. Are we clear?"

Argent opened his mouth to speak, and she held a hand up to silence him before revving the engine and roaring back up the lawn and into the garage. The engine cut off, and she walked calmly out of the garage, helmet still on her head as she went around to the side of the house, muttering. She just wanted so badly to hit something. Anything. She was positive that beating the crap out of something would help her bleed off some of the frustration.

Aurelian walked behind Argent as he let out a small sigh and followed. A loud cracking sound echoed through the night and the men gave each other a sidelong glance before bolting around the house to investigate. Two more loud cracks echoed out before the two of them rounded the corner and came to an abrupt stop, nearly bumping into one another at the sight before them. There were several impressive fist-sized holes in the siding of the house now, and Jilah was drawing back for another blow before she noticed them.

Mira blurred to stand next to Argent, and Orlando dropped down from the roof, his boots making a heavy thud as he hit the ground. His wings folded back behind him as he looked over to see what the fuss was about.

Jilah glared at them and snapped, "Can I have a fucking minute?"

She then commenced smashing more holes into the side of the house, her indigo and white braid whipping around as she forcefully slammed her fist into the wooden siding again and again. There was an almost relaxing cadence to her rhythm as she worked, and she punctuated every angry utterance with a fist.

Yes, it was childish, but it was starting to make her feel better.

Mira opened her mouth to say something, but Argent quickly cut her off, growling, "You would be ill-advised to speak."

Better his lover's frustration be directed towards something inert than continuing to eat away at her. If this was what she needed to calm down, he was more than happy to give her the space she needed to do it.

Argent turned and began making his way back to the front of the house. "Just get in the bus."

As they walked along the lawn, Aurelian gave a low whistle and commented, "Man. She's got issues."

Argent's response was harsh. "And I assume that you would handle a similar situation with quiet grace and dignity? You've been a Selkie since birth, Aurelian. She has not had that luxury. A great many things have been dumped on her in a very short period of time. Most of them unpleasant. She has many things to deal with."

Aurelian's eyes widened in honest surprise. "You've changed a lot since we last saw you, Strigaisha."

Mira nodded, adding, "There was a time when you would not have given such a creature a single moment of your precious time."

Argent glared at her as they reached the bus, his voice tight as he responded, "Seventy years in seclusion has affected me in ways that I could not have predicted. Do not, however, make the foolish mistake of thinking that this makes me less capable. Or less dangerous."

Mira lowered her eyes, taking a respectful step back. Were it not for the fact that she was extremely efficient and capable in her duties, he would've eliminated her during his first reign. She could be socially impossible at times and was insolent as hell, but she was a remarkably useful asset. Such individuals were needed to maintain order amongst the sociopaths he would soon be dealing with on a regular basis again. It would also be a shame to remove the last of her kind from the earth, and he couldn't bring himself to do so, yet.

Orlando reached over to open the door for him. Argent climbed up on the first step, his tone stern as he said, "Watch her until she's ready to board. Keep her safe."

The boy nodded and stalked off, walking back towards the side of the house.

Jilah was finally beginning to calm down, now that she'd wrecked a substantial portion of the bleary wood siding of the house. She stood back and surveyed her handiwork, taking a long, deep breath. She spotted Orlando out of the corner of her eye, moving to lick the blood from her knuckles. The silver-haired boy stood silently before her, his posture relaxed, but his eyes were alert.

Jilah reached down to collect the helmet from the ground at her feet, cocking her head as she came up and asked, "You're not much of a talker, are you?" The boy shook his head silently. "Outstanding. The other two talk too damned much."

Jilah strode past him, feeling much better now as she called back, "I guess we'd better head out." She could almost swear she'd spotted a momentary grin.

She then collected the laptop case and duffel bag from the garage and walked over to the bus, closing the garage door behind her. She turned and looked back at the house, feeling a strange sense of loss. Yes, it was a hovel, but this had been her place, her den. It had become home. It felt odd to leave it like this.

As she stepped up into the bus, she couldn't help staring at the overwhelming gaudiness of the main cabin. The interior of the front cabin was a riot of bright splashes of yellow, red, and orange organza fabric draped in jaunty swag swings over black walls with swirls of multicolored glitter. The driver's seat was covered with crimson faux fur and skirted with red tassels and silver bells that quivered and clinked around the bottom of it.

The gearshift and dashboard were covered in a swirl of crimson, yellow, and orange sequins that were encased beneath resin so that the elaborate decoration didn't come off with use. It looked like something that had rolled off the set of a darker, stranger version of Priscilla Queen of the Desert. Jilah peered over at the red and orange dangling fuzz balls that traced the top of the window, her eyes suddenly transfixed by a hula girl in a fiery skirt that was slowly wobbling on a makeshift pedestal that jutted out from the driver's console.

A stunning woman with platinum blond hair pulled into an upswept beehive and wearing a crimson, leopard-spotted cocktail dress winked at her from her perch on the seat and said, "Welcome to our little home away from home, honey. Do you like it?"

The woman's voice was strangely low and smoky, and she spoke with an odd accent that Jilah couldn't quite place.

"It's. Uh. Wow. I don't have words."

Jilah's jaw dropped as she noticed a small picture of the pop singer Madonna depicted as the Virgin Mary accented with colored sequins on the wall above the driver's seat.

"It's very...fiery," she murmured. She then grinned back at the woman and breathed, "It's gorgeous."

The woman positively beamed, extending a large hand with bright swirls of red, yellow and orange polished nails. "I'm so glad you like it! I'm Gigi."

Jilah was actually impressed at how the colors on the woman's nails remained uniform, wondering if they were appliqués instead of actual polish. She dropped her bags and gently shook the woman's hand.

"You have a great eye for color, Gigi."

Flattered, the woman preened, bringing a fluttering hand to her throat as she responded with a regal nod and purred, "I'm honored, Striaga. And may I say that you've got quite the flair for fashion as well, girl." The woman snapped in the air with a flourish.

Jilah grinned, then gave a mock flip of her braid as she gaily replied, "I work with what I've got."

She really liked this woman, for reasons she couldn't quite figure out. Gigi seemed entirely nonthreatening and open, which was definitely a nice change from Mira.

Jilah's tone warmed as she added, "I'm really glad to meet you, Gigi."

At this, the woman laughed and patted gently at her beehive, grey eyes sparkling as she said, "I can't tell you how happy I am that there's another woman on this trip without Permanent Menstrual Syndrome." She cast a mock glance of annoyance towards the door separating the cabin from the rest of the bus and added, "Christ honey, she really needs to take that chip off her shoulder. People will mistake it for unnaturally large dandruff."

Jilah blinked, then laughed, and soon both of them were giggling like schoolgirls. Okay, so maybe the trip wouldn't suck entirely.

Gigi giggled and nodded back towards the door and said, "Well, honey, people will talk if you stay up here. You should probably head on back and get settled, so I can get us started on our happy little dysfunctional journey home."

She reached forward, turning a key, and the floor of the bus suddenly rumbled for a moment under Jilah's feet. The engine sounded much quieter than she'd expected it to for a vehicle of this size.

Jilah nodded, grinning now as she turned to open the door to the interior cabin and called back, "Happy trails. I'll probably come up and bug you again later."

The cabin door led into an entirely different world. She walked into a fair-sized living room, spotting a wet bar over in the corner and a top of the line entertainment center along one of the walls. Argent reclined comfortably on a long, black couch on the other side of the room, his leg cocked up and an elbow resting on his knee.

The tone of his voice was amused as he sent, :: *I see you've found a new friend* ::

Jilah smiled and continued to look around the room. Orlando sat off in a corner, the boy's stone-colored, leathery wings draping over the back of the chair he was sitting in. The cherry on his cigarette brightened as he took a pull on it, the smoke twisting in a slow, sensual pattern in the air above his head as he looked back at her.

Both Mira and Aurelian were suspiciously absent. Jilah raised an eyebrow as she looked back over at Argent.

"Where are the wonder twins?"

He cast a lazy glance towards the hallway behind him, his tone wistful as he replied, "They are currently engaging in a little physical entertainment."

He slid down into the couch a little and placed his hands on his stomach, his grin slow and easy. Jilah winced at the thought, placing the duffel bag and computer case on the floor and walking over to him. She tossed the motorcycle helmet into a plush black chair before shrugging out of her jacket and letting it drop to the floor. Argent shifted on the couch, his grin becoming wicked and heated as he looked back at her.

"Oh no. You're not getting out of an explanation that easily, you undead little sex machine." She stood before him, hands on her hips as she asked, "These 'sisters' that you mentioned earlier. What exactly are they?"

Argent sighed, then moved and gave her room to sit down beside him. Jilah sat on the opposite side of the couch, watching him intently as he explained. "The Sisters have been an annoyance to my kind for centuries. Nobody really knows with any degree of certainty what they are, but it is said that they are each named for the daughters of

Zeus and Themis." Jilah frowned at the reference and he explained, "The Fates of ancient Greek mythology."

"Oh," she replied as she recognized the reference now.

"They're essentially assassins that seem to hunt only those who sustain themselves purely through the consumption of blood. Nobody really knows why. Throughout the years they've been almost meticulously precise about their strikes. This path of random destruction that they've recently engaged in is disquieting, to say the least. They are apparently eliminating every Sanguine they encounter on their way towards us. It is not at all in keeping with their usual methods."

Jilah became still, murmuring, "So that's why everybody showed up early." At least it was a viable explanation for the earlier mayhem back at the house.

Argent gave a solemn nod, his tone serious as he added, "We shouldn't run across them on the way down, but if Mira is correct and they are indeed tracking me, they will undoubtedly head back to New Orleans once our arrival has been announced."

He remained silent for the space of a few beats while Jilah slid her boots off and leaned back into the couch, a stunned expression on her face as she breathed, "Well, you did say it wouldn't be easy." She looked over at him, her expression hopeful as she asked, "Our chances should be better once we get there though, right?"

"One can only hope." He smiled shyly, eyes glittering.

Jilah sighed and slid her feet over to touch his, her toes wiggling against the pads of his feet as she grumbled, "Way to reassure me, there."

Argent peered at her curiously, "You would prefer that I lie to you about such things?"

Jilah gave him a sidelong glance, answering, "No." her tone slightly petulant. "I just wish I had a minute to get my bearings before something else life-altering happened. I know I'll get a handle on it eventually."

With a warm smile, Argent gripped her toes with his and squeezed gently. "You're doing better than you know, Jilah."

She presented him with a shy smile, her eyes sliding away to look across the room as she tried to control the erratic beating of her heart. She cleared her throat and met his gaze again, her head full of so many questions that it seemed to be spinning. There was so much knowledge to process, and since they were going to be cooped up in a tour bus for this unusual road trip, she figured a good way to pass the time would be to start sorting through it all.

Argent spent the next couple of hours patiently answering a barrage of questions about court behavior, mannerisms, and the various factions involved in the current situation. He was becoming increasingly pleased with her progress and her desire to learn as much as she could about the new life she was hurtling headlong towards. It gave him hope for the outcome of the events that would surely unfold upon their arrival in the city.

Eventually she tired of the questions and moved to lean back against him, smiling as he wrapped strong arms around her. Finding herself suddenly exhausted from the night's activities, Jilah turned to snuggle against him, murmuring softly before dropping off to sleep.

Argent leaned down to nuzzle the top of her head, feeling better at this moment than he had in the seventy years since the beginning of his self imposed exile. He sighed softly as his thoughts drifted back to his successor. Judiana had been a stunning, willowy beauty with long, wavy crimson locks and acid green eyes. The first time he'd met her, he had a hard time believing that she could ever have passed for a man. Her face was so delicate and sylvan that he'd almost mistaken her for one of the Fae. He had been the Strigaisha of New Orleans for thirty years when she'd been brought to his attention. She had been presented to him as a very rare, exquisite gift from an earnest supporter.

He could still see her in his mind's eye in that same daring black and red bolero dress, her hair upswept in a dramatic style that left soft little crimson ringlets about her face and neck. He had been quite taken with her beauty and presence. She'd been unusually tall and had moved with a quiet grace that mesmerized him. Only later, when they had retired for the evening, had he discovered her true nature, impressed that she had been able to deceive him so thoroughly. They remained casual lovers up until the day he departed, leaving control of everything in what he felt sure at the time were extremely capable hands. She'd proven to be his equal in many things and had even surpassed him in her leadership abilities, finally counseling him on a variety of matters towards the end. By then, his heart had entirely gone out of the sordid business of politics, whereas she was just beginning to flourish. She'd gone on to do things for the region and her subjects that had filled him with a strong sense of pride, once he'd gained some distance from the immediacy of the events that led up to his abrupt departure.

Although – given his state of mind when he left, he was no longer certain that he could trust the reliability of those particular memories. Argent had always hoped to see her again someday. The abrupt news of her death had stunned him.

Jilah shifted gently against him and he relaxed, happy to have her at his side but still melancholy about the losses of the past. He also found himself wondering about exactly what they were both going to have to face when they finally arrived in the city. He closed his eyes and let his thoughts drift, wanting to remember the past for a while.

Argent woke to the sound of Aurelian's voice, unaware that he had fallen asleep. The Selkie was peering down at him with a concerned expression, a towel wrapped tightly around his waist. Mira stood behind him in a crimson silk teddy.

"There's something that you need to see."

Aurelian sounded anxious, and he clutched at the corner of the towel, wet golden hair sticking to his bronzed shoulders as he bent down to pick up the remote control for the television, clicking it on. Jilah moaned softly, but remained sleeping as Argent gently shifted on the couch. He kept an arm around her while he watched the image come into focus. A female reporter stood with her hand to her ear in front of what looked like the aftermath of a bombing.

Smoke rose in great billowing clouds behind her, and the image canted to the left as the camera jerked, then righted itself. In a voice that sounded entirely too rehearsed and professional, the reporter did her best to explain the situation as events unfolded. The text ticker at the bottom of the screen identified the transmission as coming from New Orleans, Louisiana.

"I'm now standing in front of the ruins of Templeman III in the Orleans Parish Prison compound." She turned and gestured to the mess of smoking rubble behind her. "Earlier today, the serenity of this bustling tourist metropolis was ripped to pieces in what appears to be a devastating terrorist attack. As of yet, no groups have stepped forward to claim responsibility for the act, but Emergency personnel and police investigators are doing all they can to help the injured and to track down those responsible for this heinous deed." The woman then went on to briefly explain the history behind the building itself before hawkishly yanking frightened people in front of the camera to share their opinions about the incident.

Aurelian turned the sound down and looked back at him. Argent gazed up at the Selkie, nonplussed as he quietly asked, "And?"

Aurelian frowned, then quickly explained, "In the last ten years, a section of that building had been reinforced and converted into a safe house of sorts for the Tribe of the Savage Moon. They've been using it as a place to instruct pups that were hitting puberty. It was the largest sanctuary that the pack could find that could safely contain them throughout their first shift."

He looked up at Aurelian, his voice low as he asked, "Has this sort of nonsense been happening a lot?"

Aurelian looked over at Mira who quietly replied, "There have been threats, Strigaisha, but nothing like this. It is an abomination to resort to such garish human methods." Her expression hardened as she spat, "It is laziness. There is no skill to it."

Aurelian interjected, "Julian Gautreaux, the rogue leader of a faction of wolves that split from the Tribe, has been making waves about the leadership of the city for a while now. He's been preaching about the need for shifter leadership in the province. It's his opinion that because the wolves have greater numbers than the other preternaturals in the city limits, they should have the right to rule by default."

Argent frowned. "There's always somebody that isn't happy with the current power structure..."

Aurelian nodded, but explained, "Yes, but this is the first time that the violence has spilled over into the mundane world in such an open fashion. It's as if they're daring the council themselves to come and deliberate – in their favor, of course."

Argent let out a sharp laugh, "Fools."

Jilah's eyes slid open, roused by the sound of the conversation. She kept a careful eye on Aurelian as he began to pace slowly, his demeanor completely changed as he rattled off state affairs. Any remnants of the old, playful surfer boy personality had vanished as he spoke and he affected a flat, businesslike tone as he continued to explain the situation. It didn't sound good.

Argent let out a weary sigh, and Jilah leaned her head onto his shoulder, wanting to comfort him.

Aurelian continued, "Only an element of true fear can effectively quell what has quickly turned into an explosive situation. Your ability to dominate through applied terror tactics is something that the dissenters will dread and be forced to respect. There are no current residents with your particular ability, even though there are now twenty of the Sanguine that permanently reside within the prefecture."

Upon hearing this news, Argent blinked. Such numbers were unheard of during his reign; but then again, only five of his kind had roamed the city in his time. Now there were twenty?

It's a wonder there aren't open confrontations on the street nightly. The Sanguine tended to be very territorial when it came to their feeding grounds, and understandably so. But times had apparently changed.

Jilah raised her head, wiping the sleep out of the corner of an eye as she asked, "Is that a lot? It doesn't sound like a lot."

Aurelian turned towards her, his demeanor still all business as he replied, "It was decided long ago to keep the numbers of the Sanguine within city limits low so that confrontations remained at a minimum. There are several establishments throughout the city that now cater to them, for this very reason."

Mira spoke up then, adding, "Even before this detestable action, Julian was a high-profile suspect in Judiana's death. At the very least he has a well-honed sense of self preservation – he went underground when my people went looking for him. Nobody seems to know his current location, and no manner of persuasion is bringing us closer to finding him."

Jilah sat up and stretched, offhandedly commenting, "Sounds like a charming guy."

Feeling the pull of the rising sun, Argent slowly sat up, placing his elbows on his knees. "Enough for one night. We'll discuss this more in depth when I rise tonight. I leave the rest of our trip in your capable hands."

He rose from the couch, taking Jilah's hand and gently pulling her to her feet. She smiled and leaned into him, and Mira murmured, "There's a proofed container in the back, should we run into trouble during the day, Strigaisha."

Argent wrapped an arm around Jilah's waist, letting her dip down to collect her bags before giving Mira a nod as they strode towards the back hallway to bed down for the day. Argent stepped up to a door at the end of the hall and opened it into a lush bedroom that was colored in similar tones as the living room section. A large steel trunk with sleek, curved edges sat off in a corner.

Jilah placed her metal case and duffel bag on the floor and looked over at him. Her lover looked exhausted, but then he usually did when the sun was close to breaking across the horizon. Jilah swept him into her arms and walked over to the bed. Argent rested his head on her shoulder with a drowsy smile before she pulled back the covers, gently setting him down on teal sheets.

Within moments, he became utterly still and Jilah shivered. She still wasn't used to seeing him like this and hoped that she could bunch the covers between them so that she could get some sleep without being kept awake by the now-familiar chill that rolled off him in little wisps while he was down for the day. Perhaps if she got an electric blanket?

She stripped out of her clothing and padded over to her duffel bag, pulling out a pair of soft black shorts and a black t-shirt, shrugging into them before walking back over to the bed and climbing in next to him. Maybe after a good day's sleep, everything wouldn't look so bleak.

Yeah, she thought to herself as she snuggled down into the covers, *and maybe I'll get a job riding a whale at Marine Land.*

Seventeen

First Night in New Orleans

Jilah slowly roused from a deep sleep, surprised to find herself in an empty bed. The covers pooled around her legs as she sat up and yawned. She perked up at the sounds of quiet conversation in the next room. More politics. Jilah sighed and slowly climbed out of bed, wondering how close they were to the city as she peered at the small bathroom off in the corner. The shower inside was tiny and cramped, but it was at least functional.

After cleaning off, she pulled on a pair of black leather knee-length military shorts, a black cotton tank top with FTW in large white lettering across it, knee high speed-lace grinders and a set of black leather suspenders. She was still braiding her hair as she opened the door and stepped into the hallway.

Argent sat at a table in the corner of the main cabin, wearing only a pair of black jeans. It was odd seeing him in something other than black leather. He didn't seem like much of a jeans person to her, but they didn't detract from his physique. It was also probably a good thing that he was now in clean clothes. Mira and Aurelian sat across from him, obviously tense and uncomfortable as she stepped up to the table.

:: *Did you get enough sleep?* :: Argent caught her gaze with a weary expression.

Jilah smiled and walked up to him, flipping the braid over a shoulder and wrapping an arm around him. :: *Actually yeah. Is there anything I can do to help?* ::

Argent leaned into her, sighing as he shook his head. :: *I'm afraid that it's mostly political trivialities, unfortunately. Care to join us?* ::

:: *Not really, but since it's part of the job description..* :: Jilah grinned and kissed his temple as he scooted over to make room for her.

Over the course of the next hour, little bursts of information that she could follow would come through. It was sporadic at first, but her understanding increased in frequency as she listened to their conversation. The knowledge that Argent had planted in her head was apparently triggered by situational exposure. As she slowly became aware of the roles that Mira, Aurelian, and Orlando played in the governing body, she also began to understand their roles in accordance with her position as Striaga. The entire group dynamic had changed overnight.

Mira and Aurelian were now behaving with deference towards her whenever she voiced an opinion during the discussion. She wondered exactly what Argent had said to them while she had slept.

The conversation came to an abrupt halt as Orlando, who had been sitting motionless across from them the entire time, suddenly stood up.

With a soft sigh of resignation, Argent nodded. :: *We've arrived. I need to get ready.* ::

Jilah moved to let him up, brushing soft lips briefly against his cheek as he slid past her and headed into the back.

:: *Should I change?* ::

:: *Actually, you look perfect. Very intimidating.* ::

Light laughter echoed through her thoughts as she moved to follow him into the room and paused to watch him dress.

Argent proceeded to slide into a pair of black leather pants with a crimson skeletal dragon design in the leather wrapping around the right thigh, its tail ending just below the knee. The design was intricate and mesmerizing, seeming almost alive as he zipped himself up. He then picked up a form-fitting black leather jacket that accentuated the width of his shoulders, tapering down to a narrow waist as he slid it on. The same symbol decorated the back of the jacket, with smaller versions on the upper arms.

Jilah crooked up an eyebrow and asked, "Are you sure you don't want me to change? I'm feeling a little under-dressed here."

He smiled and shook his head. :: *You look just fine.* ::

The outfit definitely showed off the contours of his body. It was nice to see him in different clothes. Argent turned towards her, buttoning the jacket up before sitting down to slide on a pair of black boots. Two rows of blood red buttons adorning both sides of the front of the jacket came down in a V from the shoulders to form a three-inch gap at the narrow waist.

A strange sigil was engraved into the leather where one side of the front was unbuttoned, exposing a blood red square of leather. The symbol seemed to shift as she looked at it, making her feel a little queasy. Jilah wondered what the hell it was, but had the distinct feeling that the time for questions would definitely be after the preliminaries of entering the city were done.

Jilah smiled over at him as she playfully growled, "You really do look amazing in leather pants." She sighed and murmured, "You sure we don't have a little time to spare?"

Before he could answer, she leapt at him, and he evaded her with a mock gasp of shock as he chided, "Now, now. Manners."

Jilah hit the floor in a crouch and laughed, batting out at him with a hand before coming to a standing position again. "Oh, you are soooo going to pay for that later."

Argent chuckled softly, offering her an arm and quietly purring, "I look forward to it."

Jilah rolled her eyes and took his arm, leaning into him as they walked out of the room. "Oh, I just bet you do."

Orlando stood at the end of the hallway, his expression distant as he watched them walk towards him. Gigi strode past Mira and Aurelian, who were standing off to the side of the Guardian, her appearance now strikingly different from when Jilah had first seen her. Her platinum locks were now auburn, and they curled around her face in a sixties shag style. She was wearing a silver outfit that looked like it was straight out of a space kitten serial. Jilah found herself wondering where the woman had hidden her ray gun.

Gigi murmured something under her breath and made a few complex, jerking gestures with her fingers, then smiled and said, "Last stop. Everybody out."

She turned and began walking quickly towards the front of the bus, with Argent, Jilah, and Orlando keeping close behind her. Mira and Aurelian followed behind them. As they stepped out of the bus, the few people that she spotted didn't seem to notice their presence at all. Jilah frowned as Gigi headed off in the direction of a building that looked old, but well-restored. There was a side entrance, but Gigi kept walking towards a blank space on the wall itself.

Jilah took a quick look back and blinked when she saw that the bus was no longer where they'd left it. How can something that big just vanish? she thought to herself, blinking.

The group proceeded towards the back of the building, the six of them looking very much like a motley group of band members that couldn't quite figure out what look they were trying achieve.

She began thinking that they were all going to walk directly into the wall in front of them, when Gigi made another strange gesture with her hands. The wall itself then shimmered into reddish transparency, and an enormous gate constructed of prismatic light swirled beyond the reddish haze of the wall.

Gigi quickly waved the group on, and Orlando stepped through first, a strange energy crackling around his arms and wings as his appearance reverted back to his true form on the other side of the portal. The red haze stripped away any semblance of humanity in the boy, leaving standing in his place a much larger creature with a rough grayish hide that rippled with enormous muscles. The rest of the group paused outside for a moment as the gargoyle sniffed the air before turning back to face them and giving a solemn nod. His entire face had changed; his features now thick and craggy with a set of enormous jagged horns extending out from his forehead. His jaw protruded slightly, and a set of dangerous-looking discolored fangs jutted upward from his lower lip. His eyes appeared almost chromatic in the recesses now overshadowed by his wide forehead. His wings appeared to have doubled in size. As the rest of them stepped through the reddish haze of masonry, the gargoyle flexed his wings briefly before folding them against his back, sending a draft of spice-scented air blowing against Jilah's skin.

Power skipped along her arms and she looked around the room. The entrance was sparsely furnished, the unusual gates before them opening to a large, lengthy corridor that extended well beyond the light of the torches in the room. Aurelian appeared at her side and Mira at Argent's as Gigi gestured towards the wall behind them. It solidified immediately as the redhead moved around them. With a flourished wave of her hand, the corridor was immediately illuminated with a strange, yellowish green glow.

Her voice sounded loud in the utter quiet of the room as she trilled, "This way, ladies." Gigi then started off down the passageway, again taking the lead. The yellow-green glow illuminated the hallways as they followed behind her.

:: *Where exactly are we going?* :: Jilah felt Argent's hand encircle her own, his fingers cool as they laced with hers.

:: *I'm not sure, exactly. I do not remember any of this, but it is not at all surprising that things are so very different after all these years away.* ::

:: *What is this place? It feels almost...powerful.* :: She gripped his hand firmly as they strode through the corridor.

There was a pause before he answered with a dark chuckle in her thoughts, :: *It is an old convent once populated by Ursuline nuns.* ::

:: *What, supernatural nuns?* ::

Images of a young Sally Field in her flying nun getup flashed through her memory.

Argent actually laughed out loud as he replied, :: *No, nothing like that.* :: He paused for a moment, then continued, :: *Humans are unusual creatures. When a large group of them fosters a particular belief in a chosen deity, the very act draws from those inner protean reserves and imprints a psychic pattern or resonance that can then be utilized by that which they revere.* ::

Jilah furrowed her brow, asking, :: *So, you're saying that these nuns left behind all this excess energy for their god to feed off of?* ::

:: *Certainly not with clear intent. Certain religious paths focus on ideals and abstracts, while others are more concrete or sympathetic. Those who tend to focus on the abstract or an idea tend to scatter their collective energy. When this happens, the excess energy bleeds off into the materials around them. What you are feeling now is what they define as hallowed ground. You will usually encounter wellsprings of this nature when you find yourself on ground that is considered consecrated. If you think this is power, I should take you to the altars in Africa, or the old Incan and Mayan places of worship. Blood excites and energizes everything it touches - including those who would set themselves up as gods. When sects begin to break away from blood sacrifice, the true power produced begins to wane, but the memory of it still remains and radiates, locked in the foundation of the grounds, if you will. ::*

Jilah winced, not really liking the idea of blood sacrifice – either animal or human. It was a moral zone that she wasn't entirely comfortable having a grey area in.

:: This is simply the way it is, beloved. Blood is the conduit to power. Besides, does being what you are not present you with an unusually strong sense of irony if you truly feel this way? ::

Jilah eyed him, her tone wary as she replied, *:: I'm not going to get another lecture, am I? You know I hate it when you end up being right. :: Argent simply tightened his grip on her hand. :: And stop skimming my thoughts. ::*

Argent smiled as he responded, *:: It is almost impossible when your surface thoughts are so loud. ::*

The corridor suddenly opened up into an enormous dark chamber. A slow increase in light brought the features of the room into focus. Huge detailed tapestries of bloody conflicts between every kind of creature imaginable decorated the high stone walls next to strangely incongruous pastoral scenes. Unusually large wolves and other creatures that Jilah couldn't quite make out shared panels with regal men and women. The coloring in the pieces was incredibly vivid, and the tapestries seemed to vibrate with an innate sense of motion as she peered curiously up at the intricate designs.

A dais with steps that appeared to be carved out of obsidian led up to a large ebony throne at the far end of the room. Muted crimson light emanated from small fissures in the stones that wrapped around the top step. A canopy of sharp, jagged, black and crimson points curled up and over the back of the throne, thrusting out towards the room at different angles. The carved form of what looked like an enormous blood red lizard wrapped around the throne. The lizard's head was positioned directly under the right armrest, almost as if waiting for a loving touch from its owner. It's yellow eyes stared out at the room before it with a baleful gaze.

There were recessed openings on either side of the throne, their mosaic patterns a brilliant splash of red, yellow, and orange tiled flames. The shiny black marble of the wall extended along the length of the dais. Jilah blinked as she looked back at the lizard, amazed at how lifelike the creature appeared. She felt as if, at any moment, it might spring down from its resting place and tear their small group into wet, red, bite-sized chunks.

The mental image sent a shiver through her.

Wow, this is pretty over the top.

Argent gave her hand a gentle squeeze, raising it to his lips and kissing it gently before releasing her and walking slowly towards the dais. Orlando followed him, an ever present shadow as Argent crossed the room and ascended the steps. When he reached the top step, he paused and ran his fingers in a gentle caress along the jaw of the lizard.

:: *I had all but forgotten...* :: echoed through Jilah's mind in a soft and wistful tone as he turned to face the doorway at the other end of the great hall.

"Strigaisha."

A hushed voice echoed through the room as a tall, muscular woman with long, straight raven-black hair and mocha skin stepped into view. She slowly advanced towards the throne followed by a large, bronze-skinned man who stood almost a full head taller. They both looked to be over six feet, easily. The woman was clad in a pair of faded jean shorts that made her legs look impossibly long and a tight turquoise doeskin vest with trailings of bone and beading on the front of it.

Her companion was clad in paint-stained jean shorts and little else, showing a broad expanse of well-muscled torso and powerful legs. His hair was the same color and about the same length as his companion's. Both had sections of braids snaking in and out of their long, straight locks. Jilah noticed that they were also barefoot.

As they padded across the floor, Argent stepped down from the dais and moved towards them. Jilah raised an eyebrow as the woman darted over to Argent, crouching slightly before nuzzling the underside of his jaw, her tongue darting out to lick the side of his mouth. The man moved towards him in a similar crouch and repeated the gesture.

Argent smiled and wrapped them in an affectionate embrace as he quietly breathed, "Cynette. Alain. I have missed you both greatly."

Jilah frowned as something tipped into her memory. She instantly understood that Alain and Cynette were the Alphas for the Tribe of the Savage moon, the largest wolf shifter pack in the southern Louisiana territories. They were also the enforcers for the court. The odd greeting that she was witnessing was their way of showing respect to him. The brain dump that Argent had performed on her was proving to be useful, but was a little creepy as well.

The three of them broke the embrace, grinning like idiots and making strange little sub-vocal growls to each other. Cynette peered around Argent's shoulder at her, eyes narrowing as she cocked her head and growled. Argent made a strange noise, and the woman jerked back in surprise, immediately moving forward to give his chin another quick lick before taking a step back.

Jilah frowned as she sent, :: *Is everything okay?* ::

Argent turned to face her, a smile playing at the edges of his lips as he walked over to her. The strange pair followed behind him, their expressions intensely curious as they looked at her.

:: *Everything is fine. You'll probably see a bit more of that in the future, if not outright challenges to you directly. I can deflect most of them, but unfortunately not all of them.* ::

There was a hard edge to his expression that hadn't been there before and she frowned as she sent, :: *You look different.* ::

:: *Dealing with the court is always a power play. Unless you appear to have the upper hand in either dominance or power, you get ripped apart. Many things are frequently not as they seem. I will do my best to fill in the gaps later. This is but part of the dance, beloved.* ::

Argent walked up to her and reached out, collecting her hand in his as he turned to the Alpha pair and announced, "It pleases me greatly to present you to my Striaga, Jilah."

He turned back to her, snaking an arm around her waist. The pair crouched and hesitated as they looked up at her, as if waiting for something.

:: *They wish to greet you and acknowledge you as Striaga.* ::

Jilah's eyes widened slightly as she asked, :: *Does this mean they have to lick me?* ::

She had become accustomed to Argent's touch, but was still far from being comfortable with the touch of others. He leaned into her and gave her a light squeeze, replying, :: *It is a show of submission, or of deep respect among the wolves. It is considered incredibly offensive to refuse* such a thing because it is never offered lightly. *They are dominant in their pack, and showing submission to anyone or anything is usually an honor bestowed only on those that they vow to ally themselves with.* ::

Jilah's gaze never left the two wolves in human skin crouching before her as she asked, :: *So what are they waiting for?* ::

:: *Tilt your chin forward a little. They'll do the rest.* ::

Jilah did as he requested, and the pair nuzzled her chin, sniffing at her neckline before rubbing their faces against her shoulders. She heard them making little sub-vocal growls before they moved back to place quick licks on the sides of her mouth. They then stepped back, smiling as Alain spoke in a low rolling rumble.

"The pack welcomes you, Striaga."

Jilah released a breath she hadn't known she was holding, wondering how many more people she'd have to get all touchy-feely with during this little adventure. She relaxed as Alain wrapped a tanned arm around his mate, liking the sound of his soft chuckle as he nodded towards Aurelian and said, "So. I see you brought the jackass back with you."

The Selkie promptly grinned and gave him the finger. "Screw you, wolfman."

Argent laughed, shaking his head slowly. "I see you two are getting along as usual."

Cynette nodded, grinning slightly as she nodded and said, "Some things never change."

Argent sobered, his voice soft as he said, "And some things change a little too much. Were any permanent injuries incurred in the explosion?"

Alain grew somber as he replied, "We lost several key people, as well as one of our cubs."

His mate let out a low whine as he continued, "The pack is howling for a blood hunt, and things are getting to the point where some of the younger cubs have started taking to the streets and searching for Julian. We're certain that he and his dogs are the ones behind this."

The alpha's eyes filled with a malevolent fire, and Argent kept his voice even as he reassured them, "He will be called to account for this, Alain – as will his comrades. You have my word on it."

Alain met his gaze, nodding once. "It's good to have you back, Strigaisha."

Argent turned to look back at Aurelian, his tone clipped as he asked, "How many know of my arrival?"

Aurelian stepped forward, responding, "A very select few. The general populace has heard rumors, but nothing substantial."

Argent nodded, rocking back on a heel. "We will make the official announcement tomorrow night. There are many things that need tending to before then."

A deep booming voice echoed through the chamber as an enormous winged figure stepped into the room.

"Bienvenue maison, Strigaisha." The creature stood at least eight feet tall, a mass of bulky muscles and sharp claws.

Argent wheeled around and smiled, his eyes bright as he strode over to his old friend.

"Brigliadoro."

He slipped into a language that Jilah couldn't understand as he began speaking with the Guardian of the Court, and she smiled gently, enjoying the way the odd words sounded as they rolled off her lover's tongue. There was still so much about him that she didn't know, having spent less than a week together so far. She found herself regretting the fact that they hadn't had more time to get to know one another before everything became overly complicated.

Jilah stood silently off to the side, watching everybody as they chattered to each other, feeling extremely out of place and unnecessary. Gigi broke away from the group as the rest of them headed over to Argent. She walked over to Jilah and quietly asked, "Honey, are you OK?"

Jilah nodded and forced a polite smile. "I'm fine."

The redheaded sorceress sighed and shook her head, her tone chiding but gentle as she said, "Girlfriend, trust me. You're not. Anything I can do to help?"

Jilah shrugged as she met the tall woman's gaze and replied, "Not really." She paused for a moment, then asked, "It's that obvious, huh?"

Gigi laughed lightly, her eyebrow arching up as she answered, "Oh yeah. You've gotta learn to rein it in, or people will take advantage."

She smiled and took Jilah's hand, gently pulling her along as she began walking towards the group at the door.

"Socialize, sweetie. Mix it up. Getting to know everybody takes the edge off."

Jilah tentatively followed, pushing a little more power into her shields. If she was this easily readable, she was quickly going to become a liability. As she did this, a strange, nonsensical rhyming couplet entered her thoughts. It occurred to her that this was a tool that she could also use to clear her mind, effectively shutting out any external interference. As the pair of them walked up, Argent looked over at her with the tiny hint of a smile as he formally presented her to Brigliadoro.

At least the enormous gargoyle didn't want to lick her. A strange, nagging sensation tugged at her as she listened to the breakdowns of the various affairs of state. There was a moment of recognition before a rush of images ran through her mind, causing her to wince slightly.

A large man hefted a heavy bundle in his arms. It looked like a carpet of some kind. The red haze around him swirled with a fierce malevolence that she had yet to come across. Jilah caught the glimpse of boats and a dock. A piercing wail brought the vision to a lurching close.

When she came to herself again, all eyes were on her, peering at her with the curiosity of somebody that has just discovered an interesting kind of bug. Hands reached out but she jerked away from them, steadying herself against a wall. A talloned hand extended in a warding gesture as she tried to figure out how long it would take her to get to him. She had the strong feeling that his victim was still quite alive, but didn't know how much longer that would last.

Argent was at her side in the blink of an eye, his voice soothing in her mind as he asked, :: *Are you alright, beloved?* ::

Jilah flinched, fixing the rest of the group across the room with a wary gaze.

:: *I need to work. I don't know this city, and I need to get to this guy as soon as possible. The girl is still alive.* ::

Her head felt strange, almost as if something was buzzing in her thoughts. She didn't think she would be able to track him on her own and wasn't quite sure why. She had never had this problem before.

Argent frowned for a moment, then answered, :: *Gigi will take you. She is the only one that can effectively mask your presence when you're this unfocused.* ::

He caressed her cheek, his brow furrowing as he added, :: *I regret that I cannot accompany you myself.* ::

With a weak smile, Jilah brushed her fingers gently over his abdomen as she sent, :: *You've got your hands full. I'll be all right.* ::

Argent leaned into her, frowning as he kissed her temple.

:: *Be careful. Hunt, then come directly back. We need to maintain a low profile until the announcement is made. I don't want anything to happen to you.* ::

Gigi stepped up to them, her grin playful as she snapped fingers with silver-painted nails and said, "OK, Romeo. Time to let the girls out for a night on the town."

Argent's expression grew sharp as he grated, "Just bring her back safely, *Cagliostro*. Do not fail me in this."

The sorceress sobered, giving him a solemn bow before gripping Jilah's hand and quietly responding, "Yes, Strigaisha."

Argent then turned from them, heading back to the rest of the group.

Jilah frowned at the exchange, discomfited by the harshness of his tone. She shook it off when Gigi brightened and laughed lightly.

"All right honey, where are we headed?"

Jilah described the general area, and Gigi nodded.

"I know exactly the place."

The tall redhead began leading her back down a passage that Jilah hadn't spotted when they had first entered the room.

As they made their way through the corridors, Gigi broke the silence, asking, "I hate to sound overly nosy, but what exactly is it that you do?"

Jilah's voice echoed strangely in the long hallway as she heard herself answer, "Reader's Digest version? I, ah, torture rapists and child molesters."

Gigi blinked and stopped for a moment. Jilah looked over at her, startled at the bluntness of her own response. Gigi quickly recovered, her tone light as she replied, "Honey, you just caught me off guard. I'm not used to people being so forthright about themselves here."

Jilah nodded as they came to a stop in a small room without any doors or windows.

"Yeah. I can understand that."

Gigi made a strange gesture and the wall became translucent as they walked towards it. She kept her tone light as she asked, "Is it interesting work?"

They passed through the wall out into a parking lot. Jilah nodded as she looked around, trying to get her bearing, "It's very..*satisfying*." She looked over at her companion and asked, "You?"

Gigi shrugged and began walking towards the main gate.

"I guess you could say that I'm a sorceress, although I prefer to think of it as more like a Samantha the witch meets I Dream of Genie kinda thing, but with much better looking leading men."

She laughed lightly and looked back at Jilah, who was now standing in the middle of the parking lot and staring at something in the distance.

The mental cloudiness she'd experienced before began to dissipate and the path to her target cleared in her thoughts.

Jilah's voice dropped an octave as she growled, "Hang on."

She pulled Gigi into her arms and took off at top speed for the docks, instinctively knowing how to get there now that they were out of the convent. For some reason, the energy the place emitted had mucked up her sense of direction. With a lurching stop, she gently set the tall redhead down.

Gigi wobbled on her heels, looking mildly queasy. Jilah peered at her for a moment, then turned towards a shipyard. Her quarry was in a packing container up ahead, and the sound of a muffled scream drowned all else out.

Gigi blinked as Jilah disappeared. She then frowned, cursing herself for losing sight of the child so easily.

If anything happens to her...

She was relatively assured that the Strigaisha wouldn't kill her outright for it. He needed her talents too badly. Unfortunately, it was understood all too well that failure often came with a nasty price when it came to Mr. Valentine.

Gigi paled, shivering at the very thought of what he'd do to her if she didn't come back with his lover intact.

A high-pitched wail tore through the night air. It was just as quickly silenced. Gigi gesticulated with her fingers, making several quick stabbing gestures at the air as she gated onto the deck of the boat. Following the sounds of violence, she stood stock still as she happened upon the source of the noise. It took her a moment to process the scene before her.

Jilah appeared to be systematically slamming her fist into sections of the body of a large man on the floor in front of her. It looked as if she were slowly working on crushing every bone in his body, inch by inch, starting with his right foot. She'd gotten halfway up his shin when Gigi noticed that the man was still conscious, his mouth opened in a silent scream.

Dear god, no wonder he wants her, Gigi thought to herself as she moved into the room. *She's every bit as savage as he is.*

A little raven-haired girl, who couldn't be older than nine lay crumpled in a corner, her chest rising and falling in quick, shallow breaths. The girl's arms and legs were splayed in unnatural positions, as if they'd been dislocated before she'd been unceremoniously dropped to the floor in a pool of her own blood. She stared at the ceiling, eyes unfocused.

Although Gigi wasn't a doctor, it was obvious that the girl didn't have a chance. It was strange, she thought, how the child could be smiling so peacefully after such a horrific ordeal. She barely heard the girl's final breath leave her body over the sounds of a fist hitting meat and breaking bone punctuating the silence.

Gigi looked back over at Jilah. The avatar, after having completely ruined the man's first leg up to the knee, was now slowly making her way up his other shin. A hideous grin split her features, giving her a ghoulish appearance that sent a chill through the Cagliostro. Gigi blinked twice, no longer doubting the appointment of Striaga. This woman definitely had the same vicious, violent streak that their former regent possessed, and she apparently reveled in it as much as he did.

They were perfect for one another.

Suddenly, Jilah stopped, peering into the man's empty, open eyes before spitting into both of them. She then slumped to a seated position, one arm holding her up as she began to tremble violently. Her features, which had been devoid of all semblance of humanity before, were slowly softening as her head dropped to her chest.

In a quiet, mournful voice, she croaked, "Rot in hell, you sick bastard."

Jilah strained to master herself. There was still work to do. She slowly got to her feet and walked over to the little girl, pulling a tarp down from a shelf above her and gently covering her with it. Gigi watched the scene intently, moving closer to the man to get a better look at his features. Her mouth dropped open in a little O of shock, and she took a quick step away from the body, recognizing it.

Jilah walked over to her, head cocked to the side as she asked, "What is it?"

Gigi looked over at her and stammered, "This guy that you've spent the last five minutes pounding into dog meat? His name is Gregor. He's of Alain's pack mates."

Jilah looked back over at the man who now seemed to be breathing a little easier. He was beginning to twitch, and it looked like parts of his legs were slowly inflating. A low howl broke from the man's lips as his body began convulsing violently; a white, foamy froth was bubbling up on his lips as he scrabbled at the floor. It took her a minute to realize that this target had stayed alive a great deal longer than she had expected. What she'd seen him doing to that little girl... It was as if everything had shut down and she'd just gone on autopilot. He hadn't put up much of a fight because she had been able to catch him off guard, crippling him instantly.

Jilah frowned and asked, "Their gray matter doesn't heal, does it?"

She looked up at Gigi, who was watching the body heal with a distasteful look on her face.

"What do you mean? It doesn't look like you hit him in the head."

Jilah shook her head, asking, "If they go insane, they stay insane, right?"

If not, this was going to turn into a very long night. In her opinion, there wasn't enough that she could do to this asshole to make him pay for what he had done to that little girl. Or all the others.

Gigi nodded, her expression growing wary as she answered, "I guess. What on *earth* did you do to him??"

There was a barely discernible scent of fear coming from the sorceress. Part of Jilah embraced it, almost wanting to revel in it. The other part of her wanted to reassure this new friend, not wanting to drive her away.

Her tone was haggard and haunted as she explained, "He's been doing this to girls for the last year, Gigi. Somebody had to stop him."

Gigi was horrified that one of the Tribe would do such a thing, much less repeatedly. Hunting humans had been outlawed hundreds of years ago. Gregor was damned lucky that the council hadn't gotten wind of his extracurricular activities.

She indicated the twitching body on the floor with a wave of a delicately manicured hand, her voice hard as she said, "We need to bring him with us. Are you ready to head back?"

Jilah sighed, relieved that she wasn't going to have to perch on the asshole's chest all night. She nodded and collected the twitching body, hoping he didn't jerk so much that she lost her grip on him. The sorceress' fingers fluttered in the air, and Jilah felt a sickening wrench in her gut. It was as if her stomach was trying to force its way out through her skin, and her head spun as their surroundings warped around them. There was an almost metallic whine, as if an enormous, thick piece of iron was being bent back in on itself. The nausea was overwhelming.

Suddenly it all stopped, and Jilah dropped to her knees, letting the body fall to the ground before noisily throwing up into the grass just outside the convent.

"My god. What the hell just happened?"

She moaned and heaved as another wave of dark crimson fluid splashed out onto the grass.

Gigi looked back at her, entirely flustered and cursing herself for not thinking. Transport between was always difficult on people, especially when they weren't prepared for it.

"Oh honey, I'm really sorry. I forgot how rough that can be on people that aren't expecting it."

"Expecting *what?*" Jilah croaked as she burped and did her best to keep from throwing up a third time.

"Gating between places like that. I thought it would be wise to get you back here as soon as possible, so I..." Gigi stammered, and Jilah cut her off with a wave of her hand.

"I have one request." Jilah grated, relieved that the rest of her meal was now staying down as she jabbed a finger at the sorceress. "Don't ever do that again."

Once back in the convent, they quickly made their way through several passages that snaked toward the throne room. The body in Jilah's arms was seriously beginning to creep her out. Hair kept flowing out of the pores of the man's body in patches, only to be replaced by bare skin moments later, and she swore that she could feel the shifting and popping of bones and sinew beneath his skin. The sooner she could put the damned thing down, the better.

They strode into the throne room, surprised to find Argent sitting alone on the throne. Orlando was around somewhere, to be sure, but he wasn't in plain sight.

"Strigaisha."

Gigi's voice rang with authority through the large hall.

Argent turned to look at her with an expression of annoyance that quickly turned to alarm as he saw the body in Jilah's arms. He was beside them in an instant.

Jilah dumped the body onto the floor, shuddering as she took a quick step away from it.

"What the hell happened??" he asked.

Jilah vibrated with a quiet anger as she answered, "This was my target. I was too late to save the little girl he destroyed, but he is paying his price, and my patroness is satisfied."

Argent looked up at her, then over at Gigi, who was nodding solemnly in affirmation. He took a slow breath, then bowed his head as he mentally sent for Alain. At least they hadn't left the premises yet.

The body on the floor smelled like Alain's pack, but he could have been one of the upstarts that had broken from him and chosen to follow Julian. If this wolf was still Tribe, Alain had a serious problem on his hands that would have to be dealt with immediately.

Argent would be damned if unchecked shapeshifters killed humans in his city.

He stood slowly as the Alpha and his mate strode in and walked over to the body, cocking their heads and tasting the air as they looked down at it.

Alain's voice was soft as he murmured, "Gregor."

He knelt beside the body, touching the man's face as he growled, "Who did this to him?"

Argent's voice was cold as he responded, "The one who caught him with a little human girl that he'd tortured and killed."

Alain stiffened and his mate recoiled beside him in horror.

"Gregor was a pack brother. It is well understood that hunting humans is punishable by death, but this..."

He shook his head slowly, his voice growing angry as he continued, "is unforgivable. It is torment beyond imagining to be denied death when the mind has gone. His soul is trapped."

Jilah's answering tone was heated as she replied, "Maybe you'd like to see what he did to earn it. Slowly tearing apart that little girl as he raped her. I arrived in time to spare her the experience of being eaten alive." Her voice rose in pitch as she continued, "Not to mention the five before her. I assure you, he deserves every bit of what he's going through, and then some."

The large Alpha's shoulders shook as he fought to calm himself. The blood of his pack brother howled for retribution.

"You could show me such a thing?" he whispered.

Jilah quietly extended a hand down to the alpha.

"If you wanna look, be my guest. It's not at all pretty, though."

Alain slowly stood up, staring down at her with a baleful gaze. Jilah met his eyes, feeling the anger and accusation in their depths as she felt his hand encircle her own. She reached out to cover the top of his hand, then gently pushed the stream of images and memories into him in a single wave. To his credit, the Alpha took it all without making a sound. A few moments passed, and Jilah broke the connection, looking up into the face of the large man who now bowed his head before her.

His voice was heated as he said, "Please. Promise me that he will be allowed to die when you are finished. The only way that he can atone is to pass beyond the veil. Keeping him trapped here serves no purpose."

Jilah felt a rising tide of lust coming from the huge wolf and shivered. Unbidden, her gaze drifted down his torso. What he had seen had evidently aroused him, and the very thought of it nauseated her. She began seriously doubting her reasons for coming here.

Argent's voice echoed through her thoughts, :: *He is a wolf, a primal creature at heart. Fear is as much an aphrodisiac to them as it is for us. Perhaps moreso. Alain is a good Alpha. He will insure that this doesn't happen in his pack again, no matter how stimulated he may have been by what you have shown him.* ::

Jilah's voice was strained as she glanced back at the Alpha and murmured, "You have my word, Alain."

With that, the Alpha pair quickly departed, and Jilah turned to glare back at Argent, her tone sharp as she asked, "So – you want me to kill him now?"

Argent nodded slowly, his voice soft as he answered, "He's already gone, Jilah. Can't you feel it? The void? There's nothing left of him to hurt."

In a blurring motion that was too quick for the eye to follow, Jilah slammed her hand into the shifter's gut, burrowing under his ribcage. She yanked his heart out and squeezed the remaining crimson life in it out onto the floor with a set of vicious, bloody talons.

"Happy now?"

She dropped the heart to the floor and held her clawed hand out to him, fingers splayed. Sure, it was petty, but she was angry and more than a little uncomfortable with what had just happened. Argent let out a soft sigh, gesturing for Gigi to leave them. The sorceress nodded and began walking towards the great doors in the hall as Argent softly asked, "Are you?"

Jilah frowned and looked away.

"No."

She let her hand drop, giving her fingers a quick flick to shake off the excess blood.

"You are angry with me," he murmured.

"No, Argent. The problem is that if I'm called and it happens to be somebody that you perhaps don't want dead..." She shook her head, feeling a mixture of anger and sadness as she added, "We're going to find ourselves in this position again. You know what I am; you know what happens to me if I shirk my duty. You also know that I have no control over who the target is."

Argent nodded, his voice quiet as he breathed, "I had hoped that it was only humans. This presents an inconvenient wrinkle, but not one that is unworkable."

It also presented another possible problem. If she had known about half of the things he'd done in his formative years, would she still choose to stay with him? Would the poisonous squatter in her mind force her to destroy him? To make him atone for his misdeeds? He had mellowed substantially over the course of his life, but his prior deeds as a youth would undoubtedly be seen as those of a monster in her eyes.

In almost anyone's eyes, he had to admit.

It would all come to light someday, he knew, but for now it was definitely in his best interest to remain silent about it.

She took a step away from him and asked, "So. Where do we sleep in this place? I'm thinkin' that I really need some alone time right about now. A shower probably wouldn't hurt either."

He reached out to take her hand, sighing as she flinched before finally allowing him to thread his fingers through hers. :: *I will never be your enemy, Jilah. No matter what external forces happen to come into play.* ::

She frowned and looked away, trying not to think too hard about what had just happened – and what it might mean.

:: *Please,* :: *Argent's voice was soft and gentle as he murmured,* :: *Trust me. Do not turn from me.* ::

With a soft sigh, she nodded and let him pull her close, her voice tight as she replied aloud.

"I'm not handling this very well, am I?"

Argent stroked her cheek softly as he murmured, "Trial by fire is never easy, beloved."

Jilah laughed weakly and nuzzled his chest, a tired resignation creeping into her voice as she breathed, "Just show me where the bathtub is and I'll feel much better."

"Let's get you cleaned up."

Argent smiled gently, leading her towards one of the back passages.

Eighteen
A Plan of Action

The sheer size and opulence of the bedroom left her speechless. Jilah slowly scanned the room in stunned silence. Crimson and black fabric swept down and away from a central point in the ceiling, flowing back to the corners of the room in shiny organza and silk swags, giving the entire room an almost Middle Eastern feel. An enormous king-size bed was the dramatic focal point of the room, located against a wall draped in alternating black and crimson silk. It looked remarkably solid. Four iron corner posts with odd-looking fittings climbing up the sides of them stretched up into an opaque black organza canopy that swept over the top of the bed and spilled in a froth around the corner posts. The canopy softened the harsh, utilitarian frame of the bed nicely. As they approached the bed, Jilah found herself wondering at the function of the hooks and rings connected to the posts.

A section of the wall on the far side of the room was peppered with the same strange rings and hooks, some with solid-looking chains dangling limply from them. Argent remained silently at her side, watching her closely as her gaze drifted across a collection of whips, scourges, floggers, paddles, crops and canes. Beside this draconian display was an assortment of leather and rubber harnesses and collars, along with chains and leaders. Argent wished he'd thought to inspect the room beforehand; hoping that the equipment wouldn't trigger negative responses for her. It had been a rough night for her already.

Jilah inhaled sharpy, turned to him and murmured, "Uh, did anybody actually sleep in this room?"

Argent nodded, his voice mild as he responded, "Yes. Of course."

He paused for a moment, then explained, "Although a great many other activities have taken place in here as well." Vague was safe. If she asked directly, he'd answer, but he would rather not be forthcoming with anything that he thought might cause her further discomfort.

Jilah's lips turned down into an uncertain frown as she looked away from the wall. She blinked, "The bathroom?"

Argent padded off towards a door to the right, calling back, "Would you like me to check it out first?"

Jilah's voice was a little tight as she gave him a quick nod.

"Please."

She watched him dart into the tiled room and winced, slowly getting an idea of exactly what this room had been used for in the past.

Had people been held here against their will? she wondered. The very thought sent a chill through her, and she hugged her arms around herself, not really at all comfortable with this pleasant, yet strangely savage room. It was exceptionally tiring to be this uncomfortable this often.

The sounds of things being pulled free of tiled walls shook her from her daze. Argent quickly appeared in the doorway again, presenting her with a sheepish grin.

"The bathroom is now ready for inspection."

Jilah numbly replied with a nod and padded towards him, wanting nothing more than to sit in a nice, hot bath, then pass out. As she entered the room, she noticed a strange pattern of holes in the walls around the enormous tub.

"I'll have the tiles repaired tomorrow. I'm afraid that you're going to have to wash some of the plaster out of the tub before you can use it, though. Unless you would like me to?"

Jilah shook her head as she looked at the tub. It looked big enough to seat ten people comfortably. That was, of course, if they didn't mind being extremely friendly. She would almost be able to swim in it when it was full. Recessed lighting in the walls pointed down to provide low mood lighting. Black and red tiling and fixtures were everywhere, prompting her to say, "Pretty cliché coloring scheme, don't you think?"

Argent chuckled and shrugged, his voice amused as he replied, "I believe that Judiana found it pleasantly symbolic. We can always change it, if you like."

Jilah looked over at him, and the ghost of a smile played at the edges of her lips.

"Can I decorate it any way I like?"

The idea of having a mundane project such as remodeling began to lift her spirits a little. It might just be what she needed to focus on to get some of the weirdness of the last week out of her head long enough to evaluate everything that had happened. And control, whether real or perceived, could only help at this point.

Argent nodded, brushing his fingers gently against her arm. "Of course, beloved." He snaked an arm around her waist, slowly pulling her close as he breathed, "Anything you like."

Jilah smiled, nuzzling his chest as she wrapped her arms around him.

"Thank you. I know it seems like such a petty, silly thing, but thank you."

Argent stroked her hair tenderly, his voice honeyed and smooth as he purred, "It is not petty. Or silly. It is perfectly reasonable for you to want to be in an environment that better suits you. One that you feel at ease in."

Jilah relaxed in his arms, sighing softly as he kissed the top of her head.

"You should probably go. I know you have a lot to take care of in the next night or so."

Argent smiled and gave her a quick kiss. "You and your gift of understatement."

Jilah grinned and smacked him on the arm as she growled, "Shoo! Go play with the other vampires."

Argent laughed and disappeared, leaving her blinking and shaking her head as she turned to begin cleaning the tub out. "I hate it when they do that."

As he reached the throne room, Argent wondered how to turn this new development to his advantage. How many of the inhabitants of the city were unknowingly putting themselves into the line of his lover's sights with their actions? This added a fear factor that he could possibly utilize to keep the peace. There were far too many preternaturals that had insinuated themselves into human society now, working alongside them without raising suspicion. It seemed to be striking a positive social balance, and Argent would have to make it clear in no uncertain terms that the status quo had to be protected and maintained at all times.

The ever-present form of Orlando moved to stand behind Argent as an attractive redhead stepped through the doors at the far end of the room. Argent's heart did a slow roll as he watched her move, sighing softly as she walked towards them.

The woman's dress shimmered in the low lighting of the room as she moved. Her gait was graceful and regal, as were the lines of her face. Her bright, violet eyes glinted in the dim light and the edges of her gold-hued lips presented a secretive smile. A vibrant crimson wave of large curls swept up and away from her face into a loose topknot that was clasped in a strange metallic band with alien characters that morphed along its surface as she moved. The rest of her hair cascaded in a shining flow down to below her waist.

Brigliadoro's son moved in to protect him, but Argent held up a hand, his voice breathy as he said, "She is family, Orlando. I doubt that she has come to harm me."

Orlando stepped back, holding his ground as the woman walked up to them, her bare feet padding softly on the stones. Argent smiled, eyes glittering as he said, "S'llethe. It has been far too long."

The woman smiled, and her entire presence somehow brightened, becoming almost incandescent. Her voice had a lilting, musical quality to it that echoed softly in the large room as she responded, "We have missed you, brother. Come and greet us."

Argent went to her, eyes bright as he wrapped her in a strong embrace. He was happy to see her, but wondered what had prompted the surprise visit. He hadn't seen any members of what he'd considered his extended family since his first ascension to the throne of New Orleans so many years ago.

She hadn't aged a bit. But then, none of his unusual family ever seemed to age. She laughed softly as she leaned into him, pressing her lips against his temple in an affectionate greeting, her tone warm as she said, "You are wondering why we are here."

Argent nodded, a little chagrined as he answered, "The thought had crossed my mind, although I am not at all unhappy to see you."

S'llethe smiled, amusement playing in the depths of her eyes as she took a step back and regarded him with a pleased expression.

"You have returned home. You have also mated. She eases you, as the one who created you did. Perhaps moreso." Argent blinked as she continued, "We would meet her."

He had forgotten how easily they'd always been able to read him. Did they wish to approve of his choice, he wondered?

Argent frowned slightly as he asked, "Might this perhaps wait until a little later? I am afraid that now is unfortunately not the best of times."

The woman nodded, the amusement never leaving her expression as she replied, "We watch. We understand and will return tomorrow to attend your ascension, dear brother."

Argent gathered her hand into his and murmured, "Surely you'll accept accommodations until then? Please, stay?"

S'llethe paused then nodded, her features sharpening briefly before her lips curled into a playful grin.

"Of course, we happily accept your hospitality brother. As always, you are most kind."

Her features softened, the coloring of her eyes darkening a touch as she looked back at him.

Argent grinned, lacing his fingers through hers as he sent a mental call out to the Matron de Cour. A plain woman in a pale grey utilitarian dress appeared in the doorway shortly thereafter, bowing slightly to indicate that she was ready to show the new guest to her room.

The redheaded woman leaned in and kissed Argent softly, her voice melodious as she pulled away and said, "We shall leave you to your intrigues, brother. Until tomorrow night."

Argent watched in rapt fascination as she departed; knowing full well that her true form appeared nothing like the beautiful woman that was now padding away from him, but unable to help himself.

Beautiful creatures of both genders tended to be one of his primary weaknesses. Once she disappeared down the hallway, his thoughts drifted back to the issues at hand.

It would be a good idea to speak with Roane and Ariane, although he'd never really been big on Ariane's method of divination and problem resolution. Vodou had never been his cup of tea, if indeed he had ever had one in a spiritual sense, but he had to admit that she produced startling, albeit very helpful, results in the past.

Argent supposed that he had never really utilized her as much as he could have in the past, and this was mostly due to his discomfort with anything remotely connected to what she referred to as the Divine Mysteries. Sanguine were hardly creatures of benign purpose, and so when doing work for him, Ariane could only work directly with what she called the Petwo or hot 'mysteries.'

As he walked back to the throne, he mentally sought out the Speaker for the Dead, hoping that she wasn't currently incommunicado. As he waited for her to appear, he found himself wondering where The Sisters were. They had certainly become bold and earnest enough that he almost expected their presence at the ceremony tomorrow night.

Orlando settled into place behind the ornate throne as a diminutive young woman appeared at the door. A shock of sea-green hair was pulled back from her face in short, bouncy little pigtails that perched high on her head. Her style of dress resembled that of the young ones he had seen at the club where he'd first met Jilah.

The long-sleeved metallic top that she wore appeared to be constructed out of two separate pieces that fitted over one another, leaving an opening that showed a rather generous amount of cleavage. Her knee-high boots had metal plating on the front of the toes as well as an array of silver buckles that lined the sides; her skirt was a vibrant, electric blue material that was pleated in the front with open sides that strips of black rubber joined, leaving wide spaces of pale thigh showing underneath.

Argent raised an eyebrow, unsure of what to think of such a radical change in appearance. The last time he'd seen her, she'd been wearing a much more demure style of dress. One could have referred to it as dour.

Her eyes lit up when she saw him, and she laughed as she strolled into the room, her voice loud and a little brash as she called out, "Look at you! Wow. The Dragon's Hammer all decked out in all that sexy twenty-first century leather."

Her pigtails bobbed as she bounced along. She nodded appreciatively, her voice dropping an octave as she leaned in and added, "What a stud."

Argent laughed, decidedly pleased with this new, happier version of his old associate. Roane had never been a particularly happy, comfortable woman. There were many things about her condition and abilities that had plagued her, and it had made her fairly morose. It was decidedly good to finally see her perky. It was also quite disorienting; a sharp reminder of how much time had passed.

"Dear Roane. How you've changed!"

She did a little spin, raising her hands over her head, her voice ebullient as she asked, "Like the new look?"

He could see that her hair was shaved to the skin halfway up the back of her head, the back of her neck decorated with strange sigils of some sort that extended down into her shirt. He wondered if they trailed down her spine as well. Burnished steel goggles perched high on her head, just above unruly bangs. As she completed the turn, she placed a hand on her hip and grinned. Teal-colored lips pulled back to expose razor sharp eyeteeth as she cocked her hips and growled, "Drives the girlz wild."

She was obviously adapting far better than he would've imagined in the last century. Argent blinked as he looked her over, a little boggled as he replied, "Oddly enough, it really suits you. It's just going to take a little getting used to." He chuckled softly.

Another woman with a mixture of intense purple and teal hair that swirled through long wavy pigtails that rode high on her head strode purposefully into the room. She was carrying a large black backpack and two live chickens – one black and one white; both dangling from her right hand by their legs.

She was wearing goggles as well, although hers were white. She wore a baggy white jumpsuit that had a strange, ornate symbol on the right breast that looked like a collection of connected diamond shapes with asterisks inside them. The diamond shapes were bisected by lines that went straight up and down through them. At the bottom was a curved flourish dotted with stars around it. At the top of the design sat a single diamond perched atop a line with an asterisk inside it. The jumpsuit was practically covered with little black bungee cords and pockets, the trouser legs flaring out widely at the bottom in huge bell shapes.

Her voice was husky, incongruous with her very feminine features as she asked, "Where do you want me to set up, Strigaisha?"

Argent looked her over, startled at her appearance. Both women had changed so much during his absence. Many years ago, out of curiosity he'd once asked her why she always wore a white kerchief on her head when she worked. She had answered that it was for protection – to keep her head clear and free of anything malignant that wanted to enter.

Curious as to why she wasn't wearing one now, he asked, "Do you no longer need to cover your head?"

Ariane stopped and eyed him, caught off guard by the question. She shrugged and explained, "The dye acts as a kind of protection, and it keeps me from having to cover up and overheat."

Argent raised an eyebrow, guessing that as long as it worked, it didn't really matter. The pair of them looked almost nauseatingly cute together, and he couldn't help smiling.

"Business as usual, Ariane? No jibes or friendly banter?"

Her ice blue eyes glittered as she walked over and began setting everything to the side of the throne, her tone brusque as she answered, "Too much nasty shit is going down for levity."

He couldn't argue with this so he shrugged and asked, "What do you need me to do?"

She had always been the more serious one.

The Mambo began pulling out a strange collection of items from her backpack – an aged wooden bowl, a weathered cutting board, a sizable piece of meat, a cow's tongue, half a dozen habanero peppers, a tin of gunpowder, several other items that he didn't recognize as well as a large knife and machete that appeared to be formed out of hand-wrought iron.

She motioned to her left and barked, "Stand there. Stay still."

Ariane began laying everything out on the floor before him, her breathing controlled and focused as she handed the white chicken to him.

"Just hold it and turn in three circles, clockwise."

Argent complied silently as she stood up and began waving the frantically flapping black chicken up and down over every part of his body. As she did this, she began muttering in a growling patois that sounded like extremely bastardized French. Roane stood watching earnestly as Ariane quickly pulled the black chicken away from him and grabbed it by the neck, easily snapping it with a rapid jerk and throwing it out into the corridor across the room.

Roane went to retrieve the chicken, placing it inside a paper sack, which she then placed within another paper sack. She then disappeared with it as Ariane began tracing an intricate design in what looked like white powder on the floor in front of the bowl. When Ariane finished, Argent noticed that it bore a striking resemblance to the sigil on her jumpsuit. She then turned back to him, gently collecting the white chicken from his hand. She cooed gently to it, brushing her fingers along its feathers in a reassuring gesture. Argent cocked his head, fascinated as he then watched her loop its neck back around towards its legs.

In one deft motion, she picked up the knife and slid it through the bird's neck, holding it over the wooden bowl in order to collect the blood. More murmured pidgin French followed that he couldn't entirely understand. After a few moments, the bird stopped moving, the blood from its neck slowing down to a trickle as she moved forward to hold it over the design. She spattered drops of blood over it, turning the flour pink where it hit. She then placed the dead chicken at the base of the design, and pressed down on it with her foot.

The bird made a brief, wet, honking noise as she put her full weight on it. Argent also heard several bones give with a muffled crunching sound. After a few moments, satisfied that it wasn't going to flop around anymore, she removed her foot. When the bird stayed immobile, she reached down to dip her fingers into the rapidly cooling bowl of blood. She slid her fingers across her lips, slicking them with a dripping crimson streak. She began chanting again in the same strange butchered French singsong, swaying gently as she rocked back and forth before the bizarre mess.

Argent watched as the woman began to jerk, lightly at first then more violently. This was the part that always disconcerted him. After a moment, the woman shouted something and crouched before him, still jerking and twitching. Roane suddenly appeared again, leaning over to collect a dark red sash from the backpack. Ariane's body was still shuddering with an odd, jerking motion as Roane reached around to tie the sash around her waist.

Ariane then rushed over to him, eyes wild as she advanced menacingly at him with the machete. She was shouting a message in that same broken French, her voice now an octave lower and much more ragged as she sized him up. She glared at up Argent, jerking her head up and saying something that Argent took as a derogatory remark of some sort.

Frustrated that he'd let his understanding of the language Ariane was speaking slip so badly, he looked over at Roane, one eyebrow crooking up on his forehead as he asked, "Did I do something wrong?"

He hated having to go through a translator, but seventy years away from the language hadn't helped to him retain it. Roane shook her head slowly, her voice casual as she replied, "Nah. Ogou's just a little testy tonight. One chicken isn't enough. You're gonna have to give him some of your blood."

Roane reached down to collect the knife, and Ariane quickly bent down to slap her hand away, angrily sputtering in that same unusual language as she reached down to collect it herself.

Argent tensed as Ariane whirled around to face him, her eyes wide and a feral grin pulling her lips tight as she muttered something and jerked her head violently. Witnessing possession of any kind had always made him distinctly uncomfortable.

He quite preferred death over letting something external inhabit his body. Argent didn't know how she did it and didn't want to. He sighed and held his hand out, hissing as the blade of the wrought iron knife sliced through muscles and tendons, tearing into his wrist. Ariane then grabbed his hand, pressing the cut to her mouth to suckle and chew at it noisily.

Roane grimaced and said, "Wow. Messy eater much? Ugh."

Argent winced in pain as blood dribbled down Ariane's chin, peppering the pristine whiteness of the top of her jumpsuit as the spirit greedily fed through her. Argent swayed a little as it drank deeply, realizing that it would likely come close to draining him to the point where he would need to feed immediately afterwards.

The woman wrenched his arm nearly out of its socket with a firm jerk, and he began to feel a little dizzy. The edge of a headache started just before Ariane pulled free, her fingers still tight around Argent's wrist as she pulled him down to the bowl of blood. She dipped fingers into the blood and began painting his face with it, nodding with satisfaction when she'd finished. She then gave a gruff laugh and slapped him twice on the chest with the flat of the machete, almost knocking him over before chopping at the floor at his feet – three times on the right and three times on the left. Ariane then turned and began babbling at Roane, her expression intense as she made broad, sweeping gestures with the machete.

Roane nodded, rushing to memorize as much of the message as possible before it departed. Everything the Lwa had to say, no matter who you ended up calling, usually ended up being of grave importance, so it was critical to listen very carefully in order to gain the entirety of the message.

Ariane suddenly stopped and looked back at Argent. A hearty, booming laugh echoed out of her throat before she slumped. Roane blurred forward to catch her, gently laying her down on the floor and shaking her head as she said, "Wow. He really liked you." She looked up at him with a big grin. "Says you're good eatin."

Argent arched an eyebrow, watching his wrist with a distasteful expression as the wound started to close up. "Indeed. I thought it was going to pull my arm off for a moment."

Roane laughed, grinning broadly as she replied, "Oh, stop whining."

Argent's eyes grew wide with surprise and his jaw dropped as the necromancer looked back at him.

"What, I should treat you with kid gloves now that you're back? C'mon, there's gotta be at least one person that can chap your ass that isn't your Striaga. You'd go nuts if there wasn't."

Before he could react, she grinned brightly, then looked down at Ariane's still form and said, "Could you watch her while I take care of this stuff?"

He nodded, still reeling a little from shock as he answered, "You will, of course, tell me what she said when you get back?"

He remembered little Roane as being a handful before, but she had apparently taken it to a new level in the long years since his departure. It had been his personal policy to put up with a fair amount of grief from the pair of them, knowing that they'd never push it beyond where he'd have to react in order to keep from losing political face. That, and it was also important to remember not to get on the bad side of necromancers and people that could call down spirits that consumed blood.

Roane dipped into the backpack, fishing around and pulling out a large clay jar with a wide mouth.

"Oh yeah. He had some really interesting things to say."

She placed the jar on the floor and began pouring the blood from the bowl into it. She was very careful not to get any of the crimson fluid onto either herself or the floor as she grumbled, "Blood is such a bitch to get out of designer clothing." She then jammed the chicken in the jar and disappeared with it in a blur of motion.

Orlando lurked behind him as Argent watched the rise and fall of the mocha-skinned Mambo's chest, wondering how long it would take her to recover. Perhaps Ariane had developed a bit more of a tolerance for being ridden as she'd referred to it.

Argent cocked his head, his tone wry as he mused, "It would, at the very least, be nice to know exactly how long I have to leave the rapidly congealing blood of a dead animal on my face."

The ghost of a smile flickered across Orlando's features, and Argent raised an eyebrow, his voice dropping an octave and his lips curling into a smile as he murmured, "I saw that."

Orlando straightened, the boy's expression becoming empty again as he stood guard behind the Strigaisha. Roane came back into the room, placing the bowl off to the side.

"Okay, here's the deal. The Lwa Ogou is gonna silence Julian's tongue; his ability to rally people against you. He'll bring Julian to you."

Argent nodded as Roane continued, "Next, an unexpected ally has arrived. Not exactly sure who it is, though, so I'm not sure if knowing that really helps or not."

Argent thought about it for a moment, then nodded. "I know who it is. It helps."

Roane nodded and continued, "Third, you need to create a place of prominence in the throne room for Ogou. He wants a red and black candle, along with the bloodied machete and knife used earlier. You'll want to place these items on top of a blood red cloth. When Julian falls, you'll need to place his head on the constructed altar until it begins to rot. This is the rest of the payment for the service Ogou has done for you tonight."

She grinned, adding, "Make the presentation flashy, too. He digs that kinda thing, and you'll definitely be rewarded for it. That's pretty much it." Roane paused for a moment, then said, "Oh, and he thinks you're a snappy dresser."

Roane looked over at Ariane as she up, breathing easier.

"You have my gratitude, Ariane. Is there anything you need?" Argent watched as she rubbed at her eyes and shook her head. She slid her hands across her forehead, flinging her fingertips out and away from her face in a series of repeated gestures.

"I still have work to do. Man, he comes on strong with you. I'm gonna be loopy for a day or two," she replied in a hoarse croak.

Ariane got to her feet and collected the chunk of meat, the cow's tongue, the peppers, the gunpowder, and the wrought-iron knife that she'd used moments ago. She took the supplies behind the throne and began speaking again in that strange, pidgin guttural-sounding French. He craned his neck to look, but Roane tapped his shoulder.

"It's best if you don't watch for this part. She'll get better focus."

Argent nodded and sat back on the steps, looking back at her. "Is it permissible to remove the blood from my face now?"

"Oh, sure. Sorry about that. I get squicked when she does that too. It's funny – you'd think that by being what we are, that sort of thing wouldn't affect us."

The blood of animals smelled, and felt, different. It wasn't something that was easy to explain, but for whatever reason, the cold animal blood was making his skin crawl. He sighed as he reached into a pocket and pulled out a handkerchief, gently rubbing his face clean. "I was never particularly fond of chickens when I was among the living. I find that my dislike has only increased over the centuries. I like having their bodily fluids on my person even less."

Roane grinned as she knelt by his side, placing a hand on his shoulder as she breathed, "It's really good to have you back, boss."

Argent looked back at her, still bowled over at how drastically she'd changed. It made him intensely curious, prompting him to ask, "What happened after I left that caused you to change so completely? You were always so dour and quiet."

Roane laughed, then replied, "Judiana had a nice long talk with me about fashion and the lighter side of life. She also helped me realize that Ariane was in love with me. It was weird, at first; realizing that it wasn't just the fact that she was my ghoul that tied her to me."

Her expression fell, her tone becoming somber as she continued, "Judiana may have been a sap, but she was right about a lot of things. I miss the hell out of her."

"As do I, Roane. As do I." Argent wrapped an arm around her, letting her lean into him as they embraced.

The woman's sea-green pigtails trembled slightly as she rested her chin on his shoulder and said, "You were a real shitheel for leaving the way you did, but I guess you had your reasons. I'm just glad you're back. All else is in the past."

It was the best welcome he'd received thus far. Argent smiled sadly as he held her tighter.

Jilah stepped out of the bath and toweled herself dry and looked herself over in the mirror. Her hair was clinging to her back and sides in a spidery web. She froze at the sound of something falling in the other room and wrapped the towel around herself and slowly crept over to the door. Peering out, she scanned the room. The enormous gargoyle standing immobile in the corner startled her, and she cried out, "What the hell are you doing in here?"

The creature frowned as its immense head slowly turned towards her, regarding her for a moment before answering, "Garder vous." Its voice came out in a low, rocky rumble, sounding as if two large pieces of masonry were being rubbed against one another.

Great. She padded over to it, noticing that one of the leather implements had come off its hook and landed on the floor in a tangled heap.

"Come again? This time in English, okay?"

The gargoyle frowned as if trying to find the appropriate words in English before it answered, "You guarding I am." It then stared back out at the rest of the room.

Jilah sighed and turned to see that all her luggage was now positioned at the foot of the bed.

"I need a guard?" She muttered as she strode towards the bed and reached down to grab one of the suitcases, tossing it onto the covers and opening it and rummaging through the contents. She searched for a moment before finding something suitable to wear to bed. Since she now had a permanent guest, she'd be damned if she was going to sleep in the nude. She pulled out a large t-shirt that read 'I feed on the blood of the living, and I vote!'

It used to be black, but the rigors of multiple laundry cycles had long ago faded it to a sickly grey color. Shirt in hand, she stalked back towards the bathroom, wondering if she was going to have a permanent shadow the entire time they were here. She grated her teeth as she realized that this was merely protocol until the official ceremony tomorrow.

If Argent thought that she was going to get intimate with him while anybody, or anything, was watching them, he was sadly mistaken. She could protect herself. Jilah quickly shut the door behind her as she stepped onto the cold tile of the bathroom floor, tossing the towel behind her before shrugging into the shirt and quickly braiding her hair. When she opened the door again, she peeked her head out, eyes narrowed.

Yep. He was still there.

Damn.

There was really nothing left to do but to try to make the best of it. She dimmed the lights, then walked over to the bed and quickly leapt under the covers. As she settled in, she re-evaluated her previous opinion of the state of the bed. It was the most comfortable mattress she could ever remember sleeping on. There was a strange pull to it that made her feel as if she was sinking into the downy softness of it. Overcome with exhaustion, her eyelids slowly slid shut as she felt the anxiety from the day's events slowly melt away.

Argent quietly slipped into the room; giving a respective nod to Brigliadoro as he padded over to the bed, the leather jacket slowly sliding down his arms. He deposited it gently on one of outer hooks that decorated the four posts of the bed then paused for a moment, looking down at Jilah. He watched his lover sleep, smiling at the sound of her slow pulsing heartbeat. She stretched and turned away from him, settling back into a deep, restful sleep. His gave a happy, satisfied sigh as he pulled the remainder of his clothes off and slid under the covers.

Tomorrow was going to be a busy night.

Nineteen
Introduction to the Court

"Wake up, beloved. It's time to get ready."

Argent had been trying to wake her for the last few minutes, but the only results to come of it so far had been her curling up into a tighter ball. Perhaps the sleeping wards on the bed were a little too strong. He would have to talk with Gigi about cutting them back a little so it would be easier for Jilah to rise in the future.

Argent grinned as his lover finally seemed to rally, slapping at him weakly before growling and rolling to the other side of the bed. She rubbed at an eye with the back of her hand and sat up abruptly with a petulant frown as she turned to look at him.

Wait a minute. Why is he already dressed?

"Whattimeisit? HowlongdidIsleep?" she croaked.

Why was she so disoriented? When they'd previously shared bed space, she had always woken up at least an hour or two before he did. The fact that he was now up and dressed startled her.

Argent presented her with a broad grin as he flopped back on the bed, turning to look up at her.

:: *All day, and part of the night. It's the wards on the bed. They're supposed to soothe you to sleep, but the effects are apparently a little stronger on you than I'd expected.* ::

Now that she was actually awake, she noticed that she no longer felt at all tired. She moved to stand up, stretching briefly as she asked, :: *Did I miss anything?* ::

:: *Not yet, but people will begin arriving soon and we must make our grand entrance.* ::

Almost as an afterthought, he casually added, :: *Oh, and Gigi designed something special for you to wear tonight...* ::

Jilah raised an eyebrow at his mischievous expression then looked around the room. A flash of color caught her eye, and she gasped as she spotted an outfit hanging on the bathroom door. She darted over to examine it, her fingers flexing. It was glorious.

A clipping hanger held up a black leather corset with indigo and purple accents that tapered into a point in the front. The skirt had a back panel that went from hip to hip, connecting to a front panel that swept down in a four-inch drape of fabric that looked like it would stop just below her knees.

The fabric rippled as she gently trailed a finger along it. It was softer than anything she'd ever touched. When she pulled it down from the hanger, the light played against the fabric and complimentary hues of teal, indigo, and purple seemed to roll through the fabric. It was mesmerizing. Burnished steel blue buckles down the front of the corset offset the overly feminine tones of the outfit, giving it a soft, yet battle-ready appeal. Jilah whistled approvingly.

:: *Do you like it?* :: he asked, knowing her answer and grinning.

Her smile was positively incandescent as she gently pawed at the dress. "Wow. I mean, WOW." She itched to try it on. :: *Oh yes. I like it very much.* ::

She had never seen anything like it and knew of no natural cloth that could drape and move in such a fashion. The fact that Gigi had created this for her, after what the woman witnessed her do last night, brought up a lump in her throat. Jilah took a deep breath, giving silent thanks to her new friend. She hoped that there was some way that she could repay the kindness. It was almost enough to make her cry. Nobody in her life had ever done anything this nice for her before. Argent chuckled softly behind her, and she leapt over to the bed, jumping on top of him and kissing him fiercely as a tear trickled down her cheek.

Startled at the change in her emotions, he brought a cool finger to trail gently along her cheek, wiping it away.

:: *Does this make you sad somehow?* ::

Jilah sighed and shook her head with a wistful smile. :: *No, not sad. I'm just not used to such open generosity from people.* ::

Argent traced her face with his fingers, murmuring softly, :: *It is something you most assuredly deserve, beloved.* :: He grinned and raised an eyebrow, sending, :: *What are you waiting for? Try it on.* ::

Jilah giggled like a giddy schoolgirl as she rushed back over to the dress. She took a quick look around, insuring that the enormous gargoyle was no longer in the room. She then whooped and pulled off her t-shirt, tossing it into the corner. As she touched the hanger a pair of stockings dropped to the floor. She dipped down to collect them, marveling at their texture and color. Their hues changed in the light as well.

She sighed softly at the feel of the fabric against her legs as she slid them on. There was a wonderfully sensual texture to them that sent little shivers up her spine. After clipping the skirt on, she then collected the corset from the hanger and slid into it. As she began clasping the buckles down the front she looked down and turned towards Argent.

:: *Doesn't really leave much to the imagination, does it?* ::

Argent grinned back at her, his expression hungry as he nodded.

Jilah laughed, asking, :: *She didn't happen to make matching underwear, did she?* ::

Argent dangled a small piece of fabric from his fingertips, his grin becoming sharp as he crooked a finger at her, beckoning.

Jilah sighed in mock annoyance as she took her time adjusting the stockings, doing her best to give him as much of a show as possible. She then slowly sauntered towards the bed. She shook her head, as if admonishing a small child.

:: *Oh hell no. Are you insane? I'm so completely not fighting with you in this outfit for the last shred of covering.* ::

Argent supposed she could always walk out on his arm as she was, but begrudgingly held up the garment for her to collect.

She leaned down and kissed him, snatching them from his fingers and quickly shifting her outfit to slide them on. She laughed as Argent made a pained noise, holding his hand to his heart, as if it had been pierced by a cartoon arrow. She turned and walked back over look at herself in the bathroom mirror, amazed at how the fabric felt as against her skin, spilling around her legs as she clipped the stockings to the garters dangling from the corset. Argent appeared in the doorway holding a pair of shiny, black, knee-high steel-heeled stiletto boots. The toes came to cruel points that nearly made her drool.

"My god, you really are Prince Charming, aren't you?"

:: I know how fond you are of such things and am enjoying watching you luxuriate in them. ::

Jilah turned to lean against the door as he knelt before her and began sliding them onto her feet. As he finished, she noted that his hand began to wander upward. She laughed and playfully slapped it away, stepping away from him. Argent sighed and stood in a single smooth motion.

:: How quickly you wound me with your rejection. :: He sighed dramatically and sat back down on the bed.

After a quick application of makeup and hairstyling, she was ready. She stood up and turned to inspect the full force of the outfit in the mirror, happy with the effect of her upswept hair; long ringlets of indigo and white framed her face as the rest of it curled into a loose roll around the top. It was perfect. She couldn't have asked for better. When she turned around, Argent's jaw dropped.

Jilah was simply stunning. It hit it him all at once with the force of a hammer between the eyes. He let her know the affect it had on him with a heated look, smiling as she flushed and fidgeted. Her heart fluttered as he offered her his arm. She paused a beat before smiling and leaning into him. Argent placed a soft kiss at the nape of her neck as he led her out of the bedroom.

:: So, how bad is this going to be? :: she asked, beginning to get nervous as they made their way into the hall. The idea of royalty was all fine and good if one looked at it from afar, but up close? She wasn't sure if she was ready for it, much less ready to be part of it. Now, all at once, the reality hit her as well as the volatile possibilities of screwing up.

:: I mean, is it going to be all hoity-toity and refined? ::

She grimaced as an imagined train wreck of socially catastrophic images collided in her head.

Oh, this could end up being so much worse than having a dream where you show up naked in your high school gym class. She plucked nervously at the hem of her corset. What if she fell over? What if she burped, or became so nauseous that she threw up? Royals didn't really care for that sort of thing, after all.

Argent chuckled beside her, covering her hand gently.

:: *This is not the same as a human royal court. Keep in mind that this is an entirely different dynamic. There are many protocols that differ vastly from the idea of monarchy that you're thinking of, if your thoughts are gravitating to the example of the lines of Elizabeth, Charles, and Diana.* ::

Jilah looked over at him, her eyes widening. :: *They're not, I mean... are they?* ::

Argent laughed and slowly shook his head. :: *No, they are very much human. It's just that most Americans tend to view the Queen Mother's family as being the exact picture of monarchy. Our kind governs an entirely different way. There is less fanfare and a great deal more violence.* ::

Jilah frowned as she walked alongside him down the dimly lit corridor.

:: *When you say more violent...* ::

:: *Disputes are often settled with a brutal and deadly finality. Preternatural creatures aren't big on discussion when they disagree about issues of leadership. There is usually no room for mistakes, for hesitation, or for dissent that would call into question the authority of the governing body.* ::

"Oh." The sound of her own voice in the corridor startled her momentarily, and Jilah gripped his arm tighter as she slipped back into thought speech. :: *So, if I slip up in there..* ::

Argent stopped and turned towards her, cupping her chin gently and kissing her as he slid an arm around her waist. :: *You will do magnificently. Remember to trust your instincts. React quickly if you need to. Do not worry about what anybody is going to say or do. You are now among creatures that respect intelligence as well as merciless and vicious response. I've seen you work. I know without a doubt that you have the capacity to handle anything that might happen tonight.* :: He pulled out of the kiss and smiled back at her, again offering his arm.

She took a deep breath and reached up to wrap her fingers around it, hoping to god he was right. She'd been pretty certain up until this point that once they were in the throne room, she would be under dressed. Her outfit was gorgeous, but downright scandalous. A hush went through the room as they walked in, and her eyes widened as she looked out at the gathered congregates that filled the enormous throne room. For a moment, Jilah wondered how many fire codes this crowd was violating.

She was intrigued at the fact that only some of the members of their collected audience looked as if they were patrons in a goth club. There was a surprisingly wide variety in the styles of dress in the crowd, but there were also elements of the throng that wore outfits a great deal more revealing than what she was currently showing off. It helped her to feel a little less self conscious.

All the showy, flashy scenes from the various vampire movies she had seen scrolled through her head in a blur. In none of them did any of the people have expressions as intent or openly fascinated as these creatures before her. Jilah felt as if she were being heavily scrutinized, which she imagined went along with the territory. She felt considerably more self conscious as she realized that the majority of them were examining her for immediate flaws, for weakness. It wasn't something that she could explain, but she could definitely feel it.

She pulled her shields tighter around her, feeling them as an almost physical presence against her skin as she strengthened them and began mentally reciting the rhyming couplet she'd discovered earlier. She found that with a little practice, she could run it in the back of her mind without it hampering her ability to function and listen clearly.

All eyes followed them as Argent led her to the throne. Jilah looked over to see Mira, Aurelian, and Gigi standing off to the left. Mira was dressed in a black leather catsuit that looked as if it had been painted on her small body. A red Chinese dragon spiraled up her thigh, its head ending just above her groin.

Aurelian stood closest to the throne, wearing black leather pants and an untucked maroon shirt that looked as if it had been created with the same material as Jilah's skirt. The first three buttons of his shirt were undone, revealing a glowing red dragon emblem blazing on his sternum. Gigi was now in a black vamp wig, her eye makeup the vivid color of peacock feathers. She was in a black PVC corset and a skirt that looked like a long, fluffed out tutu. Tall black PVC platform boots adorned her feet. Chrome buckles crept up the sides of the boots.

My god, it's like something out of Vogue - The Otherworld, Jilah thought to herself as she checked out Cynette and Alain to the right of the dais. They looked pretty much the same as when she'd first met them, but she noticed that they wore matching pendants with small, intricate red dragons coiling around themselves. She wondered why her outfit didn't have any dragons on it, since it seemed to be the theme tonight.

Argent stopped by the right side of the throne, squeezing her arm gently before releasing her and moving to stand before it. His expression remained empty as a woman smaller than Mira stepped into view holding a strange-looking device in her hand. She looked extremely out of place in her charcoal grey business suit. A set of shiny black hair sticks protruded out of the top of her hair, which had been swept into a severe blue-black bun.

After tapping on the front of the device in her hands several times, she spoke in a loud, clear voice that seemed incongruous with her tiny body.

She proclaimed, "A new applicant, Argent Valentine, has stepped up to claim the title of Strigaisha of the New Orleans Prefecture."

The courtiers remained silent as the woman's voice rang throughout the room. Jilah felt something tickle the tiny hairs on the back of her neck as the wind went up her back. She scanned the crowd for uneasy faces as the woman finished.

"Should any gathered under this roof wish to dispute this, the Council urges you to step forward now in challenge."

As the woman's voice faded, Jilah looked back out at the congregation. She wondered who, if anyone, would end up speaking out or stepping forward. Argent's expression remained inscrutable as several moments ticked by, a period of quiet that brought the slow thump of her heart jumping into her throat. She almost jerked when the herald's voice broke the silence.

"It is so noted by this officer that there is no challenge to this claim. Let the record show that Argent Valentine is now openly accepted by both the Council and those assembled as Strigaisha of the Court of the New Orleans Prefecture."

Jilah let out a slow breath as Argent stepped up to the throne and slowly sat down, his posture regal and relaxed as he set a hand on each arm of the chair. As if this was exactly where he should be. His rightful place in the world. What thoughts were going through his head as he'd taken the throne? She would have to ask him later. He had closed himself off, becoming mentally untouchable to anybody in the room.

So far so good, she thought to herself as the woman spoke again.

"Jilah, the Strigaisha's chosen consort, is now presented to the court as claimant for the title of Striaga of the New Orleans Prefecture. Should any gathered under this roof wish to dispute this, the council urges that you step forward now in challenge."

Jilah felt herself pale inwardly at the announcement, hoping that she didn't let it show. Having the entire crowd's attention focused on her was uncomfortable, to say the least. She could feel the almost oppressive weight of their collective gaze, and a cold pit started swirling in her stomach. She took a slow breath to bring her thoughts into focus, to clear her mind. A hush fell over the room, and she stayed still as she waited for somebody to speak out. To say something, anything.

The sound of the herald's voice caused her to jump slightly this time, and Jilah silently cursed herself for being so easily spooked. As the woman spoke, Jilah caught a blur of movement out of the corner of her eye, and her eyes narrowed. Something was speeding towards her, almost too quickly for her to track.

What the fuck? Something enormous and shaggy slammed into her, knocking her across the floor before she had time to react. Her head smacked the marble hard, bringing momentary bright flecks into her field of vision.

A burning fire ripped through her side, and she felt her heartbeat crank up as she tried to figure out what the hell was going on. It was obvious that she was being attacked, but what on earth was it? Several more searing slices tore through her as she did her best to fight back. Whatever it was, it was for damn sure cleaning her clock. She began to feel dizzy, and a sliver of fear jangled her nerves.

Holy shit. This thing's gonna kill me.

A familiar presence pressed itself against the inside of her skin, and Jilah felt a strange sense of working in tandem with something inside her. It had been a while since she had needed to let her reaction time happen in tune with whatever it was in her psyche that now wanted to come out and play.

Jilah shifted beneath the creature and pushed, irritated that it wouldn't let go. A sharp pain blazed through her shoulder, and she felt teeth scrape her collarbone. The creature then began worrying its head back and forth until Jilah saw spots. The edges of her vision began to go gray, and she felt her heart race in her chest as she slipped into unconsciousness.

Argent felt her drifting and shifted on the throne; his expression cold and calculating, he looked back at the creature that was mauling his lover. He tightened his jaw as he felt a burst of familiar energy shake its way through her. It had all happened within the space of a few moments. He wanted badly to intervene, but knew that if he did, he'd face the full wrath of the assembled gathering. In the eyes of the court, she would either have to prove herself by defeating the challenger or die. Anybody who stepped in to help would be ripped apart.

Still, he was damned close to throwing caution to the wind when a low growl echoed out from Jilah's throat, sounding entirely alien. It was oddly reassuring and let him know that the fight wasn't yet over. He watched as clawed hands darted out to stab repeatedly into the sides of the attacker. Her hands moved in a blur, and the furred beast quickly released her shoulder and was now moving to protect itself. It began shrieking and howling, opening more cuts in her arms and legs as it tried desperately to get away from her. Ropes of gray intestine were now spilling out of one side of her opponent's gut as Jilah moved in and began ripping holes in its abdomen. In a few moments, the contents of its stomach spilled out onto the marble. Her hands were a blur as she pressed the attack on her challenger. The creature continued to scrabble and kick at her furiously.

Argent watched as she yanked its right arm out of socket. With one arm down, she quickly did the other, then leapt astride it, forced the head aside and buried her teeth in its neck. The body bucked beneath her, but Jilah held fast, drawing deep. Argent nearly winced at the rush that flooded her system as she fed. He let out a small breath of relief, his expression sharp with grim satisfaction. The alien presence seemed to shift in her, and Argent felt Jilah snap into stark awareness. He felt her surprise, but was pleased that she kept feeding. She was going to need it. He could see the various wounds that the creature had inflicted beginning to heal over already. The beast beneath her finally began to weaken.

Jilah pulled away from the creature, peering down curiously at it. She definitely didn't want the fucking thing coming back, and the easiest way to achieve that seemed to be to take the heart. She jammed her talons up into the chest cavity, digging and rooting around for the heart. When her fingers closed around it, she yanked hard. The wet pop it made as it came free made something inside her smile. She pulled it out of her opponent's ruined body and sucked it dry. She tossed it into a corner, licking her fingers as she watched the body closely for any further signs of life.

When she was assured that it was well and truly dead, some of the pain began to bleed back into her synapses. She took a shaky breath as she looked down to see the extent of the bodily damage she'd incurred and winced. She desperately hoped that it looked worse than it actually was.

Pressing her palm against one of the more gruesome wounds to staunch the flow of blood, she looked back at the crowd with an acidic gaze. She saw several individuals nod almost imperceptibly with approval, but the majority of the court remained impassive.

Assholes. The very least they could do would be to react with something other than that carefully constructed facade of mild interest.

:: Are you okay? ::

Argent sounded really concerned, and she found herself wondering how bad she looked overall. There was an awful lot of blood – enough so that she felt that she should probably be getting dizzy or passing out real soon, but she felt fine.

Well, except for the pain; which was beginning to creep in a little more.

Helluva way to find out that I'm not indestructible, she grated internally. The fucking thing had damn near punched her ticket. She wondered exactly what had happened during the time she'd passed out. The herald began speaking again, as if none of it had happened.

Jilah took a deep, slow breath and glanced over at Argent. He was looking over at her curiously, and although she realized that he couldn't afford to show more than that in his expression, she was a little hurt. But then, she knew that she really couldn't afford to feel or show that either. Now wasn't the time to be comforted, or to seek comfort. Now was the time to be strong so that nobody else got the bright idea to jump her tonight. She wasn't sure if she would survive another confrontation. The thought truly frightened her, and she did her best to not let it show.

It was definitely high time she started honing her reaction time and fighting skills. After months of hunting nothing but pale shadows of the creatures she was now going to be dealing with on a regular basis, she'd pretty much assumed that she had no limits. That she couldn't really be hurt. Now she'd just had an effective, almost deadly lesson to the contrary. It scared her enough to make her want to train for the contingency of having to fight like this again in the future. She wasn't sure how often this kind of crap would end up happening, but she was damn sure going to be ready for it next time.

:: I'll live, :: she sent in response as the end of the herald's statement rang through the room.

Having asked again if there was a challenger for the position of Striaga, another period of silence extended into what felt like minutes. Keeping the cold anger in her eyes as she looked back at the gathered crowd, Jilah waited for another challenge as she centered herself and wrapped her awareness around the room. After another couple of seconds, she realized that there was now nobody else in the throne room that was willing to contest her appointment.

Well, for the moment, that is.

Jilah stood ramrod straight now, her hands at her sides as the maddening itching of the healing process began in little patches all over her body. The itching grew worse as the official pronouncement was made. She gritted her teeth against it as the assembled gathering bowed their heads in obeisance to the new Strigaisha and Striaga of New Orleans.

:: It – It nearly killed me.. :: she sent to Argent as she tried desperately to keep from shaking and scratching everywhere at once.

:: I should not have brought you here. :: Argent replied, furious with himself that he had so nearly lost her.

:: We'll talk. Later, :: she replied quietly, trying to reassure him. It had been her choice to come.

It took an extreme force of will to keep herself upright and stoically silent as the herald proceeded to list off various new laws, protocols and proclamations now that somebody again sat in control of the prefecture. Jilah listened halfheartedly, wanting to go back to the bedroom, anywhere that she could be alone to fall apart for a few minutes.

Although the encounter had shaken her, she couldn't help but notice that pieces of the material from the corset and skirt were fusing into the wounds. She dreaded having to pull them out after they'd fully healed. The process would be nowhere near as bad as the pain of the initial wound itself, but she was pretty sure it would be unpleasant. Just when Jilah was starting to think that the droning spew of political dross would never end, the herald stopped. Jilah blinked and looked over at Argent.

:: *It is almost over,* :: he murmured softly in her thoughts. He sounded almost defeated.

She sighed and tried her best to smooth out what remained of her outfit as courtiers began lining up in front of the throne to pay their respects to the new leader. They first knelt before Argent, who politely greeted them. After a few congratulatory and some possibly simpering remarks, they made their way over to her, again kneeling and declaring fealty. Or so she thought. Who knew with some of them? Not everybody spoke a language that she could easily understand.

The entire scene reminded Jilah of a bizarre version of what married couples had to endure at their receptions. She sighed softly as she looked at the size of the line forming behind the current well wishers. At least the guests at this reception were as varied as the different kinds of creatures she'd skimmed over in the library when she had first started to research herself and her nature. She reminded herself to begin amassing a collection of stories about supernatural and mythical creatures to see if she could figure out the differences between the recorded myths and the reality that now surrounded her.

The man currently before her was smiling and falling just short of prostrating himself. As he stood back up, he purred in a silky, hissing voice, "You are as swift and deadly as you are beautiful, Striaga. It is my honor to serve you."

Jilah mentally recoiled as she forced a smile. She took a breath to steady herself and sent, :: *Please tell me that they aren't all like him.* ::

Argent's response was somewhat somber. :: *After your earlier display, you can probably expect quite a few responses to you that follow in a similar fashion. You were, after all, suitably inspiring.* ::

Jilah nodded to another well wisher, smiling just enough as to be polite.

Twenty

Duty Calls

As the last few attendees filtered out of the throne room, Jilah looked over at Argent nervously.

:: *How often can I expect challenges like that?* ::

Argent frowned, his eyes not meeting hers. :: *Can't say. Everyone's reaction to you will be different.* ::

At the surface of her thoughts, he found that she understood why he hadn't been able to jump in to help her during the challenge, but she was still disappointed. He quickly explained, :: *It is likely that you've put a great many detractors off with the way you handled yourself tonight. It was an effectively gruesome display. The throng usually reacts positively to such things.* ::

Jilah nodded and took a tentative step towards him. Argent finally met her gaze, his anguish plain on his face.

:: *This will not happen again. I swear it. Even if my intervention causes the death of us both.* ::

She closed the distance and wrapped her arms around him.

:: *Just teach me how to fight. If I actually know how to fight, you might not need to back me up.* ::

Argent looked up at her as she added, :: *And I won't get another gorgeous outfit shredded to hell and back.* ::

He breathed a sigh of relief at her smile. She gently ruffled his hair as she stood beside the enormous, ornate chair and Argent leaned into the touch.

:: *How often will this sort of full court appearance thing be happening?* ::

:: Court convenes sporadically, when need demands. During the majority of our time spent here, I will be involved in diplomatic negotiations with other Prefects, settling disputes between individuals and groups, and personally enforcing general order when such measures become necessary. Large events such as these do not happen often, for which I am very grateful, but there will be enough busywork to keep me occupied for long stretches of time until order is restored. ::

Although Jilah had almost died tonight, Argent had to admit that his original appointment as Strigaisha had been a great deal more vicious. It was the night that he'd earned the moniker thrust upon him by the denizens of the prefecture – The Dragon's Hammer. The memory brought up a bittersweet remembrance of times past – once again he realized how much things had changed. Some, for the better – others, he wasn't so sure.

The enemies who had wanted his head on a pike when he'd abdicated – would still want some form of satisfaction or revenge. He assumed that any dissension from this point forward would be covert and shadowed, which always ended up being worse than outright confrontation.

Argent frowned as he noticed the bits of leather and cloth that were now embedded in Jilah's side, the wounds having healed completely around them as they were tending to affairs of state. It would hurt a great deal to dig them out, but she'd heal again. He found it reassuring that she had been able to keep her wits about her throughout the healing process. The itching must have been maddening. He reached over and tugged gently at one of the larger pieces, and Jilah let out a yelp.

"Ow! What the...?" She frowned and slapped his hand away, stepping away from him.

:: Cut it out, dammit. ::

He could tell that the wounds still prickled a little, even though the worst of them had fully healed over. Jilah plucked at a section of skirt that trailed in a tattered length from a spot in her upper thigh.

"What a pain in the ass," she grumbled, wanting the bits of cloth out, but not really sure if she was ready to start yanking roughly at them to get them the hell out of her body.

Argent gripped her wrist and pulled her closer. :: *They will have to come out. It's better done sooner than later.* ::

Jilah narrowed her eyes at him. :: *You're entirely too eager about this. You might get carried away.* ::

His hand crept slowly towards her side, and she slapped it away again.

:: *Moi? Carried away?* ::

He was the very picture of innocence as he batted his eyelashes back at her.

:: *Don't you have things to do? Places to be? Proclamations to write?* :: She waved him off dismissively. :: *Go write a law or something.* ::

Argent grinned and slid off the massive throne, slowly prowling towards her, his moves smooth and fluid as he extended a hand out to try to yank out another swatch of cloth. :: *I'm pretty much done for the moment, and I do believe that you could do with a little harassing.* ::

He mirrored her movements step for step as she maneuvered toward the back corridor, and Jilah couldn't help smiling now. Argent stopped and she stood stock still, waiting for him to make a move, her grin getting wider. :: *You are going to be soooo sorry if you don't cut it out.* ::

:: *I highly doubt it.* ::

Jilah eyed him, then broke for the hall, giggling now. :: *You're such a shit.* ::

:: *Eloquently stated.* ::

Argent grabbed her as she reached the mouth of the corridor. She squeaked, spinning around to elude his grasp. She kicked out at him, and he dodged effortlessly. He wrapped an arm around her waist and nuzzled her ear as his fingers plucked at the fabric at her waist. He gave a sharp yank and she cried out.

"Ow, dammit!"

She tried to throw him, but he just held on tighter. She jammed her heel down at his foot, and he deftly moved it aside. Her heel met the floor making her teeth clack together. Every move she made, he countered with ease. She couldn't stop laughing. Finally, she spotted an opening and with a few quick moves, she broke his hold, grabbed him and pushed him back into the throne room.

With a hearty laugh, she yelled, "HA! Too slow, Chicken Merengo!" and sped down the corridor, whooping with laughter.

Argent appeared next to her just outside of the bedroom, a wicked grin curling the edges of his lips as he whispered, "Boo."

"Holy crap!" Jilah leapt back, startled. He grabbed her again, bringing her up and slamming her forcefully up against the wall. The impact jarred her momentarily, but she quickly recovered, writhing in his grasp.

:: No fair, you're older! ::

Argent stopped and looked at her for a moment, confused.

:: And what, exactly, does that have to do with anything? ::

It gave her enough of an opening to grab his shoulders, and she rammed him against the other side of the hallway.

:: Nothing, actually. I just needed a distraction. ::

Argent laughed and looked back at her as he grasped another piece of fabric and yanked, causing her to cry out.

"OW! Goddammit, that hurts!"

Argent laughed and yanked out several more pieces before she could stop him.

:: Oh, that's it! Now you're going down. ::

They began wrestling in the hallway, laughing and playfully knocking each other around. They eventually ended up on the floor, grabbing and slapping at one another and giggling like idiots. Scraps of bloody fabric littered the floor around them like gruesome confetti.

Argent rolled onto his back and she straddled him, pressing his wrists to the floor. "Okay! Okay! I'll get the rest of it out myself, dammit! Piss off!"

Argent looked up at her and grinned. Jilah flushed and smiled back at him, leaning down to brush her lips against his.

:: You really are a pain in the ass. ::

He growled happily, arching his hips against her as she kissed him. Jilah released his wrists and placed her hands on either side of his face. Another sharp pain flared in her side, and he grinned up at her as he quickly pulled several more pieces of her embedded corset out of her skin. She slapped at him and laughed again. He chuckled as he continued to try to pull the rest of the fabric out of her healed wounds.

:: Ow! You are sadly mistaken if you OW! think that this is a valid way to get into my pants. Cut it out! ::

:: Surely my method of removal is far more entertaining. ::

Argent now furiously pulled and yanked at the various embedded bits of fabric, figuring that the faster they came out, the quicker she'd heal and have it done with. Besides, the distraction kept it from hurting her as much as it would if she'd done it herself. Jilah continued to slap at him, her laugh throaty and warm.

:: This is absolutely..OW! The worst date I've ever been on. You'd better pay for everything, mister! ::

They collapsed into a fit of giggles. A throat clearing behind them caused them both to freeze and turn towards the source of the sound. Alain stood looking down at the two of them, his expression perplexed.

"Strigaisha, I apologize for interrupting, but there is the matter regarding Julian that needs to be addressed."

Argent didn't think he'd ever seen the Alpha this flustered by anything in the entire time he'd known him. In the past, Argent had been very reserved in public, and his current behavior probably shocked the Alpha. Being around Jilah made him feel young again, and he couldn't remember the last time he had been able to express this side of himself.

Realistically, even when he was a child, he had never truly been able to let go and enjoy himself in such a manner. But then, a great many things had changed within him in the last seventy years. They would all have to get used to him again.

Argent stood up and offered Jilah a hand, pulling her up and snaking an arm around her waist. Her voice was soft in his thoughts as she placed a hand on his hip and squeezed gently.

:: You should go, check it out. I've got things I need to take care of as well. Meet you back here later and we can pick up where we left off? ::

Argent grinned back at her and chuckled. *:: It's a date. Make sure to wear something that you will not mind having ripped off. ::*

Jilah shivered and grinned back at him, trying to express something that wouldn't come with words.

Argent smiled, his voice a warm purr in her thoughts. *:: Me too, beloved. Me too. ::*

Jilah glanced over at Alain and gave him an awkward nod of acknowledgment before running into the bedroom.

Argent watched her go for a moment then turned towards Alain. "What's the current situation?"

"The whelp apparently had a meeting of his own last night. According to our sources, there were a record number of attendees. More shifters appear to have switched to his side after hearing about your consort, and what she was capable of doing to a pack brother."

Argent took a deep breath and leaned up against the wall. Damn. He thought something like this might happen. He had hoped that the news wouldn't have spread so rapidly. Argent turned to look back at Alain, watching the large man's broad features tighten as he spoke.

"Julian is taking full advantage of what happened by spreading the seeds of fear through his mongrels and to anybody else who will listen." The Alpha steeled himself, his voice low and quiet as he continued, "Many are responding to his message. There are those in my own pack that I've had to bring to heel for speaking in agreement with him."

Argent's brow furrowed. His new lover did come with some serious baggage. In the beginning of his initial reign, he'd been surprised when the Tribe of the Savage Moon had offered fealty to a blood drinker as the head of this city. Most preternaturals were well aware of their penchant for mental manipulation, and he was pretty certain that the last thing the wolves wanted was a ruler that could force them to think and behave in certain ways, somebody that could manipulate them easily.

Not all Sanguine had the same talents, but none of them were too eager to spread that particular fact around. It helped keep people on their toes, made them a little more manageable. It wasn't until Argent realized exactly how badly the Tribe outnumbered all the other preternaturals in the city that he understood the enormity of what they were offering him. An individual with the proper mental talent could easily subdue several pack members at a time, but any more than that proved to be taxing, if not downright fatal. The wolves tended to be very much of the 'keep your friends close, and your enemies closer' persuasion.

The wolves of any given city were not a group to be trifled with and, unwittingly, his lover had stepped into a hornet's nest and taken the court with her. Now he had to try to insure that his people could roll with the resulting fallout.

"How much damage control is needed at this point?" Argent asked, almost not wanting to know.

"They fear her because she snapped the mind of a pack brother without a care that his soul would remain in limbo. They wonder if Gregor still suffers for his crimes, even though she dispatched him. He had no chance to take with him his lessons learned from this Run – to be among us again in a different form. To do such a thing to any living creature, to take that choice from them; is an abomination. It goes against everything we believe in. To have destroyed Gregor in such a manner is an unforgivable offense." The Alpha shuddered as he continued, "His soul has entered the Dreaming broken and unaware of itself."

Argent came to a dead stop in the hallway, very careful to keep his expression neutral as he looked over at the Alpha. This was definitely something he hadn't counted on. For therianthropes, the Dreaming was defined as the time after, beyond the fur and the flesh, when they could reflect on the events endured on the current Run. It was a time of reunion, when old friends and family long past would see each other again before they decided to take their next step on the great, grand Run of living.

Argent found himself wondering if Jilah knew, or would even care, about what happened to the souls she cracked open during the course of her work. Did this happen to the humans she tracked down as well? And even if Jilah did care, would the ebony-skinned demoness in her head? After all, she was the one running the whole show. Jilah was very likely seen by it as a puppet to be utilized until her usefulness came to an end.

Argent wanted to discuss this with her at some point but wasn't sure how to broach the subject, much less how to offer a solution, if there was one to be had. Alain's voice was cold and calculating as he took a step back and said, "Considering the circumstances, I believe I have a right to know what she hunts for. It is the only way that I can be sure to contain the threat that they all seem to see in her."

Argent became distant, his voice guarded and wary. "Contain the threat?"

Alain continued, his tone softening. "If I know what she seeks in those that she hunts, I can insure that this is not a problem within the ranks of my pack. Within limits, of course."

The tension that had been building between them eased, and Argent hooked his thumbs into his pockets. "She preys on those who sexually brutalize human women and children."

The Alpha's shoulders dropped slightly, his posture becoming less rigid as he gave Argent a curt nod. "I thank you, Strigaisha."

The large man turned and strode purposefully down the hallway. Argent wondered if now that it had been made clear that his lover's targets weren't only human, he wondered what would happen if Jilah ever found out about his extremely questionable past? Would she hunt him, too?

He shivered as he realized that yes, she very likely would. He was certain that the entity that squatted in her mind would ensure that she had no choice. Argent sincerely hoped that it would never come to that.

Twenty One

Land of Swine and Roses

As the last few pieces of leather came free, Jilah felt a chill go up her spine.

I almost died tonight.

Her own thoughts echoed in her mind, rattling her again. She groaned and tossed the bloody remains of her corset into the trashcan in the bathroom. It was a damn shame to lose the outfit. She imagined that Gigi would understand that loss, though. Jilah turned the shower on, wincing as she looked down at the collection of bodily fluids gathered on her skin. Although none of her injuries really hurt anymore, she was appalled at the image she presented in the mirror.

Something else occurred to her. The Dark Lady in her head was remaining oddly silent. Jilah figured that she'd be pissed that her vessel had almost gotten herself permanently knocked out of commission, but she felt nothing coming from her patroness. Jilah frowned as she let her hair down and stepped into the shower. Letting her head rock back, she grabbed the soap and began scrubbing at her skin.

She shivered at the memory of the beast's teeth sinking into her shoulder. She scrubbed harder, forcing the image from her mind. She was shocked that he had done so much damage to her so quickly, although there was almost no trace of it left on her skin now. There were a few small patches where the skin had closed up after having the fused bits of fabric yanked out of them, but for the most part her skin was now clean and unbroken.

The sound of the water became louder, the volume slowly cranking up as she felt a familiar lurch in her gut. "Ah crap, already?" She muttered to herself as she felt her legs wobble.

Jilah's gut wrenched again, sharply, and she slapped a hand against the tile as her quarry's location flared in bright images through her head.

What, no recovery time? That's hardly fair.

A discordant thrum through her mind gave her the distinct feeling that she shouldn't push it.

Through the flashing images, she could make out a raggedy shack in what looked like the middle of a swamp. She could hear dogs barking, but the noises were muffled and distorted. She couldn't tell how many there were, but they sounded big. Small, empty eyes stared out from between the bars of what looked like a small pet kennel. It looked like a child, but one that was completely spaced out.

She pulled herself to her feet from where she had slid to a crouch on the shower floor as the images had cascaded through her mind, shaking her head to get rid of the ringing in her ears.

"Okay, OKAY! I'm going already!" she growled, stepping out of the shower and shutting it off.

She searched for something simple to throw on and found a bra and black tanktop. A familiar sound echoed through her thoughts. It sounded angry.

She pleaded with her patroness, :: *Could you tone it down on the stabbing pain with the visions? Just a little? I don't mean to sound ungrateful, but..* ::

The Dark Lady's voice cut her off mid-thought. The voice of her patroness whipped through her psyche, and Jilah winced as she spoke.

:: *I require something different from you this time, daughter. A show of appreciation for your gift, I think. You didn't seem to think much of almost throwing it away earlier, so I believe that a grand gesture on your part would reassure me that you are still grateful.* ::

That doesn't sound good.

As Jilah continued dressing, she shivered. :: *And, that would be?* ::

:: *A trophy.* ::

:: *A w-what??* :: she stammered in response.

:: *Bring me his head.* :: The Dark Lady crooned softly. It set Jilah's teeth on edge.

The image of a nondescript table with black cloth, and a collection of implements; a sword, a hangman's noose, a small platter and a wooden bowl, flickered through her mind. Jilah blinked rapidly, taking a minute to realize what she was being directed to do.

:: *You want an altar.* ::

:: *Yes daughter. This is not a polite suggestion. I insist.* ::

But, where the hell would she put it? Not to mention that this 'trophy' was going to get pretty gamey in short order. Rotting meat always had a distinctive, telltale odor, and there wasn't much that she could do to cover it up once it started getting funky. In a building full of people with extraordinarily keen senses, it would be damn near impossible to pull off. Jilah made a distasteful face at the very idea of the stench.

The image of a passageway, and a hidden opening, flickered in her mind's eye. :: *It will be safe there. This will be enough to appease my ire at your earlier carelessness.* ::

Jilah frowned and asked, :: *You're angry that I came here?* ::

Her patroness' response was sharp and harsh, :: *It is a mild irritant, or at least it was until that creature almost cracked you open and spilled my precious gift out onto the cold marble of that chamber. I do not take kindly to having my vessels mistreated – by anything. Including themselves.* ::

The voice shifted, continuing in softer tones, :: *You have put yourself squarely in harm's way by coming here, daughter. Moreso than you would have encountered in the regular pace of your nightly duties. You are my precious gift to this world, seeing you hurt puts me in ill temper.* ::

Jilah answered softly, "I understand."

The Dark Lady's tone became almost loving, :: *Go work my will this night, daughter, my most precious weapon.* ::

Jilah pulled the rest of her clothes on and headed out into the hallway. She paused, unsure of how to find her way out of the convent without Gigi. The avatar turned in the direction of the throne room, preparing to send a mental call out for Argent before she paused and closed her eyes. Something in the resonance in the room had changed and her head no longer felt clouded as it had the night she'd first arrived. She followed her instincts and turned to the right.

Is it me, or was that turn in the hallway not there the last time I walked through here?

Jilah followed the turn and came to a dead end. She stepped forward and placed a hand on the stone. It was surprisingly warm. She reached forward, touching her fingertips to the stone. The wall shifted in response, becoming opaque.

Jilah shook her head as she stepped through the wall to the outside.

Her destination turned out to be at the edge of a bayou. The sounds of various night critters thrummed in the air like an eerie heartbeat. At least she had been able to get here without having to use a boat of any kind.

As Jilah crept around to the back of the building, she could see how someone could easily lose their way back here in the sticks, getting stuck in the bogs, or worse, if they didn't know their way around. At least she hadn't run into any alligators. Yet.

Jilah stood at the back door of the shack, listening to the symphony of myriad bayou denizens singing in the night air. She steadied herself and took a deep breath to prepare herself for what she thought she was going to find.

A cry sounded from inside the cabin, freezing her in her tracks. It was followed by something thumping heavily on the floor. It sounded almost like two people wrestling.

The dogs playing, perhaps?

Jilah reached forward to grip the door handle, her fingers lengthening into sharp-tipped claws. The sounds of muffled yelling now pricked her ears, and she scanned the room inside to make sure that the dogs weren't at the door. A loud slap followed by another thump that sounded suspiciously like a body hitting the floor urged her on.

With a growl, she kicked the door off its hinges. It flew into a dingy kitchen full of dishes and soiled takeout containers, clattering to the floor. The lock in the doorframe splintered away from the wood, hitting the floor with a metallic thunk. Jilah heard the dogs before she saw them; feral growls and the clicking of claws on tile echoing from the next room as the animals pounded their way towards her.

The rottweilers were enormous and wild-eyed. One of them tripped over the door, the other climbing over it and leaping at her. She snatched it out of the air, snapping its neck with a savage shake, then quickly dispatched the other one, leaving their furred carcasses quivering on the linoleum. Damn, and I like dogs, too.

It was just something else she would have to pay the bastard back for. A pungent scent assaulted her nostrils, and she suppressed a gag as she walked through the kitchen. Jilah rounded the corner, her eyes widening at the scene before her. A small collection of filthy cages held what she could only assume were children in cramped, crouched positions. They were definitely too small to be anything else. The children looked to be at extreme stages of malnourishment and abuse, their expressions wan and distant as they stared blankly through the bars of their makeshift prisons.

Not one of them looked older than eight or nine.

All of them had ugly bruises, welts, and cuts covering their bodies, in varying stages of infection. They all had the same haunted, empty expression. She felt a part of her begin to crack inside as what looked like one of the newer arrivals extended a hand out to her, screeching from under a mouth full of duct tape.

A very young boy was on the floor, holding his ribs and shuddering so strongly that she thought he was having a grand mal seizure. The rancid odor of the place was so overwhelming that her eyes began to tear up. It smelled like a charnel house. How could anything live here and not notice it?

In the corner, a wet bundle of skin covered in black ichor and mold wriggled in a cage. Several mottled, strangely shaped pillows lay next to it in the cage, and it took her a moment to realize that they were amputated body parts that had been left in the cage to rot next to the body they'd been taken from.

With a dawning sense of horror, she looked back over at the boy in the middle of the room. A dark red pool of blood was spreading out across the floor from beneath the boy's hips, and Jilah's conscious thought completely shut down.

She quickly began backpedaling, her jaw opening and closing like a stuttering ventriloquist dummy as she thumped up against the wall behind her.

It was too much. Her mind started spinning, and a high-pitched sound bubbled up out of her throat. A violent shake brought Jilah back to her senses, and her patroness howled through her consciousness with incoherent rage. She winced in pain as the voice ripped through her gray matter.

The man she saw in her vision appeared before her, yelling something she couldn't understand as he slammed her back into the wall and backhanded her. With a snap, something in her other took over, pushing her emotional reaction to the back corner of her consciousness. It became a dull buzzing as the man continued yelling at her. Jilah couldn't make out what the man was saying.

She figured that he was likely bitching her out for killing his dogs and busting his place up.

Her hand snapped up, claws clutching the man's throat and squeezing as she picked him up, holding him out and away from her. She peered up at him as his feet kicked at the air beneath him. Screaming in rage, she tossed him across the room where he collided with a chair, knocking it over and breaking it. The man's eyes widened and he began trying to get away from her. She darted over and grabbed one of his ankles, pulling him beneath her and straddling him, pinning his arms with her knees as she squatted malevolently on his chest.

Her eyes blazed as she gazed into the depths of the man's soul, finding nothing but a monstrous need to use and consume within it. The sheer number of faces and names that swept through her mind as she began drawing them out of him nearly broke her heart. She gritted her teeth against a virtual tidal wave of grief and anguish for so many broken bodies. So many dead.

All of them children.

Jilah shook her head to clear it. She would have plenty of time to grieve for them later. Now was the time to take care of business.

The man had been engaged in this horrific business for quite some time. Jilah reeled at the realization that most of the children in the house were considered old stock. He considered himself a trainer of sorts, seeing his job as 'breaking in' new prospects so that they'd be pliable and docile for their new owners.

There were several people in the area, as well as a rather large client list from outside the state, who came to him with certain unusual requests on a regular basis. His associates could be more than a little rough on their purchases, and the demand for fresh ones when they'd broken the old ones kept him in business.

Most of the remains ended up in the swamp when these men were done with them. After all, alligators were always hungry – and they usually didn't leave much after consuming a meal. The bones would just end up mired in the depths of the swamp, removing any trace of the children.

The idea that such a person could exist – that there could be a group of human beings that would do such a thing.

The Dark Lady was showing Jilah their faces, telling her to kill all those within easy reach, to fill her altar with their heads.

Jilah could think of no finer tribute, her tone reverent as she shivered and breathed, "Yes, Mother."

A righteous fury shook her to the core of her foundation. It flooded through her in a blistering wave, feeling better than almost any other sensation she had ever experienced. It had always felt so good, so cleansing in the past when she ended up angry, and rightly so. Divine Justification was sublime, after all. But this was something so far beyond her previous experience.

It was rapturous. Glorious.

Every neuron in her synapses felt as if it were firing at the same time as Jilah roared and forced an instantly crippling wave of images and emotion into the man's cortex, her face radiant with joy as she howled above him. Her body shook with the sheer pleasure of it – the utter delight as she felt his soul immediately splinter and shatter from her onslaught, almost sending her over the razored edge of release.

A small part of her shrank back from the experience, sickened by what it found there, this was dancing on the path to true evil. Reveling and gaining this much pleasure in the anguish and pain of another; it was what her prey did to their victims. Something didn't seem at all right with it and part of her lurched and cracked; just a little.

Jilah's patroness howled with laughter in her head, and her thoughts were filled with the woman's, reassuring voice.

:: You need not concern yourself with the morality of your task, daughter. You are now an instrument beyond mere human principles. You have been assigned a holy task, one that only such as yourself can fulfill. You are the only reason that these animals are being called to account for their actions,

otherwise they would continue their work at destroying the innocent. They are FAR from innocent, and their punishment is just. Remember this, daughter. Remember. ::

Jilah shivered and looked away from. Yes, the punishment was just, but was she really any better than him at this point? Her patroness was right, but how she had reacted to the man's utter terror and pain felt so alien, so evil.

And yet, a part of her crooned, so goddamned DELICIOUS.

The flare of orgasm flashed through her body, taking her entirely by surprise. Jilah threw up almost immediately, her gut churning as she retched violently, over and over. When the worst of the wave of nausea had passed, she forced herself to breathe slowly, in and out. In and out.

She wiped her mouth with the back of her hand, closing her eyes as a tear trailed down her cheek. She didn't want to turn to see the rest of the room, the rest of the house. She wanted so badly for none of this to be happening, to do anything that would make it a dream. Unfortunately, there was so much work to do.

Please let me be strong enough to make the end quick and painless for them, Mother.

With a heavy heart, she got to her feet and set about doing what needed to be done.

Jilah stood on the back deck of the cabin, shuddering so hard that the wood beneath her hands splintered.

It had been considerably worse in the basement. The man kept a surgical table off in a corner so that one of his clients in the medical field could discreetly visit and conduct experiments on some of the 'inventory.'

The things that they would do with the bodies on that table after... Jilah thought that she would never truly be able to eat again.

She held a shaky hand to her forehead; tears spilling down her cheeks, she gasped for breath as she wept for the children that she'd had to euthanize. Jilah told herself that there was nothing else she could have done for them. The few victims that were still living were so mentally fractured that they were little more than quivering, long-suffering meat.

Several were so badly injured that their wounds had become septic – to the point that they were only days, if not hours, from death. Most of the 'stock' that the animal had left over were already dying. He had been waiting for another shipment to come in a day or two, from god only knew where. Whether the few that were barely alive could have been physically rehabilitated, it was certain that none of them would ever be aware of themselves or their environment again.

She had been as quick and merciful as possible, and every time they sighed in release it broke a little piece of her heart. Even the boy she'd broken in to rescue had died in her arms as she tried to comfort him in his last moments in this godforsaken place. His wounds had bled out too quickly for her to stop his passing.

Jilah was certain that no amount of good or happiness could ever cleanse this blight from her emotional memory. It was a stain on her soul that would never rinse off, never come clean. Sometime in between killing her target and going through the rest of the house and methodically euthanizing anything left alive, something inside her had definitely snapped, twisting her perceptions of people into warped, one-dimensional puppets.

Perhaps Argent was right. Maybe they are only good for meat.

With a steely resolve, she pulled a book of matches out of her coat pocket, opening it and striking one of them. She felt a cold wind blow through her heart as she held the book over the flame, tossing it into the kitchen when the entire pack caught. She blurred away to a safe distance as the kerosene she'd spread throughout the house ignited. Flame crept out of the hairline cracks in the foundation; and a loud rupturing noise thundered through the night air.

The generator tank went up, taking the house with it.

The fire was purifying in a way, taking with it the foul stench of what had transpired in this house. The fire also effectively covered her tracks. The noise from the exploding tank would likely tie up local officials long enough for her to continue her hunt throughout the city proper without interference. She watched the conflagration for a good ten minutes before turning her back on the remainders of the blaze and heading back towards the hazy pink lights of the city. It was going to be a long night. And, she still had to eat.

The very idea of drinking any of the viscous fluid that flowed through that malignant pig's body had been utterly repugnant to her. She was thankful that her patroness hadn't pressed her on the feeding thing in this particular instance. It was bad enough feeling the rhythmic thumping of the man's severed head against her leg. She'd put it in a pillowcase after wrapping the head in plastic wrap so that it wouldn't start seeping through the cloth. She now understood with horrible clarity why the Dark Lady wanted his head as a trophy.

Picking her way through the swamp to her target had been less than appealing, even though she'd been shown the way. Tromping back through it again wasn't something that she wanted to do anytime soon. When it was finally behind her, she hoped never to be in a position to have to walk through another one.

When Jilah stepped within the city limits, she felt a familiar pull as the second blaring vision of the night flared to life in her head. Mercifully, there was no physical pain associated with it this time. Perhaps things were looking up.

Jilah stood with her hands on her knees, her breath coming in hitches as the last of the images faded out. This one was close. Her target was fast asleep in his bedroom, next to his loving wife.

Jilah let out a low growl and began to run.

Twenty Two

The Killing Dance

Ah, suburbia.

Jilah walked around the perimeter of a large white house with a wrap-around porch. She crept silently as she moved into the backyard.

Back door entry, take two. No dogs this time, please, she thought to herself as she peeked in the back window. She really didn't want to kill any more animals.

She gave the handle a gentle turn, doing her best to make as little noise as possible. The door popped open without a sound, and Jilah let out a little breath that she hadn't known she'd been holding. Once inside, she was relieved to find it in much better shape than the last place.

How the man in the swamp could live in the utter feculence he'd mired himself in was beyond her. Jilah felt a small wave of nausea at the memory of the corrupted scent of the cabin come up before she could force it back down. After a several deep breaths, she squared her shoulders and pressed on.

Jilah cat-footed through the kitchen, peeking around the corner into the darkness. The living room was standard and nicely devoid of people and animals. She spotted a staircase off to the right.

So far, so good.

She froze in place as something rubbed up against her leg. Looking down, she spotted a marmalade tabby that appeared to be enjoying itself a great deal as it pawed playfully at her foot. Letting out a small sigh of relief, she reached down to give the cat a gentle scritch on the chin before slowly making her way up the stairs. The cat gave a petulant mew at being rebuffed so quickly, then padded off into the kitchen in search of food.

As Jilah crept up the stairs, she noted that they weren't creaky. Another good sign.

At the top of the staircase, Jilah scanned the hallway, trying to figure out where the master bedroom was located. As she moved through the hallway, she briefly peered into each room, checking them out to make sure they were empty. The second room she looked into was like a punch in the gut. The guy had kids, but they weren't in their beds – two boys, by the look of the room's decor.

An ugly smile curved the edges of her lips as she made her way to the last room at the end of the hallway and poked her head around the corner of the doorframe. Hubby and wifey, sound asleep and floating in blissful dreams. It made her sick to her stomach. Jilah wondered if his wife knew. If she did, Jilah would kill her too, without hesitation.

She moved closer into the room, gently placing black-booted feet on beige padded carpeting as she crept over to the man and looked down at him. He was sleeping deeply, his body in a fetal position, the covers curled in his hand. Jilah glanced over at his wife, who was sprawled out on her side of the bed, her hand on her chest. She looked completely relaxed and at peace. She probably didn't know.

In the blink of an eye Jilah was on the bed between them, her hands clapped over their mouths. They both woke with a start, wriggling beneath her, and she hissed at them, her voice sharp as she grated, "If you move, I'll kill one of you while the other one watches. Am I clear?"

The woman began weeping but nodded quickly before looking over at her husband, her eyes wide.

The man gave a scared nod, but Jilah watched anger creep into his eyes as he glared up at her, this insolent woman that had invaded the privacy of his house.

"Good. Outstanding even. First things first."

She looked over at the wife and purred, "Sleep, and forget." Jilah felt something in her mind push into the woman's thoughts, gently imprinting her command on the woman's gray matter. The woman lurched for a moment, then dropped into unconsciousness.

So that's how it's done, she thought to herself.

She then looked back at the man who was now staring over at the sleeping form of his wife, he looked back to Jilah, his eyes wide with fright. She straddled the man's chest as something sensual and deadly began speaking with her voice.

"You've been a naughty boy, haven't you?" Jilah let out a sinister chuckle, trailing a lengthening claw down the man's cheek, the nail biting into his skin sharply as she reached his jawline. The man cried out, and she backhanded him savagely, shuddering with pleasure as she heard the bones in his cheek shatter. "How many children have you gone through, I wonder?"

Her voice was a poisonous, honeyed purr as she leaned into him, riding his fear and lapping it up as she sucked a drop of his blood off the tip of her finger.

"I visited your supplier earlier tonight. Turned out he had quite the selection. It really was a shame to see it all go to waste, don't you think?"

It was almost admirable how the man tried to talk through the pain, his voice difficult to understand as he slurred, "Whuuh taa.. whuuh meea?"

"Oh, come now. Don't pretend as if you don't know what I'm talking about. It insults both of us." Jilah spat at him, her voice still thick and sultry as she continued, "I must admit that I'm wondering, how a man with your curious predilection has children anyway? Were you getting tired of the empty-eyed little darlings that señor motherfucker out in that putrid little cabin in the swamp kept billing you for? Were you perhaps cultivating your own?"

Jilah smiled as the man's eyes grew huge, tears brimming at the edges. His voice was hoarse, cracking as he muttered something unintelligible that sounded a little as if he were begging her not to hurt them. Jilah laughed and jumped off him, gripping his arms and pulling him into a sitting position.

"Such a caring and devoted father," she mocked, sneering at him. "If I wasn't aware of your other crimes, I'd almost be moved to not kill you and take your head. As it is, I'm afraid that I'm going to have to leave your children fatherless. Given your past record, it really is the best thing I can think of to ensure that they grow up in an environment in which they remain unmolested."

The man was weeping openly now, his body shaking as tears rolled down his face. The display disgusted her, and she snapped, "How dare you? How. Fucking. DARE you beg me to spare the lives of your children, when you knew what that pig in the swamp was doing? When you yourself bought and traded children as if they were items to be used and discarded. Did you think that because they were the offspring of the truly impoverished that it was somehow okay? That they didn't matter as much as your own flesh and blood?"

The man was now yowling and pulling away from her.

"What's wrong, asshole?" she growled, "Don't like somebody forcing you to see your dirty little secret in a way that isn't so flattering?"

She released his wrists and began moving around the bed like a cat stalking a mouse as the man tried to scramble across his unconscious wife to get away from her. Jilah placed her hands on her hips, her expression cold and calculating.

"You been takin' out a great deal on your karmic loans, prick. Tonight you pay up."

The avatar roared and jumped at him, grabbing his arms and rolling off the bed with him, straddling him as they hit the floor. The loop was much smaller with this one, but no less painful for her to bear. It stunned her that he had children of his own and had engaged in unimaginably horrific acts with kids of the same age. It was inconceivable.

As the loop took hold of him, she hungrily bit down, drinking deeply and in earnest. Unfortunately, there was nowhere near the amount of red stuff in him that she was going to need. She would have to feed on the next target, and the next. After all, there were several more to go before she'd be finished with tonight's busy schedule. Jilah pulled back after a few moments, wanting to give him plenty of time to suffer before she collected his head. As she stood up, she found herself wondering what his wife would think when she woke up and found his headless body on the floor.

Sighing softly, the avatar sat next to the poor woman as she slept, plucking out the images from tonight so that she wouldn't be able to identify her husband's assassin. Taking it a step further, she gently placed the knowledge of what her husband had done, hoping that the woman would do the right thing and go to the police with the information. If she didn't, Jilah would come back for her head as well.

There was a noise behind her, and Jilah spun to see the marmalade tabby standing in the hallway, an expectant look in its green eyes. The cat peered up at her and meowed, then walked over to the man at her feet and began licking tentatively at the ragged ruin she'd left in the man's neck. Jilah chuckled and leaned on the bed, resting back on her hands as she watched the cat eat. After all, there was no sense in letting perfectly good, fresh food go to waste; and it certainly seemed to make the cat happy.

The tabby started purring loudly as it tore a bloody sliver of skin from the man's neck and swallowed it down. "Bottom's up, kitty. There's plenty to go around."

By the time her rounds were completed, Jilah had run into two more dogs, another cat and an enormous Hyacinth Macaw, of all things.

She was grateful that she hadn't had to kill any of them.

The weight and ungainliness of the heads was now becoming annoying, not to mention the whiff factor of the intestines of the last man she'd dispatched as well as the other items that her patroness had bid her to round up. The Dark Lady had wanted those as well. Last minute additions to her tribute. Everything was beginning to smell a little too vivid.

Jilah had placed the wet, cloth-covered body parts into a trash bag and was making her way back to the convent when she heard the wail of emergency sirens. It certainly sounded like there were a lot of them. They seemed to be coming into the city.

Jilah cocked her head for a moment, wondering why they were heading back this way. The explosion in the swamp was probably seen from quite a ways away. She figured that it would have kept them busy for awhile. Perhaps the wife of the first victim had roused early for some reason and had then called the police.

In any event, the cops were now apparently hot on the trail of something big. She felt that it'd be best if she were indoors instead of standing in the middle of the street with a fair amount of damning evidence bouncing against her hips and back. The first shining fingers of dawn were starting to make their way across the sky, and she put on the speed, blurring all the way back to the convent.

It took her a few minutes to figure out how to get the wall to open again, but once she stepped onto the gray stones of the corridor, she let out a sigh of relief. When she reached the intended place within the tunnels for the altar items, Jilah gently placed the trash bag at her feet. She collected the bowl, the sword, and the hangman's noose that she'd fashioned out of thick cord that she had found in one of the targets' basement, setting them off to the side. The avatar then reached in and pulled a sizable section of black cloth.

I'm afraid the table's going to have to wait.

Jilah began laying out the cloth on the floor as neatly as possible, placing the three items on it in a crescent configuration. The heads were next, with the first head of the night completing the crescent as she set it down next to the bowl. The other five heads she arranged in two piles off to either side of the cloth. She draped a ropy loop of intestines around the entire display, snaking them in and out between the items and the heads. Although it was more than a little ghoulish, she had to admit that the layout had its own particular flair.

Jilah stood up to inspect the makeshift shrine and nodded respectfully as the Dark Lady's voice echoed through her thoughts.

:: You've done very well tonight, daughter. I am pleased and honored with this display. It is suitable. ::

"Thank you, Mother."

Jilah's tone was reverent as she knelt in front of the shrine, kissing the ground before it and bringing her hands up to her lips, kissing her fingertips and again touching the ground with them.

:: Your duties for tonight have been discharged, vessel. You have earned a rest. ::

Jilah gave a heavy sigh as tears started rolled slowly down her cheeks. She touched her head to the ground in front of the altar, then stood up and began walking back through the hallway, wanting badly to be rid of the memories that now plagued her. Now that everything was over, she didn't feel at all strong or confident. Her legs struggled to keep her upright.

Where was the cool, easy, commanding presence that brought all those men to their final end, earlier? It had fled, and she was left to deal with the vicious emotional aftermath as she began slowly collapsing inside, unable to come to grips with the enormity of the horror she'd borne witness to tonight.

Jilah stumbled along the hallway, dazed and dry heaving, not really feeling the passage of time or being aware of much of anything except her heart and soul cracking open for those poor kids. She could've sworn that somebody was calling her name, but it sounded as if it were coming from very far away. The sound was muddled, as if she were hearing the call while trapped under several feet of water. It distracted her enough to bring her gaze up in time to see Gigi running towards her.

The Sorceress was in club clothes and looked like she had just come back in from a long night on the town. Jilah tried to say something, but the only thing that came out sounded like a gurgling choke before the floor came up to meet her in slow motion. Everything sounded muted, as if the sounds were coming from very far away as Gigi fluttered around her frantically, terrified at her new friend's condition. Jilah looked up at the sorceress and trembled, immediately breaking down in tears as she curled into a fetal ball at the woman's feet.

"Jesus, Mary and Joseph, child, what in god's name did this to you? I'd ask if you were okay, but the answer's obvious."

Jilah tried to answer, but the only sound that would come out of her throat was a horrible croaking. Besides, what could she tell them? Sharing the horror of an experience didn't always help. Jilah looked up to see Gigi making strange little jerking motions with her hands and was startled to find herself rising off the floor. Her eyes grew wide as she tried to figure out what was happening.

Gigi purred, "Babydoll, everything's going to be all right. You're home. You're safe. I'm just going to get you cleaned up. I mean, I can't exactly pick you up in my best outfit, can I? You're caked to the gills with gore."

Jilah relaxed, letting the anguish pour out of her as she floated down the hallway behind her friend. The world turned into a disorienting collection of images and moments as she drifted along. Jilah faintly remembered Gigi turning at some point to look over at Argent who was curled up under the sheets, her voice catty as she trilled, "Isn't that just like a man? Always sleeping when he's needed."

After Gigi undressed her and scrubbed her down, the sorceress then let her soak in the tub for a little bit, keeping watch over her. Jilah drifted in and out of awareness, catching snippets of a strangely comforting story about the adventures of a very odd woman named Auntie Mame that Gigi read to her in an attempt to cheer her up, or at the very least distract her from what was so obviously breaking her apart inside.

A part of her remembered and was profoundly grateful.

Afterwards, Gigi had pulled her out of the tub and toweled her off before carrying her over to the bed. Jilah wept quietly as Gigi placed her next to Argent, her voice hoarse as she breathed, "Thank you."

Gigi smiled down at her, depositing a red, glittery kiss on her forehead, smiling as she stood back up. "You, beautiful lady, are most certainly welcome."

The bed quickly worked its peculiar magic, and within minutes, Jilah was fast asleep.

Twenty Three
The Big Comedown

As Jilah slowly came to awareness, she looked around to find the source of the voice calling her name. Her mind was groggy and her eyelids felt as if they weighed a ton. She tried to push herself up and felt something squish against her fingers like oatmeal. It was as if she was mired in the stuff – and if her senses were to be believed, a rat had apparently died and festered in her mouth overnight. Christ, what had she eaten?

Her body responded sluggishly; as if she'd been drugged. When she tried to speak, a dry croak echoed out of her throat.

What the hell?

A face swam into view, and she frowned at the expression on it. Argent was peering back at her, relief coloring his features as he saw that she was finally waking up.

:: *Beloved, what is wrong?* :: His mental voice was thick with concern as he brushed a wisp of hair out of her eyes.

Jilah blinked and squinted as she looked around the room, dazed, wondering what they were doing on the floor. It had never been this difficult to wake up before. What had happened? :: *I don't know. I can't..* ::

And then it hit her.

The images from last night came back in a scalding rush that assaulted her senses, snapping her wide awake. She scrabbled across the floor away from him, her back slamming up against the wall as a trickle of blood trailed out of her nose. Argent appeared next to her as her claws lengthened and began digging into her legs. Tears spilled down her cheeks as her expression collapsed in dismay, her breath coming out in heart-wrenching sobs.

:: *What happened to you last night? Try to think. Please, let me help you.* ::
Argent gently pulled her into his lap and held her tightly. :: *Beloved, I am here. You are safe. It's over. Whatever happened, it is over now.* ::

Jilah looked up at him, her expression so very lost and full of pain. He smiled down at her, holding her tighter as he began crooning a soft French lullaby. Jilah wrapped her arms around him, holding on to him as if they were adrift in a vast, icy sea and he was the only thing keeping her from slipping into the cold, watery depths.

Argent held her tightly, kissing the top of her head. He wondered what had damaged her psyche like this. There was a tear in her mind that he could feel. Had the dark squatter in her head finally pushed her too hard, breaking her? He gently rocked her back and forth, cooing to her as he brushed his fingers along her arm. The sound of footsteps echoed down the hallway. Agent looked up to see Aurelian's head pop around the corner. The Selkie looked more than a little unsettled.

"Ah, Strigaisha, there's a problem."

Argent snapped, "Tell me."

Aurelian walked over to him, his tone wary as he began, "There are reports of multiple attacks on humans last night in the city – several of them being prominent figures in either the business or political community. Headless bodies were left in plain sight. Some of them disemboweled with inner organs missing. It's all over the news.

"I spoke with the Chief of Police briefly about it. He says that the wife of one of the victims apparently woke up to find the family cat happily chowing down on the remains of her husband. That colorful tidbit didn't make it into the news reports. It had to be an interesting sight. The heads have yet to be found, which is baffling the local authorities. Apparently one of the bodies was completely gutted as well. The intestines were conspicuously absent. The cops are thinking that they've got a psycho head collector out there with a possible political agenda. The media has already started referring to the perpetrator as the Headless Horseman. Catchy, huh?"

Argent quirked an eyebrow up, his expression curious as he asked, "So, am I to understand that this brigand rode around town on a horse collecting heads in a bag?"

Aurelian responded with a weak smile, shaking his head. "No, but that'd definitely make him easier to catch. Spree killers in and of themselves are kinda hard to track. A spree killer on a horse, however, would be much easier to spot – especially if he was one of those obsessive-compulsive types that had to have the horse. But, I digress. Some media asshat likely thought that the title had a better ring to it than anything else their marketing goons could come up with."

Argent sighed and looked down at his lover. Jilah was beginning to breathe normally now, her grip becoming less desperate as they talked.

"Does there seem to be anything that ties the victims together?"

"Not yet. The attacks appear to be totally random. This one's making the cops pretty skittish. They really hate mystery motivations. She okay?" Aurelian's expression was concerned, but not overly so.

Argent nodded, gathering her up in his arms and getting to his feet. He needed time to help her, to clean up the mess that was quickly building in the city, and time to get his political legs under him. He was apparently going to have none of it, so he would have to carve it out himself. He had known that coming back here was a supremely bad idea, but he hadn't expected that things would get this out of hand so rapidly.

"She'll be fine. Is there anything else?"

Argent walked over to the bed, sitting on the edge as he continued to cradle his lover's body.

"No, Strigaisha. I'll keep an eye on the situation."

Outstanding, Argent thought to himself as he watched Aurelian depart. He kissed Jilah's temple gently, and she looked up at him, her eyes full of a pain that seemed very familiar to him. She looked so very lost.

:: *Can you tell me what happened?* ::

Jilah shuddered in his arms, her head moving to rest gently on his shoulder. She clasped his hand in an almost painfully tight grip, as her voice crept through his thoughts, timid and shaky. :: *I don't know if I can do this anymore. I don't know if I can take it.* ::

Argent squeezed her hand, stroking her cheek softly as he waited for her to get it all out.

:: *I think last night kinda broke me.* :: She let out a heavy sigh and began playing with the drawstring of his pants, her movements more like that of a distracted child now than an interested lover.

:: *Jilah...* :: *Argent hated seeing her like this, feeling so helpless.* :: *What can I do to help?* ::

She slowly pulled away from him, tears brimming her eyes as she looked up at him. She hated crying, but she couldn't seem to stop. :: *Do you trust me?* ::

Argent smiled gently and nodded. :: *Of course* ::

:: *I don't think I can explain what happened without breaking down. I'd have to show you...* ::

He kept his expression neutral as he softly replied, :: *Then show me.* ::

She gave him a sad smile before closing her eyes and opening her mind to him. She gritted her teeth painfully as the images flooded through her mind and overwhelmed her lover. Argent gasped beside her as he took it all in, not ready for the torrent of emotion that came with it.

The assault on his senses abated as he pulled back a little, throwing up a mental damper so that he could dispassionately sort through the images and watch them play out instead of being bowled over by the enormous swell of rage, heartsickness, and nausea that accompanied them.

He was now extremely distressed about her emotional state. The images that flickered through his thoughts hadn't come close to evoking the same response for him. He again wondered why she cared so much. After all, he had been watching humans act this way, and worse, towards one another since long before she was born.

Human trafficking of all sorts had always been a reality along the fringes of almost every culture – and people's needs had only become more exotic and dangerous over time. What they did to one another no longer surprised him. He'd long since gotten over any shock about how humans conducted themselves amongst their own kind.

They were like any other animal, preying on one another and victimizing those weaker than them. In many cases, they behaved far worse than animals. Animals didn't have ulterior motives; didn't act purely out of spite. Another glaring difference about humans that rang true for him was that they had something that animals didn't have the luxury to indulge in. Hope that things would get better; that something was watching out for them.

He knew better. He also now knew who the police were looking for.

For whatever reason, events were rapidly hurtling to a head. The damage control on this was going to be difficult, at best. Not only had she gone completely outside the rules of his own prefecture, which he figured would happen soon enough; she hadn't bothered to hide any of the evidence. Given her current mental state and what he'd come to know about her in the short time since they'd met, he guessed he couldn't really blame her. But he would still have to do cleanup. He would also have to ensure that nobody outside of the immediate court ever found out.

When the images ceased, he looked back down to find her crying softly on his shoulder, her tears trickling slowly down his chest. He tentatively probed the surface of her thoughts, relieved to find them a little less frantic and shattered. She would still need time to recover, though. The best thing for her at the moment was more sleep.

Argent turned to place her gently down on the bed, caressing her forehead with smooth, cool fingers as he kissed her and murmured reassurances that everything was going to be all right. He sent out a mental call for Brigliadoro as she looked back at him with a weak, weary smile. She dropped off to sleep, and the guardian's hatchling arrived, along with Aurelian.

The Selkie was white as a sheet. "Julian has arrived and is demanding an audience with you, Strigaisha. He's making..." Aurelian looked over at Jilah and quickly brought his eyes back to meet Argent's eyes. "Outrageous claims."

And so it begins.

This would at least give him a chance to remove Julian directly from the equation. Argent stood, his tone brusque as he brushed past Orlando.

"Guard her. If anybody but myself comes looking for her, ensure that they leave quickly. If they cannot be made to leave, destroy them."

Argent's expression darkened as he stepped into the throne room, his eyes blazing. The room echoed with the sound of the brash ranting and raving of a man that he assumed could only be Julian. The word 'cur' came to mind as his gaze swept Julian's frame. The whelp looked all of about twenty-five; his clothing and hair was disheveled and torn in the manner only high-priced designers could pull off. He was strutting around, talking loudly to no one in particular, and gesticulating wildly.

Great. Yet another arrogant child that loves the sound of his own voice.

Argent looked over at the boy's supporters who were equally grungy, but on them it looked realistic. Street kids. They were agreeing in angry, loud voices with everything he said. They were puppets, and therefore of no consequence.

Argent thought it likely that most of Julian's supporters were little more than bullies or weaklings who thought that their position in the chain of power deserved more recognition. They were individuals more easily coaxed into 'rebellion', eager to join the madness of the throng when it came time to shoot or hang those they perceived as wicked tyrants. Brigliadoro moved to flank Argent as soon as he walked past the throne. Alain stood off to the side watching the scene unfold, his posture careful and wary. He was waiting for Argent to make the first move.

"So. You're the big baddie that's come home to roost. Have to admit that I don't see what the fuss is all about." Julian presented him with a lazy expression as he rocked back on a hip and slid his hands in his pockets.

Argent blinked. How had things gotten so entirely out of hand that a non-Pack-affiliated cur would even think of behaving in such a fashion without reprimand? In a blur of movement, Argent appeared at Julian's side, wrapping cold, sharp claws around the mongrel's throat. Julian's eyes widened, and his jaw opened and closed as he tried to speak, but he could only get out a pained croak. Apparently the boy wasn't used to being openly treated as persona non grata, much less as an outright enemy of the court.

Argent growled and forced him to his knees. In a cold toneless voice, Argent spat, "You will keep a civil tongue in my court, dog. Am I understood?" He then released Julian with an expression of distaste.

As Julian clutched at his bloodied throat and gasped for air, one of his followers growled, then leapt. Argent easily sidestepped the attack and the boy slammed into Brigliadoro. The gargoyle grabbed him by the throat and squeezed. There was a muffled snapping sound before Brigliadoro released his hold on the attacker's neck, letting the body fall to the floor, motionless.

Argent looked back at Julian's wayward pack brothers, his expression empty. "Are we done with the pissing contest, or are you going to continue to attempt to assert a position that you clearly don't have?"

Julian took a hitched breath and faced Argent, his eyes filled with stunned fury. The man's voice quavered as he growled, "Your bitch..."

"Be very careful, dog."

Julian's face twisted with rage as he took a deep breath. He slowly stood up, pressing a hand to his ribs.

In a strained tone, he grated, "Your mate," he spat, "is responsible for killing humans, defying your own law." His tone was petulant. Petty.

Argent regarded him with a detached curiosity as he asked, "And how exactly did you happen upon such information?"

"One of my boys saw her. She was running around town with several garbage bags that reeked of meat puppet last night. He followed her." A young boy with tousled brown hair nodded as he took a shaky step forward. Watching one of their own die so easily had taken a considerable amount of fight out of them.

Julian began to smile as he continued, "Oh yeah, she was a busy little girl last night. She hit three more houses after that, then disappeared. We lost her sometime around dawn."

Argent looked over at him, his expression carefully neutral. "Exactly how am I to believe such a carefully constructed little fable? And why would you bring this to my attention, even if it were true? You're a known dissident."

Julian shrugged. "I go where it benefits me and mine best. At least Padmajai understood that, cut us a little slack. I'm just letting you know what's what. So you can lay the smackdown on those who need punishing."

"How very helpful of you." Argent's voice was thick with sarcasm.

He frowned, not knowing why Julian had chosen to come here – to deliver such an unwelcome message. It made no sense. Did the cur have no sense of self preservation? Then remembering little Roane's words after that wretched bloody ceremony, he smiled. Ariane's spirits could be unpleasant to deal with, but he had to admit that they always came through with results.

Julian's answering laugh was an ugly sound. The man pulled himself up to his full height with a cocky grin. "Just consider me a citizen doing my civic duty."

Alain growled, narrowing his eyes and flexing his fingers. Argent caught the flash of a surface image through Julian's thoughts. Judiana?

Julian turned to smile at the raven-haired Alpha and smirked, his hand sliding his thumbs into his back pockets before he turned and began walking towards the door, calling out, "Anytime I can help, you just give me a call."

The Alpha watched Julian go, his eyes blazing as he turned to look at Argent. The Sanguine gave him a grim nod, rocking back on a heel as Brigliadoro and Alain moved to intercept him, blocking the exit.

Julian spun to face Argent, irritated. "What's this all about, man? I just gave you valuable information. Information that if given to the right people could have you out on your ass. Don't make me..."

Argent blurred forward, neatly slicing Julian's throat open. The boy choked, dropping to his knees as blood spilled down his shirt in a red wash. The mongrels with him stood petrified with fear, their eyes huge as they watched their leader slump to the floor. Argent stepped back and licked at his clawed finger, his voice smooth as silk as he purred, "You are obviously laboring under a rather foolish misunderstanding. This is not a democracy, boy. It is a dictatorship. There will be no revolution."

Julian sputtered, choking on his own blood as he tried to speak.

Argent crouched down, grabbing a handful of the whelp's hair and yanking him up to peer into his eyes.

"Don't worry, your injury isn't fatal. Well, not yet anyway. Now let's see what you've got in that horrid little head of yours about Judiana."

Julian's eyes widened and he tried to pull away, hands and arms scrabbling for purchase on the floor, which was becoming slick with his blood even as the wound in his neck began healing over. It only took a moment to locate the information he needed. The cur had never been taught how to keep people out of his head, which came in very handy in this particular instance.

Julian had apparently made what he thought at the time was a rather lucrative deal with The Sisters: they kill Judiana, he gets the run of the Pack and the City. Of course it didn't shake out that way, but then how far could one really trust hunters when dealing with elements of the world they hunted within?

Unsurprisingly, Julian would've liked a much more beneficial situation than the one that proceeded Judiana's death, but all things considered, he really couldn't complain. After all, he'd been able to manipulate things so that he held a certain amount of power. Judiana's successor had not been at all ready to assume the mantle of leadership. It had been the crippling blow that he'd needed to insinuate himself into the position he had wanted so badly for himself.

The thing that mystified Argent was – how? How had everything become so weak, so quickly? During his reign, this mouthy pup would've been butchered, his hide and head hung on the wall as a reminder to wayward dissidents who chose to follow in his footsteps. Judiana had always been a bit of a soft touch in comparison, he had to admit, but didn't she have any sense?

Well, not anymore, obviously, he thought angrily to himself. This cur had personally seen to that.

Argent's eyes glittered as he pulled away from the boy, his entire body tensing as he stood up. He motioned to Alain who roughly jerked Julian to his feet.

"You betrayed her to The Sisters for nothing, dog. You'll die in this room, as will those that accompanied you on this fool's errand."

Julian cried out in outrage, now realizing that Argent meant every word. Alain and Brigliadoro stepped up and held Julian against the wall as Argent calmly walked over to the throne. Argent collected several items from a panel hidden under the seat, then turned to face Julian with a gruesome smile. Before the pup could say anything, Alain placed a long, razor-sharp claw under his chin.

Argent held up two large silver spikes, letting Julian get a good long look at them before he dropped them to the floor along with a wicked-looking war hammer. The sound of the hammer sent a loud thunk echoing through the room as it hit, and cracks in the stone spidered out from beneath the head. Argent then looked up as a chain began lowering from the ceiling. Two large, very nasty-looking silver hooks dangled at the end of the links. Julian's eyes widened, unsure of what was going to happen next, but pretty positive that whatever it ended up being, it was going to hurt very badly.

When the hooks came down far enough for Argent to grasp them, he waved Brigliadoro and Alain forward. They wrestled Julian over to him, holding him still while Argent grabbed the man's right wrist and slowly forced one of the hooks through it. Julian struggled fiercely in their combined grip, screaming as the Sanguine then impaled his left wrist on the other hook.

Argent then took a step back as the chain began scrolling back into the ceiling, taking in the slack and pulling taut before finally wrenching Julian off his feet until he hung about a foot off the ground.

Aurelian then stepped into view with a small stepladder, a large silver skinning knife, a two by four that had an eye bolt at the middle, and a device that looked like a cattle prod. He placed the stepladder at a point where Argent could climb up on it and be face-to-face with the betrayer. The boy was still screaming and kicking as Brigliadoro and Alain moved to grab his legs, holding his feet back against the board.

Argent looked over at Julian's companions, who were now watching the scene before them and whining like dogs that had been given a sharp kick. One of them turned away and Argent growled, "You will watch, or the same will happen to all of you. Am I understood?"

Two of Julian's companions grabbed the one that had turned away and forced his eyes to the front, remaining silent in their terror. They had apparently never borne witness to such a thing. Argent was pleased that they were being properly motivated by the sight of their leader being reprimanded.

Argent moved to collect the silver spikes and hammered them into Julian's feet, splaying the man's legs wide apart with the eye bolt on the board positioned towards the floor. Howls of fury and terror filled the room as Aurelian attached the eye bolt to a length of chain that came out of the floor, locking it down and pulling it taut so that Julian could now no longer move. Julian strained and stretched as he tried even now to free himself. The pain had to be unbearable.

Argent stepped up on the ladder and nodded at Aurelian, who proceeded to jab Julian roughly with the cattle prod. There was a loud zap, and the smell of ozone crackled through the air as the sounds of the man's howls rang off the cold stone walls.

The familiar wet, popping sounds of the change began as Julian started shifting, his bones sliding and reforming under his skin as Argent made the first precise cut down the man's torso.

Julian's flayed remains were left chained up off to the right of the throne as an example to any other parties interested in fomenting dissent in the ranks. The remains of his pelt draped over the spikes on the enormous throne, the seat now slick with the treacherous therianthrope's blood. As tribute to the Vodou Lwa that had brought his enemy to him, Argent had Julian's head placed on a long iron spike within a large black cast-iron cauldron. Candles illuminated the garish display, as well as throwing jittering shadows along the back wall.

It was important at this crucial time for the residents of New Orleans to know that the Dragon's Hammer had indeed returned.

The business of justice having been concluded, Argent had offered freedom for two of Julian's followers, knowing that the stories they spread would be a very effective way to get his point across to the rest of the community with a minimum of effort. Spreading terror through word on the street was always fairly easy. All manners of creatures loved to gossip and nothing went around faster than bad news. Argent had disemboweled and taken the others' heads, resting them at the still dripping feet of their leader.

Feeling a little better now at having resolved the immediate situation, he turned to Aurelian and asked, "Has anything further been revealed about last night's beheadings?"

The Selkie looked over at him and took a slow breath before quietly answering. "Nothing else, Strigaisha."

Argent was covered in blood from head to toe. He ran a crimson-stained hand through his hair, squeezing some of it out onto the floor, his voice growing cold and distant as he replied, "Stay on it. Use every contact in the various organizations throughout the city that you have. I want to know what the police know, and what actions they will be taking."

An efficient-looking woman in a gray dress walked up to him and handed him a towel, which he gratefully collected. He began drying himself off, not wanting to track more blood all over the place.

Aurelian looked at him expectantly, and Argent silently murmured, "This is not a safe question to ask me, nor a safe topic to broach, Aurelian."

The blond gave him a curt nod before walking out of the throne room to attend to his duties. Argent turned to Alain, his voice soft as he spoke to his friend.

"Does this satisfy your pack's prix de sang?"

The Alpha nodded with a slight smile, reassured that there was now somebody in power that would do what was necessary to make things right.

"Outstanding." Argent took a deep breath, hearing a little bitterness creep into his tone as he growled, "Now, if The Sisters would just give me a night or two, I should be able to..."

A soft, musical voice cut him off in mid sentence, and he looked back to find S'llethe walking towards them.

"Brother. We would have a word with you."

Argent raised an eyebrow as he turned towards her, wiping his hands off and placing the towel around his neck. "Of course. Is something amiss?"

S'llethe smiled; this simple action bringing a peace to him that was both calming and reassuring as she replied, "Your Striaga. She suffers. We feel it. We would offer our help."

Argent gave a brief nod to Brigliadoro and Alain, then took S'llethe's hand and led her through the throne room, towards the back corridors. "Yes, she suffers. There is little I can do to remedy it, and it pains me."

S'llethe replied with a warm smile. "You do not have the capability to restore in her what is broken, brother. But together, you can rebuild each other."

Argent frowned, unsure of her meaning. Her kind tended to be poetic and lyrical as opposed to getting to the point of the matter. "But if I am unable to restore her, then I do not understand."

S'llethe laughed lightly as they walked through the corridor, her voice warm as she breathed, "Many things are better done first, and explained later." Hearing this did little to reassure him.

As they entered the bedroom, Argent tensed when he looked over to see Jilah tossing and turning in the bed. He was surprised that the bed hadn't knocked her out completely. He moved to go to her, but S'llethe held him firm. He always found himself surprised at how strong the members of his extended family were. They all looked so fey and winsome, but they were easily capable of pulping him if he got out of hand. He still remembered several rather embarrassing times when he'd had to be taught harsh lessons by his unusual brothers and sisters.

"Brother, do you trust us with her?"

Argent nodded, his tone somber as he answered, "Of course."

He trusted them – all of them, with his own life and now the life of the woman he loved.

S'llethe smiled brightly, her lavender eyes shining as she took his hand and led him over to Jilah's side of the bed. "Then come with us, help us heal her." The woman placed a gentle hand on his lover's head, and Jilah popped awake at the touch, her body instantly covered with a fevered sweat. Jilah looked up at both of them, bewildered. She scrutinized S'llethe thoroughly, unsure of Argent's reasoning behind bringing a strange woman into their bedroom when she was already in an emotional tailspin. And why was Argent covered in blood? What on earth had happened?

The woman's voice was serene and gentle as she murmured, "Striaga Jilah. We are honored to meet our brother's chosen."

Jilah gave her a strange look, reassured that the woman had referred to him as brother, but confused that there was absolutely no family resemblance. She relaxed as S'llethe continued, "We feel your pain and we wish to help. Will you allow us to do so?"

Jilah regarded the woman with a wary eye, croaking, "That would depend on your definition of the word help."

Considering the abruptly life-altering response to the last time she'd called out for help, she wasn't entirely certain that she wanted it from an unknown source again. Not that she wasn't grateful for intervention, but life had definitely taken on several rather rough turns since she'd started working for her patroness.

S'llethe smiled, looking over at Argent. "She is much like you, brother. Very stubborn."

"She is many wonderful things. We are well matched." He leaned over Jilah and kissed her forehead.

:: All will be well, love. She is family. I meant for you to meet under different circumstances, but life has become most unpredictable lately. ::

:: Is she a queen or something? Why does she speak as if there's more than just her? ::

Jilah felt a gentle mental nudge; something unpleasant was trying to make its way through to her conscious thoughts but she couldn't quite remember what it was. The only thing clear in her mind was the current moment, which was strange enough in its surreality. She pushed the nudge aside as Argent answered.

:: They are a unique race. Uncountable years old. They speak as one because even alone, they are as one. They stay always connected somehow. I have never really figured it out. ::

S'llethe smiled as she watched their mental exchange and squeezed Argent's hand lightly. "We should start now, brother. The longer we wait, the longer it takes hold in her and the harder it will be to remove. This displacement is very much like a disease that works to consume her."

Argent looked back at her in shock, wondering if she was referring to the ebony-skinned hellbitch that was currently taking up residence in his lover's head.

S'llethe shook her head gently and replied, "No. That we cannot remove. That will have to choose to go or stay of its own volition."

"Then what?" he blurted out, and S'llethe waved him silent with a delicate hand.

"The memories?" Jilah breathed, her hands starting to shake as she felt the beginning of something unpleasant tapping and scrabbling as it tried to force her to acknowledge it. "Maybe she's talking about the memories."

S'llethe looked back at Jilah and cocked her head, her tone soothing as she asked, "Would you be rid of them?"

Jilah selected her words carefully. She'd played into the hands of her current patroness in a similar fashion, and didn't want to fall into the same kind of situation. One external governing force in her life was plenty.

"I want to be rid of the pain they cause, but the memories themselves need to be something that I can access when necessary. I just don't want them to come up without me choosing to have them manifest. I don't want to be victimized by them anymore." That seemed the safest way to put it.

S'llethe nodded and smiled. "We understand and will help."

Jilah wasn't so sure that the help that this odd woman kept referring to was such a great idea. *In for a penny, in for a pound,* echoed through her mind – and for the first time in six months she was the only occupant of her head.

It was disorienting, and she wasn't sure that she liked it. She had grown accustomed to the snakelike voice of her patroness and now that it wasn't rolling back up, it was making her nervous and tense. If anything was capable of rousing it, she would've been sure that this would be it. Perhaps her patroness was sleeping, or off tending to something else. Jilah screwed up her courage and reached out for Argent's hand. Enough strangeness had happened already that it was becoming almost old hat to grit her teeth and jump feet first into a new, potentially life-threatening experience.

"Okay, lady, do what you're gonna do before I..." Jilah's mouth opened wide in a silent 'O' as S'llethe began humming a strangely familiar tune. The contact with Argent felt electric, and her hand tightened in his grasp, almost breaking his fingers. Argent responded by slumping over her on the bed. It felt almost as if somebody had poked her head open and had inserted a straw, as if her mind had become one of those foil pouch tropical drinks.

Jilah arched on the bed, whining softly as she felt an increasing tugging sensation. She remembered a blinding flash as she screamed out, then nothing.

Much later – feeling extremely groggy and worn out, Jilah groaned and rolled over, wrapping an arm around the waist of her lover as he

lay beside her. She sighed and pulled him closer, snuggling up to his back gently before realizing that he was ice cold.

Frowning, she slowly sat up and ventured a look. Argent was curled up as usual, dead to the world. He had also found time to clean up, apparently. There wasn't a trace of blood on him anywhere. For some reason, this time his body temperature didn't creep her out. It took her a minute to realize that she was burning up and the cool touch of his skin was helping to bring her temperature down enough so that she could get back to sleep.

She sighed and kissed his shoulder, then wrapped herself around him with a dreamy smile as she dropped back into blissful unconsciousness.

Twenty Four

An Unusual Connection

Feeling movement in the bed beside her, Jilah slowly brought her arms up and stretched, splaying her legs out against the sheets. She looked over to find Argent turning towards her, his eyes growing wide as he looked back at her. She pulled back for a moment, wondering what was wrong.

A sudden flood of confusing images, thoughts, and words overwhelmed her. Startled, she realized that they were coming from her lover, unbidden. He was so happy to see her, so happy that she was no longer hurting and that her mind was at peace for the first time since he'd known her.

Along with those selfsame thoughts, he was bewildered at the fact that he was able to see all this effortlessly. His surface thoughts were an open book that poured over her, and she brought her hands up to her temples to try to shut it all out. The images, emotions, and feelings swirled in a disorienting blur when taken in and mixed with her own. It was impossible to tell what she was feeling, seeing – and what was him. The blending of perception made her dizzy.

She was suddenly startled as a ghoulish parade of savagely butchered women swam through her thoughts, and she frowned as she realized that she'd never personally seen any of them. A great many of them were costumed in styles of dress from various points throughout history. They flew by in a blinding blur, indistinguishable as she heard her lover growl beside her.

Argent reached and touched her. The physical contact muted the sensation to the point where she could concentrate on something other than the feeling of being so mentally off balance. The doubled mental images slowly bled back to her own thoughts, her own feelings, and she relaxed a little.

:: *What the hell was that?* :: She asked, covering his hand with her own as she scooted closer, hoping that the more contact they had, the more she would be able to control this weird perception shift.

Argent exhaled shakily and wrapped an arm around her.

:: *I have no idea. Do you remember the other night? When you were so upset?* ::

Jilah nodded, frowning. As she thought back, she could touch on the memories, see them playing out before her, but she was unable to connect to any intense emotion. It was as if her mind had completely disassociated itself from the negative intensity of the experience, like watching a movie where somebody that looked like her had the lead role.

:: *Yeah. But I'm not upset anymore.* :: She looked back at him, her expression curious as she continued, :: *There's...nothing now. It's almost as if it happened to somebody else.* ::

For a brief moment, she wondered if this was how the girl she had saved in the graveyard felt now.

Argent watched her carefully as he replied.

:: *Then for all intents and purposes, it worked.* ::

Jilah frowned as she tentatively tested the other memories in her mind, slowly working her way through them back to that first fateful night. Not a one of them brought up an overly negative or stressful wellspring of emotion.

For the first time since her unusual night job began, she didn't feel the familiar oppressive shudder of disgust or anguish anymore. But it was more than that.

She felt – whole. It was as if a part of her that had been missing, had been found and finally clicked into its proper place.

There was no longer a part of her that dreaded hearing the Dark Lady's voice anymore. Something in her now also felt secure in the fact that this 'fix' wouldn't go away; that she didn't need to worry about any of it coming back again.

Her mouth dropped open slightly as she said, "Huh." Well, how 'bout that? She laughed quietly.

:: *It doesn't hurt anymore. None of it.* ::

Jilah smiled back at him and Argent blinked as he looked back at her. :: *I'll be damned.* ::

She relaxed as he smiled and hugged her. Argent let out a long sigh as tears slowly started streaming down Jilah's cheeks. Argent gently kissed them away, his fingers tracing the delicate curve of her face.

She leaned in and kissed him. He smiled against her lips in response, sliding his hands down her waist.

:: *This new revelation appears to have given you a bit of an appetite..* :: A warm chuckle drifted through her thoughts, setting her skin tingling.

Jilah nodded, pushing him onto his back, straddling him.

:: *Gimme a break, I've behaved for..oh, hey, that's new.* ::

She felt something flicker to life in her, something that was now allowing her to add his experience of her to what she was already feeling. It effectively laid out a road map to all her lover's erogenous zones. She looked down at him, her hands on either side of his head, disoriented at seeing him before her in addition to experiencing his own perception of her. The blended imagery far outshone what she had received back from any mirrored reflection. She blinked slowly before moving to kiss him again.

Argent reached up to cup her breast as she kissed him and through the connection Jilah felt his body respond, trembling at the touch. Her lips left his and he leaned in to nip at her breast.

Jilah was startled at the ghostly feel of her own nipple in her mouth as she felt him bite down playfully. He began to pull her down to him, sucking gently.

Eager to try something now, she gently pulled away from him. She could feel his disappointment as he asked, :: *Where are you going..?* ::

His question trailed off when she began slowly kissing her way down his chest. Argent arched into the touch of her lips, groaning at the soft kisses she trailed down to his waist.

Jilah slid her fingers slowly around the one warm spot on his body. She gently squeezed, thrilling at the way that he pulsed in her hand and at the feel of her own fingers curling around flesh she had never been physically equipped with. Moving down to let her fingers play further south, she let her tongue trail over the tip of him, shuddering at the nearly electrical rush that clutched low in her belly in response to the touch.

Argent let out a low, hoarse growl as she slid her lips over him and she moaned in response, shaking slightly. She'd always been curious at how it felt for men when they had received such attention and now found herself thoroughly pleased with the results of her endeavor. She could feel her own hot mouth wrapping around him/her. She groaned and shuddered at the contact, reacting along with her lover as he twisted and bucked underneath her.

My god, no wonder this drives men crazy.

For a moment her mind tried to explain this duality. The idea was quickly lost when she rasped her tongue along the sensitive bundle of nerves just under the tip, delighting in her partner's moans as he shuddered against her – as well as the returned sensation along her own nonexistent flesh. She clutched at his hips, slowly sliding her tongue along his length and sucking gently, enjoying the scent and the taste of him.

Argent's fingers began digging into the sheets as her ministrations forced him quickly to the edge.

Jilah growled as she tipped closer to the edge with him, her body shaking in time with his movements as her fingers slid up his chest. They were both so painfully close. She gently squeezed his nipple, sucking him harder before pinching the now taut nipple roughly between her fingers. Argent roared as his pleasure rushed through him in a fiery wave, his voice haggard as she yanked him over the edge and cast him into a place that set every one of his nerve endings on fire. He spilled into her and she drank him down, pulled over with him as she screamed around him.

They both slumped to the bed shaking as they slowly began to recover.

:: Wow. :: Jilah giggled.

Argent let out a throaty laugh, and flopped his head back on the bed with a very satisfied sigh. He was still a little out of it, and began grinning like an idiot as he relaxed into the sheets.

:: I swear you're going to be the death of me someday, but what a way to go. ::

Jilah grinned, pleased as she rested her head on his stomach, her fingers playing gently along the lines of his hip as she murmured, :: *Such a daredevil, riding that razor's edge.* ::

:: *When it feels like that, you're damned right. At this rate, I shall be very lucky if I live to see my next birthday.* ::

Jilah laughed and gave him a playful pinch before sliding her hand up his torso.

:: *It feels different now. So much stronger than it was before. I mean, I know you said that it'd only get better over time, but WOW.* ::

Argent smiled slid his fingers through her hair.

:: *This is different. It is like nothing that I have ever experienced with anyone else.* ::

Jilah sighed and writhed slowly against him, enjoying the dual sensation of her body against his legs. She now had what she considered a very well-shaped body and it was intensely interesting to feel it from such a wildly different perspective. Beyond wanting to explain it, she was in no mood to stop anything that felt this good anytime soon.

:: *You're not just saying that, are you?* ::

Argent reached down and slid his fingers underneath her chin, gently pulling her up to meet his gaze. His expression was utterly serious as he responded, :: *What just happened; I've experienced a fraction of it before, but nothing as* :: he paused for a moment, then continued, :: *There is a duality to this that I have honestly never shared with anyone else before. I never thought it could be like this. Had I known, I would definitely have come for you a great deal earlier than I did.* ::

Argent grinned and pulled her up to him, kissing her deeply as he slid his hands down to cup her ass. :: *You constantly amaze me.* ::

Jilah purred contentedly as she moved to nuzzle her cheek against his shoulder. :: *So, you think this is me? Something in me that's making this possible?* ::

Argent shrugged then moved his hands lower, sliding his fingers along her slickness; enjoying the way she shivered against him and moaned in his ear.

:: *I have no idea. Does it really matter at the moment?* :: Her body pushed away the rest of any sane, rational thought as it quickly responded to his touch. In the end, she guessed it didn't. The only thing that mattered was that he keep touching her – and that he never stop.

They were interrupted by a sharp knock at the door, and Jilah growled in irritation. Things had been going so well and now the only thing she wanted to do was to choke the life out of the person that had interrupted it.

Argent sighed, then turned to look over at the offending door with a baleful gaze. He mentally reached out to see who it was, unsurprised to feel Aurelian's presence in the hallway. The Selkie's thoughts were always a little too jumbled to dip in lightly. It would probably be easier to just get up and answer the door. He desperately hoped that nothing was happening that required his immediate attention.

:: *Unfortunately, I have to answer that.* :: Argent turned back to her and sighed. He frowned and she gently pushed him to the edge of the bed.

:: *Go ahead. It might be important, and whoever it is, they've already ruined the moment.* :: The avatar grumbled as Argent slowly got to his feet.

:: *It's Aurelian. I'll see what he has to say, then I'll get rid of him and make it up to you.* :: He grinned back at her and she laughed as she curled her legs under her and pulled the sheet up to cover herself.

Argent was well aware that that he had various affairs of state to attend to, but at the moment he just wanted time to conduct an in-depth examination of all the possibilities that Jilah's new condition had afforded them. After all, who knew how long it would last? If it happened to be temporary, he wanted to take advantage of the connection while they still had it. He hoped that the distraction could be dealt with quickly so that he could get back to more preferable activities.

Argent didn't bother to dress as he made his way to the door, throwing it wide and glaring at the Selkie who was standing in the hallway with an expectant expression.

"This had better be something important."

Aurelian's eyes widened as his gaze slowly slid down Argent's torso and he gave his head a brief shake before snapping his gaze back up to meet the eyes of his regent. "Did I come at a bad time?"

Argent's eyebrow arched, wondering why the blond was so flustered. The man had seen him naked before, what was the problem? He heard Jilah gasp behind him and was startled to realize that she'd somehow tapped into a long forgotten memory of the pair of men being intimate. It rose up, spilling over him in an overwhelming wave as both he and his lover experienced it in its full glory again.

Argent grasped the side of the door, fighting to clear his vision.

Where the hell did that come from?

The overload of sensation almost made his knees buckle with the intensity and he fought to keep from crumpling to the floor.

"Strigaisha!" Aurelian cried out, reaching out to Argent who quickly held up a hand, warding him off.

"Don't." Argent croaked, taking a step back into the room and pressing his back up against the wall. He shook with the effort of remaining standing.

Jilah was watching them with wide eyes, her gaze quickly flicking back and forth between the two men. Argent watched as she tightened her fingers around the sheets in her hands. Aurelian quickly stepped into the room, closing the door behind him.

He looked over at Jilah who was now watching him with a very intent and hungry gaze. She remained immobile, her eyes following his every movement like those of a snake watching a small wounded bird as it made its way to safety. Argent wouldn't turn to look at him as he slowly made his way back to the bed.

Aurelian's voice was urgent, his expression concerned as he blurted, "What can I get you? How can I help?"

Argent climbed back under the covers and Jilah pulled him close, wrapping herself around him protectively. Her eyes followed Aurelian as he cautiously moved to the edge of the bed. Still in the throes of long ago forgotten memories, Argent shivered and groaned, clutching Jilah tightly as his body quickly responded to the visceral flashback of the two of them. She placed her cheek on his forehead, rocking him gently as he took long, deep breaths in an attempt to master himself.

"You should go." Jilah's voice cracked slightly as she spoke.

Aurelian's voice became husky, dropping an octave as he replied, "You're not acting at all like somebody that wants me to leave."

Aurelian turned to look over at Argent, his features softening and becoming almost dazed with heat. Argent shivered as Jilah accessed intimate memories and emotions without meaning to. It couldn't be helped. He could tell that Aurelian was completely thrown by his behavior; equally worried and excited at the same time. It was also clear that this wasn't an entirely pleasant sensation for the selkie.

He winced as his mate reacted to the bittersweet taste of what he and Aurelian had once shared and was shocked as she now dipped into Aurelian's thoughts. The selkie was remembering what it was like to be in Argent's arms, to feel the Sanguine's cool fingers on his skin. He often missed it now, a great deal more than he wished others to see.

With this realization, Argent let out an anguished cry.

:: *Please. Stop. Whatever it is that you are doing, stop. It hurts too much.* ::

Over the years, Argent had greatly missed the people he'd left behind, but he hadn't taken into account how much his absence would wound those he had once shared his life with. To know that Aurelian still kept that memory close to him, that the reminder still burned – it was almost more than he could bear.

He felt her fear as she sent, :: *I can't. I don't think I'm doing this. I can't control it.* ::

Argent gripped her tighter, unsure of what needed to happen next. He felt like a fledgling again, remembering the painful learning process of adapting to new abilities. He could hear the liquid thrumming thump of Aurelian's heart and badly wanted to set that rhythm free, to have it splash on his tongue in a crimson spray. The sexual tension in the room cranked up sharply, and Jilah drew in a shaky breath as she looked back over at Aurelian.

The Selkie was now slowly pulling his shirt over his head. Jilah let out a strangled cry as Aurelian put a hand on the bed and slowly began crawling towards them.

Aurelian begged her, his voice hoarse with the effort of speaking. "Please."

Jilah blinked quickly, licking her lips as Argent watched the selkie. The man was mesmerizing, his well tanned skin stretching tightly over well-formed arms and shoulders, his soft platinum locks spilling over his shoulders and brushing against his arms. The sanguine watched the muscles on his back writhe as he crawled, so slowly, reaching out to them. His fingers brushed Argent's calf and she felt her lover's body stiffen against her.

Argent could feel the need radiating off the man in a hot pulsing current, but knew that if he saw the raw desire that was surely showing on Aurelian's face, he would be lost. There would be no controlling his actions. The touch set off a fiery collection of emotions that went along with the memories. Aurelian seemed to be holding back as he waited for a signal of acceptance and approval. It was making him suffer considerably.

Argent relaxed as Jilah gently sent, :: *It's been a long time. And you've both missed each other in ways that I wouldn't have understood, before now.* ::

Taking a deep breath, Jilah reached out and took Aurelian's hand. He was hot to the touch and she shivered at the thrill of his warmth. The Selkie felt like a furnace in comparison to Argent. Aurelian let out a shaky sigh as she pulled him closer, happy that he was finally here where it felt like he belonged. *Where did that come from?* she wondered, as Argent slowly turned to look over at Aurelian, his expression heated but wary. They were both being so very careful of her.

With a shock, Jilah realized that she was naked and in bed with two very attractive men who were now looking up at her with pleading expressions. What the hell did they expect her to do? Referee?

The thought made her laugh, and she quickly clapped a hand over her mouth. They looked back at her with strange expressions and she tried to explain, "It's just...well, you both look like you're waiting for me to drop a flag or something."

The men looked back at each other, then slumped against her, laughing. She grinned as the tension between them dissolved, then began giggling as they pressed up against her, feeling softly trailing fingers along her stomach.

Oh hey, this is new, she thought; the laughter cut off by a soft sigh as the two men now matched each other, move for move, along the curves of her body. She shuddered as she experienced the shared emotion that her lover felt towards the man on the other side of her body. Jilah watched as the pair smiled across at one another, now seemingly in familiar territory. In what looked like a smoothly choreographed move, Argent moved up to kiss her, while Aurelian began kissing his way down her torso. She moaned into him as she felt the Selkie reposition himself, gently spreading her legs apart and sliding hot hands along her inner thighs, squeezing gently.

Argent smiled as she shuddered, delighting in her soft little whimpers and moans as Aurelian's fingers gently tickled the slick curls between her legs, his thumbs sliding along her slickness as he dipped his head down to taste her. She arched up against the sheets, crying out. His mouth was hot, so very hot, and his heat began spreading up her torso in delicious, shivering waves.

Being able to see herself through Argent's perception was the most erotic visual she'd ever encountered. Argent moved to capture her cries with his mouth as Aurelian pulled pleasure through her with his own heated kisses. For a moment, the pair of them broke contact with her and she opened her eyes in time to watch them kissing with a passion that startled her. While she was not at all used to seeing men kiss, she slowly realized that it definitely did something for her.

A great deal, in fact. She shuddered at the ghostly taste of herself on Argent's tongue, and now wanted to kiss Aurelian herself to see if he tasted as good directly.

Argent smiled as she sat up and moved forward. He reached out to slide his hand along Aurelian's shoulder. Aurelian looked back at her for a moment, his gold eyes glittering as his gaze swept her body. He then reached out and pulled her into a savage kiss that caught her off balance as it sent a rush of heat through her. She couldn't get over how warm he was; how hot and vibrant he felt.

Aurelian moaned, she could hear his heart hammering in his chest as she slid her hand down his torso, over his pants and gently squeezed the hard length of him cruelly trapped behind his jeans. The Selkie cried out, and she could hear Argent laugh lightly behind her as she felt cool hands cupping her backside. She helped Aurelian quickly free himself from the rest of his clothing, shuddering as Argent slowly slid his hands up her back. Argent curled his fingers, running his nails along her back, then moved his hands around to her hips, causing her to groan and shiver.

Jilah wrapped her fingers around the Selkie's curved length, pulling him closer. It felt like an ember in her hand. Aurelian growled, moving to grab a fistful of her hair as he pulled her into another rough, passionate kiss.

:: He picks up very quickly on what people like. ::

:: Jesus, you ain't kiddin'. :: she sent back, raking the nails of her other hand along the smooth tanned skin of Aurelian's torso.

The Selkie gave a self-satisfied laugh, biting her lip and suckling it as he smiled into the kiss.

Jilah pulled away, presenting Aurelian with a sharp-toothed smile. He looked back at her, his expression bold and open as she trailed a finger along the side of his neck. She slid a hand up into his hair, gripping it tightly with her fist as she grabbed his shoulder and yanked him forward, her tongue darting out to lick along his neck in a long, cool line. The man tasted exquisite.

She began nipping at his neck, wanting to release the rich red spice just underneath, wanting to watch it spill out over his skin. Argent's cool fingers slid along her slickness, and she moaned against Aurelian's neck, tightening her fist and smiling as he cried out. She held her tongue along the pulse in Aurelian's neck now, shivering as she wrapped an arm around his waist, roughly pulling him closer. Responding to an intriguing image in Argent's mind, she pushed Aurelian down onto the bed, smiling as she slowly crawled up his body. The Selkie grinned as she reached his stomach, growling as she nipped him hard. Behind her, Argent pulled her hips against his own, pressing himself gently against her slickness and squeezing her hips. Jilah growled as she reached Aurelian's neck and nipped lightly.

She breathed in his scent, basking like a cat in the warmth that radiated off the large man's body. Again, she wrapped her fingers in his honeyed blond curls and pulled his head to the side. Aurelian groaned and she flicked her tongue out quickly before biting down. Hot crimson fluid splashed onto her tongue, and Argent growled as he slammed into her, his fingers digging into her hips. She felt Aurelian's hands move to cover Argent's as her lover roughly pumped into her from behind.

Her senses reeled as the Selkie's blood rushed through her. The quickness it sent through her veins made her jittery. Within moments, the three of them crashed over together and Jilah felt a mixed swirl of fire and ice rush through her, sending a wind along her skin that made her hair stand on end. Goose flesh swept along her body as she screamed and passed out onto the hot skin of the man beneath her.

Argent felt a swell of power shake through her and was startled to find himself sweating with exertion. When she collapsed beneath him, his eyes grew wide. He was shaking like a leaf at the realization that he wasn't in any way weakened, although by all rights he should be.

Instead of spilling his energy out with his release, she seemed to have filled him up – he felt positively drunk with it. He wasn't too worried that she'd fainted. He'd come damn close himself with that much over stimulation. She would probably come back to herself in a couple of minutes. He gently rolled her off Aurelian, brushing a damp strand of hair out of her face.

He looked over to see if Aurelian was all right. Although it was already beginning to heal, the wound was deep and ugly. His lover had torn into him pretty badly. He quickly leaned over to suckle the bite in Aurelian's neck, and the wound quickly closed over.

As he pulled away, the Selkie looked up at him, incredulous, his mouth opening and closing before he breathed, "Jesus. Is it always like that with you guys?"

Argent frowned back at him, shaking his head. "I am afraid not. Why are you staring back at me so strangely?"

The Selkie blinked, raising an eyebrow. "Your eyes. They've changed. It's almost as if you've overfed, but to a kinda drastic degree."

Something out of the corner of his vision drew his attention back to the body of his lover, passed out on the bed. Argent looked down and shuddered as he saw an indigo hue slowly start to flush across Jilah's skin. The color came in brief flashes, then was gone. A flicker of something slid underneath her skin; as if something thick and snake-like was swimming around within the mass of her muscles, breaking the surface to press up against the alabaster film of her skin. Argent reached a shaky hand out to touch her, his fingers gently brushing her shoulder as another flicker surfaced. He quickly jerked back as if burned. He'd felt it through his fingertips, thick and scaly.

Aurelian turned to look at what he was reacting to, then peered at him strangely. "What's wrong?"

Argent's voice was a hushed whisper. "Something is inside her. Beneath her skin."

Jilah stirred and looked over at them, her voice low and husky as she frowned and asked, "What's wrong? You look like you've seen a..." She blinked rapidly, "Whoa! Your eyes! Are you okay?"

The two men looked back at her, their eyes widening as Aurelian quietly asked, "Ah does she usually look like this after sex?"

Argent's voice was shaky as he answered, "No. Something is most definitely amiss here."

Jilah frowned and pushed herself off the bed, wondering what the hell they were talking about. She felt fine. More than fine, actually. She was almost dizzy with the elation she felt. The avatar grinned and stumbled away from the bed, wanting to see for herself what was causing such a reaction.

"Look, I'll agree that the sex was amazing, but I feel fi..." her words trailed off as she gaped at her reflection in the bathroom mirror. She had, within the last few minutes, grown a pair of small, two-inch long blue-black horns that jutted out of her forehead, curving upwards. Her eyes were now entirely jewel blue, shining brightly back at her as if something flared remotely in their depths, making them unnaturally luminous. She gasped when she saw her teeth.

Her canines were still jutting out a bit from the rest of her teeth, and when she prodded one with a finger, a drop of blood welled up on her fingertip. Her hand crept up to her forehead, gently touching the horns. They were smooth, and very sharp.

"Holy shit." she breathed to no-one in particular.

"Holy shit." Louder now.

Jilah held onto the counter, steadying herself before she ventured back out into the bedroom. She faced the men on the bed, stammering, "Uh, what exactly are you guys seeing when you look at me?"

Perhaps she was hallucinating on the Selkie's blood. She hoped to god she was. After all, she had gotten strange hallucinations off of the gargoyle's blood back at her old house. Argent's answering thought was understandable, although she only caught images and ideas. She breathed a sigh of relief that she wasn't seeing in her what he had.

Aurelian quietly asked, "You mean other than the horns, the eyes, and the tail?"

"TAIL?" Jilah cried out, covering her mouth in shock.

She hadn't meant to shout. She ran back into the bathroom and turned to the side, yelping as she saw that there was now a thin, indigo tail that sprouted from her lower back at the top of the swell of her buttocks. The skin along the tail faded to black, ending in a little arrow that forked back into little points. The tip reached down to her calves. It almost looked like a comical little demon tail. It swished back and forth, like that of an angry cat.

"What in holy HELL is going on?"

She walked quietly out of the bathroom. After taking a long, slow breath, she then made her way over to the bed, her gaze fixed on Argent. Her voice was tight and strained as she said, "So. About that... fix last night."

Argent shook his head slowly, unable to come up with an answer for his current condition, much less hers.

:: *S'llethe would not have done anything to endanger either of us, but her people; the power they channel sometimes...* ::

The connection between them flared before he could finish, and she stiffened. She stared back at him, stunned. Unable to keep her out, Argent winced, cursing the situation. The realization that he'd been holding something back from her about the healing that the strange woman had offered made Jilah's blood run cold. Before she become truly hurt or angered, however, she followed his train of thought and frowned, slowly comprehending. She understood his unspoken apology, and accepted it. It wasn't something he could have done anything about.

She had been so eager to keep the feeling of horror that had crept up on her from getting worse that she hadn't even given herself time to listen to the voices of her own doubts. To their mutual relief, the mental double perception didn't seem to be as strong now. At least that was something. Jilah let out a heavy, tired sigh, her eyes narrowing as her tail began twitching furiously.

"Man, I hope that this is something that wears off over time." she grumbled.

:: *Your family has a strange way of defining the word help.* ::

Aurelian looked over at her, fascinated. "You know, that tail is kinda sexy."

"Oh, shut up," she snapped at him as she walked over to the bed and sat down. The tail flicked out and slapped him hard in the chest and she eyed him, "At least it's good for something."

Argent chuckled, wondering where S'llethe had gone off to. Something had definitely gone awry, and he hoped that she could help sort it out. He was still shivering with the sheer amount of energy that coursed through his veins, his teeth chattering as he wrapped his arms around himself.

:: *What's wrong? Can't you just get rid of the overflow like you did last time?* :: she asked, concerned.

:: *For some reason, it's different. I can't concentrate,* :: he replied.

Jilah went to him, unsure of what she was going to do when she touched him, but she knew there was something that she could do to help him bleed off a little of the energy that was crackling behind his eyes. Straddling his legs, she leaned into him, placing her temple against his.

:: *Are you sure this is a good idea?* :: he asked as he watched the idea quickly form in her mind.

:: *I know it'll work. I don't know why, but I do.* ::

Jilah looked down and gave a little jump at the sight of the thick, bright purple line that stretched from her chest to his now. It hadn't been there a moment ago. She tapped into it without thinking, pulling some of the energy from him into herself. The flow between them seemed perfectly natural, as if this was something she'd done all her life. She utilized what she could from what she'd bled off him, sending the energy he needed that he gained when he fed back to him. She felt a strange pull as the zippy feeling from Aurelian's blood changed to a more grounded, stable hum.

She watched as Argent's eyes fluttered shut, once again becoming aware of the Selkie's presence beside them. As the transfer slowed to a trickle, she looked over at him and grinned.

"Much better."

Aurelian raised an eyebrow as Argent's eyes opened, breathing out a sigh of relief as he realized that they no longer looked flooded with all that black. Argent blinked several times, then looked over at Jilah, who was now smiling peacefully.

:: *How did you..?* ::

She laughed and shook her head. :: *No idea, but hey - it worked. Do I still have horns and a tail?* ::

Argent nodded slowly. Jilah let out a little disappointed huff, and Argent reached up to trace his fingers along the contour of one of her new horns.

"You know, they're actually quite appealing."

Aurelian grinned and nodded his assent, his voice a warm purr as he added, "Don't forget the tail. It really is kinda hot."

Jilah looked back at him with a stricken expression. "Are you both cracked? I look like...like a demon pinup girl!"

"Exactly." They responded in unison before looking over at each other, then back at her with wide, hungry grins. She backed away from them, hands up.

"Oh hell no. Once with you two was enough for me to sprout horns and a tail. Who knows what'll happen if we start up again?"

Argent's voice was a soft rumble as he purred, "It will be a great deal of fun finding out, wouldn't you agree?"

Jilah leapt off the bed as they crawled over the sheets towards her.

"Oh, sure, the sex is great, but I don't want to see how much worse this gets before I know what the whole story is. Enough has happened in the last..." she paused for a moment. Holy crap, had it been less than two weeks? She shook her head vigorously, standing her ground with her arms crossed.

"No. There will be no more 'knocking of the boots' with me before we get this shit straightened out. GET IT?"

She glared at them, and they paused for a moment. Argent looked at her quizzically. In response, Aurelian leaned over and whispered something to him, making Argent grin in response.

"Ah. Another interesting colloquialism."

Aurelian looked back over at Jilah, his lips close to Argent's ear as he quietly asked, "So, how quick is she, anyway?"

Argent crooked an eyebrow and looked back over at his lover. "Sadly, I think this particular chase will have to wait."

Argent sighed and leaned back into the bed, his gaze sliding over to meet Aurelian's. The Selkie settled next to him and chuckled.

"Ah well. Another time, hopefully." He grinned over at Argent and raised his arms over his head, stretching before he looked back at Jilah. "I'd really like to try that tail out."

Jilah glared at him, resting her hands on her hips.

Aurelian laughed, asking, "What?"

This time, Argent laughed, explaining, "She thinks you're an uncouth pig. Give her time to get to know you."

"What the hell's that supposed to mean?" Jilah barked, tapping her foot in annoyance. Aurelian was smiling back at her with a self-assured expression. His arrogance was infuriating.

:: *He can be a brash, cocky youth at times. But you have also seen how he can be at other times, through me.* ::

Jilah softened as she looked back over at Aurelian, who was now grinning back at her. Something in his body language had changed, as if he had toned the lewdness down, and she relaxed a little.

She grumbled petulantly, :: *I'm still not coming anywhere near you two until we talk to your sister.* ::

:: *Do you not trust us, love?* ::

Argent looked back at her, doing his best to maintain the innocent look.

Jilah laughed out loud. "Not as far as I can throw you."

Argent chuckled and Aurelian slid closer to him, resting his head on the pale man's shoulder. She felt the interest between the two men began to heat up again as she moved around the room, looking for clothing as she desperately tried to ignore the sexual imagery and sensations that bled into her psyche through the enhanced connection with her lover.

:: *There has got to be a way to crank that down a little.* ::

She pulled on a pair of loose gray sweatpants, and yanked a gray tank top with a fuchsia skull and crossbones on it over her head. To accommodate the tail, she had to let the sweatpants rest just underneath it, which was uncomfortable.

She turned away from the bed, but could now feel Aurelian's mouth on Argent's through the connection; the feel of the selkie's hands on Argent's body as they slowly slid down to grip him and squeeze gently. As she felt Argent's body respond to the touch, she quickly ran for the door. There was no way she was going to find herself drawn back into bed with them again, but she also didn't want to spoil the moment for them.

Perhaps she could track Gigi down and thank her for being so kind to her the other night.

Jilah darted out into the hallway, closing the door behind her. In her head, she could still hear them groaning, and it made concentrating damned difficult.

Jilah hoped that Gigi could help her find the mysterious woman who could possibly answer the myriad questions that now swirled in her mind. She turned and gave a little jump as she spotted Mira standing at the end of the corridor. The woman was watching her.

What the hell is that all about? Is she keeping tabs on her boyfriend?

Jilah winced, suddenly feeling very guilty.

Come to think of it, she probably should, considering what just happened. Mira acknowledged her presence, giving her a slight nod of respect.

OK, that's weird. She hates me, right? Unless that's changed as well.

Jilah took a slow, steady breath then headed down the hallway, towards her. What do you say when you'd just boned somebody else's boyfriend? Her face burned with shame. The woman had every reason to hit her now, although Jilah really hoped that she wouldn't.

"Is everything okay?" she croaked, clearing her throat.

Mira regarded her quietly for a moment, then responded, "There is news, but I don't want to disturb them."

"Anything urgent? Is it bad?" Jilah was practically shivering with the desire to go back into the room and join the boys, feeling bodies rocking and sliding along sweat-slicked skin through her psyche. She didn't know how much more she could take.

She jumped again when Mira asked, "Are you alright, Striaga?"

Jilah did her best to smile and nod without breaking a sweat. *Christ, I'm well and far away from them now - shouldn't I be able to shut it out just a little?*

Perhaps she needed more distance from him. Her voice cracked a little as she said, "Let's go somewhere that we can speak. This hallway isn't the best place in the world to receive...news, after all."

Mira replied with a brusque nod and murmured, "Follow me."

Twenty Five

A Steep Learning Curve

A question nagged at the back of her mind as Jilah followed Mira through the corridor. She wasn't quite sure how to address what had happened earlier without offending the woman, but felt that she needed to.

If Mira had been down the hallway earlier, there would have been little doubt about the activities that had just played out. Jilah wasn't at all quiet during sex, and her voice usually carried pretty well. She blushed and another wave of shakes swept through her as the boys' sexual gymnastics continued to keep her on edge. She took a long slow breath to collect herself.

"You have a question."

The statement hung in the air between them, and Jilah's jaw dropped as Mira spun to face her, her expression expectant.

Jilah had to backpedal in order to keep from bowling the smaller woman over. She presented Mira with an apologetic grin, her voice a little higher than she intended it as she cleared her throat and asked, "Ah, are you the jealous type?"

Mira peered up at her with that same strange expression of intense scrutiny. After a moment, the woman replied, matter-of-factly, "I am not jealous of you."

Wanting to inquire further, but not wanting to seem overly nosy, Jilah responded with a quick nod, and Mira turned back around and began striding down the hallway in that same quick, official walk.

As she followed, Jilah wondered where they were going. The corridors of this place seemed to go on forever, and they never seemed to go in the same direction twice. Again, she came to a jarring halt as Mira stopped suddenly. The woman had an annoying penchant for stopping on a dime, not seeming to care that someone was following behind her.

Another flash of images and sensations shuddered through Jilah and she let out a little moan, quickly covering her mouth with a hand.

Mira looked back at her, crooking an eyebrow.

Jilah slid her fingers from her mouth, resting her hand on the side of her cheek. She blushed furiously as she croaked, "Sorry." She winced as the woman nodded towards an open doorway.

Jilah walked into the small room. She had no idea where they were now. The room was grey and bleak except for long, grooved, claw-like marks in the surrounding stone. Ruddy stains and splashes swept across the wall in spatters and swaths of varied lengths. There was a steel chair and table in the room, but little else. Frowning, Jilah looked down to see deep scratches in the surface of the metal. With a start, Jilah realized that this was an interrogation chamber.

She shivered as she turned around in time to see Mira close the door behind her. She tentatively asked, "You sure you're not jealous?"

Shit. If only Argent had taught me a couple of moves, she thought. With that scream and the flying head, the bitch could probably clean her clock without putting much effort into it. Jilah felt her tail twitch around her legs nervously.

Mira responded with the barest flicker of a smile, again shaking her head. "Aurelian, while being my consort, is free to do as he wishes. I have no animosity towards those whom he chooses to bed."

Jilah eyed her with a slight frown. Her brain switched tracks of thought, and it occurred to her that she should be jealous of Aurelian, actually – seeing as how Argent was currently entertaining himself sexually with him. She relaxed as she realized that she wasn't jealous at all. Quite the opposite, she was happy for both Argent and for herself.

The connection between them made it feel as if they were both still together throughout, so she had no reason to feel left out. This both reassured her and for reasons that she couldn't quite explain, also made her feel uneasy; but since so many things had occurred that she had not been unable to figure out or quantify, she let it drop. There was no reason to pick at this particular issue if there was nothing broken. Besides, there were too many other important things at hand that needed to be dealt with.

She looked over at Mira, who was now peering at her with a strangely curious expression. The woman's tone was careful as she quietly said, "This room is safe. Nobody will listen in."

While not necessarily comfortable with the idea of being in such an enclosed space with a woman that had sent her howling across her own bedroom in abject terror several days ago, Jilah realized that with Argent otherwise occupied, it was probably a good idea for her to try to keep tabs on things so she could fill him in later. He had explained that the actual coronation, as it were, would be tomorrow night. Envoys from various parts of the country, as well as different parts of the world, would be showing up to witness his official declarations as the new Strigaisha of New Orleans. She thought it would be good for him to take the night off to get in a little recreational time beforehand.

"Several prominent members of the European Council have arrived early. While this in itself should not be cause for alarm, I have run across several conversations that were most intriguing." She paused for a moment, gathering her thoughts. "There are certain things that I need to inform you of, and while I recognize that you are acting Striaga, I would prefer to disclose the more volatile information directly to the Dragon's Hammer himself."

Jilah frowned, unfamiliar with the term. "The Dragon's Hammer?"

Mira looked at Jilah with a strange expression. Suddenly very aware of her new physical additions, Jilah reached up to run a finger along one of her horns. Making the assumption that the woman was just now noticing this, she opened her mouth to explain – but before she could say anything, Mira asked, "You mean you don't know?"

"Know what?"

Mira looked back at her, incredulous. "Your lover was once the most feared regent that the southeastern region of the United States has ever known. You've really never heard of The Dragon's Hammer?"

"I only just recently met him – all of this is new to me..."

Mira waved her hand in dismissal, starting over.

"It is unimportant. Given the current circumstances, it is vital that the incidents that have drawn so much attention in the media of late come to a halt." She took a step back and squared her shoulders. "If they continue with the members of the European Council here, it will be seen as an inability of the Strigaisha to control the situation."

Jilah regarded Mira with a wary expression, careful to keep her tone empty as she asked, "The bombing that happened on our way here?"

Mira responded, "Between that and the beheadings last night, the city proper is in a state of shock. Aurelian was to speak with the Strigaisha about the details earlier, but as you well know, his message was...delayed."

Jilah's arms stiffened at her sides as another nearly overwhelming wave of sensation rushed through her, this time making her sway on her feet. She hoped the boys hit an end point soon, so that she and Argent could finish up and get down to the business of fixing this – whatever it was.

"Striaga, are you certain that you are all right?"

Jilah nodded, taking in another deep breath as she balled her hands into fists and tried to walk it off. A shiver shook her body and her voice tightened as she answered, "I'm good." She unclenched her fists and began patting her palms against her sides. "I need to get some air."

Mira gave her that strange scrutinizing look again, and she couldn't help feeling that she was being inspected. The woman's tone was flat as she answered, "Try to keep from going around town, cutting people's heads off and leaving bodies for unsuspecting civilians to find. In the event that you find yourself unable to properly dispose of remains, we have damage response teams that will."

Jilah blinked.

"What, does EVERYBODY know that it was me now?" She stammered, "I was..."

Mira held up a hand, cutting her off. "The reasons are not something I need to know about, Striaga. Sometimes things just need to be handled with a certain finality. I'm no stranger to it myself; however, I must reiterate that if you need a cleanup crew, call me. Conducting business in a sloppy manner brings unwanted negative attention on the Strigaisha, which is the very last thing we want to do."

Understanding now that she wasn't getting dressed down for doing her job as much as the manner in which she'd done it, Jilah relaxed and nodded.

Mira pulled a black cellular phone out of her pocket and handed it to Jilah, explaining, "There's only one number programmed into it. If you run into a similar situation again, call it and tell the person that answers that you have a carpet that needs to be replaced. Give the address, then immediately hang up and destroy the phone." Her eyes narrowed as she added, "Do not use the phone for any other reason – and never answer it if it rings."

Jilah frowned as she looked down at the phone. "Do I get an exploding pen and laser watch too?" she asked.

Mira let out a harsh laugh. "This isn't a movie, Striaga."

Jilah thought about offering an explanation about the previous night's activities, but realized that it would fall on deaf ears.

"What else needs to be done?" she asked.

"The Dragon's Hammer has seen to Julian, so he will no longer be an inconvenience; nor will his compatriots. The Strigaisha's actions have destroyed the fight left in them. The only thing left to do at the moment is remain vigilant and react with extreme prejudice against anybody that wishes to act up or do anything stupid that might jeopardize things while the visiting delegates are here."

Jilah wondered what had happened with the rogue werewolf, but wasn't going to ask. She had already revealed a great deal of her political throat to Mira without intending to this evening, simply by being caught so completely off guard. She was very lucky that the woman wasn't taking advantage of it and tearing her apart. Jilah figured that it would be more prudent to ask Argent for details when they had a spare moment.

Suddenly, the feeling of her lover driving himself into Aurelian crashed through her, causing her to cry out. The sensation was indescribable; it practically fried her synapses for a few seconds as her legs buckled and she slumped to the floor.

She propped herself up with her hands as she came to her senses. "This shit has got to stop." She'd be no good to anybody if it continued. Hell, at times it was almost as if she hadn't left the room at all.

There was a rap on the door, and Jilah turned to see Gigi's poke her in. She had on a sea-green vamp wig and her makeup was done in shades of gold, emerald and light green. Her lips were coated with glittering emerald lipstick that made them look like slick jewels.

She met Mira's gaze first, her tone casual as she said, "You called?"

Mira crooked a finger at her, then pointed down at Jilah, who was hidden from the view of the door by the table.

"What, are you done with another..?" Her words trailed off and she gasped in shock as Jilah looked up at her with an apologetic smile. Gigi's eyes grew wide as she quickly moved to help her up, brushing her off as she wobbled on her feet.

"My, how you've changed in such a short time. So, missy, what's with the new horns? And the tail??"

As if on queue, Jilah's tail began whipping around nervously, and she replied, "I can't explain, but I need to get out of here. I need to get away from this place for a little bit."

The sorceress placed her hands on her hips with a stern expression. Jilah couldn't help but admire her fashion sense. The short, slinky black dress Gigi wore was cut high enough so as to be almost illegal. Long black opera gloves adorned her arms and a set of sea-green garters held up black fishnet stockings. Knee high combat boots completed the look.

She looked like a force to be reckoned with.

Gigi gently took Jilah's hand and led her out of the room. "Come on, sweetie. Let's get you back to your boy before he kicks my ass for letting you wander around all sick and," she waved her hand to indicate Jilah's new changes, "jacked up again."

Jilah looked back to see Mira breathing what looked like a sigh of relief as the sorceress pulled the avatar out into the corridor.

"But..." Jilah stammered, unsure of exactly how much she wanted to disclose. She was still embarrassed that she'd bedded Aurelian at the drop of a hat and wasn't sure how Gigi would respond to her if she knew. She stopped in the hallway, bringing Gigi to a halt as she explained, "He's not, ah, he's busy."

Her tail cracked her in the leg, and she let out a little yelp, rubbing at the sore spot.

The sorceress raised a carefully sculpted eyebrow, picking up on Jilah's tone as she responded, "Busy? Without you?"

Jilah blushed fiercely, pulling her hand free of the tall woman's grip. "It's okay, I'm not jealous, it's just that, well it's hard to explain."

Gigi's expression grew concerned, and she placed a gentle hand on Jilah's shoulder. "Honey, what's wrong? You're not all fidgety for nothing."

Jilah held a hand up to her chest, letting out a low, throaty moan. Gigi looked back at her, startled. "Good lord. Are you on something?"

Looking back at her friend nervously, Jilah brought a shaky hand up to her stomach to try to steady herself. The sensations she was receiving were reaching an almost unbearable crescendo again, shorting out her synapses and making it impossible to vocalize. Her knees began to buckle again, and Gigi quickly moved forward to catch her, sweeping the Striaga into her arms. The woman's eyes grew wide as Jilah began wailing and writhing, her eyes rolling back in her head as she let out a husky scream.

Gigi tried her best to restrain Jilah, doing what she could to avoid being impaled on her horns or whacked by the tail as it thrashed about. It made a couple of close passes at her head, and Gigi grabbed it, holding it tightly against Jilah's side. Jilah tasted blood on her tongue, hot and scalding as she felt Argent climax through their shared connection, and then everything went black as she went limp in Gigi's arms.

"What the holy hell?"

She turned to walk down the hallway and started slightly at the sound of Mira's voice.

"I wouldn't." Mira warned, her tone flat as she walked up to them.

Gigi looked back at her, annoyed. "You wouldn't." She rolled her shoulders back, continuing, "I, however, am." She gave Mira a sidelong glare before turning on her heel and walking down the hallway, her tone catty as she added, "Please feel free to follow, if you like."

A smile quirked Mira's lips as she watched Gigi proceed down the hallway with a haughty stride. This would be well worth watching.

From a respectful distance, of course.

Argent relaxed back into the bed, letting out a satisfied sigh. It was indeed very good to be home. He had missed it more than he had thought possible as he looked over to watch Aurelian scratching his stomach and stretching his legs out in the bed beside him.

The Selkie's voice was a whisper as he rolled over and slid an arm across Argent's stomach.

"Thank you. Thank you for coming back."

Argent took a slow, sated breath before running now warming fingers through the waves in the Selkie's platinum blond hair.

"I have missed you as well. A great deal more than I thought I would." He smiled into Aurelian's upturned face, pulling the man into a gentle, soft kiss. "And I am so sorry that I left in the manner I did."

Aurelian grinned and pulled out of the kiss, resting his head on Argent's chest as he murmured, "It's okay. God knows you had enough reasons."

Argent sighed and rested his cheek on Aurelian's forehead, his voice soft as he breathed, "I hurt you. I will endeavor to keep from doing so again."

Aurelian's responding smile was brilliance itself, and he sighed happily as he pulled Argent closer, chuckling. "I need to congratulate you again on your choice in Jilah. She's definitely something. What a hellcat." At this, they both chuckled.

"You have no idea. NO idea. I am indeed very fortunate to have found her." Aurelian propped himself up on an elbow beside him as Argent continued, "For her, I would cross oceans, join battles, and fight the devil himself."

"Wow, you really are gone on her." Aurelian's watched him, his expression amazed as he continued, "I don't think I've ever seen you like this."

Argent laughed, curling his fingers around the Selkie's arm, slowly sliding them up to his shoulder.

"I don't think I've ever truly been like this before. She brings many things out in me that I didn't know were there. It's not something that I can easily put into words."

Aurelian smiled, resting his cheek on Argent's shoulder and brushing against it lightly before looking back at him. "I like you like this. Rough and soft at the same time. It'll take a little getting used to, but

I'm sure I can handle it." As Aurelian dipped down to kiss him there was a sharp rap at the door.

They both looked across the room and Argent growled, "Who the hell is it this time? It's starting to feel like a damned bus terminal in here."

The Selkie laughed and gently pushed him towards the edge of the bed.

"You should see who it is. It might be important. I know it was when I interrupted."

Argent looked back at him, frowning. "Why didn't you say anything?"

Aurelian sat up, placing his elbows on his knees. "It wasn't as if I had much of a choice, as I remember." His eyes glittered as he presented Argent with a boldfaced, sated grin.

Argent's lips slowly curled into a smile, "There is that."

He didn't know if he would've been able to remember to deliver an urgent message either if he'd walked into the same situation. He stepped up to the door, grabbing the handle and muttering, "This had better be good."

He flung the door wide, ready to tear into the person in the hallway, but at the sight of Jilah limp in Gigi's arms, he quickly stammered, "What happened?"

Gigi looked back at him, her eyes widening nearly to the size of saucers before she quickly shifted her gaze and caught sight of Aurelian naked on the bed behind him. In a blur of movement the Selkie was standing beside Argent, his expression concerned as he looked down at Jilah.

The sorceress recovered quickly, taking a breath before explaining, "We were walking down the hallway when she began having what looked like a seizure of sorts. She just screamed and passed out."

"Ah..." Argent took a step back and breathed a soft sigh. He remembered feeling her reaction through the connection, hoping that it wouldn't end up embarrassing or inconveniencing her, but unable to really do anything about it in the moment. Aurelian eyed him, trying to figure out why he looked so guilty. Argent looked up at him and snapped, "What?"

Aurelian raised an eyebrow, his tone chiding as he replied, "You look like a kid who just raided a cookie jar and got caught. What's up with that?"

Argent winced again, irritated that he was being so transparent. His tone was defensive as he said, "I didn't think that she would be this strongly affected if she wasn't actually..." His mouth snapped shut and he looked back over at her.

"Wait, you mean that she..?" Aurelian's expression relaxed as he suddenly realized what happened. He then proceeded to laugh uproariously, padding back over to the bed.

"That's AWESOME!" he shouted.

Gigi glared back at both of them. This only made Aurelian laugh harder. He was now clutching at his stomach as he leaned back against the bed. Argent threw him an irritated look before moving to collect Jilah from Gigi's arms.

"Thank you for bringing her to me." His kept his tone quiet as he addressed the sorceress, not entirely sure how much he should tell her about what had happened. It seemed that he didn't need to, however, as he watched her flush, her hands fluttering up to her mouth in astonishment.

Gigi's voice was slightly husky as she breathed, "My god. She reacted like that to the two of you and she wasn't even in the fucking room?? Holy Mary Mother of God."

Argent watched her flush deepen as she crossed herself and his eyes widened at the accompanying images in her head. Aurelian was giggling now as he sat down on the bed.

"That, is the best thing ever. Oh man."

Mortified, Argent now wanted to throw something at him. Jilah was right. He really could be insufferable at times, but Argent also had to admit that it was impossible to stay truly angry with Aurelian when he was like this.

"She'll be okay, Gigi. Please leave us."

The sorceress was still shaking her head, stunned as she turned and walked back down the corridor. Argent slowly closed the door and looked over at Aurelian, his expression stern. Aurelian looked back at him, sobering a little.

"Do you think she's all right?"

Argent sighed and walked to the bed, gently setting her down. "I think she'll be fine, but I should have known that something like this would happen."

Aurelian looked back at him with a slight frown. "What – has this kind of thing happened before with her?" The Selkie placed a gentle hand on Jilah's shoulder, peering down at her, curious.

Argent sat next to him, watching her carefully. There were no colors that rushed across her body this time, and the sliding entity he'd seen under her skin before didn't seem to be resurfacing.

"No, not until tonight. But then, we've only been together for the last couple of days. She is the only individual that I've been intimate with in a long while. No, this is different."

"So you didn't really know that it would happen, right?"

Argent looked over at him, presenting him with a sheepish grin. "Yes, but while I was with you, I felt her as well – and could feel her reaction to what we were doing. I knew it was hitting her strongly, but..."

Aurelian rested a hand on Argent's shoulder, his tone reassuring. "Don't go beating yourself up because you were too far gone to stop. I know I definitely was." He paused for a moment, then continued, "Besides, it sounds like she enjoyed the hell out of herself."

The Selkie grinned and looked back down at her, chuckling. "Lucky girl."

"What was it that you wanted to tell me when you came to the door earlier?" Argent looked back at him, frowning slightly.

Aurelian shrugged and replied, "We have delegates from Europe arriving already, the current popular topics of discussion seem to be alternating between the bombing and this 'headless horseman' that the media keeps going on about."

His gaze darted down to Jilah for a moment, before moving up to meet Argent's eyes again.

"Apparently, the prevailing feeling is that the resultant media fallout is reaching a critical point. It's been said that if the situation isn't contained quickly and efficiently that the council proper will look into setting up shop here for one of their own. I seem to also remember overhearing something about meat or cows."

"The Butcher." Argent's voice came out in a hushed whisper. He understood that the situation probably looked serious to an outsider, but was not at all convinced that things needed to be taken to that level of extremity. Had the council taken complete leave of their senses? Perhaps they'd become a good deal more reactionary during his self-enforced exile.

The stories of old about the Butcher told of a bogeyman of sorts – a creature the Council would utilize from time to time when a city was considered beyond help. According to accounts of legend, it was an entity that was capable of conducting a completely bloodless, bodiless slaughter, immediately consuming everything it was tasked with destroying. It was like a supernatural vacuum cleaner of sorts that the council would use to raze the preternatural denizens of a city to the ground in order to start over.

Of course, he wasn't certain if it actually existed. There had been many colorful stories, centuries ago, but there had never been any eyewitness reports. Any mythology about The Butcher had been passed on purely through rumors, idle speculation, and generational stories.

Argent had hoped that The Butcher was just a scare tactic, intended to terrorize a regent into weeding out problem children within their given domain – but if it was real? That was another matter entirely.

The idea that even a fraction of the stories could be right, that the council would employ such harsh methods in this particular instance shook him. He remembered that they could be heavy-handed, but did not think that they were completely without sense. Julian had been firmly dealt with. Those who had witnessed the act of retribution were already working quickly to convince the rest of his wayward pack of mongrels to shut up and sit the hell down. So far, all accounts of further opposition had stopped completely. He'd cut the problem off at the root and was very pleased with the results.

His lover, however, was another story entirely. When she recovered, he would have to speak with her about ensuring that she left no further evidence behind when conducting her duties. He understood that she had a job to do, but leaving bodies behind all over the place was simply bad business. Surely even her patroness could see that.

"Do any of the delegates need to speak with me before the ceremony tomorrow night?" he asked, feeling very tired all of a sudden.

Aurelian shook his head slowly and reached out to place his hand over Argent's. The Sanguine smiled at him, sighed and said, "Good. I suppose Mira has things well in hand?"

The Selkie grinned and crooked an eyebrow at him. "Oh yeah. She's definitely not fuckin' around. We worked hard to track you down and bring you back here, and she'll do what she needs to do to ensure that you stay on the throne. She was more than a little disappointed that you didn't give her a crack at Julian, though."

"She is more than welcome to go into the throne room and poke what's left of him with a sharp stick if she feels that will help allay her frustration at being left out."

Argent presented him with a wry grin and Aurelian laughed. "Nah. You know how much she likes her meat to quiver and scream when she plays with it. My little sadist."

Argent nodded. "I do indeed."

The sheets rustled and they both looked down to see Jilah moving slowly. Argent brushed his knuckles gently along her forehead. She slowly opened her eyes and looked up at them, blinking as she frowned and muttered, "Well, that sucked. I now feel like an enormous slut."

She closed her eyes, groaned and asked, "Gigi isn't angry at me, is she? I hope I didn't embarrass her too much."

At this, Aurelian started laughing again and Argent smacked him. Her mental connection with Argent flared to life and the scene with Gigi at the door replayed for her from her lover's perspective. Jilah flushed and placed her hands over her face.

"Oh my god. I'm mortified."

Aurelian, still laughing, asked, "But was it good for you?"

Argent glared at the Selkie, who just started laughing harder. Argent rolled his eyes at him and turned down to look at his lover. A single jewel-toned eye peeked at him through a crack in her fingers, her blush deepening. She was embarrassed beyond belief.

:: *Can we please talk to your sister now??* :: she begged.

Argent nodded, depositing a gentle kiss on her forehead before he slid off the bed and began getting dressed.

:: *I am sorry, beloved. That was very selfish of me.* ::

:: It's all right. It was something you both needed. I just wish I hadn't been so... affected by it in public. :: Jilah reddened as she watched him dress, letting out a soft sigh.

Aurelian's laughter died down and he frowned as he asked, "Where are you going?"

"We need to discuss something with an old acquaintance."

Argent slid into a pair of black leather pants, zipping them up and pulling a black tank top on. "I need you to stay around the delegates, find out the gossip and what other rumors are being shared."

Aurelian nodded, his tone becoming official as he moved to collect his clothes from the floor.

"Gotcha."

After sliding a pair of black engineer boots on, Argent looked back over at Jilah, who was now curled up in a semi-fetal position on the bedspread.

:: Ready? ::

Jilah sat up slowly, feeling a little dizzy. *:: As ready as I'm gonna get tonight. ::*

Argent presented her with that boyish grin she'd grown so fond of, then walked over to Aurelian as the Selkie was pulling his shirt over his head. A bright spill of honeyed platinum locks popped out of the top of the shirt. Aurelian smiled back at him as he slid the shirt down to his shoulders. Argent then pulled him into a slow, tight hug.

Jilah rolled her eyes and grated, "Don't start that up again, or we'll be here all night."

Aurelian spun around and pulled her into his arms, kissing her fiercely. *:: Is he usually this affectionate? ::*

Argent's answering chuckle rolled through her thoughts. *:: Think of him as a big puppy - one that's a really good swimmer, among other things. ::*

Jilah pulled out of the kiss, looking up at Aurelian's goofy smile. She laughed and swatted at him. "You really are a huge dork, you know that right?"

The Selkie shrugged and grinned, his tone easy and happy. "Oddly enough, you're not the first person who's said that. You guys have fun storming the castle, or whatever it is you plan on doing." He walked slowly to the door. "And if you end up having another party like this again, you know where to find me."

He gave a joyous whoop as he opened the door and walked out into the hallway.

Jilah looked over at Argent and murmured, :: *He really does grow on you.* ::

Argent nodded, laughing. :: *Indeed he does.* ::

Twenty Six
A Family Affair

They made an odd pair as they walked down the hallway. Jilah's long blue-black tail whipped quickly from side to side, and Argent watched it out of the corner of his eye, crooking an eyebrow at it. Knowing she was nervous, he laced his fingers with hers and hoped that S'llethe would be able to do something about the tail, if nothing else. The new appendage made Jilah's emotions transparent, which made her vulnerable.

Granted, she had been able to fend off her first attacker, but not everybody would be as bold or open if they chose to move against her in the future. It was disconcerting, being in Argent's head throughout this thought process, and Jilah gripped his hand tightly, choosing to communicate with him in words to try to distract herself from it.

:: *I don't want to be somebody that can be used against you politically because of this. If she can't..* ::

He cut her off, softly answering, :: *We'll figure something out, love.* ::

The passageways and tunnels of the convent continued to be indistinguishable from any of the others as they made their way toward S'llethe's guest quarters. Jilah was beginning to think that she would never learn her way around. The entire place felt like a gigantic rabbit warren or a stone habitrail of sorts. Every corridor looked exactly the same, and they all seemed to shift directions from time to time. It was amazing that anybody could actually get where they were going. She wondered if there was a trick to it.

:: *Actually, there is. And you've figured it out before.* ::

Argent's response made her jump a little but she kept in stride with him as she looked over at him.

:: I have? When? :: A memory slowly surfaced and Jilah frowned. :: Wait. Every time I've needed to leave, or find a place in here, it's like I knew where I was going, but only after I'd figured that I was already lost. ::

Argent smiled and replied, :: Exactly. As long as you're connected to the inner court, you'll always end up arriving where you need to be. ::

Jilah frowned, turning to watch the corridor slowly retreating behind them as they walked along.

:: So, how exactly does that work? ::

He explained, :: It is a resonance imprinted in the structure itself that remembers where everything is. The corridors themselves know where they lead. When a member of the inner court needs to know where they're going, for whatever reason, the stones respond and lead the way. ::

:: So, what would happen if I wasn't a member of the court? :: She asked, thinking that she already knew the answer.

:: You would become hopelessly disoriented. Every passage would end up leading to the same outside exit. ::

Jilah thought about this for a moment, then asked, :: How can they tell that I'm a member of the court? ::

:: It is a bit like a coded imprint of sorts. ::

:: What, like a security access badge or something? ::

It was a strange concept that Argent could see clearly in her thoughts, and although he'd never seen one himself, the shared idea did seem similar.

:: Something like that, yes. ::

:: What, so there's like a chip, or a thing that I have on me somewhere that..? ::

Knowing where her train of thought was headed, Argent replied, :: It's a psychic attunement of sorts. Gigi dispenses them to everybody when they arrive. ::

Jilah looked over at him, shocked. So, she'd been zapped with this attunement sometime between when they'd gotten off the bus and now, but she couldn't remember anything distinct that stood out. When had Gigi had the time to do it? It seemed like something that would take a little time, or that would've at least registered as a blip that she would've questioned. Maybe it was done while she was asleep?

:: *It doesn't have any side effects does it? 'cause I've had just about enough of those to last me a lifetime.* ::

Argent squeezed her hand, chuckling. :: *There are no side effects. It's just a minor transparent addition.* ::

Jilah sighed and plucked nervously at the hem of her shirt with her free hand, her tone a little distressed as she sent, :: *It's difficult for me to get my legs under me with everything that's going on. It'd be nice to catch a break sometime in the near future.* ::

They turned a corner, almost bowling Gigi over, and Jilah let out a small yelp of surprise. The sorceress grinned at her and exclaimed, "Striaga! I'm so glad to see that you're feeling better."

Jilah blushed, wincing a little as she said, "Sorry about earlier, I just..."

Gigi cut her off with a flourish of her hand and replied, "There's no need to apologize, honey. Trust me when I say I don't blame you at all for your reactions. You got some fierce men around you."

Gigi eyed Argent and raised a sharply manicured eyebrow. "And you should be ashamed of yourself, sending the poor girl out like that."

Argent dropped his jaw in surprise. Surely she didn't think that it had been his fault. After all, both men would've been more than happy to have Jilah stay with them.

Before he could respond, Jilah squeezed his hand and said, "I was the one that left, Gigi. It wasn't like they threw me out."

Gigi eyes widened, and she rocked back on a heel. "Are you crazy leavin' two fine men like that on their own? You just know they're only gonna get into trouble," she gave another sidelong glance to Argent, giving a quick snap of her fingers. "Which they did."

Jilah couldn't help laughing, mostly due to the irritated expression on Argent's face. Jilah chuckled and responded, "Trust me. If I find myself in a similar situation again, I'll know better to stay in the room."

:: *If?* :: Argent's tone was almost disappointed.

Jilah quickly amended, "When, that is."

She could feel Argent's relief at her statement and smiled.

:: *Are you kidding? Knowing what he means to you, I wouldn't keep you from each other.* ::

Argent squeezed her hand in response, his sheepish grin mirroring her own now.

"Go on, girl. Make me proud. Or at least give the rest of us a standard to try to live up to." She winked and then walked past them, humming a familiar tune that Jilah couldn't quite place.

She felt her face flush and a halfheartedly guilty smile crept along the edges of her lips. Her eyes darted over to Argent.

:: *What does it say about me that in less than a month I've gone from being an entirely sexless entity to jumping into a wild, gymnastic session of sex with two guys?* ::

Argent chuckled and responded, :: *That you are learning to enjoy yourself.* ::

He gently pulled her along as they continued along the corridor again.

:: *I just feel like I'm walking around with this big neon 'Ho' sign on my forehead.* ::

Argent looked over at her, his brows knitting. He was unsure of her meaning. He failed to see how gardening implements brought anything to bear on the current situation. His thoughtful reflection trailed off as the meaning came through the connection.

He frowned and sent, :: *The connotation that I am seeing in your thoughts does not make sense. You are hardly a fallen woman because you chose to have more than one person in bed with you. Mira is well aware of Aurelian's penchant for being with many others besides herself and feels no lack because of this. But still, you feel as if you've done something wrong.* ::

Jilah winced, realizing that he was right but still feeling a twinge of guilt in spite of it. She wasn't really hurting anybody by being with both of them, but something about it still seemed wrong. Although she'd never been in a relationship before, she had always pictured the possibility as her and one other. That just seemed the way that it was supposed to be. What she'd done earlier seemed wrong somehow, again because she'd had no previous frame of reference for such things – but then when it came to social interaction, she had to admit that her relationship ideals were pretty warped.

Argent smiled and looked over at her, his mental voice smooth and reassuring.

:: *I realize that this is all a great deal to adapt to, along with everything else. However, this particular action is something that has no bad association attached. It is one thing that you can just let happen, without worrying about the consequences.* ::

They came to a stop in front of an ornate, mahogany door. Jilah frowned, positive that the door hadn't been there a moment ago. There were strange fluid images carved into the wood, an unusual collection of sculptures in the grain that flowed smoothly from one form to the next. Jilah blinked at the design as she peered at it, positive that something in the pattern had shifted.

Wait, did that..? There!

She definitely saw it that time. The grain in one of the designs shifted slightly to the right. She raised a hand to run her fingers along the design and jumped as the door opened inward, revealing the familiar face of the beautiful woman that had assisted her last night. Jilah noticed for the first time that the woman's eyes were a brilliant shade of amethyst.

S'llethe smiled back at them, her voice lilting and musical as she invited them in.

"We have been waiting for you. We imagine that there are many questions."

Jilah frowned, her tail coming to a stop in a curl at her thigh as she looked over at Argent.

The woman continued, "Please, come in. We will explain as best we can."

Argent stepped into the room, gently pulling Jilah behind him. She peered inside, her eyes scanning the room and finding nothing overly remarkable. The room was a great deal more spartan than she expected.

:: *They are a very non-material folk.* :: Argent explained.

:: *Ah.* ::

Jilah looked back at Argent's strange sister. There was a mesmerizing beauty within the woman that confused Jilah. For some reason, Jilah had a strong urge to throw her arms around this strange woman. She wanted very badly to have this woman hold her, hugging her in what would assuredly be a comforting, loving embrace.

:: *Um, Is that normal?* :: she asked Argent, her tone wary.

She had never been comfortable with physical intimacy in social situations, and although she could understand the desire to put her hands on a man in that manner, she wasn't certain what was prompting her to have these feelings towards this particular woman. Jilah couldn't remember even feeling this way towards her own mother. There was nothing remotely sexual about the feeling – it seemed to be more about sharing reassuring physical contact. It was causing a conflict in her that she didn't really want to think about.

Argent nodded as he stood beside her, letting his thumb play over the back of her hand gently. :: *It is with them.* ::

S'llethe was still smiling back at both of them with a beatific expression, her hands clasped at her waist as she watched them. "Dearest sister, we are pleased that you no longer bear the pain of the past – but we sense that all is not entirely right."

Jilah looked back at the woman as if she'd sprouted two heads. Was she kidding? Her new tail was now twitching back and forth angrily, and Jilah grabbed it and held it in front of her.

"What, do the horns and the tail give it away?"

S'llethe looked uncertain for a moment, almost as if unable to comprehend her frustration.

"This is simply part of the joining, the healing." she replied, as if that explained it all.

Argent spoke up, his tone careful as he asked, "Joining? What exactly is this joining that you're referring to?"

S'llethe was now beaming again, her eyes shimmering as she replied, "We have made whole what once was fragmented."

Jilah wasn't sure she liked the sound of that. Her eyes narrowed slightly as she asked, "What was fragmented? Me?"

The woman inclined her head gently towards Jilah. "We have merged you with the force that animates you so that you are now no longer at odds with it. You are now in balance."

Okayyy. That definitely didn't sound good. Jilah frowned and asked, "The force that animates me?"

S'llethe remained patient and smiling as she explained, "You are now one with the dæmon inside you. The outer surface has begun reflecting the inside."

Stunned, Jilah gaped back at the woman, her eyes growing wide as she blurted out, "DEMON?!?"

Her mind reeled as she looked away, the news hitting her with a surprising amount of force. Her body rocked with it and her legs began to shake as the familiar laugh of the Dark Lady crawled through her mind. She felt Argent shudder beside her at the sound of it. An intense discomfort radiated from him at being unable to break the connection. She could tell that he was definitely not happy that he couldn't get away from her unusual head occupant. She felt something in him skitter away at the sound, and for the first time she realized that he was more than wary of her patroness.

He was scared of it.

S'llethe cocked her head, her brow creasing slightly as she asked, "You did not have this awareness already? That you were half dæmon?"

Jerked abruptly out of her thoughts by the woman's voice, Jilah absently let go of her tail and yelped as it whacked her in the back of the leg again.

"My god, no. I had no idea!" She whirled to face Argent, sputtering, "Did you? Did you know?"

Argent looked back at her, his expression distant as he responded, his voice quiet and tight, "I knew that you were different. But this? No. I was unaware of this."

He didn't understand why she was so flustered at the idea. Dæmons were notoriously hard to kill; remarkably durable. It would only end up helping with their given situation, in his opinion. At the moment he was a little more preoccupied with the mental connection between them, distinctly uncomfortable with the fact that he was now trapped with the sound of that cold, chittering voice. It was bad enough that Jilah had chosen to live with such an entity in the confines of her own mind, but sharing head space with such a creature was not at all what he was prepared to endure.

Disoriented, both from this new revelation as well as her lover's rather visceral reaction to her patroness, Jilah turned back to face the woman that stood across from them, taking a slow breath in an attempt to master herself. After a moment, she quietly asked, "So, these bells and whistles," she waved her hands to indicate her new body parts as she continued, "they're not going to go away, are they?"

S'llethe's expression softened, her tone muted as she answered, "These things you speak of, they are now part of you and therefore will not fade. This is something that you are displeased with?"

Jilah ground her teeth, not wanting to shout but finding it increasingly difficult to hold back. "Well, yes, a little. I mean, it's just that.." her voice sounded so very small as she continued, "I'd just gotten used to this body."

She wasn't sure how to verbalize it without sounding like a whiny, petulant child, and she didn't want to go there. Things were bad enough without that kind of drama.

She took a deep breath and slowly counted to ten.

Now more than a little curious, Argent quietly murmured, "This change seemed to manifest itself when she consumed a great deal of energy. If it happens again, will her appearance change more?"

S'llethe's expression was serene as she answered, "It is not for us to say. The Vaya works in its own way. We only conduct the flow."

Jilah let out a strangled laugh, her voice cracking as she said, "Great. That's just great."

She began rocking back and forth on a heel, hands on her hips as she muttered quietly to herself. Yep – looked like she was going there whether she wanted to or not.

Argent looked over at his mate with a pained expression. There was unfortunately nothing he could say or do to help with this. He could only watch her deal with the situation and be there for her. He took a breath and asked the question that he was most dreading the answer to.

"There is a mental connection that exists between us now that was not there before. Is it part of this joining?"

The woman brightened, her smile warm and wide as she said, "Oh yes. As we have joined her to her other half, we have also joined both of you, one to the other."

Argent became very still, his voice quiet as he asked, "What exactly do you mean?"

"We have been waiting for the day when you would find the compliment to your spirit, brother. Now that you have found her, we have bound you to each other. With this connection, you will be able to share everything freely, making for easy, fluid, unbroken contact. You are now mated as we mate. One to another until one of you passes beyond the reach of this sphere." Her laugh was joyous, a palpable wave of ecstasy that rolled through the room. "We are so very happy for you brother. This is our gift to you."

Argent's eyes widened as he stood before her. Gift? They thought this was a gift? It was a curse.

There were reasons that even well-suited couples couldn't read each other's minds, and all of them flooded through his mind as he closed his eyes and pressed fingers gently against his temple to try to figure a way out of this. He loved Jilah dearly, but if they ended up trapped with each other's thoughts, they would both go insane. Not to mention the fact that she had something that thought it was a dark goddess taking up residence in her head that scared the bejesus out of him.

The strained silence that followed was broken by a loud whoop of laughter. His eyes flew open in time to see Jilah gesticulating wildly, her voice high and strained as she finally snapped.

"Oh, this is just great. I'm fucked. FUCKED. We're fucked."

She turned to him and continued to laugh, her expression slightly crazed. "Your.." she waved at him in frustration, "Thing is tomorrow night, I have a tail that has pokerface written all over it, this connection or whatever the hell we have is going to end up driving us both batty eventually. And, if we have sex – or if I work again, who knows what little physical additions are going to pop up?!?"

His mate had been holding on so tightly to the last vestiges of her ability to cope throughout the last week- he could feel her relief when it all finally came to a head and she was free to rave like a lunatic. There didn't seem to be much else to do but just let her get it all out until it burned itself out. Jilah pointed her thumb savagely back at herself and growled, "They're going to slaughter me. And you in the process. Why the fuck did I come here? What the hell was I thinking? Oh god..." She clutched at her stomach and began muttering angrily to herself, furious at the world.

The faint sounds of wicked laughter rang through his own head as well as hers now, and her thoughts begin to spiral. Unbidden, the connection opened wide between the two of them, and Argent winced at the ferocious dismay rampaging through her mind.

As he watched, her thoughts ripped and tore at each other. It reminded him of the dark whirlwind he had first encountered in her mind. Jilah stood in the middle of it all, an Amazonian blue-skinned demoness. Her horns had grown long and sharp as they curved gracefully up and away from her forehead. Her indigo and white hair stood out in stark contrast against the darkness as it whipped around her in a swirling mass of color. Her tail also appeared thicker and more menacing as it whipped furiously from side to side. Argent noticed that she'd also grown at least a full foot taller. Enormous, leathery wings curled protectively around her arms and sides. He could only imagine how wide their span would be if she fully extended them. It was a look that definitely suited her.

She was trembling and crying before him, her eyes tightly shut as she tried to fend the whirlwind off. Argent made his way towards her, boldly stepping into the whirling mass that now began opening tiny cuts all over his arms, face and shoulders as he reached out to her. She was going to tear herself apart if he couldn't pull her back. Jilah cried out, a mournful howling sound, gnashing her teeth at something off to her right as Argent grabbed her hand, gripping it tightly. She wrapped his hand in a fierce grip, holding on to him as the wailing winds around them slowly died down.

Jilah sobbed as he pulled her towards him and embraced her. The maelstrom then died out altogether. He felt a strange serenity as he held her, her great wracking sobs shaking him as she bent her head down and wept into his shoulder. A rush of frightened images flowed from her and he responded by sweeping her off her feet and moving to sit cross-legged on the floor with her in his lap. He sat there, rocking her gently and responding with a stream of reassuring images and feelings.

It was an unusual way to communicate, he had to admit, but it was most definitely efficient – especially for this sort of situation. Argent began to feel her frustration and anguish fade as he continued to rock her. Jilah relaxed against him, sighing softly. In the same wordless moment, she apologized and he accepted, reassuring her that it was okay. She had so many doubts and arguments. He rebuffed them all gently, letting her know that no matter what happened, they would get through it.

Together.

She raised her head from his shoulder and looked down at him, a tentative smile beginning to curve her lips, and he was suddenly...

...back in his body, startled to find himself in the same position on the floor in S'llethe's room. Jilah came back to herself with a start as well, but happy that he was still holding her.

Okay, that was really weird. Weird, but good.

They looked up at S'llethe, who was now nodding and smiling, her eyes shining as she breathed, "You see? It is indeed a gift, brother."

Argent turned towards her and stood up with Jilah still in his arms, gently placing her on her feet beside him. "Is there any way to cut it back or mute it a little? There are times when the intensity becomes inconvenient, if not dangerous."

S'llethe looked back at him, not comprehending.

Argent continued, "We are not capable, as you are, of sustaining this level of mental intimacy indefinitely. We are creatures of singular consciousness. It is not in our nature to be so linked. We will need to be able to shut it off from time to time, in order to maintain a level of sanity."

The woman remained silent, watching Argent intently as he quietly added, "And there is an entity in her psyche that I wish to have no part of. Although I love Jilah, her chosen burden is not mine to bear. It will not bring me anything positive to engage it in any way."

Finally gaining comprehension, the woman's eyes flashed a vibrant dark purple. "Apologies, brother. We will then rectify this as best as we can so it is pleasing to both of you."

She stepped towards them, her voice soft and reassuring. "We will teach you how to do this."

Jilah was about to ask her exactly how she intended to teach them when the woman reached up and gently brushed their temples with her knuckles. A strangely resonant tutorial of sorts flashed through her thoughts, and a sense of clarity dawned on both of them. The realization that she would now be able to restrict the connection, as well as shutting it down when necessary was reassuring, but it also came with the knowledge that if either of them experienced something intensely stressful or strong, they would have to run a strange, sequenced chant of sorts through their minds in order to accomplish this.

Along with this, she understood why the physical modifications were permanent. Something about the nature of the joining didn't allow for reversals, only adaptation and addition. Argent felt something give, knowing that he would now no longer have access to the part of Jilah's mind that housed her unusual resident. The thought of such a thing squatting in his lover's mind sent a chilling shiver across his skin.

He quickly cranked the connection down to where he still had a mild awareness of her and breathed a sigh of relief, relaxing as he realized that he didn't have to worry about surface thoughts being transmitted so openly anymore. Some of the revelations that she'd accessed through the connection had been uncomfortable for her. He could breathe a little easier now that he didn't have to worry about any of it hurting her. He was thankful that he could release his iron grip on the old damning memories of his past.

Jilah blinked in shock as she felt the connection drop to a manageable level. She could still feel him, his presence in her mind light, barely registering. It was more like a friendly reminder than an overwhelming torrent.

She relaxed and rested her head on his shoulder, her voice a little shaky as she sent, :: *Thank god.* ::

Argent squeezed his arm against her waist gently. :: *Better?* ::

Jilah sighed and nodded, leaning into him. :: *Much.* ::

A slight frown quirked the corners of her mouth as she added, :: *Although the tail's gonna be a bit difficult to get around.* ::

As in response, it slowly curled back and forth, the tip twitching gently around her knees.

:: *We will find a way around it, beloved. Don't fret.* ::

She looked over at him, letting out a nervous laugh. :: *So, are you sorry you ran into me yet?* ::

:: *I do not think that there is anything that could happen between us to make me sorry that I sought you out.* ::

Jilah's heart hammered in her chest as Argent looked over at S'llethe, who was now beaming at them again. Her voice had a strange harmonic that sounded as if several voices were speaking as one. "There is balance. Is it well with you both?"

Jilah's gaze swept the woman's frame, as she once again experienced that strange desire to go up and hug her, to gain comfort through her embrace. It wasn't an entirely pleasant feeling, and she stayed her ground, unwilling to give in to it as she squeezed Argent a little closer to her.

She nodded, quietly answering, "It's as good as it can be at the moment. If no other little nasty surprises pop up, I imagine I can count myself lucky."

Argent grinned at her response, agreeing. What they needed at the moment was a string of utterly dull, unimportant events to fill the time between now and tomorrow night's ceremony. He hoped like hell they'd get them. Unfortunately, he had duties that needed his attention.

Now that his Striaga was mostly sorted out, he needed to go engage the delegates that had already arrived. Putting in a personal appearance would set their minds at ease. The diplomatic situation was tenuous enough already without something else going wrong.

:: *There are some things I need to take care of, but I want to make sure that you're alright.* ::

His expression was apologetic as he moved his hand down to the small of her back, gently brushing a thumb against her skin.

:: *I'll be good. You go take care of what needs takin' care of.* ::

Argent leaned in and kissed her quickly, then released her and slid his hand down her arm to gently grip her hand. He cocked his head and looked her over, then smiled.

:: *The horns really do suit you.* ::

She swatted at him, and he ducked out of the way, grinning as he looked over at S'llethe. "I don't wish to be abrupt, but..."

The woman with the violet eyes replied with an open smile, "All is well, brother. We understand that there is much for you to do."

Argent turned back to Jilah, his eyes glittering as he asked, :: *You don't have to work tonight, do you?* ::

Jilah shook her head, her tail now moving gracefully back and forth as she quietly answered, :: *Not so far. I think I'm going to be given a bit of a break after last night. Why do you ask?* ::

:: *If you do end up working, please try to cause a little less of a stir?* :: He looked very much like a little boy pleading for a cookie and made her want to laugh. She sighed and nodded, feeling bad that her untidiness last night was causing such difficulty for him. She also vowed to take the phone that Mira had given her out on any future hunts, just in case.

:: *I promise to be discreet, if that happens.* ::

Jilah felt the tension in him release and she smiled. :: *It'll be okay. Go on.* ::

He bowed slightly to both of them and departed, leaving the door open.

Jilah looked back over at Argent's 'sister.' She felt that same mixture of discomfort and the need to rush into the woman's arms. Her voice cracked slightly as she took a step back and explained, "I should get going too. I mean, thanks for the dæmon parts and all, but I really gotta..."

S'llethe interrupted, her voice soft and smooth. "Sister, we understand that we make you uncomfortable. Please know that this is not our intention."

Jilah let out a little nervous laugh and responded, "I know. A lot has happened in the last couple of days. I need a little breathing room."

The woman nodded, her hair catching the light of the room and reflecting it back in little crimson shimmers of color that ran through the waves that spilled over her shoulders.

"It does not have to be daunting, sister. You are becoming what you are meant to be."

Sensing that there was more that was coming, Jilah held up a hand, cutting her off.

"This isn't a conversation I'm prepared to have right now. Can we talk about this later?"

How about never? Never sounds good.

The moment the thought entered her head, she felt guilty. She didn't want to be rude. Although things had gotten way out of hand and gone off on tangents that were startling the hell out of her, the woman was only trying to help.

S'llethe smiled and nodded again as she moved to clasp her hands at her waist. "We can indeed, sister."

Jilah breathed a sigh of relief and politely excused herself, ducking out into the hallway. She closed the door behind her, then leapt away from it when she felt part of the grain writhe beneath her hand. She shook it off and started walking at a brisk pace through the corridors, no longer wanting to be in this part of the convent. Her tail whipped back and forth as she padded down the hall, and Jilah began wondering what she was going to do with herself for the rest of the night.

It was likely that Argent was going to be kept busy until sunrise, and she didn't want to sit around doing nothing. There had to be something interesting that she could do to get her mind off things. She rounded a corner and let out a startled yelp as she almost barreled into Gigi again. The sorceress was with a pair of girls that Jilah hadn't seen before. One of them had a set of sea-green pigtails that rode high on her head, bobbing smartly around a set of black goggles. Her outfit consisted of straps and strategic bits of cloth that barely covered up the naughty bits.

Next to her stood a girl with flawless mocha-colored skin and long purple and teal hair that had been pulled back into high pigtails. The ends of the pigtails tapered into black as they reached the middle of her back. She was dressed in a similar manner, but there was a harder edge to her look. In this one, there seemed to be a little more intensity than flounce. Gigi was decked out like a long, reedy Tank Girl with knee-high combat boots, ripped fishnets, tight black booty shorts, a single black kneepad, and a very tight, bright red tank top that went with her short blond spiked hair perfectly.

Jilah looked back at the three of them, stammering, "Oops."

Gigi gave her the once over, then shook her head and made a tutting noise. She turned to her two companions and crooned, "Now ladies. Does this look like the outfit of a woman that's ready to kick up her heels and go out on the town?"

Her companions chuckled, shaking their heads in unison.

Gigi continued, "Striaga, my dear..."

Jilah cut her off, pleading, "Please. Just call me Jilah."

The title didn't feel comfortable when people she thought of as friends used it.

Gigi nodded slowly, then said, "Jilah, my dear girl. You are going to march into your boudoir and go through your wardrobe, which I happen to know is both extensive and fierce, and you are going to get yourself dolled up. We are going out."

Jilah looked up at her, stricken. "What, like this?" She indicated the horns and the tail.

Gigi waved her hand with a flourish. "We'll have none of that as an excuse. It's high time we had a ladies night. Things have been tighter in this place than Sister Mary Margaret's ass. I, for one, am done with it and need a little air, and you are going to join us."

Jilah grinned as Gigi's companions gave her openly appreciative looks. Without realizing she was prying, their surface thoughts came through loud and clear, and she began blushing furiously. Whoa.

She looked back over at Gigi, her eyes growing wide as she blurted, "But, I have nothing to wear that will accommodate..." miserable as she held up her tail. She hadn't considering having to change her entire wardrobe, but now the thought depressed the hell out of her.

Gigi gave her a quick wink, taking her hand and practically pulling her down the hallway. "Don't worry. Auntie Gigi will handle everything, darlin'. You just sit back and enjoy the ride."

Jilah ventured a glance back at the two girls following behind them. Both were watching her tail swish gently back and forth and grinning, entranced. They looked like a pair of hungry cats.

What am I, a weirdness magnet? Jilah stumbled and quickly recovered, turning to watch where she was going now as the girls behind her chuckled softly.

If nothing else, it would definitely present one hell of a diversion.

Twenty Seven
Ladies' Night

In addition to her other numerous talents, Gigi was also an amazing stylist. The generic black PVC outfit that the sorceress had initially pulled out of Jilah's closet had seemed dowdy in comparison to the almost peacock-ish finery of her new friends. By the time Gigi was finished with – whatever it was that she did – the material flashed with the same iridescent sheen of Jilah's outfit from her first night at court.

Vague outlines of what looked like tribal dragons curled along the fabric of both legs as Jilah slid into the pants, and she sighed at the delicious feeling of the material against her skin. It was surprisingly comfortable and soft. Gigi had created a slit and snap in the back that fitted around the tail perfectly as well. The colors of the designs shifted with the light as she turned and inspected herself in the mirror, seeming almost alive as she zipped them up. The top was a mesh see-through midriff tank top that accentuated a black leather bra with shiny silver buckles underneath.

Jilah grinned appreciatively as the light sent shimmering patterns of glittering blue and purple playing across the surface of the fabric. Black knee length combat boots poked out from under the cuffs of the pants. She pulled on a pair of iridescent elbow pads, turning back and laughing at the image in the mirror. She felt as if she were dressing to attend an absurd, dark disco goth rollerball function of some sort.

Still, she loved the look. Pulling her indigo and white tresses into a tight ponytail high on her head, Jilah looked over at the girls who were now clapping and making earnest catcalls. She felt better already.

Although it was apparent that the sorceress' two companions were ogling her somewhat, she found that she didn't mind it so much. It felt more complimentary than pressing, as if the pair didn't expect her to actually hook up with them but were more than happy to just entertain the idea. This reassured her, and she turned to look over her shoulder at her reflection.

It looked like the tail was part of the pants themselves as the tip of it slowly curled up and down at the backs of her knees. And she had to admit that with this outfit, her new extras looked pretty good. Still, with strong enough shields, she should be able to mask them from anybody that looked at her. Gigi had also done something that she said would easily mask them from the view of anybody that wasn't already a 'friend of Dracula'.

Jilah looked over at her new friends perched on the bed and cocked her hips, doing a little step and turn as she rocked her head back and laughed. Oh yeah, she was feeling much better now.

She silently blessed them as she crooked an eyebrow up and said, "Hell yes."

Gigi looked her up and down, then crowed, "Girl, we gonna light that place on fiyah"

The two girls nodded and grinned, saying, in unison, "You damn right."

Gigi gasped and whirled around on them, quietly hissing, "Shut yo mouth."

The girls stood up and purred, "We're just talkin' 'bout Shaft."

There was silence for the space of two beats, and then the three of them began cackling as they walked out of the bedroom. Jilah grinned, shaking her head as Gigi took her hand and purred, "Girl, we are gonna have ourselves so much fun tonight, you just don't know. You're gonna tear that crowd apart, honey."

Jilah chuckled, feeling a little odd that she now found herself with such easygoing women who actually wanted to hang out with her. It wasn't something that she was at all used to. The women she was most familiar with were outright bitches, or scared little mice who barely opened their mouths to talk to anybody. She couldn't remember a time when she'd gone out with a group of women socially in her entire life. She found it a very pleasant change to be among people that just wanted to go out and have a little fun.

Jilah watched the three of them curiously as they walked through the convent halls, laughing and talking happily with one another. The girl with the bobbing sea-green pigtails introduced herself as Roane, and the girl beside her with the teal and purple hair was Ariane, her girlfriend. Jilah thought they made a good couple as she relaxed, falling into step with them.

There was nothing threatening or discomfiting here; just four crazy women who desperately needed a night off. She warmed to the girls as quickly as she had with Gigi during their initial meeting.

The group reached the end of the corridor, and Gigi created a portal to the outside. Jilah slowly opened the connection with Argent to let him know that she was heading out. She felt him perk up and then was momentarily disoriented as the furnishings of a very ornate room, resplendent with rich tapestries and red and black drapes, slowly bled into her vision, creating a strange ghost image of sorts over what was really in front of her. She wondered if she'd been transported somewhere else for a moment. She had to squint to focus on the portal in front of her. She was happy that Argent welcomed the diversion, grinning as he asked, :: *So, where are the ladies taking you?* ::

Jilah pulled away from the visual of the connection and watched Gigi and the girls step through the portal.

:: *You know, I didn't think to ask.* ::

Gigi was on the other side of the portal, motioning for her to come through. Jilah quickly followed, asking, "Where is it that we're going again?"

"To the land of supernatural drinks and eye candy, gorgeous." The sorceress winked and placed her hand in Jilah's, squeezing and crooning, "You'll love it. Trust me." Gigi let out a breathy sigh as her other hand fluttered dramatically to her throat. "It's just what a working girl needs on a night off."

She could feel Argent's smile and chuckled as she replied, :: *It's my first night out like this. I feel like I should be nervous, but I'm not. It's kinda nice.* ::

In all honesty, Jilah wasn't really sure what she was expected to do in relaxed social situations. She'd never really had friends who wanted to spend any amount of time with her, much less drag her out all over the place. In the past, when around other women Jilah usually became tense and uncomfortable, at least when she'd still been human. Tonight, she felt accepted and relaxed. With these women, there was no pretense, no social bullshit, no games. It was an interesting feeling.

:: *It sounds like we're going to a bar.* ::

The four of them kept in step as they strode into the street, looking like an unusual glam rock band. Gigi's portal had dropped them less than a block away from the source of a low, throbbing beat. Jilah's expression became dreamy – happy that she was now going to dance again, for the first time in what felt like forever. Her body hummed with anticipation.

Argent laughed and said, :: *Enjoy yourself, beloved. I should go. I am in the middle of something, and keeping the connection with you open will distract me too much, I fear. I will see you when you arrive home, if you get in before sunrise..* ::

She felt Argent pull back, the connection gently diminishing. Jilah quickly slid her shields in place to keep from disturbing him further. Once aware of her surroundings again, she blinked as she spotted a long line snaking around the corner of a large building up ahead; their destination, she supposed. It looked like a warehouse. She wondered if Argent danced as well as he sang. She certainly planned to find out someday soon.

The winding line that led to the club was peppered with an assortment of people in bondage gear; punks, goths, and graver kids who looked a good deal more animated than the same old empty shells she was used to seeing in the clubs in her hometown. Everybody here seemed so lively and vibrant.

As they walked closer, Jilah noticed a large sign on the front of the building. It was an enormous, rusty metal plate that had utilitarian-looking letters cut out of its center with a blowtorch. The sign was backlit with bright, neon green light that spilled out of the letters, spelling out the word Impulse. Other than the sign and the line, there were really no other defining features to the building.

Come to think of it, there were no other buildings in this neighborhood that were showing any signs of activity. It looked as if this club was seated squarely in the middle of a section of the city that shut down entirely at night.

It was an advantageous location, Jilah thought, considering how loud the music was. She realized that Gigi was still holding her hand as they made their way to the front of the line amid a collection of protests and groans from the kids standing behind the security rope that wound around the building.

An enormous bald man collecting IDs at the door looked at Gigi, then nodded them through. As they passed him, Jilah looked back in time to see him give her a quick wink. Jilah quickly turned around so that she didn't run into the frame of the door as Gigi opened it and pulled her inside.

The music was a shock to her system, hitting her like a physical slap, and Jilah stiffened. It was a little overwhelming.

Gigi squeezed her hand. Jilah looked up at her as the sorceress guided her further into the club, Roane and Ariane trailing behind her. The low, liquid thump of the music rolled through her body in a sensual wave, the beat bringing out an animalistic need to grab somebody, anybody, and wrap around them to the rhythm of the music.

She pulled free of Gigi's grip, balling her hands into fists as she took a long, deep breath in an attempt to bring her reaction back to a manageable level.

:: Striaga? ::

The foreign voice in her thoughts caught her off guard, and she fixed on it, seeking its source. Roane was talking to her.

Jilah frowned and looked back at the girl with the sea-green pigtails, wondering why she hadn't noticed before. The girl was a Sanguine, and Jilah had completely missed it. Granted, she had figured that if Roane was a member of the inner court that she couldn't possibly be human, but the thought of her being another Sanguine hadn't crossed the avatar's mind. There was something else about the young woman that piqued her curiosity, but Jilah couldn't quite figure out what it was.

There was something other underneath the blood, the hunger. It coiled around itself inside the girl in cold, dormant coils, but it wasn't something that Jilah could quite put her finger on. There was a feeling as if it was waiting for something, but there was no sense of menace to it.

Jilah shook her head to clear it, nodding as she responded, :: *I'm OK. The music's just really strong.* ::

She continued to breathe deeply, comforted more by the action itself then by any need to get more oxygen into her system. :: *I haven't been out in a while, that's all.* ::

Feeling a little more in control now, she smiled and added, :: *Thank you. And really, call me Jilah, OK?* ::

Roane grinned back at her, nodding. :: *Deal.* ::

Her three companions never stopped smiling, acting for all the world as if they were just out for a good time. The entire scene had a very 'nothing to see here' feel to it. As she noticed it, something else in her head clicked into place. They were in public, therefore none of them could afford to look alarmed, because it would telegraph their Striaga's state to people that would be more than happy to take advantage of such things. Jilah felt her tail go still as she pulled herself together. She couldn't afford to appear weak or out of control here.

With this, Jilah also became aware of other preternaturals in the club. She could feel them; their presence a dim tickle in the back of her mind. She wondered if, with practice, she would be able to pinpoint their locations around her without having to see them. It appeared as if tonight was going to serve several purposes at once, she thought to herself as she took another breath and slid her hand back into Gigi's, cranking her smile up a notch as she said, "So who's up for some dancin'?"

The sorceress laughed and said, "Girl, I thought you'd never ask."

The group snaked their way through the main hall in time with the beat as they waded into the vast sea of people before them. Jilah's gaze swept the room, taking in the scenery. The dance floor was a huge, open space punctuated by several small stages that sat off in dark corners of the room with pinpoint spot lights on them. There appeared to be several floors above with burnished metal railings that allowed people to peer down at the dancers on the main floor. Women and men in black leather straps writhed around in several small, metal cages suspended high above the dance floor.

It was the most eclectic gathering of people she had ever seen in one place. Punks and goths waded through the crowd, heading down a hallway that she assumed lead off to another room within the club. The place was enormous. The majority of the crowd in the main room were either rocking against one another to the rhythm, or engaged in some of the most bizarre behavior that Jilah had ever witnessed. As she looked around, she slowly began to understand what all the equipment on the wall of the bedroom back at the convent was supposed to be used for. A curvaceous nude woman with mahogany hair was chained up against a wall, hissing as a man traced a very sharp, dangerous looking knife over her breasts.

Jilah's eyes widened as a drop of blood welled up near the woman's nipple. The woman, however, seemed to be reacting positively to this. The man grinned and bent down to place his lips over the wound, and Jilah quickly looked up at Gigi, careful to keep her expression neutral. She wanted to say something, but the music was so loud that she would've had to shout. She was startled that such a thing could be done in such a public place without either of the participants being arrested. She ventured a quick glance back over at the woman whose mouth was now open in a large O of pleasure as the man began sliding a gloved hand down her torso.

Gigi's expression never changed as she looked over at Roane, and Jilah once again heard the female Sanguine's voice in her thoughts.

:: It's easier to communicate like this. Loose lips, y'know? ::

Jilah's mind kept flashing back to the woman. She shivered as she looked back in time to see the man's fingers sliding boldly between the woman's legs.

Jilah's responded, her tone sounding stricken. :: What? Loose what?? ::

Light laughter rolled through her thoughts before Roane answered, :: Sink ships. It's an old saying. What I mean is that communication is both more seamless and secure this way. Besides, we'll go hoarse if we try to scream at each other over noise like this. ::

Jilah felt a little of her tension evaporate, frustrated with herself that she was so easily spooked. Her tone became quiet and tentative as she asked, :: What is this place? ::

Roane grinned and wrapped an arm around her girlfriend's waist, responding, :: *It's many things to many people. This section is the most mainstream, since it's the largest dance floor in the club.* ::

Jilah's eyes widened a little as she mentally blurted, :: *This is more mainstream?* ::

She looked back over at the man and the woman, choking back a small cry as she watched him lap at a trail of blood that had snaked down the woman's stomach into her thatch of dark-colored pubic hair. The woman definitely seemed to be enjoying it, which confused her.

Jilah quickly turned to face Roane again, her voice tight as she squeaked :: *Is there a section where we can go where that isn't happening?* ::

Roane looked back at her, her brows knitting slightly as she replied, :: *Why do you ask?* ::

:: *Because it's distracting, and not in a good way. I can't relax with that going on.* ::

Jilah looked away, unable to meet her gaze. :: *It's just..* ::

Roane smiled and touched her shoulder, her voice soothing as she answered, :: *It's okay, that won't be a problem.* ::

Roane looked up at Gigi, who nodded and began clearing a way for them through the crowd. Jilah noticed a phenomenon similar to the one that had happened the night when she and Argent had first met. The crowd parted easily around them, like water gently moving around rocks in the middle of a stream. As they made their way to one of the far corners, a slow, grinding song came on, and Jilah was swept up in the rhythm.

Jilah sighed and looked over at Roane, who was now nodding her acknowledgment and sliding her arms around her girlfriend. Jilah watched as the two women began moving against one another in a slow, rocking motion, before sliding her eyes shut and letting the music thump through her; her movements liquid as she matched the beat with her body. She lost herself in the rhythm, shutting eyes as she danced.

A long while of dancing and drinks later, the four of them were sitting around a high circular bar table. They were giggling like loons, recovering slowly after Roane had finished sharing a particularly riotous story about Argent. Jilah was covering her mouth with her hand, trying not to laugh as she imagined what Argent's reaction would be if he knew that the four of them were sitting in a bar cackling and swapping embarrassing stories about him. Sure, he'd probably be annoyed, but the idea was insanely funny. This was mostly due to the fact that she was a little tipsy. She finally howled with laughter, unable to help herself.

This set the others at the table off again and they all ended up whooping and laughing hysterically. Although not really drunk, Jilah was definitely feeling the nicely numb, silly feeling of the alcohol. It wasn't necessarily a bad feeling, and she was warmed by the laughter of the women sitting with her.

She reflected about times past and sobered, her expression tinged with a little sadness as she murmured, "You guys are the first true friends I've ever really had."

The laughter at the table slowly trailed off. Gigi frowned and asked, "What about before?"

Jilah reached out for her drink and pursed her lips, pausing to think about it for a moment. "What, before coming here?"

She took a quick sip, growling a little. The alcohol still burned as it went down.

Roane placed her hand gently on Jilah's wrist, her tone soft as she answered, "No, she means before you turned."

Gigi continued earnestly, "Honey, surely you had friends before that."

The sorceress' jaw dropped as Jilah silently shook her head.

"What about family, sweetheart? Weren't they..?"

Jilah gave them a sad smile, again shaking her head. "I'm not really a people person. I've never been socially adept."

Ariane spoke up this time, startling Jilah. The woman hadn't really said much the entire night, and Jilah was struck by how smoky her voice sounded. "You're doing just fine with us tonight."

Jilah nodded as she slid her fingers down the side of the glass in front of her, the tips getting slick from the moisture that collected along the sides.

"It's just kind of mind-bendingly ironic that this is the first time I've ever felt truly comfortable or welcome in a social situation like this before." She forced a smile and laughed weakly. "I don't mean to bring everybody down. This is honestly the most fun that I can remember having in my life."

The women looked back at her, unsure of how to respond as she quickly added, "Well, other than with Argent, that is."

Jilah's face flushed, and she let out a nervous giggle as she looked at them with a guilty smile.

Roane laughed, startling everybody. "Man, has he changed."

The three women nodded, chuckles as Jilah cocked her head a little. "Has he? I mean, from what you were saying..."

The three women looked at one another, then began laughing hysterically. Jilah frowned, wondering what she'd missed.

Roane replied, "He used to have a real stick up his ass, back in the day. A real hard-on about the job. Towards the end, he was..." she trailed off, and the three of them grew very silent.

What's that all about? Jilah wondered, wanting to press her for more information. Roane's voice in her head brought her up short.

:: *Just trust us when we say that he's changed. And all for the better. He's actually fun to be around now.* ::

Jilah looked back at them, wondering what they were hiding. :: *Towards the end of what? What happened?* ::

Roane gently cut her off, shaking her head. :: *That's something that you'll need to talk to him about. It's his story to tell, or to keep. He wouldn't appreciate me filling you in, and although he's currently being all mister kinder and gentler Strigaisha, I still wouldn't want to test it.* ::

Before Jilah could inquire further, two rather large men caught her eye and made a strange, unfamiliar gesture towards her as they walked past the ladies' table. She frowned, now remembering several times throughout the night where other people around her had done the same thing. The motion was subtle, but enough for her to notice. It was beginning to bother her.

She turned to Gigi, whispering, "What the hell is all that about anyway? People keep doing that, and I can't for the life of me figure out what's going on."

The sorceress grinned and explained, "It's an honorific gesture. They're paying their respects to your position, girl – although not in those grand flourishing queenie movements that they do when they're at court. When it's a mixed scene, everybody behaves a bit differently about that sort of thing."

"Well, it's annoying." Jilah picked up her glass and knocked back another swig, continuing, "I wish they'd cut it out."

The ladies at the table chuckled, and Gigi pretended to cool herself with a large invisible fan as she drawled, "It's the price one pays for fame and power, darling. I'm afraid you'll have to get used to it. Or, as my aunt Fanny used to say, 'Suck it up, sugar – at least they're not shootin' at ya'."

Jilah peered at Gigi intently for a moment, then nodded sagely and said, "She sounds like she was a pretty sharp lady."

Gigi cackled and replied, "She was a stone cold bitch from the wrong side of the tracks. The rest of the family hated her. I want to grow up to be her someday."

A very attractive woman with intense hazel eyes and a shock of pink hair walked by the table, and Jilah winced inwardly as the woman made the same strange odd gesture as she passed.

"It's just that..." She set her glass down and turned to watch the woman as she walked into the other room. The liquid movement of the woman's hips was almost mesmerizing. "Well," she turned to face them again, "it's kinda creepy."

She paused for a moment, reflecting before she added, "But then if I think about it, what about this trip hasn't been creepy, right?"

Roane and Ariane laughed and picked up their glasses, raising them in a mock toast, "To creepy!" they shouted as Gigi and Jilah quickly moved to clink their glasses together, laughing and downing the rest of their drinks.

Jilah giggled and announced in a warbling Southern accent, "Ladies – stick a fork in me, ah do b'lieve ahm done."

Gigi gasped in mock horror, bringing her hand fluttering to her throat as she croaked, "Surely you're not ready to pack it in this early?"

Her eyes narrowed as she reached into her purse and dug out a timepiece. "Dear god, look at the time."

She quickly knocked back the rest of her drink, then stood up and said, "It's pumpkin time, ladies. Collect your glass slippers and follow me," as she began ambling towards the exit.

On their way out, Jilah passed several more people that made the same strange motion to her and she just gave them a slight nod, not really knowing how to properly respond to the gesture. She waited for a moment for the knowledge that would surely pounce on her brain at any moment, giving her the answer, but no such help was forthcoming. She sighed and placed her hand in Gigi's, thinking that she could ask Argent about it when they arrived back home. Or maybe...

:: *So, you wouldn't perhaps know the way that I should be responding to all these people that feel this overwhelming need to salute me, or whatever it is they're doing, do you?* :: she sent Roane, hoping that the girl could help her out.

:: *The thing is – we haven't had an actual Striaga in this prefecture in so long, I don't know if anybody knows the proper protocol for responding to the presence of one. People seem to be defaulting to giving you the same kind of gesture of respect that they'd give the Dragon's Hammer.* ::

Jilah frowned as Gigi pulled her out of the club into the night air. There it was again. Perhaps she could get an explanation this time. She decided to play it innocent, :: *The Dragon's Hammer? What's that?* ::

Roane looked back at her, perplexed as she answered, :: *This is another one of those things you'll need to ask the Strigaisha. Let him explain it.* ::

Jilah crooked up an eyebrow in response, :: *What's with all the mystery?* ::

Roane shrugged and replied, :: *Just know that there are some things we can tell you and some things he just needs to explain to you.* ::

:: *Fair enough. I'm still getting the hang of how everything works down here, after all.* :: The women made their way down the street as Gigi created a gate back to the convent with a deft movement of her fingers.

:: *Don't get down on yourself, chica. You're doing really well for somebody that's been tossed headfirst into a shitstorm. As long as you keep your head above water, you'll do great.* ::

Jilah smiled and tentatively took Roane's hand, squeezing it as Gigi pulled her into the gate. :: *Thanks. I can't tell you how much hearing that means.* ::

When she stepped out onto the parking lot at the convent, she looked back and found Roane grinning back at her. :: *Just be happy together. You make him sane.* ::

Later, she watched the three of them walk back down the corridor before she stepped into the bedroom, still grinning. It had been the perfect end to a long, rough night. She looked over at the empty bed and sighed.

Jilah knew he'd be joining her soon enough. She suddenly felt exhausted as she peeled herself out of her outfit; tossing the clothing onto the mahogany chest at the foot of the bed. As she slid under the covers, she sighed happily, kicking her feet and making the covers rustle gently before settling down and snuggling her head into the pillow.

He makes me sane too, she thought to herself as she dropped off to sleep.

Twenty Eight

It's Always Darkest...

Jilah was in the midst of a vivid, strange dream. She was a small tawny alley cat in search of a very fat, delicious mouse. She'd been throughout the entire house and at every turn had been foiled by the mouse who, strangely enough, had the face of her former boss, whom she had utterly despised. The idea of such a tasty meal, as well as revenge on somebody that had treated her like garbage in the past, had her mouth watering as she cornered the rodent and prepared to pounce.

She was about to leap when her senses became muddled and everything went out of focus. Suddenly, something was shaking her roughly, and she could hear a strange, muffled voice that sounded urgent. The image of the dream winked out as awoke to find Aurelian violently shaking her.

"Dammit, Striaga, wake up!" he roared, hauling her out of the bed forcefully.

"What the hell! I'm awake already!" she snapped as Aurelian placed her squarely on her feet, his expression startled.

"Is this how you usually wake people up? Because you suck at it!" she growled as she wiped at one of her eyes to get the sand out of it.

He backed off and Jilah took a deep breath, counting to ten before quietly asking, "Now, what exactly is so important that you had to shake me so hard that my teeth ache?"

Aurelian began rattling off a rapid string of facts and bits of news that she found very hard to follow due to both the speed and sheer volume of information being shared. She held up a hand and pleaded, "Wait! Slow it down a little. I mean, I just woke up and all."

The Selkie responded, his tone curt. "Well if it hadn't taken me almost fifteen minutes to wake you up – this includes the shaking, by the way, I wouldn't be so rushed."

Jilah eyed him and sighed. "Okay. Now I'm ready. Just put the brakes on it a little, okay? My brain doesn't race to catch up with information so well after it's just been jarred awake."

Aurelian looked back at her, explaining, "Paranormal incidents are happening throughout the city. People are starting to see things that shouldn't be seen, and it's happening with enough frequency that the police are beginning to compare notes. For some reason, the preternatural population seems to be losing its collective mind. They don't seem to care that they're revealing themselves to the humans around them."

Jilah's brow furrowed as she frowned and asked, "What kinds of stories are we talking about here?"

"The milder stories include a toilet in a woman's dormitory that has apparently begun sexually assaulting the people that use it. On the darker side, multiple bodies have been found in the French Quarter, face down in the gutter. Clear, definitive bite marks were left in full view on rather obvious, easily seen body parts."

Jilah winced as he continued, "A shop clerk supposedly underwent a full shift as she stood behind the counter, only to chase her screaming customers out of her store while yapping at their heels. She's a recent immigrant given low status ranking in the pack and her demeanor was usually very quiet and unassuming. Reports I've received from the pack members that knew her stated that this kind of behavior was completely out of the ordinary for her. Nobody seems to know what caused it. Shall I go on?"

"Wow. That's a whole lotta freaky goin' on. I would imagine that it's kind of hard to explain these things away to people on the street," she responded, her tone uncertain.

Aurelian looked back at her, his expression nonplussed as he smiled thinly and replied, "Ya think? What's worse, the authorities are becoming more than a little hinky about keeping us informed about these incidents since we no longer seem to be able to keep it all under control."

Jilah looked back over at Argent, wanting him to be awake so that he could handle this.

"What time is it?" she asked.

Aurelian responded, "There's at least a half an hour until the sun goes down."

Jilah groaned.

She turned and sat down on the edge of the bed, her thoughts racing. What was she supposed to do to fix this? She'd never been in this kind of position before. She gently rubbed her temple with her right hand as she asked, "Is there anything that you can think of that would make the preternaturals in the city act this way? Any kind of event, like a bad storm or an earthquake or something?" Aurelian looked back at her, completely befuddled. "You know, like how animals that go crazy when a tornado or an earthquake is about to hit?"

He appeared to be more than a little insulted at her statement, and his response was snippy as he responded, "Comparing us to animals with their generic little natural quirks isn't earning you any..." His eyes narrowed, and he breathed, "Oh shit."

"What?"

Aurelian quickly checked the stack of papers in his hand, riffling through them and stopping when he came to the middle of the pile.

"The Sisters. They're the only possible thing that could checkmate the threat of reprisal that the Dragon's Hammer or the Council would have over the residents. If that's what's causing people to flip out, then it's likely that they're already within the city limits, although the reactions to their presence this time are far more extreme than the last time they were in the city."

There was that term again. Still, there were more important things at hand.

"Hold up a sec. Are you really telling me that the presence of these Sisters would cause people in the city to go insane? For no other reason?"

Aurelian thought about it for a moment, then explained, "It's been said that The Sisters have a strange affect on some of the younger

Sanguine, which sometimes causes them to get a little crazy. When the blood suckers start going schizo and draining everything they can get their hands on, which is what seems to happen with those who are affected, it makes the rest of the paranormals within the radius of their feeding pattern more than a little nervous."

Jilah frowned, not really understanding as Aurelian continued, "There is a balance in nature between predator and prey. When either one starts bugging out, it tips the balance and tweaks out the remaining individuals because they no longer have an established pattern of behavior to operate from. Everything tends to domino effect from there, thus.."

"The crazy and weird," she finished, nodding as she reached an understanding that she wasn't at all comfortable with. She let out a frustrated sigh and quietly said, "Well that's just great. First week on the job, and the city goes to hell in a hand basket."

Aurelian looked back at her, silent for a few moments before prompting, "Tell him everything we've spoken about when he rises. There are other things that I need to go take care of."

Jilah nodded again, a cold spiral of doubt creeping into her stomach as she watched the Selkie depart. She wasn't really sure what she was supposed to do; there was little she could think of but to wait for her lover to wake up so she could pass on the bad news. She found herself hoping fervently that the incidents reported were a few select instances instead of being the beginning of a slowly rising tide.

Unfortunately, only time would tell. There wasn't much that she could do in order to stop things from coming to a head.

Hopefully Argent would know what to do.

Awareness came in a flood of conflicting images and ideas. Argent could only understand small snippets and snatches; nothing really useful. He winced as he mentally reached out and cranked the connection with Jilah down to a dull roar so that he could concentrate. He opened his eyes to find her hovering over him, looking distressed and concerned.

:: *Open up. I'll try to be a little more coherent. You need to see this.* :: her voice trailed off in his thoughts as he slowly opened the connection back up, now able to make a little more sense of the stream of information.

An angry frown marred his features as he sat bolt upright in the bed. He paused for a moment, then leapt out of bed, quickly starting to dress. Jilah watched him quietly, wanting to say something but not knowing the right thing to say.

:: *It was only a matter of time before they arrived. Still, it would have been much less irritating if those damnable bitches had waited another day or two.* ::

Aurelian was suddenly at the door, walking into the room and delivering a full report. The incidents had gotten much worse in the last thirty minutes. He quickly explained that council Mediators were now on their way to contain the situation. Out of the corner of his eye, Argent watched Jilah flinch at the anger that flared through the connection between them.

"They'll be here in fifteen minutes. The current word on the street is that The Sisters have taken down at least three Sanguine in the city so far. There is now talk of the Council locking the city down and declaring martial law for all humans and supernaturals. The flow of information and eye witness accounts have already been subverted to ensure that the news doesn't spread to the rest of the country through any means. The other prefectures have already been put on alert to clamp down on any unauthorized information coming into their regions. The council doesn't want anybody outside the city limits getting too interested in the things they're hearing about the happenings here."

Argent paused for a moment, realizing that if they were willing to go this far, the Council would likely have representatives throughout the city mentally interrogating people and wiping the resultant eerie experiences from their memories. The entire region would now essentially be cut off from any outside contact for as long as the Council needed to ensure that order was restored. How well he remembered the process from so very long ago – although the world had changed so rapidly around him since he'd left that it had almost been difficult to keep up.

Argent nodded, his expression empty as he replied, "The Council's reaction is understandable. With this kind of activity it is only a matter of time before news spreads so far that we are unable to control the damage without seriously taxing the court's resources."

He paused for a moment, his tone becoming icy as he continued, "Have the ones that have already broken the law been brought here yet?"

Aurelian shook his head quickly. "There hasn't been time. Mira and her guard…"

"Make time. Find somebody that can go collect them. If the denizens of this city do not realize that they need to fear me far more than The Sisters, then this prefecture will indeed fall."

Aurelian blanched and took a step back, nodding curtly before rushing out of the room.

Argent turned to Jilah and quietly said, "You'd better get dressed. We have a long night ahead of us."

Jilah asked, "What does he mean when he says that they're going to lock the city down?"

She was afforded a very brief, but informational glimpse that rang a little too sharply of Big Brother for her comfort. The mind wipes themselves sounded entirely unpleasant, and an old memory surfaced before Argent could shut the connection.

The image of a young man came to her. He was wearing a style of dress that she didn't recognize and was shaking as he stood before two individuals in crisp white uniforms, spittle bubbling and frothing from his lips. His hands clawed at the air as the strange men just looked at him blankly, clipboards in hand.

She shrank back from the visual, and Argent gently placed hand on her arm. :: *It was a long time ago, and times were more barbaric then. The young man was also an extreme case. Surely they've come up with better methods by now.* ::

His voice was gentle and reassuring, but Jilah was extremely uncomfortable that this sort of thing was now happening throughout the city.

The witnesses had done little more than be in the wrong place at the wrong time, and because of this they were going to suffer as those memories were viciously plucked out of their heads to ensure the safety of a grand secret.

This didn't sit well with her at all, but if it was a choice between that alternative or humanity itself rising up and destroying creatures like herself, it was something she figured she was going to have to live with.

:: *There are several matters that I must attend to in order to prepare for what now looks to be an inevitable meeting. We still do not know what it is about me that has The Sisters so eager to wreak such destruction here, and I need to do a little research as well. Will you be all right on your own for a few hours?* ::

Jilah nodded and forced a smile. :: *Yeah. Call me when you need me.* ::

Argent gave her hand a quick squeeze. :: *My deadly beauty. Be careful.* ::

She sighed as she watched him go, wondering what she could do, if anything, in the next few hours to help. A collection of ideas ran through her thoughts before a headache ripped through her head. She gasped for air as familiar images and messages flitted through her thoughts, gritting her teeth as she cried, "Dammit. Not tonight. Please."

Even as she said it, she knew that there would be no choice. She would have to go out and track her quarry down, no matter how inconvenient it happened to be. The pain stopped abruptly, and she gulped air for a few moments.

Well, at least this would keep her busy.

As Argent made his way through the hallway, he recalled a variety of strategies – checking them for feasibility, ticking them off when every single one of them ended up with his head separated from his body.

The Sisters rarely missed when they began pursuit of their target, this he knew well. He had no illusions of his chances. What he couldn't figure out was why they didn't just assassinate him discreetly. It was their usual method of operation, and he had to admit that he was a little shaken that they'd broken so thoroughly from their previous hunting tactics.

Why had they so suddenly become erratic? Throughout the years, the faces of The Sisters changed; new recruits always came forward to replace the fallen. Their methods, however, remained static. Until now. It baffled him, making all the scenarios in his head suspect. If he couldn't depend on an enemy to act a certain way, it became much harder to prepare to eliminate the threat. Usually, he would find this a bracing challenge, one he would enjoy finding out if he was up to. There was too much to lose now. It wasn't worth gambling over.

At the moment, The Sisters seemed content with causing general mayhem and panic in the streets. When would they direct their swath of destruction in his direction? Something nagged at the back of his thoughts, long forgotten, and he picked at it, hoping to dig it out. After a few moments of hearing his heels click on the stones of the passageways, it hit him. The enormity of it almost knocked him off his feet.

Is it fair to ask such a thing of her, after what she's been through? he asked himself, not entirely sure that he wanted to breach the topic. Without realizing it, he found himself outside the door to Roane's room.

And so it appears that this needs to happen, whether I wish it or not.

Argent took a slow breath in and stepped into the doorway, watching the teal-haired Sanguine's fingers deftly flicker over the buttons of the game controller in her hand. He grinned as he watched the action on the screen, fascinated. Technology wasn't something he was particularly adept at, and it fascinated him that she was so comfortable and well-versed with it.

He cleared his throat, and she leaped out of her chair with a yelp.

"What the fu..." the rest of the words trailed off as she met his eyes, and she quickly paused the game and whipped the controller behind her back. Roane then presented him with a sheepish grin, and explained, "I was, ah, well it helps relieve stress." she finished, lamely.

Argent chuckled and shook his head gently. "It's okay. The purpose of this visit is not to catch you doing something you shouldn't be doing." He took a step into the room, his tone quiet and confidential as he added, "And I am not your father, you know."

Roane let out a nervous laugh, and tossed the controller onto the bed beside her.

"So, what's up? What brings you down to visit the help?"

Argent's expression sobered as he replied, "I need to speak with you about something."

Roane cocked her head to the side, her eyes narrowing slightly. "That doesn't sound good. What'd I do?"

"It's nothing that you've done, Roane. It is something that I might need you to do for me. For the prefecture." he reassured her.

She frowned at him, wondering what he was getting at. "You're acting awfully weird tonight. Have you eaten yet?"

Argent shook his head, dismissing her statement. His heart was heavy in his chest as he replied, "In the event that things go very badly, I will need you to do the one thing that you swore you would never again do."

She stilled, her voice quavering as she asked, "How can you ask me this?"

Argent sighed softly, hoping that she would understand as he breathed, "If The Sisters were to kill us all, would that not be worse?"

At that she stared back at him, her jaw dropping. "Sisters? As in The Sisters? What, they're HERE?!?" she cried, hugging her arms around her midsection.

Argent gave a solemn nod then quietly waited for her to respond. She hopped off the bed and paced for a moment. He could sense that she was having a difficult time composing herself as she asked, "How bad is it?"

Not wanting to keep anything from her, and given the sacrifice that he was going to ask of her, he explained everything that had been relayed to him earlier. He watched her reel as she processed it all.

"Please realize that the only reason that I would ask you to do such a thing is if there was no other way."

Roane stiffened, taking a deep breath as her eyelids fluttered shut. Either The Sisters would destroy them, or the Council would. There really was no other choice that she could see. Her reply was toneless and gray.

"I understand, Strigaisha, and I'll do it if you need me to."

Argent reached out and gently took her hand, giving it a light squeeze.

"I haven't the words with which to thank you. Suffice it to say that I do remember what we spoke of in the past. I know this will cost you a great deal." He paused and softly murmured, "I am very sorry that I have to ask it of you."

Roane opened her eyes and looked back at him, letting out a breath that she'd been holding.

"Ariane's gonna be pissed. You know that, right?" Her expression was almost challenging as she gripped his hand with a ferocious intensity.

Argent smiled gently and responded, "I imagine she will be. And rightly so. But, still – if it must be done..."

Roane nodded and quietly replied, "She'll understand. She won't like it, there will likely be lots of yelling – but she'll understand."

Argent slowly stood up and pulled her into a hug. She let out a wry chuckle and said, "I swear, it seems like you exist for the sole purpose of getting me in trouble with my girlfriend."

Argent gently pulled away and looked down at her, his tone a little more relaxed as he answered, "I think that it would be safe to say that she will be a great deal more angry with me than with you."

At that, Roane laughed and grinned. "Oh yeah. You can definitely count on that. And thank god for small favors. She can get pretty rough when she's on a tear. I'd much rather have it directed at you this time."

He smiled and wrapped an arm around her waist. "In this particular instance, I am happy to oblige."

"You should totally have your head checked out. I think you've taken one too many blows, dude."

As they walked back to the throne room, he chuckled and nodded. "You might be right on that account."

The city was so quiet that it unnerved her.

The usual sounds of traffic, pedestrians, and street music were absent as Jilah made her way through the French Quarter. Feeling a bit as if she'd found herself on an empty movie lot, she jumped slightly as a cat sprinted across the street into an alley with a flickering street lamp. Her boot heels clunked on the pavement as she continued down the street, making her way to the address in her head. It was like walking through a ghost town. Any other time, she might have been able to enjoy taking in the surroundings without the distraction of all the people and noise, but now it just felt wrong.

Were people locking themselves up in their houses to escape the madness that was slowly crawling through their city, or were they in the throes of anguish as memories were yanked out of their heads with surgical precision? The image from earlier flickered to life and she winced, forcing it away. Psyching herself out wouldn't do anybody any good. She had her own job to do, and the quicker she did it, the quicker she could be back at Argent's side to help.

Upon arriving, she looked up at a wrought-iron balcony covered with dark party lights. Up or in? she mused as she wrapped her shielding tighter around herself. Up would probably be easier. It'd be less of a dog and pony show to get through the glass than a heavy-duty door lock.

Jilah paused for a moment, then leapt up to the first balcony. One more hop and she grabbed the railing; kicking her legs up and over. She crouched down as her feet hit the balcony floor. Her lips curled into a wicked grin as she realized that the occupant had left the door open in order to let some of the night air in.

It was always nice when they made it easier. After a quick heartbeat check to ensure that the target was alone she stood up and quietly slid the door open and slipped inside.

The place reeked of stale Chinese takeout and a familiar-smelling smoke. She spotted what appeared to be the recent remains of a very sloppy dinner on the coffee table. Off to her left, a TV was on, but the sound had been muted. The Creature of the Black Lagoon was heading towards the cameraman, arms extended. A coughing sound echoed out from one of the back rooms. Jilah spun towards the hallway and cat-footed her way towards the source of the noise.

A man's voice, rough from coughing, croaked out, "Man, that's some high quality mountain kind." He let out a small whoop, then she heard the sound of a water pipe.

Undoing the top snap on her leather vest, she stepped into the doorway, her tone warm as she purred, "I see you've got the Mercedes Benz of bongs there. What, does it take you a pound a day to get high?"

The guy looked to be about thirty. He was sitting on the edge of a bed nursing one of the largest purple water pipes she'd ever seen. A thick column of smoke swirled in the pipe as he pulled his lips away from it, his expression stunned as his eyes slowly swept up her body. When he reached her face, he broke into a broad grin and began laughing.

"Whoa. Is this shit hallucinogenic or what?"

He reached out a hand, beckoning her over, and he began giggling when she took his hand. "Man, this is some powerful chronic."

His eyes glazed, and she crouched down in front of him, slowly removing his fingers from the water pipe and placing it off to the side. "Am I in heaven?" he breathed, fascinated.

Jilah grinned back at him, cocking her head to the side as she released his hand. "I would imagine that heaven is a relative term – wouldn't you think?"

The guy's expression blanked for a moment, then he nodded slowly, his voice almost reverent as he answered, "Yeah. That's... whoa. That's... that's really deep, babe."

He continued nodding for several seconds as he stared off into space. After a few moments, he was all smiles again, giggling as he added, "Wow, hot and smart. Total score."

There was no red haze that she could see darting around him. She frowned and dipped into the guy's thoughts, finding that it was his roommate she sought. According to the incredibly high man before her, the roommate would be home momentarily. The man had apparently gone off to purchase an 8-ball from a dealer that lived two doors down.

Jilah's smile became warm, and she began laughing softly with him as she nodded and said, "Yeah. Total score."

The sound of the front door latch unlocking snapped her attention into sharp focus, and she smiled back at the very stoned roommate, explaining, "I need to go get something that'll totally make this better, okay? I'll be right back. You stay right there."

The guy grinned and nodded happily, reaching for the bong as she walked out of the room.

"Aw, goddammit John, did you have to eat all the fucking takeout?"

The voice was strongly annoyed, but not truly angry. Jilah's lips curled into a wicked grin. There'd be plenty of time for him to get angry. As she reached the end of the hallway, her target whipped around, his eyes wide.

"Who the fuck are you? How the hell did you get in? JOHN!!"

The man's eyes rolled around the room, his expression highly agitated. She could feel his paranoia crawling through his head.

Jilah cocked her hips and leaned into the wall, her voice a smooth, honeyed drawl as she asked, "What's the matter, baby? Don't you want to party?"

The man looked her over, growling, "I don't know who the fuck you are, but you need to get out of my place now, whore."

This was going to be a tough sell, and she since didn't have time to play with her food, she came right out with it. "You've been a very naughty boy, Matthew. Does your mother know what you do with your copious spare time? Does anybody?"

The man's eyes widened and she felt a flare of anger.

"Just who the hell are you? How do you know my name? Fuckin' bitch comin' up in my apartment and giving me the third degree? Hell no. You need to shake your ass the fuck ou..."

The words died on his lips as Jilah punched him in the face, pulling it at the last minute. She didn't want to shatter his skull.

He crumpled to the floor and Jilah muttered, "You're getting off light because I don't have time for this bullshit, asshole. It could've been a lot worse. Better luck in the next life, pal."

She crouched down and picked through his head, forcing him back to consciousness. It had been surprisingly easy. She forced him to his knees and held his chin as she started the memory loop in his head. He immediately began going into a full seizure, and foam flecked his lips as she dipped down and sank her teeth into his jugular.

There was a high-pitched scream behind her. She drank deep for several moments before whipping around and catching the gaze of the stoner roommate who was now flapping a pointing finger at her – his mouth a wide, round O of alarm. She found herself thinking that he looked a great deal like Donald Sutherland at the end of the Invasion of the Body Snatchers remake.

Jilah blurred over and cold cocked him, knocking him out. The body slumped to the floor with a heavy thud. Turning her attention back to her target, she spat at the twitching body at her feet and grated, "Try not to be such a rapist prick next time around, will ya?"

She didn't have time to stash the body, and she figured that it'd just be chalked up to yet another frenzied vampire attack. It would get lost among the others and would be forgotten.

At least there's one upside to this madness, she thought to herself as she glared down at the body.

"Step away from the victim, please."

An authoritative voice snapped her out of her routine, and Jilah spun around to see a very pale man in a business suit with a clipboard standing by the window.

Her eyes narrowed as she looked back at him and snapped, "And who exactly are you?"

The strange man looked back at her, his expression befuddled. His tone was hesitant as he answered, "Council monitor twenty-seven."

Oh. Those guys. She'd forgotten about them.

Jilah wiped the blood from her mouth and asked, "So, sheriff, are ya gonna take me away?"

The man peered at her strangely, then riffled through his paperwork for a moment before regaining his composure and stating, "This city is currently under lock down, and all preternaturals are to gather at the Court for examination, debriefing, and punishment, if it's deemed necessary."

Well, that was easy enough. Heading back home with an escort, no less.

"Fair enough. Ready when you are."

With a deft flick of his fingers, a set of nasty-looking manacles appeared on her wrists. A heavy link chain connected them, weighing her arms down. Jilah eyed him, growling, "This is the kind of treatment I can expect when cooperating freely?" The sound of her teeth grinding echoed in her head.

The man answered with a wry smile. "One can never be too cautious. Precautions are necessary, of course."

Jilah opened her mouth to respond, but before she could say anything, there was a disorienting wrenching feeling, as if her guts were trying to flip themselves onto the outside of her body through her skin. It stopped abruptly, and she found herself heaving what felt like a pint of blood out onto the concrete beneath her.

Jilah growled, "I swear to god, someday I'll kill every last one of you bitches that does that shit to me without warning again."

Her angry mutterings trailed off as the sounds of conflict clashed in her ears. Jilah wiped her mouth with the back of her hand and looked over towards the source of the sound.

A teeming sea of struggling bodies clashed out in the courtyard of the convent. The streets were thick with fighting, the walls around the building had been destroyed, and it was hard to pick out individuals amongst the fray. Everything had become this horrific, hairy, writhing mass of rage and conflict. Growls, howls, and gnashing teeth provided a morbid soundtrack for the scene before her.

Jilah kept seeing flashes of platinum blond hair dart throughout the crowd with remarkable speed. As they snicked through the throng, several bodies crumpled to the ground in their wake. Her heart dropped as a familiar roar echoed through the night air.

:: ARGENT!!! Where are you? ::

Her lover's mental response was startled and bewildered. Jilah saw through his perception the events that had unfolded while she'd been gone, although they were hard to piece together through the nausea.

Apparently The Sisters had arrived at the convent moments ago, and all hell had broken loose. Through their shared connection she saw a young blond woman rushing towards him, murderous intent in her eyes. Jilah felt her heart race as her eyes registered the thick wooden spikes in the woman's hands. A loud ring of recognition rolled through Argent's mind, and Jilah felt a cold fear build in his heart. This was one of the fabled Sisters that everybody had been talking about.

Jilah quickly stood up, then promptly slid back down to the ground.

NO! goddammit why can't I MOVE?!? she screamed in impotent fury in her head as her body slowly recovered from whatever the bastard had done to her.

Jilah looked around for him, but he had disappeared and left her sitting on the grass – an open target in what had become a harrowing combat zone. Her heart hammered in her chest as the connection flared again, and she watched the stake descend with blinding speed, breathing a sigh of relief as Argent evaded. The woman quickly recovered and redirected her attack, but the body of a hulking beast blocked her. It howled out with rage as the wood plunged deep into its shoulder.

Christ, she's as fast as he is.

From what she could figure out from Argent's sending, The Sisters had driven a rather large wave of maddened preternatural creatures before them and she was seeing the resultant fallout. In a moment, he confirmed for her that the blond blurs that she had seen darting in amongst the fighting were indeed The Sisters themselves. More of the combatants standing close to the convent were dropping. Jilah shuddered as she watched a large splash of red spatter along the side of the building in a garish slash.

An unearthly shriek pierced the night, and Jilah's eyes widened as she spotted a greenish blue creature with multiple eyes peppering its forehead turning towards her. She jerked back as it turned its body towards her. She found herself thinking back to the imagery of the Creature of the Black Lagoon from earlier.

"Oh, that's just great," she growled. "Creature Feature's heading this way, and I can't get out of these goddamned handcuffs."

Jilah fiddled with them, desperately looking for a locking mechanism. The strange green blue creature was now being followed by an enormous wolf and something else for which she had no visual frame of reference.

"C'mon, come ON!" She yelled, as the blue green monstery thing hunkered down, then leapt at her. Her clawed hands came up, reaching out to eviscerate the thing as she braced for the impact. Something flared in her field of vision, and everything went a dazzling white. Jilah was immediately surrounded by a sea of bodies, all sharp claws and vicious snapping teeth.

OK, fuck this noise.

With a roar, she yanked her hands apart roughly. Momentarily startled at how easy it was to break the chain, she was bowled over by a large snarling, snapping thing. Jilah reacted by grabbing it and tossing it off of her, relieved to see Argent standing over her and extending a hand down to her.

:: *And where, exactly, have you been all this time?* :: he asked as he pulled her up and swiveled to face off with an enormous black werewolf.

He raised a strangely ornate metal hammer that emitted a crimson glow as it swept through the air. When it connected with the head of the animal, it flared bright red and knocked the beast to the ground. It didn't get back up.

:: *Handy, that.* :: Jilah commented as she wheeled around, placing her back up against his as she delivered several swift kicks square in the face of a rabid, frothing man clad in an extremely revealing leather outfit. She had a moment to wonder where the moves had come from. She'd certainly never learned them at any point.

:: *Indeed it is. I am glad you are here.* ::

:: *Not going so well, is it?* :: Jilah asked, boxing the ear of a six-foot tall shaggy thing with a wolf's head as it moved in to take her throat out. It was a little easier to out-maneuver her targets now, and she briefly wondered why.

:: *Unfortunately, no. For the moment, I believe we are barely holding our own.* :: She felt a wave of regret and sadness from him. :: *We will prevail, but I fear that it will be at a rather large cost.* ::

Before she could ask him to explain, a set of fanged jaws found their mark in her right thigh. She cried out in pain, reaching down and grabbing the beast's head, giving it a quick turn. A satisfying snap followed, and it slumped to the ground. Fur and claws became a blur, each fight blending into the next with dizzying speed. Her thigh was a white hot, maddening itch, and she wasn't sure how long she could maintain this pace. Further conversation would have to wait until the threat was dealt with. Jilah hoped that there would be time enough for questions afterwards.

She had a pile of them.

Twenty Nine

Full-on Stomp

They were besieged on all sides. The remaining Sanguine, wolves, and other preternaturals that hadn't been affected by the presence of The Sisters fought fiercely beside her and Argent. Screams and howling shrieks chilled her blood as she parried a vicious-looking set of black claws that swept away from her and caught a furred thing next to her under a shoulder blade.

Jilah ducked and gutted the creature with a swift upward motion, digging her claws deep into its belly. It made a most unsettling noise as its innards spilled out in ropy strands and hit the pavement at her feet with a wet splash. Stumbling up against Argent as a sharp, blinding pain hit her in the left shoulder, she screamed. Jilah had a moment to recognize the blond that had blurred into existence before her as the woman's other hand cocked back, another stake at the ready.

Something snapped inside her. She felt a familiar, cold presence in her rising quickly to the surface, crying out with a fierce joy as it took over. She heard high, chittering laughter – the kind of laughter that bubbled out of the throats of crazy people – and shivered when she realized that it was coming from her.

The disconcerting thing was that there was now no familiar slide to the side that she usually experienced. The presence seemed to burst inside her, and she howled as a surge of adrenaline flashed through her system. A stream of incoherent language started falling from her lips, and she continued to laugh like a hyena in between phrases while her hands darted out and disemboweled the woman. Jilah howled with savage laughter as the woman's eyes went wide, her lightly tanned hands darting to her stomach as she crumpled before the avatar. Jilah then dropped four of the strange, shaggy creatures around her in a matter of seconds.

This time there was no feeling of distance, of disorientation as she sat back and watched the reaction of her body. She was fully in the moment now, sliding and darting in around claws, weapons, and teeth with a deft precision that was startling. Jilah reveled as bodies began dropping around her as she twisted their heads off, pulling limbs from their sockets with gruesome, wet popping sounds. A savage joy raced through her like a fire blazing out of control. She honestly didn't think that she'd ever been as truly happy and in her element as she was right now. The word ecstasy seemed to have been created for moments such as this.

Argent took a brief look back and was stunned at the sight before him. Jilah was moving so quickly that it was hard for him to track her movements. She was glorious. He shivered as his body responded. He took a moment to forcefully bring himself back under control and look around to assess the situation. Now that one of The Sisters had fallen, things descended rapidly into chaos. A howl went up through the crazed throng. Argent watched with a horrified fascination as several members that had initially started out fighting for the court turned to fight their compatriots with equal fervor.

Members of the crowd were now sliding into pure berserker rage at the Sisters' continued presence and more combatants were joining the fray. Where the hell were they all coming from? Even with his lover dropping bodies as fast as she could, there was no way they could keep up and hope to survive.

Argent made his choice.

:: Roane! ::

:: Strigaisha? ::

:: I must ask you to do what we spoke about earlier. There is no other way. Already our supporters begin to turn against us. ::

He had directed sea-green haired Sanguine, Ariane and Gigi to stay well out of the range of attack for this very reason. The possibility that she might actually have to do what she now was being asked to do hadn't felt real until now. Roane took a slow breath, trembling as her lover's hand slowly entwined her own. She looked over at Ariane, her wide eyes asking an unspoken question.

Ariane's response was even and soft. "Do as you must, my love. We fight for our very lives now."

Roane had only utilized her ability in such a widespread, uncontrolled manner once before – and that had been due to a forced merging with her sire when he turned her. It had resulted in the raising of every interred body within a two-mile radius. The resultant panic had been the reason that the Council had used for the immediate destruction of her sire. Since then, Roane had been extremely hesitant about doing such a thing again, but the situation was growing desperate. Ariane's grip tightened slightly, and a tear slowly trickled down the necromancer's cheek as she made her decision.

There was a flash of indigo and white off to her left, and as a mighty roar pierced the night Roane reached out with her senses.

It felt oddly comforting, after so long without reaching to touch this part of herself. At the edges of her consciousness, she could barely make out the notes of a haunting melody as uncountable tiny points of light flickered to life in her mind. She could feel them all, a pulsing presence all around her in the cities of the dead in the surrounding area.

At the touch of awareness, a resonant bass boom rolled through her, shaking her to the foundations of her very soul. She gasped as she felt the flickerings flare into a blaze that threatened to consume her, and she could hear scrabbling, scratching, and cracking noises echoing through her head. They were quickly becoming deafening.

Roane swayed on her feet, brought a little back into her body by a painful jerking motion on both arms. There was an unearthly mournful keening noise whose tone threatened to break her heart, and she found herself wondering where it was coming from. What could make such a sound?

Even worse, what would have to happen in order to bring that kind of soul agony out in someone? After a moment, realized that it was issuing from her own throat. Her eyes snapped open – she hadn't even been aware that she had closed them. Her eyelids fluttered as she looked over at Ariane, instantly recognizing her and clutching at her for support.

Suddenly, an overwhelming pressure slammed into the back of her neck, feeling almost as if it wanted to crack her head open so that it could get inside. This had never happened before. Roane shuddered, her body jerking in stiff movements as she let out a frightened scream. She wasn't sure she could stop it, and the feeling of invasion made her skin crawl.

Ariane roughly slapped a wet hand to the back of her neck, and Roane felt a slight burning on her skin as the sensation immediately stopped. There was a loud sucking sound, first in one ear, then the other. She felt hands press roughly down on her shoulders as Ariane began yelling something in Creole.

Whatever had just happened, it sounded as if it had really pissed her lover off. Ariane's words were fast and rough as she said, :: *Come back to me. Come back to your body. Roane, can you hear me? Roane... ANSWER ME.* ::

With that, Roane snapped out of her daze and looked over at her lover and nodded, her voice quiet as she replied, "I'm here. I'm okay."

She felt something that she couldn't quite put her finger on, but with this came the realization that there was now something wrong. Roane took a deep breath, then reached out with her consciousness, feeling the hundreds of bodies that had responded to her call. They had freed themselves from their prisons, but she wasn't really sure how she knew this to be true – it just felt right. How had they gotten past all the cement and mortar of their aboveground tombs? This was the part of the process that always mystified her.

The entire city was under the water table, and all the graveyards were above ground due to the fact that any buried bodies would simply rise to the surface. Now the reanimated bodies all seemed poised, as if waiting for something. She felt pressure on her hand again and gently shook it off.

"I'm all right. They need somebody to connect to them, to direct them, or they'll disconnect entirely and begin going off on their own."

The pressure released and Roane breathed, "My god. There are so many of them. How...?"

And as she spoke the answer came to her, her power knowing where to go and what to do. She took a step forward, and her head rocked back as the power surged out of her in a cold wave that sent chills through the crowd around her. For a moment, the sounds of fighting seemed to waver. With a singular step that seemed to shake the very earth, the dead responded in kind, moving forward. Towards their beloved. She needed them, and to be near her radiance they would do anything.

Roane remembered the utter adoration from earlier times when she'd worked with the dead on a much more limited basis, finding it unsettling when there had only been several bodies to respond to her, but this was practically making her shudder. It felt so very wrong, somehow, to have such blind adoration and worship from a single corpse, much less from such a teeming mass of dead bodies.

Shaking the feeling off, she maintained the connection, accepting and feeding their need as she sent out waves of whatever it was in her that caused the dead to respond. Roane took a steady breath and turned to her lover, her voice rough and brusque as she sent a call out to Argent, :: *It's done. They're coming.* ::

Ariane's grip tightened slightly as she pulled Roane away from the edge of the fighting. Roane looked back at Gigi, who nodded solemnly at her. The sorceress' brow was furrowed and sweaty from the concentration it took to keep the shield around the three of them. Makeup was running down her cheeks and Roane winced, knowing that after it was all over, she'd be horrified at her appearance.

The Council monitors stood well above the skirmish below, peering into the fray like hawks as they took frenetic notes in large leather-bound journals. It seemed that no matter how things turned out, they were going to come in and place a tin hat into the prefecture – one that could be easily manipulated by the Council itself. In the opinion of the Council, the city obviously couldn't be left to its own devices; and for all the fabled stories of the Dragon's Hammer, he had been able to do nothing to prevent this.

Roane almost laughed as she watched the eyes of one of the monitors widen to the size of dinner plates. The man began gesticulating wildly to the other monitors, who responded in kind as the dead began pouring into the battleground – their numbers quickly overwhelming the opposition. The madness that had struck the preternaturals in the city had apparently caused them to abandon any sense of self preservation they had as they turned in a unified wave to face this new foe.

A strange chanting echoed out through the night air, and Argent turned towards the source of the noise, his hammer hefted high in his hands. Jilah, standing to his back, noticed the uneasiness that rippled through the people fighting beside her. It kicked her out of the adrenaline high and knocked her back into a sane, clear head space. What the hell was happening? With a brief flicker, the connection with her lover flared and she paled.

All fighting seemed to have stopped for the moment, and Jilah's eyes grew large as she watched the waves of the dead advance on the edges of the crowd. Roane's voice was quiet and intense as she sent out, :: *When I give the signal, you need to destroy all those who stand between you and me. They want to hurt me. To kill me. You must destroy them utterly – but only on my mark.* :: to the now almost uncountable numbers of walking corpses.

The answering hiss from the gathered corpses sent the wind up Jilah's back, and she turned to look at Argent. :: *Oh my god.* ::

Argent nodded and took her hand with a grim determination. :: *We must now get behind our little Roane, as quickly as possible. Do not make any moves that could be interpreted as threatening in any way.* ::

:: *Right-o. Time to get the hell out of Dodge.* :: Jilah quickly followed him as they made their way back to the steps of the convent.

The rest of the members of the court and its supporters followed suit, moving to get behind Roane, who was now stepping forward with Gigi and Ariane following in her wake.

Jilah looked over to see Mira holding Aurelian up. The Selkie was breathing harshly, covered with cuts and bruises. Jilah winced and Mira met her eyes, giving her a solemn nod. He'd heal.

The chanting grew louder, and the sound of primal drums began to thrum through the night air as a sizable group of men and women in all white came into view. As they moved closer, Jilah spotted a tall, well-muscled ebony-skinned man leading them. He was clad in all black with a top hat resting on his head at a strange angle. She found herself mystified as to why it didn't fall off due to the extremely vigorous way he was dancing.

His torso was painted with a white skeletal ribcage, his face painted like a skull with enormous black eye sockets. Perched on his nose were a pair of black sunglasses that were missing one of the lenses. The chanting became singing, and the voices of the chorus in white were so overpowering that it brought tears to Jilah's eyes.

The rhythms and melodies were strangely haunting. She couldn't understand the words at all, but the vigorous calling that went back and forth from one section of the group to the other was so beautiful and precise it was hard to believe that it hadn't been choreographed.

There was a power and majesty to the singing that clutched at her heart, taking her breath away. She could see that all of them were now dancing ecstatically, some of them in such strange ways that she was finding it hard to believe that they were human. People just weren't physically capable of moving like that.

The skeletal painted leader was now laughing and grinding his pelvis lewdly as he danced forward, rubbing his hands along his legs and groin as the choir advanced behind him. A great whooping cry went up as several other men dressed similarly to the skeletal man in black began leaping their way through the crowd of people in white.

The strange, jerking movements of the people around them made Jilah think that several of them were going into grand mal seizures. The sounds of sharp ululating carried on the night breeze, bringing goose flesh to rush up her arms and legs. She turned to Argent, mystified. As they watched Roane walk forward, he placed a gentle hand on her shoulder.

:: *What's going on? I don't understand.* ::, she asked, once again feeling completely out of her element. Fighting she understood, but this? The twitching, jerking people in white that continued to advance as they danced and sang unnerved her as much as the rhythm of the drums thrumming through her soul.

:: *These are Ariane's descendants. She calls them Vodouisants - the children of the gods of Dahomey. I know of them, but in my entire time spent in this city I have never seen anything like this.* ::

Argent paused for a moment, looking over at Roane, who was still slowly walking forward, moving almost as if she were gliding through water. Roane's expression was beatific, her left hand stretched in front of her with her palm turned up, as if beckoning to something.

Jilah watched the last few stragglers scramble quickly behind the invisible line that Roane had drawn with her presence. The hair on the back of Jilah's neck stood straight out and shivered as Roane's hand slammed shut, making a tight fist that she then raised, and dropped straight down. The songs of the people in white reached a terrifying crescendo, and Jilah felt something go THOOM through the air around them as the dead shrieked and flooded into the square, instantly tearing apart every creature they could get their hands on. A scream crept up her throat, and she slammed her hands over her mouth, choking it back down.

She thought that she had seen horror before, experienced it as vividly as possible out at that little cabin in the swamp, but this was so much more harrowing. Blood poured over the asphalt as limbs were rent from bodies, heads ripped from torsos. Sinew stretched and popped, creating an almost orchestral grand guignol before her that was too terrifying to watch – yet she was unable to turn away.

Her eyes went wide as she watched the painted skeleton men stiffen in place, shaking and writhing as their tongues darted out like snakes, almost as if they were tasting the air – drinking the scene before them down in ecstasy.

The gathered throng in white screamed in celebration, but Jilah wasn't entirely sure why. Why on earth would anybody cheer on something so awful? A strangely calm, strong voice echoed through the crowd as a woman stepped forward, speaking in a strange dialect that Jilah couldn't understand. After what seemed like a formal pronouncement, she triumphantly yelled, "AYE BOBO!"

The celebrants in white rang out a thunderous response, "AYE BOBO!"

Argent nodded, understanding now. :: *She's feeding their cemetery gods with the blood of those who fall today. Apparently, they're protecting the rest of the city from the throngs of the dead who are apparently still arriving.* ::

Jilah looked back at him, astonished. :: *Still arriving? Good god – how many dead people are currently running around the city?* ::

Argent smiled tightly as he responded, :: *Apparently, all of the bodies within a four-mile radius have responded to our little Roane's call.* ::

Jilah let out a slow breath and shuddered, Argent's voice quiet in her head as he added, :: *She is a great deal more powerful than I had originally believed. I am hoping that I did not make a grievous error in asking her to do this.* ::

Jilah's eyes widened as the connection between them flared. Before she had time to reel from the full shock of what he'd said, the realization that he had no other choice became very clear. As quickly as she began to process this, wanting to reassure him that although it was awful, it had been necessary, she rocked back from the immediate clarity that he was actually seeing this as a possible advantageous event. The fact that he wasn't particularly distressed by the sheer carnage bothered her.

To him, the people that were currently being torn to pieces in front of her eyes were, quite literally, chinks in his political armor that would have eventually caused weakness within the power structure itself. It was his opinion that they were best handled quickly and effectively, and with as much of a terrorizing element as possible. In his mind, if this was as far as it went and the situation became controllable from this point forward, he would have brought the city back to heel in a very definitive manner, which would keep anybody else from moving against him – including the council itself.

He was pleased with the outcome. It unnerved her a little.

As the screams of the remaining victims of the slaughter died out, she grew to understand his train of thought through the connection and felt herself nod grimly in agreement when she realized that if the city fell to the leadership of a Council member, things would be FAR worse for the preternaturals living within the prefecture. As the connection between them flickered back to a light touch, Jilah placed a shaky hand on his arm as she ventured a look over at Roane.

Argent's hand covered hers, and she could feel a wave of gratitude coming from him as she watched Roane open her hand again. She had apparently chosen to spare a sizable crowd from the gathered masses that had been butchered. The remaining people watched, mesmerized as Roane crooked a finger and issued a silent order. Several of the walking corpses, now coated in a thick, shiny covering of gore and dark red blood, bent down to collect something from the pile of limbs and pieces at their feet.

Jilah wasn't entirely certain what they held in their hands as they made their way over to Roane. Argent released her hand and moved towards the little necromancer, his stride steady and bold.

:: *Stay here. I'll be right back.* ::

Stepping up to Roane, Argent gently bowed at the waist and raised a hand to his chest. Roane smiled brightly as three of the corpses shambled forward – wet, red prizes in their hands. Argent leaned down, collecting the strangely round shapes from them, gripping them by a strangely stringy material as he hefted them into the air with a roar.

"The Sisters are dead! Will order now be restored or will the Dragon's Hammer have to resonate again?"

His voice boomed through the streets. A shiver crawled up Jilah's spine as she suddenly realized what he was holding aloft. Three heads. The heads of The Sisters. The echo died down, the remains of the gathered throng going silent for several moments.

Ariane then stepped up to Argent, leaning into him and whispering something into his ear. Argent nodded, walking with her over to the painted skeletal men who were now watching the two of them with a quiet intensity. Jilah watched as Ariane touched his shoulder, gesticulated several times, then directed him to place the heads of The Sisters on the ground before the men in black. The leader of the skeletal men nodded and crossed his arms, then began bellowing with laughter. He roughly clapped Argent on the shoulder, then dipped his fingers into the blood on the heads and streaked both of Argent's cheeks with crimson lines. He then smacked his knuckles genially against Argent's chest several times, still laughing in that oddly thunderous tone, starting to dance lewdly as the gathering turned in unison and began singing as they headed back into the darkness.

Jilah felt somebody press up against her, sighing as she realized it was Aurelian. She leaned back into him as the Selkie wrapped his arms around her waist and exclaimed, "Well if that isn't the damnedest thing I've ever seen in my life."

Jilah let out a sharp bark of laughter. Now that it was over, the nervous laughter just bubbled out. The two of them then began giggling, trying to stay quiet as they did their best to contain themselves. "You really are a total dork," she whispered.

As she continued to laugh silently, she found herself wondering what was going to happen to all the dead people that were now looking up at Roane as if she were the light of the world. Such naked, open adulation from such desiccated, destroyed creatures tightened her heart. The laughter died in her throat as she looked over at Roane, who was now looking back at the growing crowd of corpses with tears streaking her cheeks. Jilah could almost feel the palpable bond that resonated between Roane and the dead. She could only imagine what the woman was going through now that she would have to send everybody back.

Gigi stood at Roane's back, placing a comforting hand on her shoulder. "You have to send them back, sweetness. It isn't fair to keep them in this state, never being able to have what they so badly want."

Roane began to shake. It felt as if her heart would break and spill open as the cooing, gurgling sounds echoing out of hundreds of throats echoed in her ears. She was surprised to find herself wanting to be with them almost as badly as they wanted to stay, just to be in her presence. It was going to be a long, painful night.

She nodded and sighed, her smile tight as she looked back at the rotting, upraised faces, overwhelmed with emotion at the sight of the devotion and love echoed in them. "C'mon guys. Now that you've eaten, mom says it's time to get you all back to bed."

A tear trailed down Jilah's cheek as she watched Roane wade into the sea of the dead. Hundreds of hands gently reached out to touch their mistress; some of the corpses' appendages and hands now crunching and cracking at the contact. The crowd parted to allow Ariane to join her, the pair of them hugging tightly before Roane rocked back and raised her face to the sky.

Argent was heading back towards her and Aurelian when one of the Council monitors rushed up to him, asking him a veritable torrent of questions. Argent looked back at the man with an annoyed expression, then at the multitude of corpses gathered around Roane and Ariane. He said something that Jilah couldn't make out. The monitor paled and quickly composed himself before giving a stiff bow and rushing into the convent.

:: What was all that about? :: she asked.

:: It was essentially the last attempt of the Council to take control of the city. They've wanted to place one of the European elders in the prefecture as Strigaisha for a long time. After witnessing the events of this night, they've rethought their plans and have now extended warm congratulations to me on my new appointment. ::

Argent chuckled darkly as he walked up to her, taking her hand in his and kissing it softly.

:: *Well, dammit. Does that mean that we have to stay now?* :: She looked up at him with mock annoyance as she wiped a thin coating of gore from his arm.

:: *Indeed it does. Are you disappointed?* :: He crooked an eyebrow up as he flicked a patch of bloody, furred skin off her shoulder.

:: *Not as much as I thought I'd be,* :: she murmured, leaning into him.

Jilah looked over to see Roane and Ariane heading out into the darkness with their zombie army. She found herself wondering how they were going to get all the bodies back into the ground. She had the distinct feeling that the process wasn't going to be at all pleasant.

The members of the court and those who had fought beside them circled the pair of them and shouted, "Vivat Strigaisha! Vivat Striaga!" before kneeling before them.

As they turned to face the crowd, Jilah sent, :: *Uh..shouldn't we get this odious mess taken care of before people start getting all celebrate-y and stuff?* ::

She felt bad that people had to get on their knees in the blood and gore that was now littering the street. How on earth were they going to get it all cleaned up?

They both gave a gracious bow to the creatures on their knees, hand in hand as Argent replied, :: *Beloved, we've just withstood one of the more bizarre onslaughts I've ever been through – and that's saying something. Give it a minute for the victory to sink in. Then we'll clean up.* ::

Jilah smiled and squeezed his hand. He was right. It could wait.

For now.